The **Helium Kids**

Smiley Daze

IGH FIDELTY

DECCA

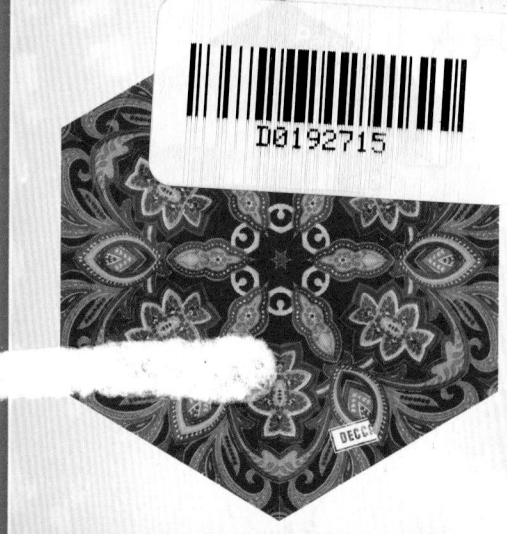

D0192715

DECCA

Low Blows in High Times

GOT LIVE WITH THE HELIUM KIDS

GLORFINDEL

HE HELIUM KIDS

The Helium Kids

Feeling the Pressure

ROCK AND ROLL IS LIFE

Also by D. J. Taylor

Fiction
Great Eastern Land
Real Life
English Settlement
After Bathing at Baxter's: Stories
Trespass
The Comedy Man
Kept: A Victorian Mystery
Ask Alice
At the Chime of a City Clock
Derby Day
Secondhand Daylight
The Windsor Faction
From the Heart
Wrote for Luck: Stories

Non-fiction
A Vain Conceit: British Fiction in the '80s
Other People: Portraits from the Nineties (with Marcus Berkmann)
After the War: The Novel and England Since 1945
Thackeray
Orwell: The Life
On the Corinthian Spirit: The Decline of Amateurism in Sport
Bright Young People: The Rise and Fall of a Generation 1918–1940
What You Didn't Miss: A Book of Literary Parodies
The Prose Factory: Literary Life in England Since 1918
The New Book of Snobs

ROCK AND ROLL IS LIFE

IS LIFE

*The True Story of the Helium Kids
by One Who Was There*

A Novel

D. J. TAYLOR

Constable • London

CONSTABLE

First published in Great Britain in 2018 by Constable

1 3 5 7 9 10 8 6 4 2

Copyright © D. J. Taylor, 2018

The moral right of the author has been asserted.

All chracters and events in this book are fictitious. References to real
people are also fictional – their actions in the book are imagined.

A CIP catalogue record for this book
is available from the British Library.

ISBN: 978-1-47212-884-3 (hardback)
ISBN: 978-1-47212-883-6 (C Format)

Typeset in Adobe Caslon by Hewer Text UK Ltd, Edinburgh
Printed and bound in Great Britain by CPI Group (UK), Croydon CR0 4YY

Papers used by Constable are from well-managed forests and other responsible sources.

Constable
An imprint of
Little, Brown Book Group
Carmelite House
50 Victoria Embankment
London EC4Y 0DZ

An Hachette UK Company
www.hachette.co.uk

www.littlebrown.co.uk

For Cathal Coughlan

CONTENTS

CONTENTS

I would love to tour the Kiev circuit

In a travelling circus show

I'm dying to be a star and make them laugh

bound just like a word on a photograph

These days are good enough, over a long time ago

Talking Heads, Road to Nowhere, 1985

Neither nothing do we want... much of... the world

here - or even in tomorrow's... of... we look... to it.

The words are art, for the listener; and it ought to be... which it is not, it we, the...

Elizabeth Bowen, The Death of the Heart, 1938

Toytruck is essentially proto... and the... engage... encroachment of home-making's machine... that to... thereit it, of a group proves... a... world to see... in... resident... routines.

Jim Dix, The... for... in... for... in, 1972

Welcome to the party, we're all here to...

Pop Group, Bite... to..., 1972

You know, in the bar I hang, and... just bought in New York, there's some graffiti in the men's room... now time you... people... not others people. "Film is King." I find... it makes... I really... if it makes me life. "I think that pretty much nails it up."

Wired, The... and, 1984

I would love to tour the Southlands
In a travelling minstrel show
I'm dying to be a star, and make them laugh.
Sound just like a record on a phonograph
Those days are gone for ever, over a long time ago.

> Steely Dan, 'Pretzel Logic', 1974

Not for nothing do we invest so much of ourselves in other people's lives – or even in momentary pictures of people we do not know ... Illusions are art, for the feeling person, and it is by art that we live, if we do.

> Elizabeth Bowen, *The Death of the Heart*, 1938

Pop/rock is essentially young people's music and the eventual encroachment of home-making usually ensures that the gang mentality of a group proves impossible to sustain beyond its members' late twenties.

> Ian MacDonald, *Revolution in the Head: The Beatles' Records and the Sixties*, revised edition, 1997

Welcome to the party, we're all just papers in the wind.

> Jo Jo Gunne, 'Run Run Run', 1972

You know, in the bar Danny and I just bought in New York, there's some graffiti in the men's room – three lines, written by three different people. 'Film is king,' 'Television is furniture' and 'Rock and Roll is life.' I think that pretty much sums it up.

> John Belushi, quoted in Bob Woodward, *Wired: The Short Life and Fast Times of John Belushi*, 1984

'Unless you let things take for ever,' Garth Dangerfield once pronounced, 'they never get done.' It was one of his better utterances – probably dating from his short-lived Zen phase – and I very nearly used it in a press release, only to be dissuaded by Stefano, who cautioned against what he called 'all this philosophical wank'. What Garth meant by it, I think, is that no human activity exists in a vacuum, that everything, necessarily, leads on to something else, that all stories are part of other stories that would take an infinity to separate out.

On the other hand, there is no harm in trying . . .

And so here I am, sitting in the dense, small-hours silence, up in the attic room of the big house in Earlham – the house my mother would have liked so much had she lived – and outside it is raining. Rain on Earlham, and the Norwich suburbs into which it feeds. Rain on the villages beyond the ring road's encircling arc, on Hethersett and Melton and the endless fields where Ralph Miniver – more about him later – wandered three-quarters of a century ago. Rain falling over Norfolk, from Yarmouth to Lynn, Cromer to Clenchwarton, and Diss to Downham, from the Broads to the Fens, and subduing even time – the clock that ticks on the shelf beside me – with its clangour.

All around me, I realise, is the baggage of a vanished life. There are laminated gold discs glinting from the wall, next to framed photographs from thirty and forty years ago. Also present, in cardboard boxes, in neatly *labelled plastic wallets, in ancient vinyl record racks and piles of cassette tapes, are the materials I need for the task in hand. It has been a long job, a small miracle of accumulation and dogged research, enterprise, tact and discrimination, but I flatter myself I have everything: the tour programmes; the stack of music-press cuttings; the vast cache of letters grubbed up by Felicia, one-time secretary to the fan club, from her hoard. (Felicia is into her seventh decade now, married to an investment banker and living in Purley, Surrey, but equally keen that all this should see the light. 'It matters, Nick,' she told me, and she was correct.) There is Garth's autobiography, there is Macdonald's mad book about the studio sessions, not to mention a whole pile of merchandise from assorted US tours, even down to the limited-edition Helium Kids barbecue-party parasol and the range of attenuated male swimwear . . .*

Above all, there is a group portrait, dating, I should say, from sometime in 1970–71, back in the halcyon days, those tornado years through which we cruised like a pack of molten gods, taken at somebody's poolside, by somebody's verdant lawn. San Francisco? Fire Island? I don't know, and the situational details – like nearly all situational details from that time – are limited. The man standing slightly to one side is Jack Nicholson. But nearly everybody who figures in this narrative is there – the boys, naturally, but also Don and Stefano, looking as if they were off to play the ugly sisters in panto, and Angie, and even Rosalind, who had somehow arrived to swell the scene. Our faces look simultaneously triumphant, exhausted and expectant, but also wary, as if already we half-suspect that the glorious prize we have managed to carry off will shortly be taken away from us.

Which is more or less what happened.

Some obvious questions. What took me so long? What stayed my hand? Why now, of all times, when half of us are dead or disappeared or reinvented into people our former selves would not have recognised? And am I telling the truth? Well, as Garth said, unless you let things take for ever, they never get done. As for the truth, granted the confessional is as artificial a form as any other, but what have I got to hide? Why, as Don once remarked, as he presented a management contract in which most of the subsidiary clauses had yet to be typed in to his five impressionable protégés for signature, would I lie to you? So this is the story of the Helium Kids, of Garth, Dale, Ian, Keith and Gary and poor, seahorse-faced Florian, of wrecked hotel rooms and bright California dawns, of Goodge Street in the psychedelic summer sun, of Ros and Lucille and Al Duchesne, of my father's corpse bobbing out to sea off the Oregon coast, of the helicopter's nervous descent onto the human ant-heap that was Ogdenville, of John Lee Hooker playing in the blues club in Columbus, of secrets that could not, in the end, be concealed and of myths doomed to shatter into a thousand fragments, and of the rain, falling on Earlham and across the world, in an endless tide, that will continue to fall when you and I and even the Norfolk villages are gone.

THE HELIUM KIDS

Garth Dangerfield rhy gtr, vocals/**Dale Halliwell** gtr/**Ian Hamilton** bs/**Florian Shankley-Walker** kybds/**Keith Shields** drms (original line-up)

Formed Shepperton, Middlesex, 1961. Even now, a dozen years into their rollercoaster career – which is putting it mildly – the jury is still out on the Helium Kids. To their admirers they are an essential part of that late-sixties *zeitgeist*, constantly adapting themselves to the new styles and influences of an ever-shifting musical landscape, and, at the height of their commercial triumphs, only marginally less successful than the Beatles (*q.v.*) and the Rolling Stones (*q.v.*). To their detractors, on the other hand (a constituency that at one time included most of the UK's music press), they are plagiarists and bandwagon-jumpers – 'a group that has clearly never had an original idea in its collective head', the influential *Rolling Stone* columnist Ralph J. Gleason declared after attending one of their concerts. The truth probably lies somewhere between these two extremes. But if hindsight reveals much of the band's early music to be highly derivative, then the force of their contribution to the nascent seventies scene has been consistently under-appreciated by critics anxious to write them off as chameleons of rock.

The Helium Kids' origins go back to St Paul's School, Shepperton, where Dangerfield (b. 19 July 1945) and Halliwell (b. 7 May 1945) were reluctant pupils. Later joined by the slightly older Hamilton (b. 3 February 1943) and Shields (b. 6 June 1943). Former child actor and musical prodigy Shankley-Walker (b. 27 August 1941), a classically trained pianist brought in by the band's manager, was the only non-working-class member. To begin with the Kids were a Beat Group pure and simple. (1), recorded over three days in the spring of 1964 with the aid of professional sessioneers, could be the work of any competent Merseyside five-piece of the era, *sans* the Liverpudlian accents, and on its second side veered close to novelty-song territory. At the same time 'Glad It's You', the first Dangerfield/Halliwell composition committed to vinyl, reached No. 3 on the UK singles chart. The US tour which followed was little short of disastrous, the band homesick and out of their depth playing to mostly unresponsive audiences in out-of-the-way venues. (2), released in its wake, is a curious *melange*, including cover versions of American R & B classics that had featured in their live sets since the early days on the west London pub circuit, but simultaneously spawning the monster hit single 'Gypsy Caravan'. By this time the band were hanging out with Ray Davies and listening to Dylan, the latter a discernible influence on (2)'s 11-minute closing track 'Watching the Raindrops Fall'.

Two more singles, 'Mohair Suit' and 'Girl You Shouldn't Know', both from the second half of 1965, kept up a certain amount of momentum, but these were difficult times for the group. There were personal tensions, many of them fomented by the presence of Shankley-Walker, whom the others disliked, and ineffectual management. (3), released in the same week as the Beatles' all-conquering *Revolver* and sounding suspiciously like the Small Faces (*q.v.*), whose Mod gladrags the boys now affected, having long since given up on their matching suits, was their weakest recording to date. The era of flower power found them treading water, although (4), with its fashionable kaleidoscope sleeve, was a surprise hit, while the group, always astutely publicised, continued to remain newsworthy. Both Dangerfield and Halliwell, for example, were supposedly present during the famous police raid on Redlands, Keith Richards's country house in Sussex, in the early part of 1967 and narrowly avoided criminal charges. The press feeding-frenzy reached its height when Shankley-Walker, who had previously expressed his intention of leaving the group, or been sacked from it – reports varied – was found dead in the swimming pool of a friend's borrowed farmhouse on 14 August 1967.

There followed an inevitable period of introspection, broken only by a cameo appearance in the Beatles' *Magical Mystery Tour* (*q.v.*), in which they can be seen cavorting on the back seats of the bus. John Lennon later remarked that they were '... fucking hooligans. Don't know why we had them on board.' (5), which dates from this time, is a period curio, largely consisting of spoken-word improvisations delivered by Dangerfield to an accompaniment of skeletal back-beats. But change was in the air. Shankley-Walker's replacement Gary Pasarolo (b. Tenterden, 12 September 1949), formerly of the Pastel Shades, was a *bona fide* guitar virtuoso. Out went keyboards, Mod cuts and King's Road stylings and in their place came leather jackets, longer hair and a harder sound. With a new manager on board – the formidable Don Shard – and, on the expiry of their Decca contract, a recording deal with EMI, the band emerged from the studio with (6) – certainly their most accomplished record to date, whose occult shadings ('Ouija Board', 'Who is This that Wakes from Slumber?') brought disapproving articles in the tabloid press. Returning to the States, for the first of several increasingly lucrative tours, they discovered that they had acquired a new, and older – if not necessarily mature – audience, attracted by the overtly 'political' material on (7). All this brought commercial rewards that were, for the time, almost unprecedented. In 1971 it was calculated that as a live act they were out-sold only by Led Zeppelin (*q.v.*), the Who (*q.v.*) and the Stones. Their extravagant stage show at this time may be viewed on *Burning Skies*, the documentary film of their notorious free concert in

Ogdenville, Louisiana, which degenerated into a near-riot, and heard – inadequate production notwithstanding – on the sprawling (8). If later albums have lacked the power of (6) and (7), then the band are still a serious proposition – both inside the studio and out of it.

(1) *Suitcase Full of Songs* (Decca 1964), (2) *Pumped Up* (Decca 1965), (3) *Smiley Daze* (Decca 1966), (4) *Paisley Patterns* (Decca 1967), (5) *Just Saying* (Decca 1967), (6) *Cabinet of Curiosities* (EMI 1968), (7) *Low Blows in High Times* (EMI 1970), (8) *Got Live with the Helium Kids* (EMI double 1971), (9) *Greatest Hits* (EMI 1972), (10) *Street Assassins* (EMI 1973). Garth Dangerfield solo – *Ragamuffin Chorus* (EMI 1970).

New Musical Express Book of Rock, 1973

Recent years have not been kind to the Helium Kids. (11)'s ill-advised foray into 'progressive' rock cost them fans, not all of whom were won back by the hastily recorded and more soul-influenced (12). An album of no-frills rock-and-roll covers (13) did reasonable business but their live appearances were by now increasingly bloated affairs, accompanied by lurid tales of offstage excess and narcotics busts. None of this was helped by persistent rumours that EMI were unwilling to renew their contract. Nadir was reached on a woefully under-rehearsed and under-attended jaunt around the US in 1977 – again hit by controversy when $250,000 went missing from the tour manager's safe. With no new record on the racks for nearly three years and the individual members apparently estranged from each other it remains to be seen whether the band have shot their bolt.

(11) *Glorfindel* (EMI 1974), (12) *Feeling the Pressure* (EMI 1975), (13) *Return to Base* (EMI 1975), *Greatest Hits Vol. II* (EMI 1976).

New Musical Express Book of Rock, revised edition 1978

PART ONE
The Big World Out There

It's a big world out there
And I am scared . . .

1. BARRYTOWN

You're asking 'bout the other girls,
And sure there've been a few
But let me reassure you babe that
Hey, I'm glad it's you.

'Glad It's You'

'Miz Rosalind, she ain't been downstairs yet,' said Dolores the coloured maid, which was what you called female domestic servants of Afro-American descent in the south-western states in the year after John Kennedy died.

'That's all right. I'll wait in the hall.'

'Mizzuz Duchesne, she don't favour people strowin' up her vesti-bule none. Says it's like a-waiting for the Kentucky Derby to start.'

'Perhaps I'd better go into the sitting room, then.'

'You kin do that, I guess. But don't you go mussin' up none of Mr Duchesne's papers. They're confidential he says.'

It was about half-past seven in the evening, but the heat was still seeping up through the parched Arizona tarmacadam and the flowers in their urns by the Duchesnes' marbled doorstep all drooped crazily to one side. In the street, a gloomy three-dozen yards away, expensive, low-slung automobiles hastened sharkishly by. When you first fetched up in Phoenix out of the desert, rolled in from Silas or Prescott, say, and found that piecemeal collection of buildings, structures so any-the-which-way disposed that it was as if Zeus had flung them randomly from the top of Mount Olympus, there was always some wiseacre on hand to inform you proudly that there were three things you needed to know: that the climate was agreeable ('never like to rain in Phoenix'); that there wasn't a traffic problem, no sir, no how; and that the natives were friendly. All these statements were, in their varying degrees, misleading.

'Now you take care, you hear?' smirked Dolores, who clearly hated young, white, visiting Englishmen as much as she hated old, white, resident Americans. Above our heads several different noises – the bopping hum of the Duchesnes' generator, the march of footsteps and what sounded like two pieces of heavy furniture crashing together – proceeded in counterpoint, and so I pressed gingerly on over smooth, tan parquet that shoe-soles struggled to grip, through acres of spongy off-white carpet, past a top-of-the-range TV set not yet unpacked from its crate and a grocery sack full of gin bottles to the Duchesnes' sitting room, beyond whose oblong latticed windows the wide Arizona sky was settling to dusk. Here hung several of the items most commonly found in the private quarters of Arizona Republican bigwigs in the early 1960s: a colour photograph of Mr Duchesne ('Call me Al') lurking deedily on the steps of Phoenix City Hall with Richard Nixon; a picture of Mr Duchesne and his bride on their wedding day attended by what looked the cast of *The Ziegfeld Follies of 1936* but were, I had been assured, Mrs Duchesne's six sisters and her seventeen first cousins, all kitted out in identical calico bonnets and knee-length organdie frocks, and a full-length portrait of Mr Duchesne taken three days after Iwo Jima where, according to legend, he had personally despatched five Japanese infantrymen. Nearer at hand, dumped on occasional chairs or strewn over the polished table top, lay objects that were more site-specific: half-a-dozen postcards of

Phoenix's favourite son staring solemnly out across Grand Canyon and Monument Valley as if he'd had them put up specially for the general benefit; sheaves of Maricopa County canvass returns with red-inked margins; a couple of boxes of GO FOR GOLDWATER campaign buttons. But this was 5 November 1964, two days after the election, and none of these items, as Mr Duchesne would have conceded if pressed, was worth a fucking red cent.

There was a copy of the *Phoenix Gazette* on the davenport, a spacious broadsheet, this, with a descending triptych of headlines that read: GOLDWATER GRACIOUS IN DEFEAT: SENATOR HAS 'NO PLANS TO RETIRE INTO PRIVATE LIFE': MRS GOLDWATER 'SHEDS SILENT TEAR'. As I bent to pick it up something shattered violently on the floor of the room above, a female voice said *shit*, which wasn't a word you heard very often in Phoenix outside a mechanics' bar or a honky-tonk, much less spoken by a woman, and with a fine to-do about doorknob rattlings and associated throat-clearings, Mr Duchesne dawdled menacingly into the room. In the light of what came later, I've sometimes tried to invest that scene in the Duchesnes' front parlour, there amid the tangled snarl of Arizonian heritage, the Navajo rugs, the antique trail maps, the cowpoke spurs and branding irons tacked to the fire surround, with more significance than it may actually have possessed. But there was really nothing to it, nothing at all – just me and a watchful old gentleman in his fifties to whom, as the father of my girlfriend – if that was what she was – and for the past couple of months my employer to boot, I owed a certain bedrock modicum of respect, eyeing each other up and making small-talk. He was an intent, nervy character with that curiously blanched look – very common to Phoenix – that comes of sitting in air-conned offices all day when the temperature outside is up in the nineties, who had no idea how to talk to men thirty years his junior and made every statement he uttered sound like an address to a political convention.

'Why, Nicholas [*Necklass*],' he now began, in his white man's version of Dolores's fantastically exaggerated down-home croak. 'A pleasure [*pleeshure*] to see you.' The stack of Goldwater postcards caught his eye and returned him to the great business of his life. 'That was good work you did on the campaign, I reckon, son. Let me say that ...' He paused a moment, long enough for me to count the chevrons on his Elk club tie, and then came out with 'You are a very fine young man.'

'It's very kind of you to think so, sir.' Which was how you addressed any white male Arizonian over the age of forty who wasn't obviously destitute.

'Uh huh? Nonsense, boy. *Non. Sense.*' There were times when Mr Duchesne sounded like what he was, which was an immensely shrewd real-estate lawyer with a finger in every municipal property development from Tucson to the Texas border, and there were times when he sounded like Hopalong Cassidy rounding up the dogies. At this precise moment he seemed a figure of enormous consequence: simultaneously baleful, kindly and capricious, a good ole boy from the back-end of the Copper State with whom you manifestly couldn't take liberties. 'Non-*sense*,' he said again, so that the second half of the word seemed to stretch out into a third syllable. 'An' you bin spending a lot of time with Rosalind too?'

'That's right, sir.'

'Taking her to the movies and such-like [*sech-lakh*]?'

'Now and again, sir. She's a very fine young woman.'

'That's OK. I guess you're the kind of young fellow I like to see her around with,' he said, without much conviction. 'Only, look here ...' But whatever he was going to add was interrupted by another terrific crash from up yonder and the arrival of Dolores to report that Mizzuz Duchesne had sent word to say that she was running late and we wuz to go ahead without her.

'Did Lucille ... Did Mrs Duchesne say how long she'd be?'

'No suh.' Dolores, so snappy if you abandoned a half-full coffee mug on her kitchen table, was always subdued around her employer. 'Said she needed time to try on a new dress or sumthin.'

'Well, we can surely wait a moment,' Mr Duchesne said, with a sudden, exceptional bitterness. He grabbed the copy of the *Phoenix Gazette*, held it up to the level of my chin and tapped it with his forefinger. 'I've had just about enough of this.'

I could see a cue when it was offered. 'Enough of what, sir?'

'Why now, Democrats grinding our noses in the dirt. Liberals pushing us around. Let me tell you that twenty-seven million American patriots voted for Goldwater and they ain't all morons [*moh-rons*]. Ole Miss, Alabama, South Carolina, Georgia [*Jawjar*], Louisiana all went 'Publican, and when wuz the last time *that* happened? The South's gonna rise again, and it'll rise up right under Johnson's fat ass. But I wuz hopin' we'd see off some first-termers. That Vance Hartke, say, in Indiana or Phil Hart in Michigan, and it ain't happened. But let me tell you I'm *proud* of what we've achieved. You hear what I'm saying?'

I heard what he was saying. It would have been impolite in the circumstances to have pointed out that Johnson had collected over sixteen-million votes more than Arizona's finest and 61 per cent of the total cast, and that Barry Goldwater, whatever his ability to beckon a few million Dixiecrat racists to the cause, had led the Grand Old Party to something approaching electoral meltdown.

'Chrissakes,' Mr Duchesne said. 'Where is that dang woman?'

Three months into my stay in Phoenix, I was used to this kind of thing: folksiness alongside steely precision; naivety framed with the basest cynicism; skyscraper buildings and a set of social attitudes that hadn't changed since old 'Laramie' Jack Swilling had crawled in off the salt flats to establish the place in 1867; all that terrible, pulled-both-ways wonder of sixties America. It was quite dark now up here in Deer Valley, where the Duchesnes grandly hung out, profoundly dark, and although the lights from downtown were blazing up through the murk you could tell that the desert, with all its murmuring silence, was only a couple of miles away. Muttering something about needing the bathroom I went out into the hallway and found Rosalind dabbing powder onto her face from a compact.

'Nick! Nobody told me you were here. It's too bad of Dolores.'

'You look very nice.' Back then, before the sixties had properly begun, the Phoenix girls were less matronly versions of their mothers and wore Alice bands over corn-coloured bobs, pearl necklaces and capacious pinafore frocks.

'Do I? Why, thank you. So do you.'

'Did I get the right kind of jacket?' The men were supposed to wear tuxedos to this evening's entertainment.

'Well, if you really must know, you could have found a better place to hire it than Schwab's.'

'On account of?'

She gave a little twitch of her shoulders, as if to show that while duly acclimatised to the prejudices of the county she didn't necessarily share them. 'On account of him being Jewish.'

'I thought Barry Goldwater was Jewish.'

'It doesn't signify *in the least.*' She leaned over and ran a gloved hand over a phantom crease in the tuxedo. 'Momma isn't coming right away.'

'So I gathered.'

'She's not quite herself.'

'I'm sorry to hear that.'

Mr Duchesne came slinking foxily from his lair, his white face grimly alight in the darkened corridor, and peered at us suspiciously. 'Time we wuz a movin' on,' he said with what might just have been a homely self-consciousness. 'Your mother will take her own car, I daresay.'

The upper part of the house had fallen silent. Outside the front door the Duchesnes' once-emerald lawn glowed beneath a tracery of fairy lights. Beyond this, and the clogged highway that ran alongside, sempiternal darkness lay over the hick towns – Prescott, Benson, Douglas – of the Arizona plain. And so, quitting the silent mansion, and Mrs Duchesne, who was not quite herself, and Dolores, who on past form would presently be pilfering Mr Duchesne's cigarettes out of the mahogany case on the sideboard, and the Maricopa County canvass returns, and the Arizonian antiquities, and Rosalind's little white-painted *boudoir* under the eaves, and all manner of hints and imputations I hadn't yet managed to get my ahead around, we packed into Mr Duchesne's gigantic Studebaker and juddered off into the concertina'd lines of automobiles winding their way down towards Main Street in the naphtha glare of the streetlamps, with Mr Duchesne grousing about the goddamned traffic as if it had nothing whatever to do with the grid-iron road layout, the absence of side-walks and gas at 15 cents a gallon on which he and the rest of the city fathers so fondly insisted, past crew-cut kids and cowed-looking Hispanics on street-corners and neon 7 Up signs and hamburger joints and late-night pharmacies with long, steamed up windows and discount funeral parlours ('Tasteful . . . Hygienic . . . Instalment plans') and attorney's offices offering $10 tax returns while-U-waited, all of them hung with election bunting that no one had bothered to take down, until finally the road swung round and we were in sight of the Corporation Plaza, around which limousines and police cars were swarming, and a banner slung over the entrance which said PHOENIX WELCOMES SEN. & MRS GOLDWATER – ALL YOU CAN EAT BUFFET $2.99.

Inside, a woolly haired butler who looked much as Nelson Mandela would look thirty years later was taking coats and inviting people to kindly step this way suh and moddom and a committee of buffed-up Republican potentates stood around shaking hands. Mr Duchesne was instantly swallowed up by this stiff-shouldered horde, swallowed up and exalted by their chatter ('Marcelle with you tonight, Eugene ...?' 'How you doin', Dale?' 'I'm good, Buck, I'm tremendous') so Rosalind and I cruised over to the bar in search of that negligible part of the Phoenix demographic which could be filed as 'anyone I know who isn't a friend of Daddy's. Here there were six-foot buckaroos in Stetsons shooting the breeze about rodeos and bull-riding, while their snub-nosed dates stood up on tippy-toes to watch, and a cine-film playing of Reagan giving his 'A Time for Choosing' speech, and I looked up at Ron – people called him 'Ron' not 'Ronnie' in those far-off days – thinking that he was an affable old ham to be sure but that no one could possibly take him seriously. I've heard it said that 1964, down in Phoenix, was the start of something, that the free market was mysteriously reborn here in the shadow of the Arizona desert and that Barry Goldwater, old Barry, was a true prophet, but let me tell you that's not how it seemed at the time. There were balloons hanging in clusters, like giant grapes, from the balcony of the Plaza's auditorium and posters all around the place proclaiming WE DID IT FOR BARRY, but none of the Arizona Republicans, the Dales, the Dexters and the Eugenes, were happy men. For here they were in a right-to-work state built on gas, cattle and segregation, where no union baron dared so much as make a phone call without some civic grandee to tell him that a basic human freedom was being infringed, with a leader who preached states' rights and the communist menace, and forty-three million of their fellow-Americans – Massachusetts liberals and Catholics and California pinkoes, yeah, but forty-three million of them nonetheless – had rooted for LBJ, a man so corrupt that it was said that back in 1960 twenty-thousand blank ballot papers had lain in the Texas Democratic Party HQ waiting for the first Republican vote totals to be declared so that whatever the figure was it could straightaway be consigned to defeat.

The 'Time for Choosing' speech had given way to clips from the Goldwater TV ads, in which Barry zestfully piloted his plane around the Arizona boondocks, ate lavish Christmas dinners with his effervescing brood at a table that adjoined parched fields of cacti, sternly inspected military installations and their hardware and looked, it seemed to me, simultaneously mad and blitzed and unreliable, and people were tearfully applauding and pounding each other's shoulders and launching sporadic whoops of admiration (*'Barry! Barry!'*). Desperate cries, they seemed to me, agonised and desperate, from somewhere far beyond the Arizona sunshine, out beyond the rim of the world. Meanwhile, there were other problems to consider, one of which was standing close by, orange juice in hand, with the light from the chandeliers shining off her hair and setting it lambently aglow.

'How was your day?'

'*Strenuous*, I guess. Naturally, I worked in the morning.' There was a fiction that Rosalind, two languid years out of high school, was taking typing classes, but everyone knew that Mr Duchesne would cheerfully have shot an elk with Hubert Humphrey rather than allow his daughter to stoop to secretarial work. 'Then I had lunch with some of the girls at Macy's bakery. Only of course Marty Knowland just had to stop by to show me his new Caddie, which is just darling.' A balloon rolled dangerously towards her over the polished floor and she took an expert little skip into safety. 'Not to mention helping Momma around the house.'

When I first arrived in Phoenix I'd assumed that its womenfolk lacked both guile and individuality. Three months later I was revising this opinion, all too aware that their submissiveness was capable of coexisting with a striking capacity for self-preservation.

The shots of Barry inspecting rocket-launchers and tumbleweed entanglements of barbed wire had given way to Barry on the porch of a Baptist church grimly attending to a foxy old gentleman in a preacher's robes who was doubtless telling him to give the Commies hell and keep those darkies in Alabam away from God-fearing white folks, but in the absence of the man himself the whoops, the hollers and the hubbub were dying down.

'What say we go on somewhere after this?' I wondered. 'Take in' – I was gaining ground on the local idiom – 'a movie or something?'

'Oh Nick, you know I'd love to but I can't.' As she said this Rosalind brought her hands up imploringly to her bosom in a gesture that would have been substantially more enticing if she hadn't performed it on every occasion that we met. 'You see, Momma wants me to go out calling with her in the morning, and then I have to be at the bureau at eleven or Mrs Oglander will tell me off to Daddy again. But we can go tomorrow evening, honey, that's for sure. Francine said why don't I go and have a sundae with her and Marty Knowland, but you can pick me up after that if you like.'

This, by the way, was what 'dating' consisted of in Phoenix the year Goldwater got trashed by LBJ, or at any rate its higher class, virgin-bride end: giggling trips to ice-cream parlours; platonic Sabbath-afternoon 'drives' to beauty spots; sundaes with Marty and Francine; a little inoffensive necking, as it was called, on the patio while Mom and Pop were out someplace and the coloured maid napped in her room. There were, allegedly, specimens of young Phoenix maidenhood who 'went too far', skinny-dipped in the Gila River, attended naked swimming parties in the basement pools of the big houses up on Shelley Heights and would end up in an abortion clinic, but Rosalind wasn't one of these.

'That's great,' I said.

All this time the Goldwater homecoming was going on around us, and the tide of variegated Republican humanity surged back and forth: damson-faced farmers with their stomachs hanging over their britches and nutcracker thighs from spending six hours a day in the saddle; little old ladies with sausage curls and elaborately clasped handbags who lived modestly in the suburbs and worshipped Ike as if he were their long-dead brother; Klan viziers and warlords with incriminating tie-pins (Barry was supposed to have repudiated the Klan, but then Barry was supposed to have repudiated a lot of things); behemoth sophomores from the local college with their Adam's apples bursting out of their throats like tomahawks ('They're good kids,' a professor met at a fundraiser had confided to me, 'but they ain't had the education. Why some of them cain't hardly write their names in the dirt with a stick.') Rosalind, I noticed, was looking at me with the kind of sympathetic yet sorrowful expression hitherto reserved for friends who were making fools of themselves with motorcycle boys from what was known, with no irony whatsoever, as the wrong side of town, and there was some kind of commotion – cacophony, dropped glasses, elbowed-aside waiters and raised voices – steadily reaching crescendo at the room's furthermost end.

In those days, back in Phoenix, afterwards in New York, even later on in Knightsbridge, I used to believe that you could import drama into your life at will, that if wished for it would seek you out in a way that matched your expectations of it. Only later did I come to understand that the truly dramatic is nearly always unforeseen, and that its consequences can never be predicted and sometimes not even understood. What happened now bore this maxim out. Rosalind did not use her sympathetic yet sorrowful look as the prelude to a declaration of love. She did not seize my hand and tell me urgently – as had happened in a movie we had seen only the other week – that I could whisk her away to a motel room and do whatever I wanted with her. Instead she said a touch brusquely:

'Daddy says he wants to have a *good long talk* to you.' Mr Duchesne was keen on having talks 'to' people rather than with them.

'What about?'

'He says he's interested to know what you're gonna do here now the election's done.'

It was a good question. There would be no more political work in Phoenix for another six months, when some of the state legislature campaigns opened up. Meanwhile, I had $50 in the First Bank of Phoenix two doors along from Al's office and the rent on my apartment was due in a fortnight.

'I'd quite like to know myself.'

'Daddy says' – and here she lowered her voice to the point where it became almost conspiratorial – 'he could help you get a job if that's what you wanted.'

And then, without warning, the known and the assimilable melted away. In fact, several things happened simultaneously. A fan which had been pulsing above our heads, winnowing the stale Republican air and setting the leaves of the gardenias that one or two of the girls wore in their buttonholes sensuously aquiver, gave an awful mechanical squeal and ground painfully to a halt. Rosalind drew in her breath sharply. A man standing next to me, sounding like Foghorn Leghorn in one of the *Looney Tunes* cartoons, said, 'What in tarnation?' Meanwhile, at the far end of the room the haphazard choreography of descending trays, tangled limbs and shattered glass resolved itself and out of the confusion, moving towards us with a swaying yet purposeful step, came a solitary female figure.

The effect on Rosalind was electric. 'Oh my good Lord,' she said.

In my three months in Phoenix I had witnessed several of Mrs Duchesne's performances. I had seen her plunge headlong down the main staircase of her house. I had seen her miss by a solid foot the ashtray in which she was trying to extinguish a cigarette and grind out the butt on the palm of her hand. I had seen her stand on the back porch and hurl a pile of dinner plates, one by one, in a wide descending arc, like a champion discus thrower limbering up. Eyeing up these displays of temperament, I had rather admired the nonchalance that seemed to lie at their core – that, and the oddly non-committal way in which they were received by the other Duchesnes. Mr Duchesne, Rosalind, Herb the beetle-browed elder brother who sometimes came over on Sunday afternoons – none of them ever seemed particularly bothered by the smashed dinner services or the spread-eagled figure on the parquet floor. It was what Mrs Duchesne did, how she behaved, part of the baggage she carried around with her, her inch-thick turtle's shell, which the others dealt with by not making a fuss about it. Here, though, it was pretty clear that, like the girls who went skinny-dipping in the Gila River, Mrs Duchesne had gone way too far.

'Oh Momma,' Rosalind wailed away. 'You *promised*.'

What had Mrs Duchesne promised? Not to follow her husband and daughter to the Corporation Plaza when demonstratively the worse for drink? Not to cause trouble in their wake? Not to appear before the Republican elders of Phoenix in what even I could see was a manifestly unsuitable costume of off-the-shoulder Manhattan party frock, surfeit of badly applied lipstick and stockingless feet? Whatever it was, she had failed, and failed miserably.

Rosalind's watchfulness had given way to a determination not to let things go any further. 'Now, see here, Momma . . .' she began.

Mrs Duchesne ignored her. This might have been deliberate. Or it might have been that she was so far gone that the faces around her were simply indistinguishable. Whatever the explanation, she whirled round on her heel with such force that the three or four people nearest to hand, all of whom had been watching her with expressions of fascinated disgust, spun nervously away. Quite by chance, or so I thought, her gaze fell on me.

'How are you, Nick? Nice to see you.'

'You too, Mrs Duchesne.'

Until this time it was arguable whether Mrs Duchesne and I had exchanged more than two-dozen words. Now, for some reason, she greeted me as if I was her oldest friend.

'Would you believe it, Nick? There was a black man at the door tried to tell me I couldn't come in. Wasn't that ridiculous of him? And then a waiter dropped a whole tray of glasses just where I was trying to take off my coat.'

'But you're all right now, I hope?'

'I thought I'd just look in. Shake some hands. See the sights. Hear what Senator Goldwater has to say. That's if he has anything to say at all.'

There was a way in which Mrs Duchesne's lucidity diverted attention from quite how stupendously drunk she was. The really odd thing, I decided, was the colour of her face. Always reddish-tinted, this now seemed to have acquired a faint tinge of apricot.

'*Momma*,' Rosalind cried again, frankly aghast.

'Don't Momma me,' Mrs Duchesne said equably. Her knees sagged a bit, but she managed to right herself. 'In fact, why don't you go and find your father and tell him I'm making an exhibition of myself? That's what you usually do. And then I can have a nice little heart-to-heart with your *beau* here. That's a good girl.'

We watched Rosalind skitter off through the throng. There was a feeling that the situation had calmed down, or at any rate could get no worse. The people who had seen Mrs Duchesne arrive in the room, and perhaps had experience of her behaving badly, went back to their conversations. The fan above our heads gave a little start and whirred back into life. Taking this as a signal, the band of white-coated musicians who had been loitering on the raised dais on the far side of the ballroom arranged themselves in formation and a tiny bald man in a multicoloured waistcoat and a pair of horn-rimmed spectacles began lustily to sing:

> In ah mountain greenery
> Where Gahd paints the scenery
> Jest two . . . kerrazy people tagether
> While you love ya lover
> Let blue skahs be ya cover . . .

'You'd better get me a drink,' Mrs Duchesne instructed, raising her voice above the din.

The bar was a heaving mass of tuxedos, worn by men who were clearly determined to tie one on before the sobriety-enjoining arrival of the senator, but there was a waiter going past with a tray full of martinis. Mrs Duchesne hoicked a glass off the edge and downed it in one. The cherry re-emerged on the tip of her tongue for a second and then, with a little dab of her head, she flicked it cruelly away.

'Al will take his time,' she said. 'Always did. Never one for a *scene*. You know, that's a beautiful accent you have there, Nick. Quite beautiful, even if you do tune it up for our general benefit. You ought to make a *rekkud* of yourself talking so that all the Phoenix ladies could listen to it and get themselves an idea of what civilisation was all about.'

She would have been about forty-five, I thought, slimline but raddled, with a nicotine-stained right forefinger and hair piled up behind a bow like Mary-Jane in the TV ads doling out cookies to the children. Searching for some resemblance to Rosalind, I found it in the curve of her jaw and the way her throat tapered away oh-so-gracefully into the skin of her neck.

The band had finished 'Mountain Greenery' and the man in the multicoloured waistcoat was loudly demanding of ice-cold Katy why she wouldn't marry the soldier. Outside on the wide star-lit plain Arizona would be settling down for the night, and back in the dead towns, in Elfrida, Turtleneck, Fredonia and Snowflake, the younger citizenry would be drinking tomato juices in the late-night pharmacies and lighting out along Main Street, while the coyotes bawled at the moon. Mrs Duchesne took a pack of Marlboro cigarettes out of her bag, and stuck one in the corner of her mouth.

'Could you kindly light this for me? Thank you, Nick. You know, I've been watching you taking in our little ways. Don't think I haven't.

Nothing to worry about. I mean, I like you, Nick. And believe me, that's something. Much better than not liking you. Al doesn't. You may think he does, but he doesn't. I suppose, now the election's done, you think he's going to give you a job?'

'It had occurred to me.'

'Well, he won't. Sure, he liked having you on the team, shaking hands with the farmers, with that gorgeous accent of yours, but believe me that's as far as it goes. Al likes people he knows. Better still, people whose fathers he knows. Grandfathers, sometimes. And then there's my daughter. My daughter *Rosalind*,' Mrs Duchesne said, as if she had countless other daughters lying around the place. She looked about for an ashtray and, not finding one, tapped the cigarette against the lip of the martini glass. 'No chance there either, I should say. She'll marry Marty Knowland. Maybe not for a year or two, but that's what she'll do. You're very fond of her, aren't you, Nick?'

It was difficult to know how to answer this. Perhaps what had done for Mr Duchesne would do for his wife. 'She's a very fine young woman.'

'Yes, she is,' Mrs Duchesne sadly agreed. 'That's exactly what she is. Just like me. I was a fine young woman once. Yes sir, every old bag of bones in this hall used to be a fine young woman. You can't get on if you're not. And you certainly can't marry Marty Knowland. Rosalind knows that. Why now, there she is again.'

Over by the dais, where the press of bodies was at its greatest, the crowd had parted to release a small procession made up of Rosalind, Mr Duchesne and a Duane and a Eugene or two eager to catch the fun.

'Get me out of here,' Mrs Duchesne said suddenly.

'What do you mean?'

'What I said. Get me out. Before I smash this glass into Al's face and tell Rosalind that she'd be better off marrying some poor booby boy from the county asylum.'

Rosalind and Mr Duchesne were only thirty feet away now. Mr Duchesne's face was whiter than ever, like candlewax. Above our heads the Tannoy crackled into life. '*Ladeez,*' the announcer wearily began over the racket of the band, '*Ladeez and gennelmen . . .*' For a split second I wondered about abandoning her, jumping ship, letting the Duchesnes fight it out among themselves, coming back later to examine the casualties. At the same time I could tell that I was in the presence of a will much greater than my own, a controlling force that wouldn't be gainsaid. Mrs Duchesne, I saw, would get what she desired, whether I liked it or not. It was only her vote that would be counted.

We reached the hotel lobby to find a wave of tension sweeping through it, like wind over corn. Flunkies came smartly to attention; the old black butler abased himself on the plum-coloured carpet. A family party, consisting of a tall, spare patriarch in his fifties, two younger men and a girl and an older woman with elaborately marcelled hair, was racketing through the vestibule. I had seen enough photographs of that husky and curiously tortured face, quite often framed beneath a cowboy hat, to know that this was Barry Goldwater. By this time the senator, flanked by a couple of aides and a man I recognised as the local Republican Party chairman, was barely a yard away. I could have reached out and touched him had I wanted to. I could have reached out and struck him had I wanted that. Straying instinctively to one side, I saw that Mrs Duchesne had taken up a position directly in front of him, more or less blocking his path.

'Why Barry,' she said. 'You're awfully late.'

Goldwater's face relaxed. 'Lucille. It's good to see you.' He put out his hand, to which Mrs Duchesne clung tenaciously for a second or two, and then, thinking that his tardiness needed some formal explanation, went on: 'We had a problem out on the interstate. Thought we were never going to get here. You with Al?'

'He's in there somewhere.' The right-hand shoulder of Mrs Duchesne's skimpy frock had twisted up, exposing her brassiere strap to view. 'I was just leaving myself.'

If Goldwater was wondering why the wife of one of his trustiest lieutenants had opted to walk out of the hotel where he was booked to speak at the precise moment he was walking into it, he was too polite to say so.

'That's too bad,' he said gravely.

Mrs Duchesne began to laugh. In the ghastly light thrown by the hotel chandeliers her face seemed to have turned bright orange. 'You'll have to excuse me, but there's something I need to tell you.'

Goldwater offered no encouragement. He seemed to understand that something was wrong. Perhaps he was used to being accosted by the dishevelled wives of his supporters in hotel lobbies. For a moment he stood sizing Mrs Duchesne up: the three-term Arizona senator who had lost to LBJ by the small matter of seventeen-million votes and the Phoenix real-estate lawyer's drunken wife, by now laughing uncontrollably and with part of her underwear showing.

'Barry,' Mrs Duchesne went on, her voice rising to a shriek. '*I'm sorry you fucking lost.*'

The cortege passed on. Outside in the street the heat was still rising from the sidewalk. The downtown traffic snarled around us. Mrs Duchesne, who had stumbled on her way down the marbled steps, clung to a railing for support.

'I never liked him,' she said, between mouthfuls of warm air. 'Ron Reagan I can just about stand. But not that sonofabitch from the John Birch Society.'

Her car was parked in a side street round the back of the hotel, with one wheel up on the kerb. Luggage lay jammed up against the rear window. Mrs Duchesne installed herself in the passenger seat and rested her head on the dashboard so that her dark hair flooded out over the plastic like a stain.

'You'd better drive.'

'Where to?'

'You decide. Anywhere but here.'

'I see.'

From inside the hotel came a burst of applause, wild cries, a bass drum eerily resounding. By degrees, and with advice from the passenger seat, we moved off. Another thing about the truly dramatic is the lessening of responsibility it brings. Here in the car with Mrs Duchesne I was half exhilarated and half struck down with terror. There was absolutely no knowing what would happen. All bets were off.

'I need to stop at my apartment.'

'That's fine by me,' Mrs Duchesne said. Bolt upright in her seat now, arms folded across her chest, face more or less returned to its normal colour, she looked surprisingly at ease. It was hard to believe that the events of the last half hour had taken place.

The apartment was on the south side of town: a stone's throw from what was unofficially known as the nigger belt. Here mouldered tenement housing, all-night diners and juke joints where old black men played country blues deep into the small hours. It took five minutes to pack what I owned into a pair of canvas holdalls and write an ambiguous note to the landlady. At intervals out in the street the car horn sounded. I switched off the light and lingered for a while in the darkness, following the trail of the streetlamp where it fell over cupboard doors, folded ironing boards, empty milk cartons and boxes of Golden Grahams. It was about half-past nine, but the day had one more surprise. On the doormat, receding into shadow, lay a white envelope. I picked it up and turned it over in my hand. The writing, not seen in half-a-dozen years but horribly familiar, was my father's. Outside, the car horn sounded again.

At some point in my absence Mrs Duchesne had raided a suitcase, for she was wearing a top-coat over her frock and had wound a chiffon scarf around her neck. She was also eating a Hershey bar.

'I thought you were never coming,' she said.

'I was wondering myself.'

I stowed the canvas holdalls in the boot, stood irresolutely on the sidewalk, climbed into the car and then, without even knowing that the trick was done, moved off from one world into another.

2. NORTH PARK AND AFTER

Going back to the place I came from
Going back to the world I knew
Going back to the dreams I nurtured
Going back to me and you

'Going Back'

The house is small. Just the five rooms, not including an eight-by-six-foot cupboard under the roof with space for a couple of boxes. My mother likes to call this the guest bedroom, although no genuine guest will ever sleep there. Downstairs are parlour, kitchen and sitting room. The cramped garden, where thin grass blanches in the shadow of monstrous gooseberry bushes, never catches the sun. We will be moving soon anyhow, my mother says brightly all through the early fifties, a little less confidently in the years that follow. We never do. Outside lurk the perils of the teeming streets: the park with its file of elm trees; the dangerous highway of Colman Road where fast cars maraud. Deep into adolescence I have a mantra dinned into my head to recite to the policemen or responsible adults who will rescue me should I stray from this quadrant. My name is Nicholas Franklin McArthur Du Pont – after Roosevelt and the general – and I live at 33 North Park Avenue, Norwich, Norfolk. The last two locations are superfluous. Everyone I am likely to meet knows where this is.

Taken together, the names are a mouthful, if not a liability. On the other hand, they are nothing like as onerous as my father's, who claims to have been baptised Maurice Chesapeake Albuquerque Seattle Du Pont in homage to the army depots where his own father, Grampa Du Pont, had done his military training. Not that there is any guarantee that my father's head has ever gone into a baptismal font. He has a kind of genius for evading official constraints or prescriptions; has, allegedly, no driving licence, passport or social security number. This provisional quality is enhanced by his not actually living in the house on North Park, but in America, possibly in Sarasota, Florida, or perhaps – my mother is vague about this – somewhere in New Mexico. Sir Winston Churchill becomes Prime Minister for the second time and King George dies in his sleep forty miles away at Sandringham. Bread comes off the ration, but my father is not there to witness it.

Despite the gaping hole of his absence, Maurice Chesapeake Albuquerque Seattle dominates my early life. There is a framed photograph of him a foot square in the uniform of 319th Bomb Group on the parlour mantelpiece. The wartime 78s presented to my mother – 'In the Mood', 'Bei Mir Bist du Schon', 'String of Pearls' – sit in a pile by the record player. From their sleeves, bland American faces stare imperturbably out. The peaked USAF cap he once wore still hangs on the coat-rack. Sometimes letters come from Florida, New Mexico and half-a-dozen other places, which my mother reads aloud to her cronies. The letters are long and full of news. My father is always up to something: planning to open a gas station; touring Montana in a convertible to watch the rodeos; negotiating to buy a mobile home. He signs off 'Your loving husband Maurice Du Pont'. My mother's friends are impressed by these budgets, but there is a feeling that distance has dulled their edge. It is all too far away, like rain falling out in the North Sea. Meanwhile, England lose 6–3 to Hungary at Wembley Stadium. Sir Winston Churchill is succeeded by Sir

Anthony Eden, who my mother, an enthusiastic Conservative, says is a 'real gentleman'.

My mother is a small, dark-haired woman: 'petite' in the cipher of the women's magazines – *Good Housekeeping, Woman's Own* – that she buys at Ragan's, the newsagent's around the corner in Colman Road in whose murky window pinned-up copies of the *Daily Telegraph* turn yellow in the sun. She likes to talk about the time she met my father at the Samson and Hercules Ballroom in Tombland, where GIs from the USAF bases out on the Norfolk plain came to dance the Jitterbug on Friday nights. My mother is from the Brecks – 'somewhere out there west of Thetford' – summoned to Norwich to work in a factory making silk canopies for parachutes. We will go back there one day, she insists, to Methwold or Feltwell, out in the wild country on the windy flat, and live in a house that looks out onto fields rather than the football pitches and the bowling greens of Eaton Park. We never do. Three months after the meeting at the Samson and Hercules Ballroom, under one of the great white pillars that flanked the stage, they get married. None of their parents attends: Grampa and Granma Du Pont because they live in Poughkeepsie, Upstate New York and there is a war on: Granny and Grandad Mickleburgh – my mother's maiden name – because they so strongly disapprove of what Henry James would call this rash and insensate step. A solitary sister escapes the net of parental outrage and comes over on the train from Brandon to be bridesmaid. Three months after that, my father is posted back to America and never seen again. Aunt Dorothy, the bridesmaiding sister, returns to 'help out'. She stays two years, before marrying an insurance agent and going to live in Southend. Once again, we are on our own. Photographs come back of a spruce, stucco house by the sea and a marram lawn where Sealyham terriers frolic, but my mother soon loses interest. She has other things to worry about.

To eke out her income, my mother takes part-time jobs. Behind the counter at the newsagent's. At the dry-cleaner's half-a-mile away in Bunnett Square. None of them lasts very long. My mother can't settle to the work. The hours don't suit, and the people upset her. One day she will get a proper job in one of the big city offices, she explains, where the men wear suits and there is a social club with a dinner dance. She never does. Whenever these part-time employments fail, an advert is placed in the *Eastern Evening News* and the guest bedroom let out to lodgers. There are several of these: Mr Standley, who works for the council's Parks and Recreation department; Mr Cadwallader, who teaches at the infants' school; Mr McNulty, who gives my mother a pound a week out of his dole money and spends his days reading the *Racing Post* and taking furtive walks in the park. My mother is distant with the lodgers, chivvies them briskly out of rooms she wants to clean, gossips uncharitably about them to the neighbours and is glad to see them gone. About this time, she takes up smoking. The empty Embassy Regal packets lie decoratively on the drugget carpet. The coupons are hoarded in a tin bowl by the front door, along with the Green Shield stamps and the Co-op's bounty. When the pile reaches the rim, my mother will exchange them for a cheap table lamp, a shoe-cleaning kit or a rickety ironing board. Aunt Dorothy's husband takes a job in Canada. Grandad Mickleburgh dies of pleurisy, still unreconciled, and my mother goes over on the train to his funeral. She comes back tearful and, it has to be allowed, three-parts drunk, saying she has had enough of North Park and wants to leave.

But North Park is not so easily left. It is a long, curving thoroughfare that follows the line of the park due west to a semi-countryside of fields and golf courses, a dense, mobile world, thronged with people: bicycling old men; children on their way to school; paperboys on their rounds; tallymen going door to door. Once one of the bicycling old men drops dead outside the house just as my mother and I reach the gate. The look on his face – a rictus of beady black eyes and peg teeth – gives me nightmares for months. The North Park men work in the boot and shoe trade, in garages and engineering shops. Their newspaper of choice is the *Daily Mirror*, which has pictures of Gina Lollobrigida, Jayne Mansfield and Diana Dors but also mention of Mr Attlee, Mr Bevan and Mr Chuter Ede. Housewives are judged by the neatness of their interiors and the freshness of their net curtains but also for the prodigality of their material goods. The first television set arrives on the road – a tiny glass screen set in a catafalque of teak, showing grainy black-and-white pictures of Muffin the Mule and the Queen launching ships on the Clyde – and is much admired. In Canada, Aunt Dorothy gives birth to twins. My father writes to say that he is thinking of becoming a ranger at Yellowstone National Park.

My mother is not without her resources. She joins a ladies' bowling club that meets on Friday evenings at the park and allows her to wear a white A-line skirt and a peaked visor as a badge of membership. There is a sisterhood of North Park women who get together in the long afternoons to play whist and canasta for sixpenny stakes. The women have names like Mrs Stagg, Mrs Baldry and Mrs Marsden. Mrs Ellington, my mother's particular friend, warns her that they are only after her money. My mother claims not to care. At thirty-five she is still good-looking, but inclining to fat, with neat black hair regularly pummelled into one of the new styles that are always coming out by Madame Yvonne, who owns the Bunnett Square salon. Madame Yvonne's real name, it turns out, is Ethel. At ten years old I have my mother's dark hair and Bugs Bunny teeth, together with my father's high forehead and wide-awake eyes. This resemblance is often pointed out by people with whom my mother shares her photographs. Shortly after my tenth birthday she packs one of them into a manila envelope and sends it to my father's last-known address in Boise, Idaho. There is no reply. A story in the *Daily Mirror* says that the most popular English dogs' names are Hercules, Rex and Tuppence. It is at about this time that my mother shows me the black lacquer box my father bequeathed to me when he left. It contains a special gift, she explains, and can only be opened on my sixteenth birthday. The key is gone, but such is the importance which my mother attaches to this sacramental object that, when the day comes, she is prepared to smash it open with a hammer. I put the box away in the corner of my bedroom next to the model aircraft kits and *The Boy's Own Book of Adventure*.

Naturally, my mother and I spend time together. North Park approves of this. It is called 'doing your duty by the boy'. On Saturday afternoons we take buses into the city and explore its dark, inviting heart. Norwich is full of mystery. In the Norman castle – now a museum – there is a display case with a Saxon skull split nearly in two by a Danish battle-axe. A stone's throw away in Elm Hill cobbled streets descend to a warren of tiny shops selling stamp-packets and antique bric-a-brac. Other times, on summer Sundays, we take the train to the coast – to Cromer, Sheringham or Great Yarmouth – and promenade along the breeze-blown front eating Sky Ray lollies and Mr Whippy ice-cream cones and peering in at the windows of the big hotels. Next year, my mother says, we will have a proper holiday in the Lake District or the Cornish Riviera, sail in a boat, climb a mountain and dine off oysters. We never do. From Canada, Aunt Dorothy sends pictures of her children and the news that she is working in some-thing called 'real estate'. A man from Ruskin Road who wins £50,000 on the football pools tells the *Eastern Evening News* that he doesn't intend it to change his life. The family moves out a month later. The black lacquer box sits on its shelf.

At ten-and-a-half I show an unexpected academic turn and pass the eleven-plus exam. Colman Road Primary, where motherly Mrs Agar reads to us out of *Moonfleet* and *The Tale of the Flopsy Bunnies*, gives way to the City of Norwich Grammar School, with its honours board and shiny, linoleumed corridors, a mile away in Eaton Road. My mother is pleased, but also apprehensive, for the Mickleburghs are not supposed to be 'clever': Grandpa Mickleburgh, in particular, is thought to have been scarcely able to write his name. The ability to pronounce the words 'sabre' and 'ptomaine' in the reading-age test is clearly down to my father's influence, an unlooked-for twitch on the genetic thread. North Park is in two minds about grammar schools. They may very well get you a job at the Norwich Union Insurance Society or Lawrence & Scott Electromotors, but they might also encourage you to 'forget where you come from'. Even with a grant from the City Hall education committee, the uniform is a trial. Despairing of the pricey school outfitters my mother buys a couple of yards of cream-coloured flannel and makes up the cricket trousers herself. As for the social experiment which this transfer represents, if half of me is quite glad of the chance to forget where I come from, then the other half is borne away on its slow, sedative current: buying the *Pink 'Un* on Saturday nights to see the football scores; my mother at the kitchen table with that week's *Reveille*, reading the stories about film stars' engagement rings and the man who was swallowed by a whale but regurgitated three days later still alive but bleached white by its gastric juices, with her mouth open in a little 'O' of wonderment, like a goldfish.

Meanwhile, change is in the air. There are houses going up all over the west side of Norwich; the fields retreat and disappear and the outlying farms are being swallowed up. Mr Attlee gives way to Mr Gaitskell. The boys stop being called George and Albert and Jack and start being called Jason and Carl and Clifford. The girls stop being called Kate and Margaret and Mary and start being called Samantha and Jennifer and Suzanne. The North Park kitchens burst out in a rash of refrigerators and washing machines. Walking into the front room of a television-owning friend, I come upon Elvis Presley for the first time singing 'Hound Dog', and am transfixed by its novelty, its sheer outrageousness, the sense of ancient codes irretrievably despoiled. The backing band are the usual crowd of demure middle-aged men with cowlicked hair, but Elvis himself is unprecedented, titanic, a moody giant in a room of pygmies. Like the dead man sprawled in the street under his bicycle, the image stays in my head for months. A dozen North Park families club together to send a girl with cystic fibrosis on holiday and are commended by the Lord Mayor for their communal spirit. The mummified corpse of an elderly lady is brought out of a house where she has lain covered in old newspapers and piles of unopened post for the past two years. Suez comes and swarthy Mr Youkomain, owner of the local fish and chip shop, who is thought to be an Arab, has a brick thrown through his plate-glass window.

My mother goes into a decline. It is as if something fractures in her and never mends. She has given up on the part-time jobs to stitch baby clothes for a mail-order firm. The blue-paper patterns are pinned up on the kitchen wall, like contour maps. Anyone can stitch baby clothes, my mother says. Still, she finds it hard to keep up with the work. The sorority of the card tables is diminishing. Mrs Baldry and Mrs Marsden go off to play bingo in St Anne's church hall. My mother has a stand-up row with Mrs Stagg, a real North Park ding-dong, with men in shirt-sleeves trying gamely to intervene, over a borrowed ten-shilling note. Mrs Ellington, the solitary survivor, is there at all hours: an eternal cross-grained presence amid the baby clothes and the piles of teacups. My father's letters grow rarer and then dry up altogether. There is no more talk of warden's jobs at Yellowstone or rodeo tours of Montana. He may now live in Maryland, or Rhode Island. Nobody knows. The last thing he ever sends is a picture postcard of the Golden Gate Bridge. On the back he has writ-ten the words *Aiming to Cross this Beauty in Style*. Mrs Ellington and my mother are very companionable together. They go on excursions to jumble sales in dusty parish halls, or take bus rides out into the Norfolk countryside. One school sports day, breasting the tape in the half-mile, I look up to find them waving to me from the crowd, their faces full of pop-eyed excitement. Like my mother, Mrs Ellington has been abandoned by a man. Unlike my mother, the experience has left her embittered, watchful and unforgiving. At fifteen, tall now, again from my father (the Mickleburghs are country munchkins), with champagne-bottle shoulders, I am fiercely protective of my mother, and at the same time annoyed by her. I am also annoyed by Mrs Ellington, the piles of baby clothes, the plumes of cigarette smoke and the jar of sixpences that makes do for a savings account. At school we read *Dombey and Son*, *The History of Mr Polly* and *Nineteen Eighty-Four*. The plane carrying the Manchester United squad crashes at Munich, killing twenty-three passengers, eight of them players. Mrs Ellington, coming home across the park at dusk, stumbles over a cigar box containing dozens of fossilised white pellets. My mother identifies them as baby-teeth.

My mother rallies for my sixteenth birthday. Even in her semi-collapsed state, its significance is inescapable. The jar of sixpences is raided for funds to buy me a copy of *The Fellowship of the Ring*, and there is a cake from Oelrichs, the genteel baker in Bunnett Square, with my name picked out in blue icing. The black lacquer box lies between us on the table as I attack the first slice. Picking up the box for the hundredth time, I am startled once again by its weightlessness, the dry, feathery sounds that rustle from within, like the elm leaves in Eaton Park trodden underfoot, how little it seems to contain. What on earth can my father have hidden in it? For some reason, now the great day has arrived, the urgency has gone. After all, it is only a box deposited by a man not seen by either of us these past fifteen-and-three-quarter years. Almost idly, my mother and I discuss ways in which we can open it. In the end, I fetch a screwdriver from the tool-box in the kitchen cupboard, slide it under the rim and give a sharp, decisive twist. Unexpectedly, the lid springs apart. A few flakes of amber rust gently descend. Inside is a cutting from a local newspaper with a picture of my father's unit on the day it arrived in Norfolk, six $5 bills and a packet of Lucky Strikes mouldering away to dust.

I decide that I am never going to forgive my father for this.

* * *

And all the while time is marching on. 1958. 1959. Sir Anthony Eden gives way to Harold Macmillan, although my mother prefers Mr R. A. Butler, and there are race riots in North Kensington. Norwich City Football Club go on a triumphant Cup run that takes them as far as the semi-final. Twenty-thousand people travel down to London for the quarter-final replay at Tottenham Hotspur, and the queue for semi-final tickets stretches a mile around the ground. A university is scheduled for the golf course and the farmers' fields at the end of North Park, and the turf is full of surveyor's pegs and cat's cradles of criss-crossing twine. The different parts of Norwich are identifiable by their smell: the sulfur reek from the chemical factory that hangs over the North Park house-fronts at daybreak; the suffocating tang of the chocolate factory next to Chapelfield Gardens; the cats' meat stalls – these have names like 'Pussy's Butcher' and 'Purr-fect Scraps' – on the back of the market, where my mother impressionably browses. I am sixteen now, going on seventeen, and in the school sixth form studying English, History and Latin with subsidiary French. In the summer holiday of 1959 I spend four weeks working dawn to dusk in the strawberry fields, a three-mile bicycle ride away at Costessey. I spend the £12 on half-a-dozen striped shirts, two pairs of drainpipe jeans, a bum-freezer jacket and black, winkle-picker shoes. There are girls by this time – super-refined Marjorie, who attends the Norwich High School, and likes to be entertained to afternoon coffee and macaroons at the Assembly House tearooms, and deeply plebeian Greta, who drudges in a shoe shop and is quite happy with a bag of chips and a stroll around the park. Though nattily attired and pungent with scent, the girls are oddly sexless. A squeezed hand or a peck on the cheek is at far as it goes. Anything beyond this is considered 'fast'. Marjorie – plump, wide-hipped and fathomlessly ignorant – whose father is Home Fire Superintendent at the Norwich Union, intends to be an executive secretary. Greta – short, blonde and guilelessly humble – can see no further than stacked boxes and measuring tape. Each of them, after a ceremonious three-month courtship of cinema viewings and Sunday afternoon walks, writes me a polite note of rebuttal. Marjorie thinks that it 'isn't working out'. Greta has 'met somebody else'. Two hundred thousand people traipse through the Berkshire by-roads to Aldermaston to protest about the Bomb. Nothing has been heard of my father for at least five years.

At eighteen I win a minor scholarship in English Literature at Pembroke College, Oxford. The scholarship is worth £40 a year. The rest of my grant will be made up by the local education authority. Of all the triumphs of my adolescence, this is the one that lights the flame of my mother's imagination. I catch her looking at me sometimes with a kind of mazy bewilderment, as if she can't quite fathom how she has managed to produce a boy whose headmaster, admissions tutor and local authority education committee chair regard him with such favour. The letter from the senior tutor, which, in an exquisite patrician touch, is addressed not to 'Dear Mr Du Pont' or 'Dear Nicholas' but 'Dear Du Pont', is taken down from the mantelpiece and shown to visitors. Even surly Mrs Ellington is impressed. Quite what my mother believes the daily routines of Oxford undergraduates to consist of I cannot comprehend, but she begins to buy me things from second-hand shops that may, she supposes, come in handy for my new style of life. Six floral-pattern china teacups, a bootjack, a cigar cutter and a mildewed cummerbund are acquired in this way, each of them left behind on the day in October 1961 when I pack my possessions in two suitcases, take a bus to Thorpe Station, a train to Liverpool Street, the underground to Paddington and a second train to the City of Dreaming Spires.

Oxford. Green lichen on grey stone. Mist sweeping up over the South Parks Road. Tattered black gowns catching in the wheels of antique bicycles. Chapel bells a-clang and bright green grass. In a small way I am an example of upward social mobility – this phrase haunts the newspapers, along with 'existentialism' and 'consumer-materialist'. I have come from nowhere; great opportunities await me; what am I going to do with them? This is a good question. There are several views of Oxford current at the time: that it is a kind of Gothic nursery, where very clever men – and a few women – sit fidgeting themselves into neurosis; that it is an institution intended, simply by way of its architecture, to impress the people who wander around in it with a sense of their own insignificance; that it is a glorified employment bureau; that, with its swelling population of grammar-school boys, it is an interesting social experiment. For some reason I never quite get to grips with the environment of which I am a part. It is all too emphatic, too various, too violently removed from the world of North Park and my mother and Mrs Ellington fussing over the teapot, so insubstantial and kaleidoscope-coloured, it seems to me, that it might vanish under my hand at a second's notice, like a Barmecidal feast in the *Arabian Nights*. It is not the place's class distinctions or its superciliousness that baffle me, merely that I cannot crack its codes. A kind of cryptic smokescreen hangs in the air above every activity. You can see the doors, hear the key turn in the lock as other people approach, but, mysteriously, not pass through yourself. I make several friends at Pembroke, witty, worldly, amiable boys who have been educated at Eton, Harrow and Winchester. They will go on to become cabinet ministers, captains of industry, playwrights and novelists. I like them and I believe – once they have decided I am no threat to them – that they like me. They think I am 'a good sort', 'officer material', as one of them once puts it with not quite enough irony to make it tolerable, but I suspect I can never become a part of the world they inhabit.

My mother visits me once in Oxford, halfway through my second year. It is not a success. She is overawed by the place and too nervous to enjoy the treats I have arranged for her. The panelled rooms on the ground floor of the front quadrangle at Pembroke are three times the size of the North Park parlour, and she sits in them with a kind of terror, as if she half-expects some enforcer of the social proprieties to arrive and throw her out. 'Your mother's very charming,' one or two of the well-bred friends to whom I introduce her duly pronounce. They mean well, but somehow the presumption of charm is worse than any insult. After she leaves to catch her train, I sit in the empty room brooding about the two worlds that have mysteriously collided here – North Park and Oxford; red-brick council houses and Gothic battlements – and wonder which one I belong to. The answer, which I cannot see at the time, is neither.

Only once in these three years do I over-reach myself, go too far, draw attention to the imposture that these three years represent. It involves a girl called Alice Danby. There are no girls like Alice Danby now, and there were not very many of them then. Oxford runs to half-a-dozen: girls of unimaginable poise and sophistication who come to winter lectures in caramel-coloured fur coats, who are driven off to dinner at Thame and Shotover by men in sports cars and saunter into Examination Schools carrying bouquets of roses presented to them by admirers on the steps outside. I meet her at a sherry party given by a friend in a room full of short-haired men in sports jackets talking about the regiments they intend to join and the City jobs awaiting them and women complaining that the iced coffee has run out: a small, dapper girl with a nose so *retroussé* that it barely escapes from the plane of her face. She looks – and I am conscious of this at the time – like the girl in the Vuillard painting who sits at her desk under the lamp: an identification which, when made, she commends as 'awfully clever'. In these days, and in these circles, women do not 'go out' with men, much less 'date' them, they 'see something of them'. So, in a small way, Alice and I see something of each other. In a world irradiated by nicknames, where men are introduced as 'Roley', or 'old Gus here' or 'the Badger', she christens me 'Nicko'. I am not sure – maybe the 'Du Pont' helps – quite how much she underrates the social gulf between us, but she is fond, in an irresistibly bantering way, of telling me not to be so lower middle class. Her father is a diplomat, which gives her a further layer of expertise ('Quite why everyone goes on about Paris I've never been able to understand') and she is, if not intelligent, then shrewd, and – like many of the upper-class people whom the satire industry is then beginning to represent as a collection of buffoons – entirely able to look after herself. Gradually it is agreed between us that I will take her to a Midsummer Night ball at St John's College. The tickets will be ten guineas each. The protocols surrounding this event are established with surprising rigour.

'You must promise me one thing,' she says at a very early stage.

'What's that?'

'You *must* wear a proper shirt. Not one of those dreadful made-up ones.'

Determined to do the job properly, I go to a gentleman's outfitter in Turl Street and buy a stiff white shirt with a detachable wing collar and hire an evening suit at a cost of thirty shillings. This, together with the price of the tickets, means that I will have no money for the remaining three weeks of term, but I do not care. I have persuaded Alice Danby to accompany me to the St John's ball where several other men, the heirs to broad acres and ancestral seats, the sons of Tory MPs and eminent divines, have failed.

It is a frost from the outset. 'You get just the teeniest bit tired of all this,' says Alice, who leads an exhaustive social life, as we wander through the college quadrangles onto a lawn where a string quartet sits playing and a man in Pierrot costume is juggling a set of tennis balls. 'Isn't cheap champagne hellish?' she volunteers, after drinking off half a glass from a tray offered her by a waiter. It occurs to me even then that she does not mean to be rude. It is merely that she regards an event which the majority of the undergraduates milling around her believe to be the highlight of their careers to date as horribly mundane. But it is not a good start. The next seven hours pass with terrifying slowness. We dance a little, criticise the band ('Awfully loud,' Alice thinks) and find Roley, Gus and the Badger, or people very like them, in the refreshment tent. At some point Alice describes her plans for the summer. They do not include me. By 2 a.m. I have lost sight of her in the crowd. Not quite drunk but furiously angry, I walk back to Pembroke in the dawn, with the last faint strains of music borne on the air behind me, past a woman in an aquamarine ball gown with a face like a horse being loudly sick on the pavement while a bored-looking man in a dinner jacket pats her shoulder and tells her to buck up.

I decide that, as with my father and the lacquer box, I am never going to forgive Alice for this.

My mother dies suddenly – of an unsuspected heart condition – the week before I am due to leave Oxford. The telegram is delivered by one of the college servants early one morning as I lie in bed. He is an elderly, white-haired man who clearly suspects that the news he is bringing me cannot be good, and makes sympathetic noises as he presses the envelope into my hand. When he has gone I sit staring at the panelled walls of the bedroom in absolute blankness, listening to the noise of the college going about its business, the feet echoing on flagstones and the voices from the porters' lodge. Later I pack my belongings into the same two suitcases I brought with me three years before, leave a note on the desk for the scout, and march off into the sunshine to the station.

It has been a hot summer so far, and North Park is sunk in torpor. The grass on the verges is shading to brown. In Eaton Park there are old gentlemen out on the greens and the clack of the bowling woods drifts back over the treetops. Mrs Ellington lurks by the front hedge with the air of a woman who, despite maximum personal inconvenience, is determined to do her duty.

Mrs Ellington and I are old enemies, for she has – so it seems to me – bullied my mother, manipulated her and played on her good nature. Now, though, circumstance creates a curious affinity between us. We walk round the house together, turn over the heaps of baby clothes that lie on the sofa, inspect the pile of unopened mail. Upstairs in my mother's room there is a jar of chrysanthemums on the bedside table. From the sniff that Mrs Ellington gives as we approach, I gather that she has placed them there.

'Talked about you a lot in the week before she went,' Mrs Ellington volunteers.

'Did she?'

'Couldn't have felt any pain, the doctor said.'

'Did the doctor say that?'

There is something else quietly uncoiling in the depths of Mrs Ellington's imagination. It shoulders its way to the surface when we stand in the front room staring at the sparsely ornamented mantelpiece with its photograph of my father in his USAF uniform and its picture postcards of Great Yarmouth Pleasure Beach and Cromer Pier.

'She always said,' Mrs Ellington begins, one eye still on the mantelpiece, 'that I should have something to remember her by.'

I see instantly what she is up to.

'No,' I say. 'You're not having the clock.'

A less resourceful woman would be affronted by this rebuff. But Mrs Ellington has the proper North Park spirit. We settle on the six floral-pattern china teacups. These Mrs Ellington bears in triumph from the house. I never see her again.

Over the next three days, I set myself the task of clearing out my mother's house. Oxford is a thousand miles away; I have never been there: only this is real. I pack the baby clothes in a cardboard box and send them back to the manufacturers. The rented television set I return to the electrical suppliers in Bunnett Square. Beyond this, it is hard to know what to do. In my absence, I discover, my mother has turned into a hoarder. There are cupboards full of tinned food, drawers crammed with notebooks and sheets of lined paper. The guest bedroom is home to a stack of cut-price tea-trays. All this, like Mrs Ellington's plundering of the floral-pattern china teacups, is in the great North Park tradition: grave goods from a world in which insecurity, pride, fear and futile endeavour come inextricably commingled. What I want, as I go about my work, is some glimpse of my mother's personality that I can take away with me. But there is hardly anything: just an engagement diary or two (*Nicky to school . . . Nicky doing biology project*) in which she herself barely features, ancient photographs from which parched Mickleburgh faces, grouped around farm gates and cottage gardens, stare lumpishly forth. It occurs to me that in some mysterious way I have let my mother down, that she has lavished time and affection on me that I have repaid in material success without any understanding of the person she was. All this is far worse than the telegram, the bunch of chrysanthemums in their jar or even the inexplicable note I find on the kitchen table that reads, *memo: buy three tins catfood* – inexplicable in that we have no cat.

Meanwhile, there are practical decisions to be made. I am twenty-one now: the tenancy of the house can be mine if I want it. But there is nothing I want less. In any case, I have already signed up with a university exchange scheme that offers Oxford graduates the chance to work on the American presidential campaign. There seems no reason to alter these arrangements. It is the end of June now, and time hangs heavy. Twice I take some of the house's debris out into the garden, make a bonfire of it and watch as the clutter of a lifetime turns to ash. The furniture and the fixtures go into storage. Almost as an afterthought I write to my father at the last address I have for him, notify him of what has happened and, for no reason I can fathom, attach details of the exchange scheme. The house is emptied, the forms are signed and returned, the key and the rent book go back to City Hall, and that is that. Ten days later I am in Phoenix, listening to

Al Duchesne ('Call me Al') telling me that, yeah, the polls are bad but Barry is sure as hell going to prove them wrong, making eyes at Rosalind and marvelling at the various subterfuges that envelop a middle-class American household in which one of the inhabitants is a full-blown alcoholic.

GARTH DANGERFIELD: Where we all lived, when you was fifteen, if you didn't want to work in a factory, there were only three ways you could make money. You could play football, you could train to be a boxer, or you could tea-leave. And then suddenly there was this thing called pop music.

DALE HALLIWELL: The music I like listening to is the blues. Howling Wolf. Etta James. Champion Jack Dupree. You ever heard of him? But you can't play straight blues and get into the charts. So that's why we do this pop stuff.

IAN HAMILTON: You know, sometimes I think I only got asked to join the group because of my amplifier. I had a Vox AC30 with a big speaker cabinet that you could plug three guitars into. Up until then they'd been using these tinny little things from Woolworths that were always breaking down. I think that was why they had me.

FLORIAN SHANKLEY-WALKER: I think we get on reasonably well. I mean, they're not exactly my kind of people. Musically they're fairly limited. I mean, you can say, 'This really needs a diminished seventh,' and none of them has any idea what you're talking about. But I think, in the circumstances, we get on reasonably well.

KEITH SHIELDS: My dad, when we started out, he'd say, 'Nobody ever made anything of themselves playing the drums.' And I'd say,

'What about Ringo, Dad?' We've had two hit singles, and he still says, 'Nobody ever made anything of themselves playing the drums.'

Interview with Maureen Cleave, *London Evening Standard*, October 1964

3. NIGHT BY NIGHT

She's been around a long time
Befriending all my foes
And that's what makes me certain
She's a girl you shouldn't know

'Girl You Shouldn't Know'

'Did I ever tell you about my wedding?'

'What happened?'

'We got married in December 1941. I was twenty-three. My mother said I'd left it late. And for some reason we decided to honeymoon in Palm Beach. Can you imagine that? Even then it was a kind of old folks' home. And then one day we came down to breakfast and it said on the radio that the Japanese had bombed Pearl Harbor. And Al was in the Naval Reserve, so he reckoned he ought to go back to Phoenix to register. I said he could do that if he wanted to, but it was my honeymoon and I was staying put. We argued about it all over breakfast, and a little old lady in a fox-fur cape came up to me afterwards and told me it was my patriotic duty to do what my husband said.'

'And did you? Do your patriotic duty, I mean?'

'No I did not. I didn't care. I stayed there for a whole week while Al went back to Phoenix to do whatever he had to do. Not that anything

much was happening in Palm Beach. There was a fearful panic about
the war, and the Germans invading from the east or coming up from
South America, I forget which. I used to walk along the beach and
never see a soul. Step into hotel bars on the seafront where there was
no one there but the barman. On my own, too. I think people thought
I was a prostitute. And then one day Al came back in his navy uniform
– quite the thing he looked, I can tell you – with instructions to report
to Fort Wayne, or someplace, and that was the end of that. Not much
of a way to start your married life.'

We were somewhere at the point where New Mexico slides into
Texas, quite early in the morning still, with the wild sky burning into
livid patches, crimson clouds rolling away across the horizon and the
wind playing havoc among the picket-wires, while the freeway stole on
through plains of scrub and cacti, with nothing to see except the distant
white birds spiralling in the thermals and longhorns clustered in the
field bottoms. There was roadkill every ten yards: gophers, prairie hens,
coyotes, turtles, nameless creatures pasted into multi-hued medallions
of guts and fur; and a sense that in the end none of these things could
be separated out from each other: the vast horizon; the blistering wind;
Lucille's spare, dry voice – as dry as the Texas desert that surrounded
us on all sides – talking implacably on about Al Duchesne, the old days
in Pheeny and what her mother had said to the travelling salesman
that time in 1935. Almost everything, in fact, except our current
predicament and how we might get ourselves out of it.

'Al now,' Lucille went on. Her hand, resting on the half-open
passenger-side window, looked curiously mottled, old and grey but
for all that lively, as if it were about to slither off, rat-like, into the
ripening dawn. 'He's not a *bad* man. No one could say that he was a
bad man. But I could tell you things about him that would make your
hair curl.'

A clump of advertising hoardings and real-estate signage went by,
with a couple of winded flatbed trucks idling in their shadow.

'Twenty miles to Harford,' I noted. 'We could stop there and get something to eat.'

'Fine by me,' Lucille said, who had not, as far as I knew, eaten anything in the past forty-eight hours. She whipped the stump of the cigarette she was smoking out of her mouth and lit another off the tip.

'How long until we get to New York? That's if we're going to New York?'

'Four days,' Lucille said. And then something about the tone of my voice, pitched somewhere between tenor and alto and I daresay cracking at the seams, must have struck her, for she turned to stare at me and all the chaos of the car's interior – the ripped Stuyvesant packets that littered the dashboard, the Styrofoam coffee cups that crunched and crackled underfoot and the hanks of discarded tissues – as if the wonder of it, and all the great obstacles that lay in our path, had only just occurred to her. 'Well, maybe five.'

By this time, as I recall, we were three days out on the road from Phoenix. Three days of wide horizons, cigarette smoke curling up against the bugs' graveyard of the windscreen and the ghost of Al Duchesne to haunt us. For Al was everywhere. His face stared out at me from the cabins of the passing trucks. It could be seen peering around the corners of motel doorways, and it had superimposed itself on the hoary physiognomies of the good old boys in Stetson hats and liquorice-lace ties who beamed out of the billboards imploring you to buy prime building plots in Cherokee County or lately drained swamps in the Badlands down along the Gulf. But in some ways all this was less to me than the ten minutes I had spent in a gas-station restroom early on the first morning, while Lucille dozed in the Pontiac's passenger seat and two, it seemed to me, very nearly insane characters named Huck and Wiggy loudly unpacked churns of milk from a Dodge pickup, reading the rank graffiti about Betsy-Lou and what she got up to down under the bleachers with the college boys when the coach's eye was turned, and, finally, when I could bring myself to begin what I knew would be a long and soul-sapping task, reading the letter from my father.

Dear Son,

I daresay this will come as a surprise to you. But it was certainly a surprise to me to learn that you were here in the land of your forefathers. It can only be the FORCE OF DESTINY – an instrument by which, as you know, I set the greatest store – drawing us together again. I am delighted to learn that, having completed your education, you have launched yourself out into the world of work – an enterprise which, if true, I heartily commend and endorse. I wish I had advice – wise words, sagacious encouragement – to offer, but can think of none. For myself, I am just this minute situated in New York, pursuing certain schemes – commercial and otherwise – which it would be tedious to explain at length. Enough to say that there is MONEY COMING. Needless to add, it would be a joy to set eyes on you should you venture this way. I should imagine that you are a strapping young fellow who would remind me of my spunky younger self. Bygones, naturally, will be bygones. We must ignore the future and cleave to the tumultuous promise of the present.

In every anticipation of our fond reunion,

Your loving father,

Maurice Du Pont

PS The news about your mother shames me. No more no less. But we must not repine. Salvation lies in the sky, not in the ground.

This, it had to be said, was entirely characteristic of the letters the old man wrote, or had written, back in the 1950s from whichever transatlantic promontory he had fetched up – bright and miscellaneous and somehow evasive documents in which egotism, whimsy, inflexibility of will and (that other characteristic of my father) a buried core that only he could get to the bottom of came furiously combined. On the other hand, the stuff about destiny was new-fangled enough to hint at a practically cosmic side. It was 6 a.m., I noticed, as I slid the sheet back into its envelope and took a last regretful look at a breezy quatrain about some Panhandle sophomore with the unlikely sounding name of Hot-Legs Hortense, with pale streaks in the dawn sky, and Huck and Wiggy were grousing deludedly over a brace of damaged cartons while the scent of fresh-brewed coffee stole over the forecourt and in the scratch yard opposite a flock of chickens came riotously awake. Back in the car, Lucille snapped out of her coma like a marionette jerked by invisible wires.

'Just imagine,' she said. 'Al has no idea where I am. *None at all.*'

'Shouldn't you let him know?'

'There's time enough for that,' Lucille said. 'Just for now, though, Al can go to hell.'

I explained about the old man's letter, gripped by a sudden, primitive urge to track him down. 'So maybe we ought to head for New York.'

'Fine by me.' Everything was fine by Lucille, from the eight-lane Texas freeways to the 20-cent glasses of orange juice you found lined up on the motel breakfast tables, each no taller than a raised finger, that had clearly been left out there the previous night. Everything, that is, except the reasons that had brought her here and seemed guaranteed to take her still further away. I paid for the gas ('Why, thank ya suh'), bought a loaf of erratically sliced bread and some Albuquerque pickle which was about all the grocery counter ran to ('Why, thank ya suh'), held the door open for Wiggy as he staggered across the portal with a dozen leaking cartons clutched to his chest ('Why, thank ya suh'), pulled the car out in the wide, meandering highway and headed east into the sun.

*   *   *

We stayed mostly in motels. The Jacaranda. Nite-Stop. Stay-Over. The Texas Snuggle Sack. Modest establishments of the kind that, several years later and in more prosperous times, Stefano used to call Fuck-off Joints. A dozen rooms, say, arranged in a square around a half-filled swimming pool reeking of chlorine and a rusty sign saying MANAGEMENT TAKES NO RESPONSIBILITY swinging in the breeze. There was much that management took no responsibility for. At first, I had assumed that a forty-five-year-old Arizona mother of two and an Englishman under half her age travelling together would seem conspicuous, that questions would be asked. But these fears were misplaced, and the motel staff scarcely gave us a second look. If I'd been black, on the other hand, I daresay neither of us would have got over the state line unchallenged. The problem of who was to pay for this succession of one-night stopovers in single rooms, so narrowly squeezed up to each other that I could hear my travelling companion's every restless turn, was settled by Lucille with the aid of a pilfered Diners Club card. 'Won't Al cancel it?' I asked, the first time this happened. 'He wouldn't dare,' Lucille said proudly. And mysteriously this vagrant, expense-account life, funded by the angry little man in Phoenix, was allowed to persist. What I remember is extraordinarily variegated, dense and partial, small things and large things mixed: the breakfast waitresses settling their caps on their heads with tender hands; rain streaking the smeared-up windows; a gleam of sunlight flying off Lucille's abundant hair once as she lingered in a doorway; a postcard sent from Amarillo and addressed not to Al but to Rosalind, with a picture of John Wayne in *Stagecoach* on the front which said: *This is what you shall do: Love the earth and sun and the animals, despise riches, give alms to every one that asks* . . . (which I didn't then know was a quotation from Walt Whitman), *Love, mother.* And, above all, those conversations.

Those conversations. Sometimes they were about the people she had left behind in Phoenix.

'Did you sleep with my daughter?'

'I can honestly say that I didn't.'

'That's a pity. It might have knocked some of the starch out of her. I can't stand starch in a girl.'

'Did anyone ever knock the starch out of you?'

'With me, it was mostly the other way around.'

Another time, dancing out of her room in a spasm of excitement with a stack of picture postcards clutched in her hand, she said: 'We need to confuse Al. We need to throw Al off the scent. That's what we need to do.'

And so another half-dozen communications were despatched to confidential friends in Denver, Rhode Island, Billings, Montana and Chesapeake Bay, who would presumably send them on to Phoenix, where Al sat in puzzled abandonment beneath the branding irons and the cowboy spurs, white and ghastly in the fading light. What she really thought of Al I never truly understood. Sometimes she gave the impression he was a buffoon she had taken out of pity. Other times she would calmly represent herself as the poor country girl – her family came from out in the boondocks, real Tucson-and-then-some Tar Heels – dazzled by city sophistication. Meanwhile, to the mounds of carefully ciphered contempt could be added an odd solicitousness. 'Al will be getting his supper just now,' she observed one evening, thirty miles short of Oklahoma City. 'Or having dinner at the club.' She was like a Stone Age tribesman huddled over a fetish, I thought, terrified of all that the wisps of bone and skin might portend but desperate not to let it out of her grasp. And every so often, pulsing through her chatter like a warning light, you would get a reminder that this wasn't a world you were used to, and that beneath its surface – not so very far beneath, if it came to that – lay an elemental land-scape of reparation and spilled blood, spunk, steel and sawdust.

'My mother shot a man once.'

'Why did she do that?'

'It was back in the old days. *Way* back.' The 'old days' in Phoenix time, by the way, could mean any year up until Eisenhower's second term. 'I don't suppose the place was even a state then. They certainly hadn't built the Roosevelt Dam. He was getting fresh, and wouldn't take no for an answer, and she took my grandfather's gun off the wall and shot half his hand off.'

'What happened then?'

'Nothing. Sheriff came and took him away. My mother made a joke of it. She said that his two fingers lay in the dirt for a while and then when someone went to look for them they found the yard dog had taken them. They never did get those fingers back. And my grandfather said that if he ever saw the fellow again he'd do the same himself. Only maybe it wouldn't be his hand he shot off.'

And I thought about Al Duchesne ('Call me Al'), scion of the Arizona Badlands, Scorpion Al, heir to blood, stone and primeval rage, who had killed five Japanese at Iwo Jima, and what he might do to me. But coming out of the motel rooms at first light, with the wind gusting in against the quivering panes and tugging at the door handles, there was never anyone there. Never anyone, just the same regiment of tarnished pick-ups parked anyhow in the auto-lot, the same rusty sign swinging on its hinges, the same scum of insect goo on the surface of the half-filled swimming pool, the same off-white light slowly diffusing into the horizon as the day took hold.

It was an odd time to be in transit across America. Only a decade had passed since Ike had built the freeways in that first great riot of post-war optimism and renewal, and everywhere the tribes were in flight. The word 'hippy' wasn't yet in common usage – older people tended to talk about 'beatniks' if they wanted to make a generational point – but the roads were full of longhairs in trucks and patched-up mobile homes, convoys of motorcycle boys in black leathers and Brando caps, and pale young faces staring from the back seats of the Greyhound buses. And behind them, in Sedan cars and sedately motoring Dodge Saloons and shark-finned Chryslers, came the families – Pa and Ma and Junior, and sometimes Grandma too, all spruced up in their Sunday best if it was the weekend, come to inspect this great nation of theirs but not much liking what they saw. You could tell that Pa and Ma were worried by the travelling kids and the long hair and the motorcycle gangs parked up menacingly on the gas-station forecourts and the newness that was everywhere to hand – the skyscrapers rising over the big cities, the houses going up on the out-of-town plots – and that they pined for that older world that Eisenhower had presided over but which had betrayed them by not staying exactly the same as they remembered it. And meanwhile, the little Texas towns where Pa worked at Get-U-Gas and Auto and Ma sold cans of 7 Up and ice-cream from a back-porch dispensary slept in the dust, each of them looking as if they had just stepped out of *The Last Picture Show*, with a church and a pool hall, a funeral parlour and a couple of flyblown stores, and no one about except a few loiterers on the sidewalk and the delivery truck bringing kerosene. Past, present and future all grimly coalescing and nobody knowing what would be the end of it all when the day came for settling accounts. And, sweeping all this to the margin of the world that was to me still the wonder of America, this picturesquely seething landscape where the horizons were wider, the skies brighter, the buildings taller and most of the assumptions about the life I would find there pulverised into dust.

It wasn't quite that nobody took any interest. There were always the traffic cops, vigilant at the kerbside in their tuned-up Oldsmobiles, noting the out-of-state licence plates, waving you down, coming to the near-hand car window and finding me in the driver's seat.

'Is he kin to you, ma'am?'

'This is my nephew, officer, driving me to Tupelo to do my Christmas shopping.'

'That a fact? Well, you take care of yourselves, do you hear?'

All this time we were heading east. Eastward under the pale sun and the wide sky. Phoenix to Albuquerque. Albuquerque to Amarillo. Amarillo to Oklahoma City, where Lucille, who I'd discovered to be a howling snob, sniffed at the passers-by and remarked that at least since her last visit they'd learned to put shoes on their feet. By this juncture we had a plan: I was going to seek out my father in the chaotic thoroughfares of Queens, which was where his letter had come from, and Lucille was going to hook up with a highly placed friend whose husband ran a creative realty firm out on Long Island. But we also had the beginnings of a solidarity, a united front against the potentially hostile world around us, a drawbridge forever waiting to be pulled up. 'I got you this,' she would briskly confide when I returned to the car from the gas-station restroom with its damaged faucets and its inked-over plywood doorframes, and there would be a carton of coffee with the black thumbprint of whoever had dispensed it still on the cardboard band, or a pack of gum, or an oily pastrami sandwich, or an oblong Snickers bar. The Snickers bars, too multitudinous for me to eat them, piled up on the dashboard, where they melted in the midday heat and froze solid in the pre-dawn chill. The nights were getting cold. Very occasionally she would volunteer to drive, sitting bolt upright with two gloved hands placed high up on the wheel like a praying mantis, nervous yet oddly forceful, cutting up the container trucks and the riggers that cruised alongside us with cruel flicks of her wrist. By this time, too, I had established certain facts about her life, or at any rate acquired pieces of information that explained what we were doing out here on the Oklahoma Interstate with the hoardings flying by and the home-stencilled placards jamming up the side of the road: JOE'S CAFÉ NEXT TURN; 30C CHEESE-BURGER – 3 MILES; BAR & GRILL: KIDS GO FREE. The first was that she'd done this kind of thing before, on one occasion getting as far as Canada before Mr Duchesne or some altruistic third party had wheedled her back. Another was that she had money of her own, tied up in

some trust fund, which gave her a degree of independence not generally allowed to the wives of Arizona real-estate lawyers. A third was
that, unlike the pale companion at her side, she wasn't in the least
afraid of Al Duchesne. Al could go hang. Al could take a hike. Al
could sit in his office in Phoenix and screw his secretary.

Meanwhile, the landscape was changing. The flat Texas oil plain,
with the rigs strewn out over the horizon and the drifting lines of
smoke, gave way to little white houses with picket fences squeezed up
against the road and then to dipping fields of arable – the buckwheat
and the barley all harvested now, but with threshers still out combing
the dry topsoil. Oklahoma City to Tulsa. Tulsa to St Louis. St Louis
to Terre Haute ('Bumfuck Indiana,' Lucille pronounced with thin
contempt, having stepped out to buy me a plastic comb and a reeking
corn dog). The thermometer began to fall, the motel swimming pools
in the early morning were layered with ice, and the sameness of the
routine – the finger of 20-cent orange juice in its plastic tumbler, the
grey thread of the highway and the ghost of Al – brought a queer feeling of dissociation, so that your mind took flight and floated free
across the interstates and the shriven cornfields to dwell on Rosalind
and Oxford and the little house on North Park Avenue, the dead
woman in the Earlham cemetery and many another broken dream
from time gone by.

Terre Haute to Columbus. Columbus to Pittsburgh. With the
radio picking up whichever local station could shoulder its way out of
the clumps of static. The big beat of Texas FM. Radio WOLD out of
Oklahoma, which specialised in country blues and the benighted
yodellings of Jimmie Rodgers, the Singing Brakeman. KMEN from
Tulsa, where the late-night phone-ins summoned palsied old-timer
voices from their distant ranch houses and pool halls to maunder
about the latest news from Kaintuck and Ole Miss and Alabammy.
('Where do they find all these retarded people?' Lucille pondered.)
The British Invasion was at full blast and here, amid the plaintive

yelping of southern songsters singing of Maybelline who hadn't been true or the little shack in Tuscaloosa where there'd be a welcome waiting for lonesome cowboy Bill, there stirred a cacophony of English voices, the sound of John, Paul, George and Ringo, the Stones, the Kinks and the Dave Clark Five, whose incongruousness only struck you once you had left the car and returned to it. As I recall, I sat fingering the plastic comb and eating the corn dog listening to 'I Want to Hold Your Hand', while dense Indiana rain slapped the bonnet, after which two announcers named Elmer and Joe-Bob started up a conversation about stock prices.

Pittsburgh to Harrisburg. Harrisburg to Reading. Reading to Allenstown. So that the cars flashing by in the dawn bore New York plates and the road signs pointed upstate to Poughkeepsie, Utica and Albany, with Lucille, mellowing now that the journey was almost done, talking about her childhood out on the salt flats where the droughts were sometimes so bad that the water had to be brought in by truck, and how true-bred Arizonians thought John Wayne was a phony who had to be helped on and off his horse, coming into the city through Bethlehem and Plainfield, with the darkness stretching out on all sides away from the lights of the freeway, and music in our heads, bright, ungainsayable English music, that drug flown in from the old country from which, although I did not yet know it, I would never again be free.

... And what sort of crowd did the Helium Kids find when they showed up at the Locarno Ballroom last week? Several hundred screaming pop-kids, naturally, drawn by 'Glad It's You' and next week's follow-up, the remarkably similar-sounding 'She's My Baby Now', but also some older types who clearly think they're an R & B outfit for whom the pop bandwagon offers a horribly convenient ride. However commercially astute this may be, it makes for a schizophrenic performance, in which cute little pop songs where if 'moon' doesn't actually rhyme with 'June' then 'heart' invariably clangs with 'apart', alternate with some absolutely savage blues work-outs, ornamented by some of the hottest bass (courtesy of Ian Hamilton) your correspondent has heard in years, and rendering keyboard-player Florian Shankley-Walker (a great hit with the female fans) largely redundant. Predictably, the pop numbers leave the blues aficionados cold, while the short-skirted girls at the front, showing more leg than is decent here in Macc on a Friday night, are just the tiniest bit mystified by 'Outhouse Blues', which they can't sing along to as its words are deeply unfamiliar. Sooner or later the Helium Kids are going to have to bridge this hulking divide but at the moment, with 'Glad It's You' still occupying the lower reaches of the singles chart and an American tour beckoning, they seem more than happy to entertain two audiences from the same stage.

Macclesfield Advertiser, November 1964

4. NEW YORK JOURNAL, 1964–5

> Face in the crowd's gonna get you
> Face in the crowd knows your car
> Face in the crowd won't ever let you
> Be the person you think that you are

'Face in the Crowd'

I found this in the loft the other day, in a pile of memorabilia. Other items included a copy of the Helium Kids' 1965 US tour programme and a press release announcing their first American single, both written by me. An authentic document, so far as I can make out. A few misspelled names have been corrected.

6 December 1964

My twenty-second birthday. We celebrate by eating at a diner round the back of Madison. Spaghetti and meatballs. Fudge sundaes. Lucille, always keen on the petty exercise of power, sends back the meatballs, which were perfectly eatable, as underdone. Toasting me with a glass of red wine, she says: 'You've got a great future ahead of you, Nick.'

'So have you,' I gallantly respond.

In fact, Lucille seems a bit subdued by New York. Is she conscious of her dowdiness when matched against the natives? The women's skirts are three inches higher here and their hair six inches shorter. I can see Lucille watching them as they go, half curiosity, half envy. Drinking a whole lot less, which is a relief.

Hotel on Eighth and Forty-Seventh. Not a good area. Prostitutes touting for hire in the streets. L seems not to notice. Fiction preserved that we are aunt and nephew, although nobody cares in the slightest. My room looks out over concrete rooftops where cats fight in the small hours. Tower cranes, construction sites in the distance. Sound of people shouting/arguing through the walls a constant.

Last night around dawn.

WOMAN'S VOICE: Why won't you give me a baby? That's all I want. Just a baby.

MAN'S VOICE: You want a baby? You have one. Have a fucking nursery full. *I* don't care.

Hotel staff transient. Hardly ever the same person on duty at reception when we go in or out. The only fixture is Doug, employed to stoke boiler, shift furniture in the breakfast room. Says 'Hiya Mr Du Pont, howya doing?' when we meet.

9 December 1964

Mixed impressions of New York. Times Square just a confluence of four shabby streets. Forty-Second Street, where I ended up walking one morning, horribly seedy. But Broadway, Fifth Avenue straight out of Hollywood. Ditto view of the Hudson River, ships' masts bunched up beneath the skyscrapers, horizon full of mist. Today we took the ferry out to Staten Island. No real aim in view. Passengers on the way back loaded up with extraordinary paraphernalia: teenage girl carrying a lute; old men with traps full of pigeons; boy with a six-foot roll of carpet slung over his shoulder.

Pictures of the Beatles everywhere (their new record is due out here next week). Even Lucille has heard of them. 'Aren't they those English boys that were on with Ed Sullivan? From Liverpool or someplace? I liked them. They were cute.' So many British groups now making inroads into the American charts that there is talk of the Labor Department refusing them visas.

13 December 1964

Making serious efforts to contact my father. Called several times from the kiosk in the hotel foyer, but phone never picked up. Finally last night at 10 p.m. someone answers.

WOMAN'S VOICE: Who's that?

SELF: Could I speak to Maurice Du Pont?

WOMAN'S VOICE: Who wants him?

SELF: This is his son. Nicholas. Nick.

WOMAN'S VOICE: Never knew he hadda son.

After which the line went dead. Today I took the subway to Queens in search of the address on the letter. Quiet street in Ridgewood, not far from the cemeteries, full of shaky-looking clapboard houses, raised front doors reached by wooden steps. Voices roundabout mostly Italian. No. 17 even shakier than its neighbours. Half-a-dozen scallop tiles missing from the roof. Two smashed window panes patched up with cardboard. No one there, so I scrawled a note on a postcard and left it in the mailbox.

L continues to buy me presents. A jacket from Saks on Fifth Avenue – one of those plum-coloured wrap-rounds that make you look like a holiday-camp attendant (she left the tag on – it cost $25). A pair of cufflinks. Expression on her face when she hands them over quite inscrutable. Can't work out what is going on in her head, or what she aims to achieve. No sign yet of any of the 'friends' with whom New York supposed to be swarming. We eat at the hotel or in cheap cafés. She always pays, for which I am grateful as down to last few dollars. Sometimes she goes away to telephone. No idea what, if anything, she is trying to arrange. Growing colder by the day.

15 December 1964

Kids in the street all with copies of *Beatles '65*. Songs playing constantly on the radio. 'I Feel Fine' heading up the charts. Do I feel fine? I'm running out of money, the person I came to New York to find has gone missing, and Lucille is hanging round my neck like an albatross.

Another visit to Queens. No one home. My note still in the mailbox. A woman shouts from the next-door porch: 'You looking for the Du Ponts? I ain't seem them for weeks. Maybe they'll be back soon.'

This is getting serious.

17 December 1964

Another gift from Lucille. The present of herself. I went back to the hotel after a late-night stroll down Forty-Seventh and another unanswered phone call to find her sitting on my bed. No doubt at all what she intended us to do. I don't think I acquitted myself too badly in the circumstances. She has curiously dropsical skin that makes you worry that if you poked a finger into her flesh the hole would remain long after you drew it out. Says nothing throughout and seems not to look at me. Not sure how I ought to feel about this experience (Pride? Shame?) but determined not to repeat it.

Afterwards L smokes a cigarette – she has cut down lately – and says: 'You need to get up early tomorrow. We're invited out.'

18 December 1964

Got the car out of the underground park where it has been sitting for the past four weeks and headed out along Highway 39 to Long Island.

A 'pre-Christmas party' at the home of Lucille's friend, the wife of the creative realtor. Not a success. Big house set in woodland with breathtakingly beautiful view down to the shore. A dozen or so New York women dressed up to the nines, drinking cocktails from trays proffered by coloured servants and admiring the giant Christmas tree. Shark-like hostess gave me several knowing looks, and another woman, whose cigarette I lit, said, disapprovingly, 'Oh, so you're Lucille's young man that we've all heard so much about.' In the end I went and stood by the drawing-room window watching the snow fall out of an iron-grey sky over the treetops and the wild garden. Later three or four girls came in. One of them, the hostess's daughter, home from Bennington, said: 'My mother doesn't like you. She says you're a gigolo.'

'And what about you? Do you like me?'

She gave a little apologetic giggle. 'I like your accent.'

Lucille drinks at least seven old-fashioneds and talks too loudly. In the car on the way back she says: 'I hate that stuck-up bitch Marjorie Draper. Who does she think she is?'

'Is she going to do anything for you?'

'Is she hell. She said Al phoned her. She told me to go home.'

19 December 1964

New York in winter. Packed snow on the store awnings. Steam gushing from the vents in the sidewalks. In the foyer of one of the big banks on Lexington, eight or nine girls in Santa Claus outfits rollerskating in a circle with charity buckets. Hot pretzels – customarily spelled 'pretzles' – at 15 cents a bag.

Lucille refuses to leave her room. Once she says: 'Coming here was the biggest mistake I ever made.' Then she adds hastily: 'I don't mean any offence to you, honey, you understand.'

Titanic quarrel in the room next door last night.

WOMAN'S VOICE: All this time you've never taken me anywhere. Not one solitary place.

MAN'S VOICE: Never taken you anywhere? This is a hotel ain't it, for Christ's sake?

WOMAN'S VOICE: You never take me to a restaurant or any place.

MAN'S VOICE: The reason I don't is that I'd be ashamed. That's right. I'd be embarrassed to take you to a fancy restaurant and have to watch the way you behaved.

20 December 1964

There is a diner half a block down where I sometimes go in the mornings. The place is nearly always empty, but today I've barely had time to blow the froth off my coffee before a small, fierce-looking man in a raincoat stalks in off the street and makes a beeline for my table. No mistaking the parched forehead and eager little glances: Al Duchesne. I have one eye on the door, but Al lays a mild restraining paw on my cuff.

'I got no quarrel with you, son,' he says warily. 'Now, where's my wife?'

I can tell that Al doesn't like New York – it's all too much for a regular guy from Phoenix, these black bellhops and the crazy men screaming in the street – and that this gives me an advantage. I tell him the location of the hotel – interesting that he wants to talk to me first – and he looks yet more wary, half of him wanting me where he can see me, the other half never wanting to see me again. In the end he pulls out his wallet – a snap of Lucille, Rosalind and her brother Herb winks from the interior – and hands me a bill.

'Here's five dollars. Can get yourself some breakfast. You hear what I'm saying?'

I hear what he's saying. It is a warning not to come back to the hotel until Al has finished whatever business he wants to transact there. Having handed over the money, Al looks appreciably more relaxed, as if a brisk chat about baseball is only a moment away. I watch him out on the sidewalk, making his way round the piled snow, which is rapidly turning to slush.

What seems like a great stretch of time later, but is actually only an hour, I head back to the hotel. Lucille's room is empty, the door ajar, the luggage gone. Going down to the foyer again, I meet Doug on the stair. 'Lady asked me to give you this,' he says with the ghost of a wink. I bear the envelope off to my room and discover another bill – $20 this time – and a note written on a piece of hotel stationery that says *It was a good time we had together. Thank you for trying to help. Lucille Duchesne. P.S. Al doesn't know.*

I think I see what she means. But there are so many things Al doesn't know that it seems queer to single this one out.

25 December 1964

Christmas Day in New York. Hotel apparently unstaffed although tape machine on reception desk plays carols in an endless loop. No snow, but bright crisp sky. Far colder than it would be in England. In the morning I walked round Central Park, bought a cheeseburger, took it back to my room and ate it while reading a copy of Dreiser's *An American Tragedy*, which I picked up in a second-hand bookstore a while back. Just beginning to get bored when there was a knock at the door. This turned out to be Doug, still in his janitor's overalls but bearing a bottle of bourbon. 'You OK, Mr Du Pont? I mean, you expecting company or anything?' He stayed an hour and a half, talking non-stop about ice hockey, his wife – now dead – and his time in Korea ('Can't look at a guy's face in Chinatown without wanting to blow it off.'). When he left he said: 'Nice talking to you, Mr Du Pont. You need anything, you let me know.'

Mysteriously, the hotel bill has been paid until the end of the month. What with the money the Duchesnes left, there is a little over

$40 remaining. I tell myself that if I can't make contact with the old man by then, I shall take one of the seven-day boats back to England.

Later. Writing this at 10 p.m. Building absolutely silent. Even the people in the next-door room have fallen quiet. Radio stations rounding up 'this momentous year' with clips from LBJ's speeches, news from the Far East, more Beatles songs. Snow starting to fall again, drifting soft against the window panes, slowly accumulating on the ledges, like a picture book.

26 December 1964

Dull, overcast morning. Another trip to Queens on the subway. Curiously, approached the street with an odd sense of assurance that there would be somebody inside. And so it proved. Light on in the porch. Fresh footprints in the frost. After an eternity of knocking, the door opened and the old man peered out into the raw air. Almost failed to recognise him. Face fallen in a bit and hair brindling to grey. But still the same old belligerent stare of the North Park photo album. Took both my hands in his and said I was a 'son of a gun', that it was a God-damned terrible thing about 'Jeanie' being 'taken', and why had I been all this time in New York without coming to visit. I was explaining about the notes and the voice at the end of the phone when he yelled 'Daphne' and a tall, savage-looking woman a year or two his junior in a shapeless woollen garment came shambling into the room running a hand through her tinted hair.

'Why didn't you tell me Nicholas had called?'

'Don't know anything about it.'

'I came a couple of times last week, but there was nobody here.'

'We got a place in Connecticut,' Daphne volunteered. 'Holiday home.'

'It's a shack in the woods,' my father said. 'We eat roadkill.' It was impossible to tell how seriously he meant this to be taken. 'This here's Daphne.'

'Please ta meet ya,' said Daphne, who sounded as if she was born in the lee of a trailer-park somewhere in the Midwest.

I'd expected some awkwardness in this parent-and-child reunion. I'd also expected that a veil of mystical sentimentality would hang over it, on account of my mother's passing. Mysteriously, there was neither. Mostly I think this is because of the old man's attitude to the people he comes across – at once casual and indiscriminate – which means that he treats me not as his long-lost son but like the mailman, say, stepping in off the porch for a chat. On the other hand, it may be a result of the very strong sensation you experience on walking into the house in Queens of having fallen head-over-heels into another world where most of the normal behavioural rules don't apply. The two main rooms crammed with junk: a row of kewpie dolls, which Daphne apparently collects, photos of the 319th crews posed next to B-25s, badly stuffed animals with their limbs distorted out of shape.

'There ain't much to eat in the house,' my father says. 'Or anything much to eat it with. But you're welcome to stay.'

'Cutlery gets left in Connecticut,' Daphne explains. Close up she is older than at first glance, nearer sixty than fifty. The tinted hair is a major mistake. We eat bowls of soup and musty crackers off trays with the lights from a tiny artificial Christmas tree winking on and off. Sometimes my father asks questions – When was the last time I had seen my mother? Had she known she was ill? What was it like in Phoenix? What are my plans? – but you can tell that his heart isn't in it, that his mind is barrelling on in some distant world where human traffic is in short supply and every so often there comes another piece of roadkill fresh for the stove. Two questions that occur to me are: *1. On what or whom is my father living?* There are uncashed federal cheques lying on the sideboard, but the amounts are ridiculous – $1.67, say, or $2.39. 2. *What is his relationship with Daphne?*, to whom he defers in arguments but on other occasions – when talking about my mother, for example – scarcely deigns to notice. It is dark before I have any inkling that the day is gone. The grey afternoon slides away and the clouds are crowding out the New York skyline. Daphne, who has been sewing desultory stitches into an embroidery sampler and then playing an interminable game of patience, looks up and says: 'Want me to tell ya fortune?'

Unexpectedly, the old man's interest is piqued. 'You need to take her up on that,' he enthuses. 'Daphne's just great at telling fortunes. The other week she told this guy we know he ought to take care of himself and the very next day he falls under a subway carriage and loses a leg.'

'Didn't thank me for it,' Daphne says. 'But ya get used to that.'

'It's kind of her, but I'd sooner not.'

'Hey there,' my father chides. He is far more animated than when he first opened the door. 'What have you got to lose? If it's a good one, you can spend the next week thinking you're going to win the lottery. If it's a bad one, well then, you know to look at the lights when you cross the street.'

Both of them, I notice, are gazing at me expectantly, like beavers gathered at the river's edge watching the first consignment of fresh logs tumbling downstream. Maybe this is what passes for entertainment on a Boxing Day in Queens. Who can tell? The old man has a stinking cheroot wedged in the side of his mouth, and the gouts of smoke that issue forth are practically curing his worn-out face so that it resembles an outsize hickory nut. How can I gainsay him? Daphne lays out the deck with painful seriousness. A tiny muscle spasm sets her upper lip tremulously a-fret. This is no easy matter. Various cards come to light: the Queen of Hearts; two low Clubs; the King of Spades; three or four more. The old man stares at them in what could be anguish or quiet bewilderment. There is no telling. The wind is banging at the window and setting the lantern on the porch a-stir.

In the end Daphne says: 'You been working for a man ah power. Important guy, but it didn't work out. There's a dark-haired woman too. Neither of them gives ya what ya want.'

'What do I want?'

'Jesus! How'm I supposed ta know that? You want to know what ya want, ya better go see a shrink. I can see ya walking outta a big old building fulla books, but that's all over. Ya life is going ta change. Can't tell how, but it will. Quite soon ya going on a journey. There's an old man involved, and it looks like he's fixin' to die.'

'Christ!' the other old man says admiringly. 'Is that me?'

Daphne ignores this. Instead she says, almost accusingly: 'Ya time will come, but not when ya expect it. Ya'll have opportunities, but sometimes ya won't make use of them. Ya find it difficult to hold on to the things ya really want. Ya must take care that people don't blame ya for things ya didn't do.'

'How do I make that happen?'

'Ya hafta do the best ya can,' Daphne says, a bit more kindly. 'That's all ya can do.' Whether this is a piece of general advice or has a specific connection with the turn of the cards, she doesn't say. 'That's all anyone can do.'

'I've heard worse,' the old man says. 'Hell and all worse.' He looks a touch undone, as if my fate, however impenetrable, has dangerous implications for his own well-being. 'You're sure the old guy who's about to die isn't me?'

'I reckon not. Older than you. *Much* older. Might even be back in England.'

I look at the pair of them: my father still faintly put out, turned thoughtful in prophecy's mystifying wake, the last of the cheroot smoke dribbling up over the grey bangs of his hair; Daphne proudly non-committal, fortune's herald, unmoved by its likely effect on the people around her.

'Getting late,' the old man says. The cloud lifts from above his head. 'We'd better fix you up a bed.'

There is a spare room, not much bigger than a closet, behind the kitchen, with a heap of ancient luggage piled up on a camp bed. Small things go scampering away at our approach. Daphne offers blankets, but no sheets. Like the cutlery, these are in Connecticut. The old man stands yawning in the doorway, slapping his hands against the cold. I fall comfortlessly asleep listening to the rats running in the roof, the police klaxons sounding in the distance, a quarrel in a nearby house that threatens to turn into a full-scale riot but eventually quietens down into the sporadic exchange of threats. Outside, the wind lifts.

In the morning there is a film of ice on the top-most blanket. The house is silent. In the sitting room, where last night's beer cans are still strewn all over the carpet, I discover the old man stark naked and in the Lotus position practising his yoga.

'On your own?'

'Daphne's gone out someplace.' Thinking that an explanation might be needed, he continues: 'She comes and goes. We ain't married or anything, you understand.'

It turns out that the old man has plans for me. An old air-force buddy who works in the music business and has an office on West Street is prepared to grant me an interview. 'He's a nice guy,' the old man says vaguely. 'You'll get on like a steak on a griddle.'

'What makes you think he'll want to give me a job?'

The old man bridles. 'C'mon, *Nick*,' he says. 'You went to Oxford University and you talk like a *dook* from an English movie. He'll lap you up.'

Over bitter coffee in the sitting room, beyond whose window icicles hang from the spindly trees, he says, 'Your mother was the love of my life. I want you to know that, Nick.' Later he does some more yoga, husky face aglow in the paralysing winter light.

*   *   *

Coming back through Queens. The sun is out, but there are vehicles trapped beneath the hummocks of snow. Men in car coats with scarves wound thrice-fold round their hands hard at work digging them out. A few children playing ice hockey with homemade sticks. Struck by how the clapboard houses look like the holiday homes at Eccles or Bacton, raised against the incoming tide. I could almost be on a beach in Norfolk, or up on the dune ridge just above it, staring out across the marram grass at the wild North Sea.

2 January 1965

Transfixed by the upper-class girls roaming in packs along Fifth Avenue. Even more socially exalted than the ones in Long Island. With their puffed-up hair, polished skin and cantilevered figures they seem more like racehorses than human beings. Alice and her friends had poise – that glacial indifference to anything that wasn't absolutely central to the world they inhabited – but nothing like this.

Fragment of conversation as two or three of them went past.

'Marcia said you had just the nicest time in Vermont.'

'It was OK. Except Greg drove his T-Bird into a tree.'

Thinking about Rosalind and the time in Phoenix. Lying on the sofa in checked shirt, jeans and sneakers listening to Bobby Darin on the record player. In calf-length skirt and matching handbag in the church porch on Sunday mornings while Al hobnobs with the preacher. Saying earnestly to Lucille, 'Momma, why don't I just make you a hot chocolate with a couple of aspirins?' Briskly rebuking me when I manage to get her blouse half open. ('Now honey, *don't*.') There are moments when I think of dialling the number in Phoenix just for the hell of it, to see who would answer. But what on earth would be the point?

*   *   *

New York starting up again after the vacation. Store windows full of cut-price furniture. Bums – mysteriously absent over Christmas – stalking the subway exits. I go over to Queens again but find the place deserted. Three days' post in the mailbox, only the mailman's solitary track visible on the iced-up step.

3 January 1965

Back from my interview with Artie Semprini in West Street. Smallish, white-haired character in mid-fifties, pleasantly – this is New York, after all – soft-spoken. Seemed pleased to see me and recalled the old man 'from the dear old 319th'. Not at all surprised to find that his old comrade-in-arms should have a son with an English accent. As the former predicted, highly impressed by my Oxford degree. On the walls of the office hang portraits of bouffant-haired crooners in tuxedos with old-fashioned radio microphones pressed to their lips. Invited to identify them, I recognise no one. Deeply unimpressed (who is this English know-nothing?), Artie pulls a portable record player out of a cabinet, plugs it into the wall and spins me a single by a British group called the Helium Kids, which is being released over here in a fortnight's time. The band themselves are quartered in a loft in the West Village, preparatory to going out on tour. What do I think? Artie wonders. The record ('Glad It's You') reminds me of everything else that flowed out of the radio on the trip from Phoenix – in rigid four-four with squeals of rackety guitar and a plaintive vocal spilling over the top – but I nod my head and opine that it sounds like the Beatles, whereupon Artie brightens (maybe I'm not the musical dullard I appear) and says, yeah, that's *exactly* what it's supposed to sound like. I go away with half-a-dozen paragraphs of Artie's notes, some cuttings from the English music papers and a brief to write the opening pages of the tour programme. If I shape up, Artie will give me a job as their publicist for the duration of the tour and possibly after it.

Back at the hotel I ask if I can borrow a typewriter from the clerk in the musty administration booth ('Sure thing, Mr Du Pont'), take it up to my room, break open a pack of twenty Kent cigarettes and set to work. Artie's notes are vestigial in the extreme – just dates of birth, eye colour, and what are coyly described as 'recreational interests'. The members of the band are called Garth, Dale, Ian, Florian and Keith. With the exception of Florian, who turns out to be a Licentiate of the Royal Academy of Music, none of them has any education to speak of, and Ian the bass player has spent time in Borstal on a charge of breaking and entering. The cuttings are more helpful, not so much for the basic information about record titles but for detailing the idiom in which this kind of material gets written up. Even better, they confirm that standards in this particular branch of the publicity business are not high. After a fair amount of thought, I write the following:

Hey there young America!

It's our great privilege and will be – we hope – your lasting pleasure to introduce you to the Helium Kids. Make no mistake – these five loveable mop-tops have been causing a regular sensation in their native land. Now they aim to bring their fine music to a whole new scene: a town near you! According to lead singer Garth Dangerfield: 'We know the young people of America are just waiting for what we have to offer, and we can't wait to bring it to them.'

The Helium Kids – a crazy name, but these are crazy guys – are GARTH, DALE, IAN, FLORIAN and KEITH. And that's right, girls: none of them is married! Back home in London town their fans include Prince Charles, His Grace the Archbishop of Canterbury, distinguished journalist Malcolm Muggeridge, John, Paul, George and Ringo and of course the 200,000 platter-pickers who bought their pulsating debut single 'Glad It's You'.

Ever-moody GARTH DANGERFIELD is 19. Likes: 'mountains and molehills'. Dislikes: 'square people who don't know
where it's at'. Favourite drink: milk ('I like it. It's real cool').

Fresh-faced DALE HALLIWELL is also 19. Dale says: 'I'm
basically a very shy person. I'm quite happy lying in a field in
summer just staring at the sky and making a chain of daisies. But
I know that when I meet the right girl it'll all take off for me and
the world will be a very different place.'

And so it goes on. Florian, a couple of years older than the others,
is naturally the 'grand-daddy of the band' and, what with his LRAM,
its 'creative brain-box'. Ian, the bass player, fresh out of Juvie, has 'had
some problems in his life', but duly maintains that 'music is helping
me overcome them'. As for Keith, the list of his accomplishments,
hobbies and opinions is so minimal that I am forced to gloss his
unsmiling portrait with: 'Tight-lipped man of few words Keith
Shields, 21, is the band's rhythmic powerhouse. But lurking behind
that business-comes-first exterior is a surprisingly warm human
being.' The whole thing concluded with a clarion call to arms:
'AMERICA – THE HELIUM KIDS SEND YOU THEIR
LOVE.'

As I anticipate, this goes down a storm with Artie. I get the job on
the spot, and a plump secretary-typist in a pair of butterfly spectacles
and purple lipstick bangs out a piece of paper declaring that I am the
accredited representative of the collective entity known as the Helium
Kids and their manager Mr Arthur J. Semprini of Utica, New York
State, and in this capacity authorised to speak to such employees of
the broadcasting (television and radio) and newspaper industries that
I or the above-mentioned Mr Semprini may judge appropriate to the
furtherance of their interests. A certain prudence cautions me to ask
Artie exactly what qualifications he thinks I possess for this role. Artie
explains that the job of a publicist mostly consists of begging favours

off disc-jockeys. 'And when they hear your accent, sonny boy, they'll play any record you like to send them.'

In the street outside Artie's office, the afternoon has bled away into twilight and the snow is transitioning into slush the colour of anchovy paste. Deciding to celebrate, I buy a bottle of Jack Daniel's and go back to the hotel in search of Doug the maintenance man. Only Doug has disappeared. The clerk says that he came in for his money on New Year's Day and announced that he was leaving: reasons unspecified. The clerk mistakes the source of my concern. 'Nothing to worry about, sir. There's another guy starting tomorrow.' But I do worry. I worry about Doug, wherever he is. On the other hand, there may be a dozen other people Doug can talk to about ice hockey, his lost wife and the gooks he shot in Korea.

Getting tired of New York. 'New York humour' simply a defence mechanism. As in Oxford, even the architecture seems purposely designed to make you feel small.

4 January 1965

Up to the West Village with Artie to meet the band. The tour begins in two days' time down in Baltimore. The loft Artie has billeted them in vast – it was previously used by a clothing company and there are old industrial sewing machines lying about under tarpaulins – and heavy with the reek of what I am now able to identify as cannabis. Artie confides to me in the cab that the boys have been smoking 'the old Mary-Johanna' ever since they stepped off the plane. He hopes it won't impair their performance. I infer that Artie is a bit baffled by this new-fangled popular music and that it may not be what he likes to think of as showbusiness. Inside there are half-a-dozen mattresses spread in a circle, with a pair of electric heaters working at full blast. It is still bitterly cold. The boys, found lounging on beaten-up sofas or making tea in a kind of galley where the roof has fallen in and half the ceiling tiles are suspended a couple of feet below their original height, are wearing their stage-clothes – for warmth, they explain, but also on the off-chance that *Variety* will be sending a photographer. 'Nick here can deal with that,' Artie says. 'He's your new publicist.'

'It's like the fucking Boy Scouts up here,' the one called Garth complains. They swear all the time, which I can see Artie doesn't quite like.

The Macy's bag he brought with him from the office turns out to contain little gifts for each of them. Garth gets a couple of airmail stamps; Dale a brace of Hershey bars; Florian a miniature flagon of mouthwash; Ian a copy of *Mad* magazine. Keith, on the other hand, is presented with an Airfix kit of a Fieseler Storch, which he immediately unpacks from its box and begins to puzzle over cross-legged on the floor.

'Is there any fucking glue?' he wonders. Artie hands him a stick.

'Keep him happy for fucking hours, that will,' Garth says indulgently.

A record player perched on top of a cardboard box plays a succession of blues records with the bass turned up.

Desultory talk about the tour. None of them has any idea of where the places are. Ian seems to think Florida is somewhere near the Canadian border and asks if you can see Niagara Falls. What have they been doing since they arrived in New York? 'Relaxing,' Garth says. 'Walking around,' Ian adds. 'And scoring grass,' someone else chimes in. Dale is alleged to be homesick for Shepperton. ''E's never been away for more than a couple of nights. ''E misses it.' 'Fancy anyone missing fucking Shepperton.' They treat Artie with a certain amount of respect – like a salty old uncle who might, if decently treated, lend them money. In the intervals of determining exactly where Montgomery, AL is on the map, I can see them sizing me up, not sure what line to take. The exception is the keyboard player, Florian – older than the others and with slightly longer hair – who at an early stage in the proceedings detaches me from the pack and demands:

'Do you know who I am?'

'Florian Shankley-Walker, I presume.'

'Then you'll have seen some of the press. I want to know what you intend to do about it?'

'What in particular?'

'I'm a *musician*,' Florian says. 'These people aren't. And I don't come from Shepperton, wherever that is. For your information, I was born in East Grinstead. You'll find,' he says languidly, 'that these things matter.'

Artie, it transpires, is not coming on the tour himself. But he intends to meet us at New Orleans, halfway through. Talk of a TV appearance on *Ed Sullivan*. Against all expectation, find myself caught up in the excitement. The sense of life taking flame.

5 January 1965

Consternation at West Street when Mrs Jabalowsky, the plump secretary, fields a call from one of Andy Warhol's people. Apparently Andy saw a photo of the boys in a magazine, heard they were in town and, obscurely captivated, wants to arrange a shoot. Artie, who knows about Warhol to the extent of having attended one of his exhibitions a while back, dubious. I say I think we should do it, on the grounds that there's no telling what it might lead to. In the end the six of us – Artie decides to stay behind – head off for East Forty-Seventh Street where Warhol has his studio. Freight elevator to the fourth floor. Foyer entirely decorated in silver foil, even down to the desk-tops. Various attendants there to greet us – 'Gerard', 'Billy', 'Cindy'. Instantly categorisable as what New Yorkers call 'freaks': floral shirts, hipster turtlenecks, pointy boots. The kind of people who would be actually arrested if they showed up on the sidewalks of Phoenix. 'Andy's out back,' one of them says. 'He's really thrilled you could be here.'

'The Silver Factory' – this is what they call it – not much more than a large loft space with a series of interconnecting rooms at the margins. Constant traffic of motorcycle messengers, girls in Pierrot costumes, workmen carrying tables. The band are unimpressed. I don't think anyone, with the possible exception of Florian, knows who Warhol is. After a long period of hanging about, Warhol emerges from a back office. Shy, startled face. Flyaway platinum hair, like one of the watches in the Tiffany windows. Chronic eczema. Voice barely audible. Tells us – echoing the assistants – that he's really thrilled we could be here. The boys, meanwhile, are getting restive, flicking Styrofoam coffee cups at each other and going off to see what's happening elsewhere on the premises. Garth comes back from one of these excursions with a glint in his eye to tell Dale that there are 'a couple of stark birds' in one of the adjoining rooms. It turns out that a movie is being shot ten yards away on the other side of a plastic screen. Intrigued by Warhol's technique, or lack of it. Prowls round the boys snapping them at odd angles, posing them in lopsided groups against the silver backdrop. Curiously, the one he really takes to is Keith, who is persuaded to spring the nozzle from a defunct fire extinguisher and balance the empty canister on his shoulder. 'Oh, that's just lovely,' Warhol enthuses. 'I just love it.' Keith looks sheepish, as if he can't quite work out if he's being made fun of. A black girl in a bikini comes out from behind the partition screen, whips Garth's cigarette out of his mouth, takes a couple of puffs, puts it back and then retreats. 'I listened to your record,' Warhol says, lizard eye on the floor. 'I really liked it. It was kind of *plastic*.'

Ian sidles over, gestures at one of the assistants who greeted us in the foyer, and says: 'Stupid fucking question, but is that a man or a woman?'

'Your guess is as good as mine.'

Odd sense of being part of an artistic ensemble piece to which everything going on in the loft – the actors behind their screen, the

motorcycle messengers coming back and forth, the meeters and greet-
ers, Keith with his lofted fire extinguisher – is somehow connected.
No formal end to the session. Warhol just mumbles, 'It's been very
nice meeting you. It's been so good. You're very wonderful people,'
and we are taken back to the silver-décor foyer and the freight elevator beyond.

Later. The eve of the tour. Settle my bill at the hotel using the $50
advance handed over by Mrs Jabalowsky. Telephone the house at
Queens several times, but there's no one at home. Gone to Connecticut,
I suppose.

Postscript 2007

All this seems to be a reliable account of what actually happened.

The encounter with the old man was par for the course for any
communication I ever had with him: that feeling of never quite knowing what you were going to get, which particular metaphorical suit of
clothes he was going to put on to receive you. Now it seems almost
sinister – the freezing house in Queens with the snow piled up against
the wooden steps like something out of a French fairy-tale; the
warring voices in the night.

Artie Semprini, I've since discovered, was quite a famous showbiz
agent back in the 1950s, a one-time associate of Sinatra and Dean
Martin hamstrung by the advent of rock and roll. In lowish water, he'd
picked up the Helium Kids at some pub gig in the West End while
on a trip to London. He was still suing them for unpaid commission
as late as 1969. An internet site called 'Starmaker' tells me died in
1983.

Mrs Jabalowsky I met again in, of all places, Oxford Street sometime in the early seventies, vacationing with her husband. She was
friendly, remembered the call from Warhol ('I tell my friends about
that and they don't believe me'), assured me that Artie was 'a real

gentleman to work for ... Not like some of those showbusiness people', but confirmed that by the time of the Helium Kids his best years were behind him.

No subsequent experience ever altered my first impressions of the Helium Kids. Garth and Dale were the creative team who dragooned the others into line. Florian was the 'educated' bourgeois along for the ride, and fantastically sniffy about the company he had to keep. Borstal-boy Ian, though biddable, could turn nasty if crossed and had to be watched. Keith was what my ever-charitable mother would have called 'a simple soul'.

The morning in Warhol's studio I remember vividly, not so much for Andy himself as for the paraphernalia and the puzzle – which could only be solved with information not then to hand – of establishing everyone's identity. 'Gerard' was Gerard Malanga and 'Billy' Billy Name. Lou Reed, who I came across several times in the seventies, swears he was present, but the history books insist that Warhol didn't meet any of the Velvet Underground until the end of 1965.

Warhol, I then thought, and continue to think, a joke. Reed, who admittedly by this time hated him like poison, told me that Warhol used to wake up every morning in terror, sure that this was the day the *New York Times* would expose him as a charlatan, the Factory would get closed down and the collective dispersed, leaving him to go back to Pittsburgh and draw shoes for footwear ads. The photos from the session, which still sometimes surface in catalogues, are terrible. Apart, oddly enough, from the ones with Keith and the fire extinguisher.

EXCLUSIVE DOORS

In the years to come, our forays into the world of celebrity went well beyond Andy, Gerard and Billy. I have stumbled through presidential palaces in my time, and marbled floors have echoed to my tread. Film-sets have found me squatting next to directorial chairs. The ante-rooms to late-night talk shows have throbbed to my urgent demands and I have drifted leisurely in the thermals of fame. Nixon I knew, and Elvis Presley. Prince Charles himself once asked me what I thought of the music of Pink Floyd. Jack Nicholson, Norman Mailer, Imelda Marcos and the members of Abba were all momentarily entangled in the web I wove to keep notoriety on our side.

Naturally, in all this mute – or not so mute – attendance at the tables of the great there were distinctions to be drawn. Nixon, patently, did not know who we were, but was advised to meet us by his aides. Presley summoned us out of pique, after we sold out Madison Square Garden faster than he had ever done himself. Björn, Benny, Agnetha and Anni-Frid were, I think, merely curious. And each of them, I hasten to add, served their purpose, were grist in the mythological mill that spun faster and ever faster above our heads, became pieces in the shiny mosaic I fashioned around us. As each tableau receded, as each familiar face faded away, as each cavalcade packed up its tents and left, communiqués followed: rarely accurate but, equally, rarely wholly deceitful or harbouring material that those implicated cared to deny. With Nixon, I wrote, we discussed the moral peril ripe to ensnare America's young. With Elvis, I alleged, we had embarked on a lengthy discussion of the influence on him, and subsequent musicians, of Arthur 'Big Boy' Crudup's 'That's All Right, Mama'. Prince Charles, I insisted, had been taught by Dale how to tune an acoustic guitar to blues scales, the better to serenade his mother.

All this worked its effect, as did the photographs of the boys in their customary poses – Garth and Dale knowing and sullen, Ian stolid, Keith dim – that appeared in newspapers. Nixon and Nicholson, the King and the Prince – none of these encounters was without its frisson, its thought of ulterior motive, its hint of embattled aliens semaphoring wildly from another world, where the sane and the well-adjusted could never hope to follow. For they were not real, those people, not at all, and their distinguishing factors seemed to have been stuck on as afterthoughts, camouflage placed there to satisfy the tourists. With Elvis the feeling that you were being introduced not to a famous man but to an exceptionally brilliant impersonation of him was exactly that: it turned out that the figure who had received visitors at Graceland dressed in what seemed to be the costume of an Egyptian pharaoh was actually Elvis's double, or perhaps even his double's double. The great man himself was incognito in Vegas, recording a gospel album in Nashville, having colonic irrigation or out of his head somewhere. You know, I forget. What I don't forget are the incidentals: the swish of damask curtains, the faces reflected back out of all-enveloping mirrors, the trays that appeared at your side and the conversations that fizzled out into a respectful silence as you drew near, all those exclusive doors, soft light behind them, tantalisingly ajar.

5. THE MOOD OF THE MOMENT

> Out on the road together
> Out with some friends of mine
> Watching the pale horizon
> Looking for a real good time
>
> 'Real Good Time'

HELIUM KIDS – US Tour 1965

7 January – Civic Theatre, Baltimore, Maryland
9 January – Doberman Sports Plaza, Lynchburg, Virginia
10 January – Lafayette High School, Charlotte, North Carolina
14 January – Robert E. Lee Memorial Hall, Athens, Georgia
15 January – Liberty Theatre, Atlanta, Georgia
18 January – Civic Theatre, Montgomery, Alabama
22 January – 'Miss Daisy's Barn', Tuscaloosa, Alabama
24 January – Grand Theatre, Jackson, Mississippi (*cancelled*)
25 January – Rodeo City Bunker, Indianola, Mississippi (*cancelled*)
26 January – Big Ed's Fun Palace, New Orleans, Louisiana (*cancelled*)

'Actually, I sometimes think my favourite composer of all is Sibelius.'

'He's very interesting, isn't he?' I had never heard a note of Sibelius.

'Do you really think so?' Florian's popping blue eyes gleamed intently from their vantage point an inch or two over the furry rim of the seat in front. 'None of my tutors at the Academy liked him at all. They used to say he was a case study in defective orchestration.'

'There's no accounting for taste.'

'You've probably noticed, but I sometimes allow a phrase or two from *Finlandia* into that dreadful slow thing we do in the second half of the set.' Florian shifted the angle of his head so that only a scattering of his rank, barley-coloured curls showed over the top of the seat. The rest of him seemed to have disappeared altogether. Soon, if everything went according to plan, he would go back to sleep. As if urgently wanting to forestall this aim, reckoning that the journey would lose its savour if Florian were somehow to be stopped from lecturing me on the merits of Sibelius, Shostakovich and Mussorgsky, plainsong, Appalachian folk music and Edgard Varèse, the coach swooped forward, hit something square on with its front-left tyre, juddered slightly and then raced away again over the white-lined tarmac.

'Jest one of them big ol' tartles,' Ed announced from the driver's seat. 'Nothing [*nawthin*] to worry about.'

Outside the window the short January afternoon was drawing in. We were somewhere near the Mississippi border, bowling erratically – a matchbox thrown on a flood tide – through a landscape of grey cotton fields. Beyond that, as in one of those stagy and over-particularised sixties filmsets on which Billie Joe is fixing to drown himself in the Tallahatchie River, came wooded country, high ridges, gathering clouds. There were birds flying south, hovering occasionally to pick up stragglers and then plunging onward. Blue eyes glinting so much that they looked ready to shoot out a stream of sparks, Florian's head bobbed into view again over the seat. Close up, his seahorse face had a greenish tinge.

'I've got some' – he lowered his voice dramatically – '*leapers* in my satchel. Do you want any?'

And here we were back in 1965 rather than watching the Ballets Russes through opera glasses or wandering through the backdrop of a Faulkner novel.

'No thanks.'

Florian was always offering you stuff: week-old copies of English papers procured from who-knew-where; Polo mints from a cache he had in his bag; set-lists with affronted little comments pencilled in the margin (*pls ask Dale to turn down his amp during organ solo!!*). As if sensing the insecurity of his tenure, he was pathetically anxious to please.

'Well, if you really won't,' Florian said. The skin under his mouth was greener than ever, while the face above it was set in the expression it had worn ever since the wagon train had corralled at Baltimore a fortnight back: peevish, put-upon, the watcher in the storm-threatened cornfield waiting for the tornado to strike. The others weren't above playing practical jokes on Florian. Oh dear me, no they weren't. A splattered prairie hen from the highway kerb propped up on his motel pillow. A condom lobbed into his bowl of Wheaties. Each was a part of the price he had to pay for being a Licentiate of the Royal Academy of Music who talked about Sibelius, Shostakovich and Edgard Varèse and wrote notes on the set-list.

Cotton fields and high ridges. Fence poles and migrating ducks. There were about thirty seats in the bus – a beaten-up tourer from the forties hired on the cheap – which meant that it was fairly sparsely populated. Langdon, the tour manager, stoical and careless of his ease, had arranged himself at a forty-five-degree angle with his arms stacked across his chest. Garth and Dale were bitchily disputing ('Nah, fuck off, you cunt') the ownership of an acoustic guitar on which they were trying to coax out a chord pattern. Ian was reading a buxom dime-store paperback entitled *Vegas Stud*. Keith, shoulders hunched against the window, hair tumbling over a set of features that looked uncomfortably like fissures etched on the surface of a potato, was fast asleep. Boredom rose in an invisible cloud above their heads. The completed model of the Fieseler Storch – a neat job, everyone agreed – lay on the adjoining seat. Outside it began to rain.

'Where the fuck are we anyway?' somebody asked.

'According to my calculations, we are between a hundred and ten and a hundred and fifteen miles east of Jackson,' Florian said with what could only have been a deliberate attempt to annoy everyone in earshot.

'Let's hope the truck's following.'

The truck, which contained the equipment and the two stalwart under-strappers who set it up on stage, had last been seen eight hours ago outside the motel where we had spent the night and could, it was freely agreed, be anywhere. For these were early days – horribly early days – for English rock groups on the road in the Land of the Free. Five years later everything would be professionalised, from the hire of the PA system to the spread of the ticket sales and the obliging ladies with fancifully small amounts of luggage whose answer to all questions was that they were with the band. Just now most of the arrangements were collapsing into chaos. Item one in this catalogue of gross oversight and flagrant dereliction of duty could be traced to Artie, who, determined to fix everything from the comfort of his desk in West Street, looked as if he had planned the tour by dangling a piece of string over the map and marking off the concerts at two-inch intervals, with no thought for geography or terrain or indeed basic human stamina. Some of the dates came in clumps – a booking at the top and bottom of some elongated southern state on successive nights, say, which might mean a 300-mile journey in between. But then followed whole stretches of time when the itinerary mysteriously flagged, leaving us with two or three days to kill smack in the middle of nowhere.

Beyond this was the question of who in particular the Helium Kids were meant to be playing to, what part of the demographic they were, in the last resort, supposed to be entertaining. Here, as well, signs of a controlling intelligence were conspicuously absent. Artie, ten-year-old copy of the *Variety Handbook of America* open on his lap, had booked us into Moose conventions, into bleak suburban gymnasia where high-school boys and their dates looked stolidly on from the bleachers, into Main Street theatres with posters for Gilbert & Sullivan in the window and the out-of-towners in the stalls wondering when we were going to set up our pedal steel guitars. None of this was particularly Artie's fault, for he was working from the prescripts of another time, that era of benign old sugar merchants in tuxes, swing bands, novelty acts, bird imitators, doggies in windows and old rugged crosses, all the paraphernalia of a bygone Tinseltown that was now coming to an end – if not quite yet here in the South, where the support act could be anything from a genuine Alabama jug band featuring ole Pa Hickory-Stick and his three sons on thimble-whacked washboards to a barbershop quartet. Worse, almost the entire tour was for some reason taking place below the Mason–Dixon line, with all the fraught behavioural protocols that this entailed. A route, by the way, that hadn't stopped Artie from employing Ed to pilot the bus, for Ed, that punctilious despatcher of straying turtles, charming, courteous Ed, was also black. I didn't give it a thought until the morning on which we rolled into a hick town outside Lynchburg in quest of a garage that would fix the tourer's rattling exhaust. 'Maybe,' Ed remarked, as he backed up the vehicle into a creosote-flooded yard where two traffic cops were shooting the breeze with a fat man who looked exactly like Elmer Fudd on his way back from a duck hunt, while a crazed mastiff strained at its leash, 'maybe one of you Caucasian gentlemen would like to attend to this.'

Pine trees rising to distant bluffs. Snow-white mansions lost among the greenery. Baptist chapels, little shacks and the ghost of Billie Joe McAllister who'd jumped off the Tallahatchie Bridge. The excruciating tedium of life on a tour bus with these five new friends, at least four of

whom seemed to possess no inner resources whatever. As for the landscape passing before us, I never really took to the South on that first
visit, and not merely because of the racial divide that was stoking its
politics up to and beyond boiling point (Johnson wasn't popular down
this way, and people were already talking about this here Governor
Wallace as a man who knew what had to be done). No, it was all too
benighted, too hidebound, too scuffed-up and set-aside and lost in
itself. We were climbing into the bus one morning in Georgia when a
crew-cut kid on a dirt bike, eyeing the party's costumes – the black
jeans and the Cuban heels – brightly enquired 'Are you the Beatles?'
and it took me a moment to realise, against all probability, that he was
serious, that he really did believe the world was small enough, and
simplistically enough arranged, for John, Paul, George and Ringo to
fetch up on the very thoroughfare where he rode his dirt bike of a
morning. Another time I was standing in line at a café counter when a
middle-aged man in a pair of grimy overalls, on which many a swamp-
bound insect had met its end, caught the unfamiliar accents flung back
from the table where Garth and Dale had established themselves,
stared hard at me and said: 'You boys from England?'

'That's right.'

'Visiting over here?'

'Surely are.' I was getting used to the local patois. A week earlier I
would have said 'Yes.'

'This yar's my son.' And here he yanked a lamp-eyed boy of about
fourteen with a twitching lower lip from his perch over by the glass
display case where the hot dogs lay suppurating, and thrust his bolster
torso between us. 'Why don't you take him with you? Give him a
chance to see the world.'

'I can't do that.'

'Sure you can. Just take him with you. Off ta see the world.'

What gave this encounter its charge was the look on the boy's face,
which was neither expectant nor astonished but only very mildly

curious. Going off to explore the world with half-a-dozen Englishmen in Beatle jackets: it was just another of Pa's mad schemes to him.

Back on the road to Jackson, there were outsize truckloads of hogs speeding by to slaughter, a dozen at least, with the animals jamming their snouts through the slats and squealing into the wind. Little eddies of cast-off straw dwindled away in the air where they passed.

'Weren't you at *Oxford*?' Florian asked, dragging himself from reverie once again. His face looked more than ever like a seahorse's, out with the mermaids, dragging the hair of the waves held back. If a human voice woke him, he would drown. 'What was that like?' Oxford was one of the things he liked talking about, along with a concerto he was supposed to be writing in his spare time and the house he shared with his mother and stepfather in Ealing.

'Never really got the hang of it.'

There was a screech from the front of the bus and a small, cylindrical object flung with startling force came whirling over the seat-rest to land in Florian's hair. It was a lit cigarette.

'*Oh mercy me*,' Florian said, genuinely scared now, who, among the countless threats and perils that lay across his path, was clearly having difficulty in getting the hang of the Helium Kids.

And here we were, set down in the US of A in the winter of 1965, the land of – to particularise – Lyndon B. Johnson and Nelson A. Rockefeller and that alluring young widow Jacqueline Kennedy, of Cassius Clay – the Louisville Lip, let us remember – and Bob Dylan, of Peter, Paul and Mary, Sergeant Bilko and *I Love Lucy*, of Norman Mailer and William F. Buckley Jr, and – infinitely removed from those scintillating cultural lodestars, whose light gently diffused above our own humble path – the Helium Kids, toiling their way across the Southern states at the rate of 350 fucking miles a day. Truth to tell, I don't remember much of that first tour. No sir, to use an expression you heard half-a-dozen times a morning, along with 'That your boy there?' and 'No coloureds in here, sir', I didn't rightly know. It was all too undifferentiated, too difficult to break down. That was when it wasn't simply incongruous – listening to Florian, say, prosing on about the Royal Academy as hailstones the size of golf balls rattled on the tarmac and the road signs advertised diversions via Shenandoah Creek. Plus, I was still trying to make sense of everything that had happened in New York, Lucille and the old man and the clapboard house in Queens and the trail that stretched back to Phoenix and its baleful host ('Call me Al'), the scent of the flowers in the Duchesnes' stultifying garden, Barry Goldwater momentarily halted in the hotel foyer under the winking chandelier, Rosalind's face caught beneath the bug-tumult of the porch lights. I was twenty-two, you must remember, and all this was new to me, so dangerously remote from North Park Avenue and Bunnett Square that it might have been taking place on another planet.

Yet more disorienting in its way was the job I'd been given to do: a task rendered just marginally less intolerable by the fact that Artie seemed even less sure of its protocols than I was myself. Every so often messages homed in from West Street – Langdon took them exasperatedly down over the payphone on a yellow legal pad he carried stuck in his belt – instructions to call local newspaper editors or sweet-talk radio producers who might be interested in interviewing 'the boys', but the data they contained was always three or four years out of date, old, stale and decomposing, and the pathways they promisingly outlined trailed away into dust. The editors had moved on, the talk-shows yielded up to country hoedowns. And this was the South, too, with its studied insularity and, it seemed to me, fundamental indifference to anything that went on beyond its borders. Meanwhile, I was getting to know the band, in so far as the band – with the possible exception of Florian – could be known, attending to the music and appreciating the very considerable difficulty they had in performing it on a stage. The question always asked about the Kids in those days is: were they any good? And the answer is that in those days *no one* was any good. Not even the Beatles when they played to 65,000 people in Shea Stadium later in the year. The PA system, hired from a connection of Artie's and prone to pick up shortwave gospel stations, kept breaking down; no concert was complete without at least one amplifier blowing a fuse. But if they weren't any good then they weren't actively bad, and a music critic from the English papers, had such an arbiter been in nit-picking attendance, would probably have said that they had two or three songs that were reasonably well put together and could stand the ceaseless repetition. Why, when things were going smoothly they could even be said to look as if they were enjoying themselves. Offstage, with the exception of Florian, they adopted a gang mentality that was quite endearing if you were an amused spectator and a serious nuisance if you happened to be on its receiving end. As for the people they came into contact with, Ed they rather liked on grounds of expertise and novelty. Langdon, who took no nonsense whatever, they respected but were not above teasing when opportunity allowed. Me they were in two minds about, the fraternity of age balanced by the fact that Florian always made a beeline for my seat on the bus and clearly regarded me as an ally against the rough boys from the council school who might just rampage into his parents' garden from the public park and steal his balloon.

And so the days slowly unwound. Rising at seven in chilly, turn-of-the-year motel rooms. Breakfast at 7.30 with blue dawn at the windows and the waitress snatching away the coffee cups as soon as you set them down. Out on the road with its squealing hog-trucks, its bosky scenery, its farm lorries cruising sedately on to God knows where, its good old boys in overalls and visor caps, or straw Stetsons and canvas shirts, its hillbilly cavalcades with eagle-eyed assassins in denim dungarees shooting gophers off the backs of pick-up trucks and its creaking charabancs full of boy scouts and church congregations and marching bands and embroidery circles. And then another

300 miles into the heart of America, with a café stopover maybe for dinner and a chance to stretch your legs, stroll down to the end of Main Street and back, maybe, and read the news in the *Georgia Sentinel*. But most of all, the long, dull afternoons in the back of the bus talking, or being talked to by Florian, about Mussorgsky, Ravel, mono-chordal middle-eights, Mixolydian modes, Oxford, the Royal Academy of Music and the sacramental oasis of his mother's house at Ealing – poor, green-tinged, seahorse-resembling Florian, who, it seemed to me, even in these early stages of a long career of drug ingestion, was taking far too many leapers than was good for him.

I woke up to find fine rain sliding in against the side of the bus. It was heading towards twilight and the field bottoms were gathered up in shadow. Vague, indeterminate structures whose function could only be guessed at loomed through the murk. These were outliers. Soon recognisable buildings would follow: gas stations; tanneries; roadside diners; Baptist chapels with flaring crosses – all the shot rubbish of the American South, looking as if it had been dumped there by some extra-terrestrial architect, his conscience untroubled by matters of harmony or scale. Langdon stirred in his seat, gave the scenery a barbed-wire grin, as if to reassure himself that nothing had been put there to confound a set of detailed instructions handed out before he fell asleep, checked his watch, brushed a few crumbs off the surface of the box file that perched on his knees, and said: 'Just about fi' miles to Jackson. We can stop for some java if you're agreeable.'

Langdon, as he had several times pointed out, was a good man to have with you on a tour: good at knowing where places were; good at getting food out of obdurate motel owners scheming to close the place down for the night; and good at facing down law enforcement officers who wanted to know if this boy was with you.

'I think that's a *splendid* idea,' Florian said, making a little cathedral arch out of his bony, interlaced fingers and then returning them to his lap. And this was another thing about Florian: his desperate air of campness. He was like the organ scholars at Oxford, with their parakeet twitter. Unlike them, he was not obviously homosexual. There were at least two girlfriends back in London to whom he sent postcards. Some of these hung around on the seats for everyone to read: *It is all rather boring . . . Nerves not good . . . A nice man called Nick is being very helpful.*

Outside, tacked onto fenceposts and dangling from bridge stanchions, the city limits signs were hastening by.

'*Oh, but this whole country's full of lies,*' Ed crooned in a reproachful tenor from the driver's seat. '*You're all gonna die and fall like flies.*'

The song – Nina Simone's 'Mississippi Goddam' – was a year old now, but it went unrecognised here in Jackson, except by Florian, who raised an eyebrow and gave me a knowing wink. The bus began to lose speed, nosed into a side-road parallel with the main track and came to a halt outside a long, low shack with tarpaper windows and a blown-out 7 Up sign.

'Usual rules apply, gentlemen,' Langdon said.

This instruction dated back to the first stopover in Baltimore a fortnight back. 'This here is the South,' Langdon had helpfully contextualised. 'You come on strong to a young lady who don't appreciate the compliment and like as not you'll end up with a piece of two-by-four wrapped round your head.'

But there were no young ladies here on the outskirts of Jackson, just a couple of gasoline trucks parked slantwise in the lot and the faint grasshopper whine of country music. Stiff-legged and blinking, the boys assembled on the forecourt. They weren't exactly tractable at these times and the air of tension that marked them as a collective unit could break out in unexpected ways. 'Ouch,' Florian squeaked, and began, much too theatrically, to massage a hand which, probably by design, someone had squashed against the door handle of the bus. Langdon looked on without interest. His job, as he had several times explained to me, was to get the bus to the concert on time, see that the concert took place and to collect any incidental expenses that were owing. Provided no laws were broken and no local sensitivities outraged, what the members of the band got up to was their own affair.

'Guess I'll buy you a Coke,' Langdon told Ed. 'Toilet's round the back, I reckon.'

The rain was easing off now. In the distance, where the land rose and houses perched on the hilltops, a series of flashes and explosions confirmed that alien hordes were whirling down out of the sky to lay waste to Jackson. There was a telephone kiosk next to the blown-out 7 Up sign. Not even trying to resist the impulse that had been welling up in me all day, a persistent itch that had survived Florian's Mixolydian modes and the discovery that I was a nice man, I fed some change into the machine, listened to the coins rattle ominously into place, took out the piece of paper with the Duchesnes' phone number and had myself put through. The phone rang a dozen times and then Rosalind's voice said in the code used even by those members of the household who weren't themselves: 'Duchesne residence.'

'It's Nick. Nick Du Pont.'

'Nick. Where in the world are you?'

I offered the bare minimum of facts about Artie and the Helium Kids.

'That's so cool,' she said, and I realised that somehow I had taken a giant leap forward in her imagination, impressed her in a way that none of the things I had done in Phoenix could ever come close to.

'What are you doing?'

'Waiting for Marty Knowland to come by.' From her tone it didn't sound as if Marty Knowland was the choicest sundae in the ice-cream-parlour window right then. 'But hey,' she said – not angrily but with a kind of wary curiosity – 'Why did you take off that night with my mother?'

It was impossible to work out just exactly what she knew, or what Al might have told her. Maybe the senior Duchesnes had sworn a vow of silence on their nervy trip home. At the same time, explanation seemed pointless.

'How is your mother?'

'Right now she's visiting with Aunt Irene at Tucson.' This was one of the organdie-swathed bridesmaids on whom Ziegfeld might have smiled. 'I haven't seen her much. Daddy said she had some kind of breakdown and he had to fetch her back. Marty said . . .' She lowered her voice almost to a whisper. 'Marty said you drove her to New York City. Is that right?'

There was nothing accusing in her voice. Again, I saw that in spiriting her mother away from Barry Goldwater's homecoming at the Corporation Plaza I had impressed her, left a calling card from a tantalising unknown world that she pined to explore. Close at hand there was a sound of doors slamming, approaching feet.

'Listen,' she said. 'I have to go.'

'Is that Marty?'

'Hell no. It's Daddy. We're not getting on terribly well at the moment. But you must call me sometime. Do you hear?'

I put the phone down. Inside the diner there was a smell of cooking fat and a doleful male voice intoning from the jukebox:

> Ah'm jest a lonesome cowboy Bill
> Mah hopes is awl behind me.
> Out awn the Colorado trail
> That's where mah fay-yate will fahnd me.

The oppressiveness of the South took different forms. Sometimes it was the abandoned screw guns, a century old now, rusting in the fields. Sometimes it was the sight of a file of huntsmen – unsmiling, green-jacketed, rifles carried two-handed at an arm's length like hedge-cutters – coming over the brow of a hill. Now it was this disembodied voice, gripped by the miseries of existence and reducing them to burlesque all at the same time.

'For Christ's sake,' Garth said. 'Turn that fucking row off.'

There were a number of possible explanations as to why, in my absence, the situation inside the diner had deteriorated. Quite probably there had been bad news about the equipment truck. Perhaps – this had happened before – Keith had lit one of his fires in the washroom. It was difficult to tell, even more difficult to know what might be the outcome. Garth and Ian had once come to blows over a bar of soap.

'All I was saying,' Florian said, in his hopeless-case voice, 'was that the point of being a keyboard player in a group is to give *texture* to the sound, and you aren't going to get that by turning everything up to *eleven*.'

This complaint had been filed before. No one showed the slightest interest. Langdon, checking off the per diems in the register Artie had given him, narrowed his gaze slightly: it was all the same to him whether Florian played his Farfisa organ or sat on the tour bus writing postcards. Coming back from the counter with a can of Pepsi, I found Garth standing in the half-open doorway lighting a cigarette.

'What's the matter?'

'It's that fucking Florian.'

'What's he done now?'

'None of the songs are written for keyboards. If he wants some that are, he'd better write them himself.'

'Why don't you and Dale try and write some with him?'

'Dale don't want to work with him. Not with no poof.'

This complaint, too, had been filed before. By degrees we returned to the bus. Here Ed had set up half-a-dozen tin cans on the rim of a cast-off tyre and, from a distance of twenty feet, was joylessly throwing stones at them. 'This here's Governor Wallace,' he announced, as the largest tin took a pebble amidships and went skittering off into the dirt.

'Oblige me by keeping it down, son,' Langdon said, in the tone he always used with Ed, making it clear that any offence caused was only to the phantom audience out beyond the lights of the freight trucks on the road. Five minutes later the bus moved off. Dale and Garth went back to their acoustic guitar; Florian sulked; Keith picked up the model of the Fieseler Storch and, with unlooked-for delicacy, began to fiddle with its undercarriage. And once again I experienced the feeling that had swept over me at the moment Lucille first swayed into view at the Corporation Plaza: a presentiment of doom, the suspicion – no, the certainty – that something deeply unpleasant was about to happen.

The Grand Theatre, reached twenty minutes later, was having trouble living up to its name. Some Elk convention or frat-house reunion or Mississippi motherfucker ensemble boisterously proceeding in the building next door had allowed the usual collection of shit-kicking regular guys with tyre-rubber necks to spill out onto the sidewalk where they milled around glassily shaking fat hands and asking each other where the hell Bill and Dexter were right now when there wuz some serious drinkin' to be done yessir d'you hear me. There were a few girls – a very few – hanging around the foyer who set up a thin cheer when they saw us, and a sign in one of the plate-glass windows that said: FROM LIVERPOOL, ENGLAND – THE HELIUM BOYS.

'Christ almighty,' Garth said.

'One helluva place,' Langdon corrected him, with what might just – all things allowed, locale, personnel and backdrop taken into consideration – have been irony. For all his sturdy professionalism, you could see that he was growing tired of his charges, yearned to be home. 'Hottest venue in Mississip. Elvis. Hank Williams. Jimmie Rodgers. They all played here.'

There was no pattern to the reception committees who turned out to welcome visitors to these Southern theatres. A husband and wife team, big Earl and docile Eulalie, say, tipping the scales at a joint thirty-five stone, with mop and pail apiece and a tray of rock buns to offer round wouldn't have been unusual. A local impresario with greased-back hair, bootlace tie and a bottle of forty rod crooked in an arthritic elbow was par for the course. At Tuscaloosa the Mayor himself had bounced into the restroom in his chain of office and declared that he was proud, mighty proud, to have us there. Here there was just a solitary black janitor to hustle us down a flight of concrete steps and along endless serpentine corridors to a dressing room where the windows had been filled in with breezeblocks. 'Now, you gentlemen kindly make yourselves at home,' the janitor said, waving a modest hand at the four chairs, the table, the plate of sand-wiches and the ketchup bottle that the room contained.

'Remember,' Garth said, who was not without a sense of humour, 'Elvis, Hank Williams and Jimmie Rodgers. They all played here.'

Overhead there was a sound of knocking and large, solid objects shifting into place.

'At least the truck arrived,' someone said.

A shuffling noise came from the corridor, and the janitor, half in and half out of the door, said meekly: 'Dey's in there, Mistah Beauregard.'

No doubt perspective played some part in what followed: the fact that Mr Beauregard, springing into the room as if he were in training for some sporting event, saw a motley collection of scuzz-bags in leather jackets, while they saw a small, fat, perspiring man in a white suit. At any rate, neither side liked the look of the other. In fact, the expression on Mr Beauregard's face was one of outright contempt. Like many another showbiz honcho down here in Dixie he clearly enjoyed despising the people out of whom he intended to make money. All the same, there was an odd look in his eye, the sense of vital information he was desperate to impart. When he had taken his bearings, glanced around the room and singled out Langdon as the figure of authority with whom the serious business of the evening would have to be transacted, he said:

'Hey, I got a piece of news for you boys. Your Winston Churchill. Seems he's dead.'

'Churchill's died?'

'It's a fact,' Mr Beauregard confirmed, not speaking to Dale, who had asked the question, but to the room at large. 'Come over on the radio a while back. Ninety years old, too. A regular Methuselah. Why, President Johnson is paying tribute to him right this moment.' There was a silence. This may have led Mr Beauregard to think that his announcement was drained of any significance it might have had. Addressing himself to Langdon, he said: 'Now, I got a hundert-and-fifty unsold tickets here that I'm proposin' to offer half-price to the shit-heels in the street. You got any objection to that?'

Langdon was starting to say that, no, that was fine by him provided he got receipts and the percentage stayed the same, when Garth interrupted.

'Well, if Churchill's dead then that's it.'

'What do you mean, that's it?' Florian asked.

'That's it. If Churchill's dead we can't play the concert.'

'Why not?' Florian, I could see, angled face glistening greenly under the dressing room's single bare lightbulb, was torn both ways, desperate not to offend his chief tormentor in the band, but equally desperate to get to the bottom of what he had to say. 'Why on earth can't we play the concert now that we're here and the truck's arrived and everything?'

'Listen you,' Garth said. 'What do you think my name is?'

'I always thought you were called Garth Dangerfield. Is that a *nom de guerre*?'

'Garth *Winston* Dangerfield. Just like John *Winston* Lennon.'

There was an uncomfortable silence in the room. Florian was getting out of his depth. Even Mr Beauregard, the hundred and fifty cut-price tickets balanced on the palm of his hand like a votive offering to some mysterious and exacting god, could see that.

'It's a great shame,' Florian said cautiously, 'that Sir Winston is dead. I'm sure we shall all remember him as a great leader. Although I seem to remember my mother told me they voted Labour in 1945. But I must say I really don't see why that should stop us from fulfilling a professional obligation to this gentleman here . . .'

A fortnight on the road with the Helium Kids, I had already seen Garth lose his temper half-a-dozen times. But these had been low-level detonations compared to what happened next. Florian was wearing a kind of frilled shirt – not the full-blown ruff that came in a couple of years later but with enough extra material to run to a small knot of flounces and ribbons at the neck. Garth grabbed this multi-coloured posy and pulled it towards him.

'It's called respect,' he yelled. '*Respect.*'

There was some debate afterwards as to what Florian should have done here in Mr Beauregard's underground lair, here in the white-washed cell beneath the dangling lightbulb. Some people said that he should have pretended to faint, or to have faked one of the asthma attacks to which he was occasionally subject. Other people said he should have thrown himself on Garth's mercy. What he should not have done, everyone agreed, was to flap the fingers of his right hand in Garth's face. It was at this point, with a kind of quiet studiousness, as if there were choreographers to thank for the way he set about the series of movements involved, that Garth picked up the ketchup from its vantage point next to the plate of sandwiches and thumped Florian over the back of the head with it.

And so the first Helium Kids US tour ended there, in the basement of the Grand Theatre, with the rambunctious shouts and hollers of the Elk convention echoing in the street outside, the pool of blood rapidly accumulating on the grey stone floor, the look on Mr Beauregard's face turning from irritation to concern and then to stark horror, and the wide-eyed janitor scurrying for help. Those were the images I took away and stored in the vault of memory. Appropriately, it was Langdon who settled everything, who decreed that Florian – not badly hurt but half-stunned – should be taken away to hospital, who squared Mr Beauregard, who saw to it, when the police arrived, that no charges were pressed on account of what was charitably marked down as a piece of horseplay that had got out of hand. The last thing I remember, curiously enough, is the moment when Florian, scalp swathed in an oozing crimson bandage, raised his head from the gurney they had laid him out on and said: 'Am I going to be all right, Nick?'

'They seem to think so.'

'That's a relief. Actually, do you know, you'll think it very strange of me to say so, but Garth was quite right to hit me.'

'What makes you think that?'

There was an odd look on Florian's face: half furtive, half sorrowful. 'I made a mistake, Nick. I misjudged the mood of the moment. It's something I've never been able to get right. I must make amends. Will you do me a favour?'

'Anything you like.'

'There's a postcard in my bag. For a . . . for a friend in London. Will you send it for me?'

It was the card which, among other things, said I was a nice man. I added a codicil beneath Florian's signature which read *Hurt in accident, but OK. N Du P.* Three days later, back in New York, I called at the house in Queens. There was nobody there, and some of the post in the mailbox was a fortnight old. Two days after that, I set sail for England.

PART TWO
The Long Afternoon

How does it feel to be one of the beautiful people?

6. SOMETHING IN THE AIR

Put in on every morning (mohair suit)
Take it off every night (mohair suit)
There's nothing in the whole wide world (mohair suit)
Makes me feel so right (mohair suit)

'Mohair Suit'

The first task I set myself when I got back to England was to work out how much money I had. As it turned out, there was a lot more than I expected. Artie Semprini had given me a parting present of $100. The contents of the house on North Park, sold at auction in my absence, had raised another £85. There was even – God knows how it had crossed the Atlantic via the *poste restante* addresses I had left behind – some backpay owing from the Phoenix exchange scheme. All this amounted to nearly £250 – a decent sum in 1965, when a London bus conductor earned £12 a week and you could rent a room in a poor district for £4. I put four-fifths of the money in the High Holborn branch of the Co-operative Bank and spent the rest of it adding to the contents of the economically furnished bedsitter on the Holloway Road, in north London, to which I now removed. My purchases included a transistor radio and a Dansette record player. I also took out subscriptions to *Melody Maker* and *Disc Weekly*. I told my landlady, impressed by the two months' rent paid in advance, that I was a student. In fact, this was the literal truth. The thing I was studying was pop music.

Why did I do this? After all, it would have been the work of a morning to present myself at the offices of the Oxford University Appointments Board and, under their direction, be spirited off into a job in advertising, the City or the professions. The streets around High Holborn, where I went to visit the bank or sign on at the Labour Exchange (how horrified my mother would have been) were full of brisk-looking twenty-two-year-olds in dark suits and black Oxfords on their way to accountancy firms in the Rolls Buildings or barristers' chambers in Lincoln's Inn Fields. Why couldn't I be like them? The answer, I suppose, is that in America I'd got some idea of the way the world was turning and the gigantic bonfire of emotion and sentiment that had been lit in the past year or so and earnestly desired to warm myself at its flames. The Beatles – and even at the time I was aware of this – had turned a howitzer on previously accepted notions of 'entertainment', and nothing would ever be the same again. Worse, or better, depending on your point of view, none of the old-style custodians of taste, the arbiters of what people listened to on their gramophones or watched on their television screens, had any idea what to do about it. They could only look on, with varying degrees of bewilderment or disgust. A conversation I had around this time with a booking agent sticks in my head. We were standing at the back of a dancehall where they were filming a programme called *Fab Gear Groove*, and the agent – he was a grey-haired character in his early fifties with a vermillion handkerchief protruding from the breast pocket of his chalk-and-blue pinstripe suit – turned to me and said, all in a rush and with a kind of hopeless jauntiness:

'I don't understand any of this. Might sound an odd thing to say, but it's true. Do you know, I started out on the Stoll-Moss circuit? That was thirty years ago now. Booking acts for variety halls. Working out whether if Max Miller was playing first house at the Acton Gaumont the taxi could get him down the road quick enough to make second house at the Shepherd's Bush Empire. And Max was on £50 a week in those days. But it's all changed now. It has though. I went to see – what are they called? – the Rolling Stones the other week. My boss told me to. "See what's going on out there," he said. In some cinema down on the south coast. There must have been a thousand people there, and a couple of hundred outside who couldn't get in. You couldn't hear anything, of course, on account of the screaming. They'd only played a couple of numbers when the St John Ambulance people had to start taking the girls out on stretchers. Could have been a riot. I was frightened for my life, I don't mind telling you. And then, when it was over, do you know what there was coming down the aisles between the seats? I'll tell you, son: a river of piss. Half the girls had wet themselves out of sheer excitement.'

And if no one apart from a few fly boys and whizz kids in the Denmark Street garrets could map out this terrifying new landscape, where girls wet themselves at concerts and parental prohibitions that had chained the likes of Marjorie and Greta to the drawing-room sofa six nights out of seven no longer applied, then, equally, no one had much idea of what skills might be needed to exploit it. Brian Epstein, famously, sold most of the Beatles' merchandising rights for a song to whoever asked him for them. Marketing, publicity, record-plugging: all the techniques with which the music business went on to caparison itself were hardly thought of. Scenting something of this, I plundered the capital stuck in the bank account in High Holborn, bought two mohair suits with sharply tapering trousers and some floral shirts at a boutique in the King's Road, and, armed with the letter of introduction that Artie – of whom quite a lot of showbiz people in London seemed to have heard – had given me back in West Street, began to call on record companies in the guise of one who possessed the key to these mysteries. Within a week I had a job as assistant publicist at a medium-sized outfit called Thames Records, with a brief to reignite the flickering flame of a singer named Dwayne Fontayne, who had enjoyed a couple of hits in the early sixties but then got left behind in the Beat Explosion. You may not remember Dwayne's 'Apples and Oranges' – a whimsical little number in waltz time with what sounds like a fairground organ playing in the background – but it got to No. 4 in the summer of 1965, and by adroitly capitalising on the deficiencies of the chief publicist and playing up Dwayne's 'bad boy' image, which involved having him dress up in pirate gear and slash at the road crew with a cutlass, I contrived to emerge with most of the credit.

All this may sound like an extraordinary imposture – wool-pulling of an altogether spectacular order. In my defence, and without vainglory, here in an industry when even minimal competence was enough to separate you from the throng of chancers and bandwagon-jumpers, I was good at my job. Some of Artie's techniques came in handy here, in particular the value of local publicity. Most of the early publicists were too grand for that: they assumed that mention of the tour dates in the *New Musical Express* was enough. By contrast, whenever anyone I represented was heading out on tour, I made a point of contacting some benighted local newspaper – the *Cleethorpes Advertiser*, the *Elgin Herald* – and brokering a telephone interview. The journalist was flattered, the artist not unwilling (provided you inflated the circulation figures). Grateful for the favour, the paper would likely as not run a second feature if the artist went that way again.

After Dwayne, the company set me to work on a band of Mod screamers from Wolverhampton called the Fiery Orbs, who were as near to being beyond the pale as a pop group could get in 1965. Their singer had already been arrested for sleeping with a fifteen-year-old girl and their live gigs were a trail of devastated dressing rooms and outraged watch committees. In fact, the word around the clubs and the industry watering holes was that the Orbs were on notice, and the only thing that would propel them to the top of the charts was a deliberate softening of their style. A plangent Elizabethan ballad with dulcimer accompaniment had been lined up for their next 45. It was left to me – no doubt presumptuously, but the deduction seemed cast-iron – to insist that the more people actively hated the Orbs the better their records were likely to sell. Accordingly, I embarked on a campaign of exaggerating their many moral and behavioural deficiencies. I wrote press releases in which, with seeming reluctance, they apologised for offences they had yet to commit. If trouble looked to be in the offing, I tipped newspapers off in advance. I issued grave-faced denials of misdemeanours I myself had concocted. On the day when, simultaneously, three members of the band were photographed by the *Sunday Mirror* urinating onto passers-by from the balcony of the hotel in which they were quartered, while the fourth was publicly condemned by the RSPCA for mistreating his cat and the *New Musical Express* printed a summary of their recent activities beneath the headline MUST WE FLING THIS FILTH AT OUR POP KIDS?, the managing director of Thames presented me with a cash bonus of £300. 'Fixing to Score', the next single, went to No. 3.

All this worked its effect. That autumn the *Evening Standard* ran an interview with me by Maureen Cleave, entitled 'PR Man to the Stars'. As a direct result of this the chief publicist at Thames got fired and I was promoted in his place, with a glass-fronted office to luxuriate in and a secretary, who had been voted by *Nova* magazine as the wearer of the shortest skirts in London, to make me cups of tea and assemble the paperwork for my thorniest assignment to date – promoting a record by a pair of conjoined twins called the Filbertson Sisters. I got the Filbertsons an interview in the *Sunday Times* by activating what turned out to be a further weapon in my armoury. You see, although this might have been a proudly egalitarian age, in which dropped aitches were strewn all over the TV sitcoms like so much confetti, the boys on the upmarket newspapers still preferred to deal

with gentlemen like themselves who had been to Oxford, could tune
up their vowels in decent company and knew what a subjunctive was.
Politesse never really went away in the sixties, it just took on different
shapes, and it could certainly be found here in the glass-fronted office
in Kensington High Street, with Miranda the dolly-bird secretary, to
whose blandishments I remained steadfastly immune, flashing her
gusset as she bent to retrieve a file, and Charteris the managing director (another dandified exquisite masquerading as a prole) barging in
every so often to borrow a handful of aspirin for his permanently
aching head, abstract promotional discs for his children back home in
Chertsey or simply come to a halt in the middle of the carpet, hands
on hips, flared nostrils at an angle like a charger sniffing the breeze, to
demand – a question you heard half-a-dozen times a day in the sixties
– 'So, Nicko, what's new?'

1965. 1966. Bright mornings in Kensington. Photoshoots at Kew
Gardens or the Round Pond or Wimbledon Common. Taxi rides to
Broadcasting House to deliver product. Train trips to tiny harbours
on the Essex coast to supply the pirate-radio ships. Blithe attendance
at the NME poll-winners' concert or backstage at *Top of the Pops*.
Dwayne Fontayne begins a forlorn descent to the cabaret circuit and
the working-men's clubs beyond the Trent. The Filbertsons' career
goes into freefall when they decide to become Jehovah's Witnesses:
the 30,000 copies of their solitary album, *Baby You're a Part of Me*,
gather dust in the warehouse. In their place come the Orang-utans,
the Cavemen, the Hootenanny Boys and Cheryl Sloane, and a tense
moment in the aftermath of the 'Find Cheryl a Boyfriend' campaign
run by an evening newspaper when the office is visited by a swarthy
man armed with a horsewhip who turns out to be Cheryl's husband.
There is, or ought to be, a moral element to all this sleight of hand, all
this subterfuge, this razor-sharp sharp practice, but somehow it always
eludes our grasp, hangs tantalisingly out of reach in the smoke-eddies

above our heads. What remains is a delightful game in which the rules can be made up as you go along. One day, everyone seems to agree – for we are all mid-century English puritans, born in the shadow of the war – there will be a reckoning, when all old prohibitions as to what can be done or said will snap back into place like so many suspender-fasteners, but until that time – which never in fact arrives – all values are purely expedient.

Picture me now in my mid-sixties peacock finery – suit by stylish Mr Fish; Cuban heels from the Pakistani shoemaker at Camden Market; hair (bushy sideburns, gaoler's-key side-parting, long over the collar) by Antonis of Ryder Street; white trench-coat from Aquascutum – trawling for gossip at the Bag O'Nails or the Scotch of St James, heading down into the East End to negotiate with promoters in pubs whose doors are guarded by burly men in straining dinner jackets and where the talk is of whether 'Ron' will be in tonight, packing up parcels of singles for delivery by trawler to the pirate ships in the freezing North Sea. The bedsitter in Holloway is long gone now, superannuated by a miniature house in a Knightsbridge mews, and the solitary nights yield up to a social life rich with colour and incident. Colour and incident, and also faint dissatisfaction. For even I can see that most of the people I have to deal with are halfwits, whom fashion's incoming tide will wash remorselessly away. In a small way, I keep up with the Helium Kids, who continue to have hit singles, but are rather a joke in the music papers for their flagrant expropriations. Certainly, *Smiley Daze*, their 'answer' to *Revolver*, sounds horribly like the Small Faces. Still, there continue to be features about Garth's occult obsessions and Keith's model kit-making. Every so often some other spectre from my past life steals up from the undergrowth to surprise me, and I slap it down.

Towards the end of October 1966, on the day the bodies were being taken out of the collapsed slag-heap at Aberfan, I was sent an invitation to a gallery launch in Cork Street. The owner was a stock-broker from London Wall, said to be operating it as tax loss, and, as a result, the guests included not merely the usual tribe of art-fanciers and scene-swellers but a dozen or so youngish men in City suits. It was a warm evening, and once the speeches had concluded and the art – mostly rather feeble attempts at homegrown abstract expressionism – had been inspected, most of those present spilled out onto the pavement. After a moment or two a small, dark-haired girl detached herself from the group of stockbrokers' clerks and came gliding confidently towards me. It was Alice Danby.

'Hello, Nick.'

'What are you doing here?'

'Oh, I'm with a rather awful man' – she indicated one of the stock-broker's clerks – 'with hands like an octopus who thinks he's going to take me out to dinner.'

A middle-class girl would have been embarrassed by this chance encounter, given what had previously passed between us, but Alice was not a middle-class girl and consequently not in the least abashed.

'You've done very well for yourself, Nick,' she said. 'Somebody showed me a piece about you in one of the newspapers. But I don't like your hair *at all*.'

'It comes with the job, I'm afraid. Like your friends over there in their suits.'

'I can see that,' she said. 'But you might at least have it cut off the collar.'

I was about to tell her that I could have my hair cut how I liked when an idea occurred to me.

'Where are you working at the moment?'

She gave a cross little flick of her head. 'Daddy's trying to get me a job at the V & A. He thinks I should be a bride of art. Until then I'm supposed to be filling in at the Belgravia Bureau. It's rather awful. Just now I'm secretary to a woman in Lowndes Square who's trying to raise money for the Vietnam orphans.'

'Would you like to have lunch with me next week?'

'That would be *very* nice.'

I selected with considerable care the restaurant on the fringes of Chelsea where we arranged to meet: bohemian enough to be attractive to a girl whose leisure was spent in a world of upper-class dullness but not sufficiently outré to scare her off. Watching her arrive, fifteen minutes after the appointed time, and casting mystified glances at the rows of cacti in their pots and the waitresses, who were got up in an approximation of flamenco gear, I saw that I had made the right choice.

'Well, this is very civilised,' she said as she sat down, which as anyone familiar with the vocabulary of the English upper classes in those days could have told you was a choice compliment.

'I'm afraid quite a lot of my time is spent taking people out to lunch.'

'Shall you put me on expenses?'

'Not unless it turns out you've a demo tape you want to offer us.'

She gave a little tinkly laugh at this, showed some of her splendiferous teeth and gave me the chance to confirm something I had half suspected in Cork Street. This was that, like many young women instinctively opposed to the social revolution going on around them, she had been forced to make certain concessions to its influence. The signs could be detected in her skirt, which stopped two inches above the knee, in the comma-like tendrils that hung down from her bobbed hair, and in her shoes, which I knew had come from a boutique in Sloane Street. Assuming that if she was, however tentatively, reaching out to an enticing new world of bohemian laxness the last thing she would want was to be reminded of the old one from which she came, I asked: 'Whatever happened to ...?' And here I named three of the friends she had introduced me to at Oxford that I had liked the least.

'Oh, they're all doing the usual things people do. Cecily Faulks is Viscountess Parmenter now. Can you imagine that? I think Alasdair got a job at Cazenove's. Somebody told me Jonty was in Germany with the Blues and Royals.' Once again, I sensed a tiny bat's squeak of disquiet with this file of mundane destinies.

'You would not believe what a boring morning I had typing out Mrs Ogilvie-Smith's letters about her wretched refugees,' she said, as the prawns gave way to the Dover sole.

After this it needed only a brisk outline of my own affairs to round off her dissatisfaction. I spent a few self-deprecating moments describing the glass-bound office in Kensington, touched lightly on the nod I had exchanged with Keith Richards a day or so ago in Jermyn Street, and waited for the seeds to germinate. All fundamentally unserious, I implied, compared to the deeply important tasks on which Cecily, Alasdair and Jonty were engaged upon, but not without its charms ... Around us the restaurant's patrons, who tended to be estate agents and Beautiful People from the King's Road maisonettes, noisily came and went and the bolero-jacketed waitresses looked more than ever as if they might be about to snap their fingers and start drumming their heels on the polished wooden floor.

'I suppose the women are rather beautiful,' she said, while the Dover sole was giving way to the strawberry syllabub.

'Of course. But they're not really ...' – and here I paused for a second or two as if in desperate search of that clinching adjective – 'real.'

'Aren't they? They always seem jolly real to me.'

Shortly afterwards, following the plan I had conceived earlier that morning, I excused myself to go to the lavatory. As luck had it this was quite near the restaurant's entrance. As I suspected, Alice was far too well brought-up to take any interest in my movements once I had left the table. And so, instead of turning into the washroom doorway, I nodded at the custodian in his cubby hole, fiddled with my jacket pocket like a man settling his cheque book back into place and stepped out into the street.

It did not take me very long to realise that, in trying to humiliate Alice in this way, I had made a serious error of judgement. It was not that I had been cruel – I had meant to be cruel – merely that what I had done had been futile. Alice might have been upset or annoyed at being deserted in the middle of a Chelsea restaurant by a man who was supposed to be treating her to lunch, but she would not be embarrassed by it. Even if she lacked the money to pay the bill she would be capable of dealing with the situation. Challenges like this were there for people like her to rise to. I could almost see her calmly explaining what had happened to the manager, settling the matter with a telephone call to her employer or her father or simply offering her name and address. In trying to expose her to ridicule, I had simply been wasting my time.

October 1966. November 1966. Pearl-grey wood-smoke rising from the Kensington gardens. Beech leaves crackling underfoot in Belgrave Square. Weekend parties at what are rumoured to be gangster joints sunk deep in the Essex boscage. Openings at Bob Fraser's gallery. Hearing Chas Chandler tell me about 'this boy called Jimi' brought back from the States and ripe to set the world ablaze. The World's End boutiques and the Portobello Road finery stores upgrade their stock: the Mod suits and the peg-top trousers are giving way to flowered shirts and chrysanthemum jackets. North Park is half-forgotten now, although my mother's face still goes careering through my dreams. The Beatles are holed up at Abbey Road, working on what is variously described as a series of sonic autobiographies or the setting of the Bible to music. From benighted Notting Hill comes fervid talk of underground 'happenings', free universities, anarchist communes taking shape behind the derelict house-fronts and ten-hour extempore space-jam freak-outs pulsing on into the night.

And then came the coup, the decisive stroke, which, far more than any stunt I may have pulled on behalf of Dwayne Fontayne, the Fiery Orbs or the Filbertsons, would establish me in my profession, make people sit up and take notice, tug away the clouds that obscured far-off Mount Olympus and leave the summit in plain view. Like many a triumph of mid-1960s music PR it was not, strictly speaking, my doing. For, looking back, I can see that I had not pushed the event into being, but merely created the circumstances in which it could take place. Providence, chance and coincidence did the rest. It involved a girl called Moyra McKechnie, known to the music press as 'the Dundee Dynamo', of whose prospects Thames Records had, over the past eighteen months, frankly despaired. She was a small, flame-eyed, limber-limbed but unexpectedly demure chanteuse from Deeside with an accent so impenetrable that when she appeared on a TV chat-show several dozen viewers wrote in to wonder why such conversations couldn't usefully be subtitled. Nonetheless, Charteris, who had convinced himself that she was 'a second Lulu' and was additionally supposed to have advanced her agent £20,000 for a four-album deal, was determined to do his best. It transpired that Moyra, a pious girl of impeccable Catholic faith ('jest a wee Pape', she had confided to one of the music papers), had in her teens spent a brief period in a nunnery, so her first album was entitled *True Confessional*. When this flopped, Charteris, who had been listening to the Shangri-Las, had the bright idea of putting her in a leather jacket and four-inch stilettos and making a single called 'My Biker Baby'. When this flopped too – a humiliation that coincided with the newspapers finding out about her mother's arraignment for operating a disorderly house in Inverness – Charteris was on the point of cutting his losses and cancelling the contract, only for there to arrive, out of nowhere, an invitation for Moyra to appear at the Royal Variety Performance in the presence of Queen Elizabeth the Queen Mother. It was a measure of the importance Charteris attached to this summons, and also of the social class in which he reposed, that he invited me to discuss this unlooked-for opportunity not in his office in Kensington High Street but over breakfast at the Connaught.

'So what do we do, Nicko?' he nervously enquired, as the platter of devilled kidneys was set before him and a second waiter asked him how he liked his eggs poached. 'I'll be perfectly frank. I'm entirely in your hands on this one.'

In later life Charteris would reinvent himself as a society diarist and write a salacious biography of Prince Charles, but just now he was enjoying himself slumming it in showbusiness.

'Junk the leather gear,' I advised. 'Put her in a nice, sensible frock. I can ask Miranda to go out and buy one if you like. See if you can get her to wear an Alice band or something. And a pair of those white stockings with holes in them. And then she can sing a nice, sensible, Scottish folk song. Something about Highland lassies skipping through the heather. The braw old banks and the bonny braes.'

'Do you really think so?' Charteris said, glistening fork halfway to his mouth. The kidneys were underdone, and his plate was awash with bloody gravy. 'I must say, I'd thought of something more . . . contemporary. What about the backing band?'

'Take my tip,' I counselled, as a third factotum plonked down an effervescing flagon of Buck's Fizz, 'and stick to a couple of girl pipers in kilts and an accordion player.'

In the end, after a certain amount of protest, Moyra was persuaded to don a calf-length confection from Laura Ashley, twist her flaming locks into a bun, concede to a tabloid newspaper that her heart leapt at the prospect of singing 'fae the Queen Mither' and perform a number entitled 'The Wee Highland Rover'. This, as I foresaw, was graciously received. Less predictable, and for which I take only an orchestrator's credit, was what happened backstage twenty minutes later. We were wearily assembled in a long, brightly lit anteroom, and the Queen Mother – game, chatty and so diminutively sparrow-bosomed that she seemed in serious danger of toppling over onto the carpet – was making her seraph's way along the line of performers. Cilla, Petula Clark, a band of grotesquely undersized harmonica-touting teenagers called the Makerfield Munchkins, an evil-looking old man who impersonated Mr Wilson and Mr Heath – all had bowed, curtseyed or otherwise abased themselves when, suddenly and disconcertingly, the lights failed. It took only a moment or two for vision to be restored, but in the mass displacement of persons that followed I discovered that I was only a yard away from the Queen Mother's silk-swathed shoulder, and that Moyra was barely a foot distant on the other side.

'Your Majesty,' I proposed, not quite knowing what would come of it, but keen that something might. 'May I present Miss Moyra McKechnie?'

There was absolutely no knowing how the parties to this transaction were going to react. The Queen Mother looked faintly baffled, but not unfriendly. For a moment I thought that Moyra – a shy girl, nervous with reporters – was going to sheer away, but then, unexpectedly, she sprang brazenly forward, seized the royal hand and clung onto it, as if they were two old cronies colliding in the slush of Auchtermuchty High Street.

'Ah'm thinkin', ma'am, that you'll be rememberin' ma grandpaw.'

By this time a flunky was on hand, ready to fling himself between them if Moyra turned nasty, but the Queen Mother was equal to the situation.

'Oh yes,' she briskly returned. 'And who would that have been?'

'Doanie Anstruther, ma'am, wad be the man ye'll perhaps recollect.'

There was a split second in which everyone froze: Moyra, whose hair was coming down at the back; the Grand Vizier of the Water Rats, or whatever he was, who had been squiring Her Majesty about; half-a-dozen wide-eyed attendants: all of them stood and stared while the Queen Mother pondered.

'Anstruther,' she said finally. 'The tall footman with the stammer. I remember him perfectly.'

'Aye, him's the man,' Moyra proudly confirmed. 'Spent twa years at Balmoral, if ah'm no mistaken, afore he left tae wed ma granmaw.'

By the grace of God, a Press Association photographer had his camera at the ready. Next day five morning newspapers carried the story and there was a facetious leading article in the *Daily Telegraph* about the servant problem. A week later a parcel arrived at the office addressed to Moyra which, when opened by her ('Whit's this noo?'), was found to contain several sprigs of Balmoral heather, sent with the fond good wishes of Elizabeth R.

Not long after this – so soon, in fact, that the two events became psychologically conflated in my mind and I could never think of one without summoning up images of the other – I got a phone call asking me if I wanted to leave Thames Records, Dwayne, the Filbertsons and the Fiery Orbs, and concentrate my energies solely on publicising what I was to refer to, in the first ever press release I wrote for them, as 'those sonic hipsters, those loveable ragamuffins and uptown delinquents, the Helium Kids'. I said yes. Wouldn't you?

7. SUNNY GOODGE STREET

My friend is dead
There lies his coffin
On bare earth rests his head
Gone but not forgotten

'My Friend is Dead'

The horses were of an old-fashioned kind: ancient stallions, black and statuesque, their plumes dyed and re-dyed so many times that they were practically purple. Stationed on the chunky gravel forecourt, grateful for the shade thrown up by the church porch, they seemed uneasy, anxious to be off. The hearse, which had come to rest at a forty-five-degree angle behind them, was a single plate-glass cylinder, like a torpedo. Bright sunshine fell in fragments, as in a modernist painting, through the gaps in the tree cover and bounced dramatically off the bonnets of the parked cars – there were fifty of them at least – that ran in wavy double-parked lines along the approach road, and which three or four men in white coats were trying to get into order.

'I told the minister – the *vicar* – we ought to have proper seating, but he wouldn't listen,' Ainslie Duncan said bitterly. 'Not my fault if we get in the church and there's a fookin' photographer been kipping in the font. Anyway, who's here?'

It was a good question, and made worse for being part of my job to answer. The cars were Aston Martins, kerb-straddling Bentleys, foxy little E-Type Jags. There was no guessing the identity of the people who had gone to ground inside them. On the other hand, I was pretty sure that the blanched middle-aged couple labouring arm-in-arm towards us were the parents of the deceased. But this wasn't what Ainslie wanted. Having long ago got beyond grief, he was prepared to settle for publicity.

'*Melody Maker* are coming. And *Record Mirror.*'

'Bloody parasites, them. No, I mean the proper papers.'

'The *Guardian* said they'd be sending someone.'

'What about that bird from the *Standard*? That Mo Cleave or whatever her name is who's always talking to Lennon? She ought to be at something like this.'

'This is a funeral, Ainslie. Not the *NME* Readers' Poll Awards.'

'I know, I know,' Ainslie said, slapping the pockets of his Mr Fish jacket as if they sheltered some excitable live thing that needed to be thumped into submission. He had a histrionic side that the job of managing a rock group, here in the Summer of Love, had never quite managed to quell and in some cases actively encouraged. 'Well, let me ask you something [*soomfin*], Nick, Nicko. How [*eyeow*] many copies of *Patterns* do you think we shifted the day after it happened?'

There were other mourners idling up the long drive now. Some of them were decently dressed in black suits and skirts. Quite a few looked as if they had been taken straight off the set of *A Whole Scene Going*. As a spectacle, they had the edge on Ainslie.

'No idea.'

'Five thousand. *Five thousand*. And then another [*anoovve*r] five thousand the next. Chap at Decca had to get onto the pressing plant . . .' He ran a forefinger up and down the seam of his blue-and-white-lozenged Harlequin trousers. 'Terrible thing for him to have died like that, though. Terrible thing.'

Later – and not that much later – memory would get busily to work and do serious things to that funeral. To be precise, memory would rapidly transform it into one of the great events of an era not exactly short on symbolic flashpoints. Memory, roaming erratically and unchecked, would eventually mark it down as the unstoppable harbinger of a whole lot of stuff that had yet to come and the farewell wave to a whole lot more stuff that had already happened. But this was not how it seemed at the time, here on a hot afternoon in the late August of 1967 whose sultriness threatened thunder, where the significance of Florian's death, at dead of night, in the swimming pool of a borrowed Sussex farmhouse, chlorinated waters closing over his curly head, still hung some way out of reach.

'Jesus,' Ainslie said, slapping his pockets again as if they had just caught fire. His eye stole beyond the shambling figures of Mr and Mr Shankley-Walker – if that was who these apparitions were – to fall mazily on a patch of grass somewhere between the gravestones at the front end of the church. Here, in unimaginable profusion, lay banks of flowers: wreaths of white lilies; amateur arrangements of pinks and dandelions in jam jars; a not that much less than life-size model of a Hammond organ with the letters F.L.O.R.I.A.N. picked out in red carnations. Set out before them on the turf were bundles of handwritten messages – *The infinite calls you, gentle traveller* one of them ran – button badges, cellophane-covered tour programmes, copies of obituaries that had appeared in the music weeklies, and an oblong square of corrugated cardboard on which someone had inked the words FEAR IN A HANDFUL OF DUST.

'Fook is all that about then?'

'It's from *The Wasteland*. The lyrics to "Fantasy Factory".'

'Jesus,' Ainslie said again. He was cleverer than he let on and almost certainly understood the Eliot reference. 'I could do without all this, I don't mind telling you.'

What could Ainslie have done without? Literary allusions? Six-foot-high walls of flowers? Death? The brittle unravelling of the past ten days? Something else above and beyond the drag put on his plans by the corpse in the swimming pool? It was difficult to tell. There were mourners heading towards the church now, some of them taking the direct road from the car park, others trailing through the graveyard. A few of them wore dark suits, but most of them were Beautiful People in boutique glad rags come to see the show. What did the men in the I Was Lord Kitchener's Valet jackets and the girls in the Biba frocks think about Florian's passing? Did they think he was a gentle traveller called to infinity? The jury was probably out on that one. Meanwhile sparrows were chittering away in the eaves and it was getting uncomfortably hot. The Shankley-Walkers, who by this stage had reached the entrance to the church, came to a halt and glanced back with a kind of fascinated horror at the tatterdemalion horde pursuing them.

'If that's Florian's mum and dad, I'd best have a word with them,' Ainslie said doggedly. 'There's some bits and bobs of his been in the office for months [*moonfs*] that they're welcome to.'

Newcomers to the Helium Kids' orbit sometimes struggled to appreciate that Ainslie was, as he sometimes put it, quite a serious fookin' geezer in his way, not to mention being a serious fookin' contender in the world through which he negligently rampaged. Like many northerners throwing their weight about down south here in the Age of Aquarius, he was embarrassed both by his origins and the depths he had to go to to conceal them from people who had already decided that he was an idiot. His father was supposed to be a Methodist minister from Hebden Bridge, and the Mr Fish jacket sat uncomfortably on his prop forward's shoulders. This sometimes gave him a melancholy air. He was also fanatically jealous of Brian Epstein, Andrew Loog Oldham, Kit Lambert and several other rival managers besides. What Mr and Mrs Shankley-Walker would make of him was anyone's call, but it was hard to think of anyone less up to dealing with two stricken parents on the day of their son's funeral.

Down in the church car park – black silhouettes under the gleaming trees – the undertakers' men were hard at work unloading the coffin from the hearse. More people were streaming up the path, even more oddly assorted than the last lot. The famous ones seemed a bit less recognisable than usual, stand-ins determined to play their parts badly. Whoever they were, Ealing was the wrong place for them. Or perhaps, when you stopped to think about it, Ealing was exactly the sort of locale where the friends and passing acquaintances and hangers-on of the keyboard player of a moderately successful rock band who had been found dead in a swimming pool should be held, for this, as every newspaper that cared about what even then were known as 'counter-cultural tendencies' hastened to assure us, was essentially a bourgeois revolution. Well, nothing could be more bourgeois than the Edwardian terraces that ran behind the church and the red bus-tops sailing away like triremes towards Acton and Shepherd's Bush. All this stirred one or two other thoughts that had nothing to do with Florian or the parched graveyard where, if everyone managed to get through with this complex operation, he would eventually lie.

'You're looking very pleased with yourself,' Ainslie said, stalking back from the church porch like a vampire out to draw blood. The Shankley-Walkers, looking even more shell-shocked than before, were shaking hands with the vicar. If it hadn't occurred to him that a husband and wife come to mourn their dead child at what already threatened to turn into a freak show might not want to be dragged into a discussion about items of the deceased's paraphernalia left in his manager's office, then his ear for emotional disturbance was sharp enough with members of his own entourage.

'I'll try to remember where I am.' There were reasons for this self-satisfaction, but they couldn't yet be explained to Ainslie, who among about a dozen other serious failings, was a hopeless gossip. Luckily his mind was still on the Shankley-Walkers.

'Florian's moom and stepdad. We had a very useful talk,' he said pompously. 'They quite understood about the cabin trunk and the typewriter at the office and they'll send someone round to get them.' A lick of wind, moving up from the gravestones, twitched at the gigantic commas of hair that ran down the sides of his bristly face and reminded him where he was. 'Told them 'ow sorry I was about everything that happened.'

It was all very well talking about 'everything'. In fact, the circumstances of Florian's death were still being reassembled, piece by fragmentary piece. Nobody knew quite what had gone on. Still less could anyone properly explain the context in which the drowning had taken place. *Paisley Patterns* had been on the racks a month. A fortnight after its release there had been a band meeting. Neither Ainslie nor I had been present. No one could remember exactly what had been said, or what state of mind Florian might have been in, only that it was supposed to have passed off satisfactorily. The next day Florian issued a statement to the music papers announcing that he was quitting the group, citing 'irreconcilable musical differences' and declaring that he was about to start work on a solo album. It was a thin week for news and the story had been splashed all over the front pages of the *New Musical Express* and *Melody Maker*. Several attempts were made to contact Florian with the aim of 'talking the fooker round', as Ainslie put it. In particular, it was necessary to clinch his involvement in a tour of Europe booked for the first week in September. But it was as if he had disappeared off the face of the earth. Shortly afterwards someone discovered that he had retired to a farmhouse in Sussex. Ainslie, who drove down to remonstrate with him, was turned away by a retainer. A week later he was found in the bright dawn face down in the farm swimming pool. An autopsy had revealed traces of various prescription drugs allowed to him by his doctor and considerable amounts of alcohol. Neither had been thought sufficient to kill him, and the coroner, diagnosing a combination of befuddlement, fatigue and poor swimming skills, had settled for misadventure.

The church bells had begun to sound now, with extraordinary violence, sending flocks of pigeons out from under the eaves. Thirty feet away the first row of gravestones shimmered in the heat.

'How are the boys taking it?'

'The boys?' Ainslie looked a bit nonplussed, as if he had charge of whole parcels and platoons of young men, uncounted households of them that it was beyond his power to differentiate. 'Well, you know the boys. They're not what you might call *demonstrative* people.' I never quite knew if Ainslie simply despised his clients, or whether the matter-of-fact way he talked about them was a kind of professional detachment. 'You know Dale wrote that poem they printed in the *NME*? *I searched for my friend in the thickets of a dark wood.* I thought that strook exactly the right note. There's talk of that being set to fookin' *music.* Keith, now. Keith's been a bit ... *quiet.*' I could never remember whether, in Ainslie's considerable list of synonyms for bad-boy behaviour, 'quiet' meant psychologically disturbed or drunk. As the mourners came streaming past us from their jaunt through the graveyard and the uncut, knee-high grass, we stood and contemplated the idea of Keith's quietness and what it betokened. Ainslie, I suddenly realised, was crying silently.

'It's Garth I worry about,' he said. 'Garth.'

The bells crashed on. There was confetti underfoot, pink, white and lilac, silted up in the crevices of the asphalt, embedded in the toecaps of my black Oxford brogues.

'Why Garth especially?'

Mesmerised by the stream of people flowing past, the clanging bells, the dust motes swaying in the dense, syrupy air – all the distinct elements of which the moment seemed to consist – Ainslie played one of his standard tricks at public events, which was to give no sign at all of having heard what had been said to him. I thought about the last time I had seen Florian. It had been a month ago, quite by chance, on a hot afternoon in Goodge Street, when I turned out of the Underground station and found him staring into a shop window, three-quarters out of it, to use one of the phrases of the time, but thoroughly pleased to see me. The shop sold party novelties, paper hats, tin whistles and streamers – nothing that would ordinarily have detained Florian for more than thirty seconds. There was no one much about.

'Isn't everyone tall?' he said.

'Yes, they are, aren't they?'

'If you and I had been alive in Dickens's time, we'd have been *giants*.'

You could never tell what Florian meant by this kind of nonsense, much less what substance he might have been outraging his cerebral cortex with. Just now he looked like something out of the *commedia dell'arte*: wide-brimmed, almost sombrero-style hat, a kind of hessian jacket embroidered with roses, billowing Turkish trousers. Shyly, like a small child keen to stay on the right side of some sinister grown-up who might turn nasty, he dug into the pocket of the Turkish trousers and produced what looked like a large, moist aspirin.

'You ought to try this, Nicko.'

'What does it do?'

'Ah. What doesn't it do?'

Florian had delved a whole lot further into the pharmacopeia since the time he had offered me leapers on the back of the tour bus. The seahorse face had had a greenish tinge in those days. Just now it was the colour of antique vellum.

'Go on,' he said, beseechingly. 'Take it.'

The pavement was busier now. There were girls with Mary Quant haircuts going by pushing prams. A man in a bowler hat flashed us an example of that terrible hysteric's glare with which men in bowler hats tended to regard the teeming world in 1967. Even by the standards of Goodge Street, this was far too weird to be borne. I put the pill on the tip of my tongue, made a pretence of swallowing it and then coughed into the palm of my hand so that the tablet came to rest between forefinger and thumb. Once Florian had stopped staring at me I flicked it away into the gutter.

'It takes about twenty minutes to do the trick,' Florian said gaily, as if he were explaining how to bake rock buns to a cookery class. 'You'll probably want to sit down somewhere.'

'I'll make sure I remember.'

'But don't take the Underground. I made the mistake of doing that once on the Circle line. You just go round and round like a carousel and for some reason your brain can't cope. I ended up thinking I was at the Nuremberg Rally. It was really rather frightening.'

'Thanks for the tip.'

Something else struck him and he said: 'Are you seeing anyone at the moment, Nicko?'

'Yes I am, actually.'

'You don't mind my asking, do you? Is she nice? I mean' – for a second he looked embarrassed – 'if it's a girl, that is. You'd be surprised how often it isn't these days. I always think that's the really important thing. That people are nice.'

'She's very nice.'

'I'm glad about that.'

He sauntered quaintly off along Goodge Street, legs sagging, as if they were tied at the knee with string, past the pram-toting girls with their Mary Quant hairdos, mysterious old women, office clerks out on errands. So many photographs of the high summer traffic of the West End were crowding out the colour supplements that it was hard not to think you were walking through a filmset. Any moment now the girls would start kicking their legs. David Hemmings would walk out of a newsagent's shop. Irene Handl would begin to swab down the pavement outside the Greek restaurant with a mop. You had to be prepared for anything. At the far end, by the turning into Newman Street, the heat had created a mirage effect so that the reflected sunlight burning off the asphalt and the surrounding buildings took on the consistency of toffee. The next thing you knew a taxi made out of newspapers would come surging along. But there were no newspaper taxis appearing on the shore, just Florian's intent, drooping figure plodding on into the heat-haze, being swallowed up by the layers of light and their caramel backdrop and then vanishing altogether.

Back in the real world of the Ealing churchyard – if that was what it was – the bells had juddered to a halt. The coffin, bouncing a bit on the uneasy shoulders of the undertaker's men, was coming up the path like an eight-legged beetle. It was time to go inside.

'You know,' Ainslie said, 'I really liked the piece you put in *The Times*.'

The Times's obituaries desk hadn't been especially keen to commemorate a dead pop star. But they had unbent sufficiently to allow a three-paragraph tribute claiming that Florian had introduced 'a rare classical sensibility to the sometimes rudimentary world of pop' and that he was 'the Rimsky-Korsakov of the Beat Generation'.

'Ains, mate,' a man in a blue serge suit and brown suede shoes beckoned as we headed towards the church porch. 'This come for you.'

Ainslie flinched a little as he took the envelope. Having once heard Brian Epstein give an order to his chauffeur, he liked to be called 'Mr Duncan'. But whatever was in the telegram seemed to cheer him up.

'From Paul,' he said. 'Nice gesture, don't you think? Seeing what great friends they was.'

As far as I knew, Florian and Paul McCartney had once talked for five minutes at a party.

'A very nice gesture,' I said. 'Want me to release it to the press?'

'Better not,' Ainslie said, altogether failing to disguise a suspicion that the telegram might not have been from Paul McCartney at all.

The church was Anglican, but sophisticated with it. There was a stone font carved in peculiar arabesques, a picture of the Blessed

Virgin Mary looking as if she had decided the whole thing had been a mistake from the start, prayer mats embroidered with fleurs-de-lys, a faint tang of incense shading into high-end perfume.

'Christ!' Ainslie said, the memory of the dissenting chapel at Hebden Bridge rising before him. 'This is a bit fookin' high, know wharramean?'

'There's no accounting for taste.'

Scared by the resplendent altar, which had been done up in satinette folds and looked like an outsize wedding cake, the high, vaulted ceiling and the phalanx of conventionally dressed mourners in the front pews, the Beautiful People had set up camp at the back of the church. Ainslie and I passed discreetly among them, shaking hands, exchanging ice-cool nods and registering pieces of small talk as we went.

'I see Groovy Bob's come.'

'And Anita.'

'Aye. You couldn't keep fookin' Anita away from a do like this.'

Only the other day, I remembered, there had been a piece in a Sunday paper about how the old England was clinging on: agricultural labourers in Suffolk villages who had never stepped over the county boundary; Empire Loyalists for whom the winds of change had never blown; mill girls in Wigan who still marched to work in clogs. There was no sign of the old England clinging on here. It had fallen off the cliff edge and burst into fragments. The back pews were filled with people from UFO, from the King's Road boutiques, from fashionable art galleries in Cork Street, from hippy bookshops in Fitzroy Square which would have closed up for the day with a regretful notice stuck up on the door in black-and-white stencil, from underground magazines with titles like *Gandalf's Garden* and *International Times*. A girl in her late teens, bobbed blonde hair so bleached by the sun that it was all but white, came skipping towards me. It was Felicia, secretary of the fan club.

'What an absolutely frightful thing to have happened,' she said.

'Yes, wasn't it?'

'I was in the office when I heard – we were getting the autumn newsletter ready – and I cried and cried. And then Dale came in to sign some photographs and he cried as well. We were going to hold a vigil to remember him, with candles and singing, but nobody could think where the best place for it was. So in the end we went to the park and took some rose petals and threw them in the fountain. Do you think that was a good idea?'

'Yes, I do. I think it was a very good idea.'

On the other hand, it may have been that the old England had clung on, in spite of everything. After all, Felicia was a lieutenant colonel's daughter from Godalming whom I had once overheard complaining about the people who didn't come to Ascot in morning dress. On this reading the Dusty Springfield hairdo and the American tan tights were simply camouflage, a second skin that she sloughed off, snake-like, whenever the old world called.

'I brought you these,' Felicia said, handing over a bulging rectangular folder on which the word FLORIAN had been written in a precise italic script. 'It's all the letters that have come in during the last fortnight. I thought you ought to have them. They're very *moving*,' Felicia said, a bit indignantly, as if she thought I was about to pour scorn on the idea of people who wrote to a pop group's fan club when one of their idols was dead.

'I'm sure they are.'

'If you want my opinion,' Felicia said, sounding every inch the lieutenant colonel's daughter from Godalming, 'I think Garth's behaved very badly.'

There were still ten minutes until the service was due to start. The flow of people coming into the church had almost stopped. In a pew not far away a man in a chrysanthemum cardigan from Granny Takes a Trip was daintily eating an apple. Ainslie, scarcely able to believe his eyes, gawped at a notice that offered confession on alternate Wednesdays. It was a very high church. I took the folder off to a seat where I could keep an eye on him and began to leaf through the letters. There were about fifty of them, nearly all from women. Some were formal expressions of regret, others yeasty fantasies of abandonment. *Now you are gone, how can there be a place for me in the world?*, one of them demanded. Ainslie laboured shiftily back from the noticeboard and squatted beside me, bony hands clasped across his knees.

'That bugger Clive has come,' he complained. 'After I specially told him not to as well.'

'Is he being discreet?'

'Hiding up the back somewhere. Robbing the fookin' poor box for all I know.'

This was another of Ainslie's oddities. Not only, in a world where nearly everything went, was he embarrassed by his homosexuality, but he was embarrassed by it on social rather than moral grounds. It didn't upset him that some of his male friends slept with other men, but that the other men they slept with happened to be hairdressers' apprentices. The fact that Clive, who minced around an antiques shop in the Pimlico Road, reposed in an infinitely higher social category than the saucy boys Ainslie stood Campari and sodas to on his trips to the West End, made his conspicuously not wanting to be seen with him in public stranger still.

'I came home the other day,' Ainslie said, letting slip the tantalising fragment that he and Clive lived in the same house, 'and he was reading a book by Angus fookin' Wilson.'

Gentle travellers summoned by the infinite. Pimlico Road antiques dealers reading Angus fucking Wilson. Colonels' daughters from Surrey with bobbed blonde hair. It was a mistake to think that the world stopped at funerals, that death and dereliction created a space where the normal rules of life no longer applied. If anything, they made the mourners even keener about the paths they were set on, even more anxious to become the kind of people they wanted themselves to be.

Organ music, welling up around us, had begun to reduce the buzz of conversation. There were choirboys filing into the back of the church, with black boots sticking out from under their surplices. The man in the Granny Takes a Trip cardigan had finished his apple and was trying to hide the core in the pages of a hymn book.

'Where are the band?'

'The band? One of them's in that fookin' box.' Ainslie could never resist this kind of joke. 'Seriously, Dale's here. I saw him having a *smook* in the car park,' he went on, leaving no one in any doubt that this was no ordinary cigarette. 'Ian'll be with him. You know how them two always tags along together.' He paused for a moment, looking bewilderedly at the extended fingers of his right hand, as if the effort of remembering the names of the people who paid his salary and whose careers he spent his days promoting demanded more mental effort than he could possibly hope to possess. 'Keith . . . Keith's been keeping a low profile just at the moment.'

I knew about Keith's low profile. 'Why's that?'

'Between you and me he's not too happy about that piece in the *Mail.*'

For nearly a year now we had been trying to build Keith up as a pop personality in the Ringo mould: not too articulate perhaps, but goofy, loveable, dependable, a matter-of-fact counterweight to the mania going on around him. It was never any good. The *Mail* article – SCHOOL DAYS OF THE STARS – featuring an interview with Keith's old PE teacher and extracts from his school reports, had not been a success.

'I didn't know Keith was so sensitive.'

'Keith is a fookin' lot of things,' Ainslie said darkly. 'Look, I know you've been doing your best with Keith, Nicko. No, I mean it. That interview where he talked about his Airfix kits, take it from me it was the best anyone could have done with, with . . .' Ainslie paused, stared hard at the tray of guttering candles that burned in a wall bracket two or three feet from where he sat, at a parched blonde girl sitting in the pew opposite who might easily have been Marianne Faithfull, at the choir, which had now, with a grotesque squeaking of boots, begun to process down the aisle, but found solace in none of them. '. . . the *material*. But let's keep quiet about fookin' Keith for a moment, shall we?'

'Where's Garth?'

'Do you know,' Ainslie said, taking another squint at the candle bracket, 'if me dad had been here today he'd have been physically sick? I'm sure he would. We shan't be seeing Garth.'

Before I could ask why we shouldn't be seeing Garth the organ gave a convulsive throb: the choir struck up 'He Who Would Valiant Be'. Heads down over their hymn books, the Beautiful People sang with surprising fervour. Just now London was full of these incongruities. Hippy cavalcades racketing along Kensington Gore. Wispy men in Harlequin gear picnicking in St James's Park. My friend Jolyon, who wrote articles for the *Observer*, had already read me a lecture on the forces of historical relativism brought into play: 'You needn't think any of this is anything new. In fact, it's absolutely the reverse. That's what my editor says. There have always been youth cults. None of this lot' – we had been watching the Beatles perform their live broadcast of 'All You Need is Love' – 'would look out of place at the Royal Academy Summer Exhibition of 1820. Isn't Mick Jagger going around dressed like Shelley? There's someone who knows which side his bread is buttered. And how long will it last? Take it from me, Nick, in five years' time they'll all' – he meant the audience, not John, Paul, George and Ringo – 'be loss adjusters or working in local government. And in thirty years' time the costumes will be in the V & A for us to laugh at.'

Later, when I had given Jolyon the letters that arrived at the management office, he would write a majestic article headed DIONYSUS

IN WI3 about hysteria, adolescent emotions, the girls who stood and wept at Florian's grave and a fortnight later would still be covering it with graffiti. Here in the church, on the other hand, hysteria was just about being kept at bay. The coffin, now being brought down the aisle by the undertaker's men, marching in step like soldiers bringing home a fallen comrade, looked far too small to hold a human being. Behind it trailed members of Florian's family: pale children; an old woman with her grandson's jaw and popping blue eyes; Mr and Mrs Shankley-Walker, arm-in-arm. Ainslie, a new and reverent Ainslie, miraculously returned to his father's chapel at Hebden Bridge, had his prayer book open at the burial service and was running his finger over the type. Outside it was starting to rain. Then thunder stirred, so angrily that the lights went dim for a second. Once the coffin had been set down on its plinth and the undertaker's men had slunk away, a girl in a white dress ran up from the back of the church and placed a single red rose on the rim.

The lesson was from Ecclesiastes, the grinders in the streets, the grasshopper a burden, the silver cord loosed, the wheel broken at the circle, and I tried to think not about whether the woman in the pew opposite was Marianne Faithfull – which she probably was – or the treat that would be waiting for me back home in Egerton Gardens Mews, but about Florian and what all this – Ainslie with his long, anteater's nose stuck in the Book of Common Prayer, the six-foot-high bank of flowers in the churchyard, the cameramen lurking in the vestry – might amount to. Apart from the fact that he was dead, it was difficult to know what to think about Florian. Was he just a supremely odd person whom the excitements and irritations of the past three years had made odder still? A sixties casualty (there were already plenty of them)? A chronic misfit desperate to find a mate? Half-a-dozen times in our acquaintanceship Florian had made some tentative bid at friendship and half-a-dozen times I had turned him down. All the same, I knew that there was a reason for this, which was that

I hadn't liked Florian, thought him absurd, not wanted to spend time in his company. There was a little guilt in owning up to this, but not much. Other people treated Florian far worse than I had. Outside, the thunder continued to roll. We sang 'Guide Me O Thou Great Redeemer' and 'Jerusalem' with considerable spirit. One of the pale Shankley-Walker children wept noisily and had to be taken out. The coffin lay on the plinth. It was definitely Marianne Faithfull. And so the time passed.

'Harrowing,' Ainslie said cheerfully as we stood in the church porch half an hour later. 'Absolutely fookin' harrowing.' He had forgotten all about the chapel at Hebden Bridge and was peering over the tops of the gravestones at the departing crowd. The rain had stopped, but there were pools of water threatening to swamp the concrete path. Carnation heads from one of the floral displays drifted over the wet grass.

'Harrowing,' Ainslie said for the third time. He was in a much better state now, and would probably want to start talking about business.

'You know they've been back in the studio?' he demanded, lynx-eyed and animated amid the typed notices about churchwardens and the diocesan synod.

'Nobody told me. What did they do?'

'As it happens,' Ainslie said, 'it was on the day he died. That very afternoon. Just the four of them. Very different, Rory said.' Rory was the studio engineer. 'Not at all like *Paisley Patterns*.'

'Very different' could mean lots of things here in the Summer of Love, but the idea of rank unlistenability usually hovered somewhere near its core. What had the boys got up to down in the studio on that August afternoon while, seventy miles away, Florian prepared to meet his death? Sacrificed a goat while someone read out passages from the *Tibetan Book of the Dead*? Conducted raucous jazz/rock fusion experiments in 9/8 time? Sung a capella versions of nursery rhymes? Who could tell? All the same, I was intrigued.

'What kind of thing?'

'A bit *loud*,' Ainslie said, as if this clinched it. 'Simon' – Simon was the record company A&R man – 'liked it. Well, he didn't not like it.'

All this raised a wider question, sometimes pursued by people you met at parties, occasionally even taken up by music journalists, which was Ainslie's unsuitability for the work he did. Naturally, there were points in his favour. As a staff writer on *Melody Maker* had once put it to me: 'Weirdest job in the world being a record company boss and having to deal with all the queer fish who swim through the door these days. You know, all those cement tycoons who've decided they can make a killing in Denmark Street or the old boys who used to book Vera Lynn for variety halls in the forties and think it's all pretty much the same now. I think when they see Ainslie with those trousers of his they find him a very nice change.' On the other hand, it was reckoned that Ainslie's lack of interest in the repertoire probably counted against him, and the manager of a rival ensemble had once won a bet in the Scotch of St James by challenging him to remember the titles of the Helium Kids' last three singles. It was 1967 now, the year of flowers in the rain, and love being all you needed, of seeing Emily play and whiter shades of pale. The times they were a-changing, and before you knew it they would change again, leaving less intrepid travellers beached and stranded in the mud. The suspicion that he might be one of them preyed on Ainslie's mind. The seam of his Harlequin trousers had begun to split, I noticed, exposing several inches of shrivelled thigh.

'I've been putting the word out for another keyboard player,' he said. 'Wondered about Stevie Winwood.'

'That's a good idea,' I exclaimed of this terrible and unrealisable scheme.

'Or the bloke from – what the fook are they called? – the Moody Blues.'

'You're on fire.' Ainslie and irony existed in remote, watertight compartments.

The crowd in the church porch was thinning out. In the distance more rain threatened. Soon the funeral cortege would be moving off to South Ealing Cemetery. Scattered around the gravestones were people even more outlandish than the ones glimpsed in the church: Dickensian figures in frockcoats and side-whiskers, women in ankle-length skirts. Ainslie, duty done, shrugged his shoulders.

'There's a private room booked at the Speakeasy,' he said. 'Thought we'd raise a glass. I'll see you there.'

It was about ten-past one. Not the best time for a private room at the Speakeasy, or anywhere else. As I went down the path, one of the Dickensian figures from the gravestones fell in behind me.

'Nick, man.'

'Dale. I didn't recognise you in that hat.'

'It's a very serious fashion statement,' Dale said, sweeping the battered Victorian stovepipe off his head and dashing the brim against his chest. 'Wear it another week and they'll be giving me a part in *Oliver!* Could do worse, of course, in the present situation. You going to this do at the 'Easy?'

'No.'

'Me neither. That Ainslie and his bum-boys getting walloped and saying it's what Flor would have wanted.' He palmed a tobacco tin out of his pocket and selected a fresh, hand-rolled reefer. 'You want a cigarette?'

'No thanks.'

'You ought to, Nick. Be the making of you. Cool you dahn no end.' Dale looked puzzled, genuinely perplexed at the thought of anyone spurning an overture in the field of drug largesse. He put the hat back on his head, where it nestled incongruously above long, greasy curls, and made a beckoning gesture with his forefinger. 'Here. Walk with me, man.'

Of all the Helium Kids, it was nearly always Dale I liked the best, found the most entertaining, the least tedious, the one with the greatest personal attack. Most of them, by this stage, had gone some way towards stylising their personal manner, but it was Dale who seemed both to have taken the most trouble from this ratcheting up of existing resources and taken the greatest satisfaction from the results. Here on the edge of Tin Pan Alley, nonchalance was an underrated virtue.

'Shame about old Flor, in't it?' he went on. Twenty yards away in the car park Ainslie had caught up with Clive and was giving him a furious ticking-off. 'Terrible way to go and all. Quite shook me up when I heard, I don't mind telling you. Lot of cock being talked about it, though. I mean, there was this face at the Scotch the other night said that some geezer did him in. Held him down in the water and then scarpered before anyone was the wiser.'

'It doesn't sound very likely to me.'

'That's exactly what I said. Catch old Flor getting wrong with Ronnie Kray or someone. Look, you were a mate of his, Nick. He was always talking about you. You know, birds of a feather. Always said how nice you were to him. So I'll tell you what happened. What I think happened, anyway. You know that meeting we had just after the album came out? Just the five of us. No Ainslie or nothink. The one he goes off in a huff after?'

'Only what Ainslie told me.'

'Ainslie doesn't have a clue. Never did. Well, there was always going to be trouble, on account of Flor not being on much of the album. Wasn't a put-up job. Just happened that way. Fucking mixes come back and there's hardly any keys, I mean. So we were expecting ructions. Only thing is that it's Garth that starts it all.'

'Started what?'

'Well, you know what he's like. That *Garth*,' Dale said, like some medieval warlord invited to admire the bloodied dungeon where a zealous underling has perhaps gone a little too far. 'Never did cut Flor any slack. Only this time he's got a kind of charge-sheet ready. That's right. Turns out he's only got that fucker Rory to tape every concert we've done in the past two munfs. And then he goes through it song by song. "This is where you come in late . . . This is where you went and played all over the vocal line . . ." That sort of thing. Went on for an hour at least. Of course, Ian and Keith never said anythink. Like they had a clue about what was going on. But what was really weird was how Flor took it. I mean, for the first ten minutes he was sort of defending himself. You know, "I didn't come in late actually . . . You was coughing, man . . ." Dale's imitation of Florian's flustered, la-di-dah voice was bang-on. That sort of thing. Only after a bit he stopped bothering. Just sat there with his eyes blinking like he'd seen a ghost. And after Garth finished and is poncing around the place like some fucking High Court judge he just gets up and says, very quiet like, "You have demeaned me in my profession."'

'Just that?'

'*You have demeaned me in my profession.* Walked out on the spot. Next morning, we get a solicitor's letter. Which is a fucking disaster, man, as it turns out his contract allows for a lump sum pay-out in the event of him being fired.'

'Had anyone actually fired him?

'Constructive dismissal, in't it? Ainslie nearly had a fit when he found out. Anyway, Flor goes down to his mate's farmhouse. Won't answer the phone. Registered letters sent to him not signed for. Gear all over the place. Friend of mine – you know that Lancelot that licks the floors at the Scotch? – saw him the afternoon before and said it was just like his dad who'd got shell-shocked at Anzio. Jittery as a skunk.'

'And that's how he died?'

Dale paused and, with surprising delicacy, Gandalf-like, blew a ring of greenish smoke that hung for a moment in the air above the brim of his hat. 'Bound to. Think about it. It's three o'clock in the morning, or whatever. He's out of his head on Bennies, or something. All over the place, anyway, of account of him leaving the band. Gets in the water, and we all know the fucker can't hardly swim. There's some scrubber girlfriend around the place but she's in the sitting room genning up on the *Kama Sutra* or something, and by the time she gets back with her tits all oiled up ready for the thirteenth gossamer caress he's gone.'

'What does Garth think about it?'

'His Royal Highness? Gone off in a sulk somewhere. Thinks it's his fault. Which it is, of course. Well, up to a point. I mean, none of it would have happened if he hadn't of got Rory to do them tapes. On the other hand, you're not telling me that Flor was ever a normal bloke. Not you-and-me normal, anyhow.'

'Now what happens?'

'Christ knows. Either he'll come back or Ainslie'll go and find him. Ainslie's very good at finding people. When I went off to Istanbul with that bird from *Ready Steady Go!* he had me back within the week.'

Back in the car park, most of the vehicles were gone. There was an Aston Martin jammed up on the verge, on which Dale's eye proudly fell.

'Anywhere I can take you, man?'

At Ealing Broadway the sun had come out and the water on the pavements had created the same mirage effect I remembered from the afternoon in Goodge Street. Any moment now a camel train would pass through on its way to the oasis. Overhead, vapour trails crossed and re-crossed. It seemed a long time now since Florian's funeral, an eternity almost since the last time I had seen him. Egerton Gardens Mews, reached half an hour later, was lost in shadow. Even the cats had disappeared. Lengthening my stride as I turned the corner, I came up to the front door at a run. Inside the radio was playing and carrier bags from the Knightsbridge boutiques lay all over the floor.

'You took your time,' a voice said. I went into the kitchen, where more sunshine was flooding in a dense, liquid stream over the table, gathering up the woman who sat at it in a hazy, aquamarine glow. 'But welcome back, anyhow,' Rosalind said.

8. LONDON JOURNAL,
JANUARY–AUGUST 1967

I'm a Helium Kid
Whatever you say that I done, I did
Everything's blooming from the seeds that I sowed
Light the blue touch-paper, watch me explode

'Helium Kids'

Unlike the New York journal of 1964, this diary is typed on foolscap paper and interspersed with press cuttings and concert tickets Sellotaped onto the pages. Again, it seems to me an authentic document.

18 January 1967

Egerton Gardens Mews, 8.30 a.m. On the wall: Jim Dine drawing bought last week from Bob Fraser's gallery in Duke Street. On the kitchen table: a dozen white-label advance pressings of the new single, 'Road to Marrakech'; *Daily Sketch* front page announcing death of Tara Browne, the Guinness heir, after his car shot a set of traffic lights – a month old now but still haven't managed to throw it away. Thinking of my mother back in the front room on North Park. My father's face staring out of its frame. The beech trees in Eaton Park. The ornamental ponds where swam the giant carp.

Hitherto I haven't taken much interest in the life of Egerton Gardens Mews. Now I see that it's nicely poised between past and present, the old world and the new. At No. 1 Major Hope-Leresche MC – some kind of stockbroking City type – and his wife. No. 2: yours truly. No. 3: Mrs Fenella Manningham, elderly lady with dyed, sugar-loaf hair, said to have 'a past' and possibly to have known Evelyn Waugh. No. 4: fashion photographer – about my age – with basement studio, who scandalises the neighbours by coming home at all hours in noisy sports car. Women constantly arriving in taxis. The other day when I took round a misdirected parcel, the door opened by blonde girl in school uniform, who couldn't have been more than sixteen.

21 January 1967

Mid-morning in the office. Beneath the window, Berwick Street market in ferment. Tarts in fur coats and high heels sullenly taking the air. Ainslie in his cubbyhole making phone calls. Norma, the secretary, sits with her skirt hitched up to reveal canary-coloured knickers mending a ladder in her tights. Cyril, Ainslie's cockney factotum, brewing the tea. Nothing to suggest that we are music people except the framed posters on the wall. Towards lunchtime Ainslie calls us together to announce his 'strategy' for 'Road to Marrakech'. Somehow, and at God knows what expense, he has got hold of the list of shops who supply returns to a databank ultimately converted into the BBC singles chart. Copies of this duly circulated. The plan is that Cyril, Norma, myself and half-a-dozen other temporary additions to the payroll will tour London for a couple of days surreptitiously buying up stock. It's what everyone does these days, apparently, 'even the Stones'. That afternoon Norma and I head out into the West End. The routine is as follows. First, I go in and buy a copy. Five minutes later Norma follows. Then we wait outside until a different sales assistant is at the till and repeat the process. By 5.30 we have amassed seventy-six copies of 'Road to Marrakech'. This goes on for a week.

30 January 1967

'Road to Marrakech' in the charts at No. 17. Ainslie cock-a-hoop. But it's not one of their better records. Even I can see that the guitar sound is robbed wholesale from the Kinks' 'See My Friend', and the keyboard figure is uncomfortably close to something the Small Faces did three or four months back. Bad review in *Melody Maker*: 'Bogged down in their attempts to re-create "the sound of the moment" – whatever that is – the Helium Kids are in serious danger of losing the qualities that, a year or so ago, made their records so distinctive.'

Garth shows up at the office. All the boys are dressing differently now, but he seems to be the only one self-consciously cultivating a 'style'. Frogged, military-look jacket, trousers in blue-and-white stripes, snakeskin boots *à la* Brian Jones. Has a bag of books with him, picked up at one of the antiquarian shops in Cecil Court.

GARTH: You ever heard of a book called *Histoire de la Magie*?

SELF: By Eliphas Levi?

GARTH: That's the geezer. Know anything about him?

SELF (*quoting from memory*): 'One who is afraid of fire will never command salamanders.'

And for once I get something never previously allowed me in all my dealings with cocksure Garth: a look of respect.

Winter routines. Boozy lunch with Ainslie in Soho. Afternoon in the office. Light fading early over the housetops in orangeade glow. Soho horribly garish and seedy. House next door, as far as we know, a brothel. Shop three doors down sells Danish pornography – the

very worst kind, apparently. Ainslie chatters blithely on but is, I
suspect, deeply worried. He is smart enough – just about – to grasp
what the music papers have been hinting for some time: that the
business is changing, that the future will probably lie not in seven-
inch singles but in long-playing records, that the old Tin Pan Alley
days are gone. Why else have the Beatles stopped touring and holed
up in Abbey Road with a limitless budget and no release date for
their next album? Ainslie can't understand this. He thinks for a pop
group not to want to play concerts is a sin against nature. Worse, the
other acts on his roster haven't lived up to their promise. If indeed
they had any in the first place. Bernadette, the Irish girl for whom he
had such high hopes, is six months pregnant and back home in Cork
with her outraged parents. The Thamesmen are playing supper clubs
beyond the Trent.

'Marrakech' stalls at No. 15. Norma and I spend a further three
days buying up copies in the West End. The next week it drops to 23.
So much for Ainslie's attempts at chart-fixing.

3 February 1967

Fairfield Hall, Croydon. Supported by Cream. Not a success. First
date this year and they sound under-rehearsed. Only two-thirds full.
Plus Florian's organ has to be turned up so loud that the notes are
constantly feeding back into the amplifier and setting up a high-
pitched squeal that drowns out whatever anyone else is doing. Furious
shouting match between Garth and Florian about this afterwards.

None of these failings helped by support act, a trio playing heavily
amped-up blues, with guitar prodigy and flailing, mad-eyed drummer.
Great debate backstage as to what the latter is 'on'. No one says
anything, but a feeling that we have missed a cue.

9 February 1967

Specimen morning in Berwick Street. Press release to music papers announcing that the Helium Kids are about to 'enter the studio' to work on a new album, provisionally entitled *Paisley Patterns*, followed by excruciating two hours with Keith ghosting a column he has been asked to contribute to *Disc* guest-reviewing the week's singles.

SELF (*takes record off turntable*): What did you think of that one?

KEITH: It was all right.

SELF: No, I mean what did you like about it?

KEITH: I don't know.

SELF (*wheedling*): Come on. There must be something in it you noticed?

KEITH: The drums were OK. And the da-da-do bit in the guitar break.

SELF: *All propulsive percussion and upper-fret arpeggios, this one has strong claims to be waxing of the week.* Shall I put that?

KEITH: Sure thing.

Shortly after lunch, Norma gives notice: 'My friend got me a job at the *Daily Mail*. The money's better, the people are nice and I won't have that Garth putting his hand up my skirt.'

11 February 1967

Yesterday morning, coming back through St John's Wood, I bumped into George Harrison. The usual Mephistophelian glint in his eye. I don't know him at all well, but he straightaway invited me to a party that night at Abbey Road 'to celebrate finishing a track'. Ainslie, to whom I confided this, *wild* with envy. 'Hobbing with the fookin' nobs. Won't make your shit smell any sweeter, you know.'

Arrived at Studio One mid-evening to find enormous crowd of people and what seemed to be an entire symphony orchestra laying down overdubs. McCartney – who can't read music – affecting to conduct: real work, naturally, being done by George Martin. Whole thing concluded with what somebody said was a twenty-four-bar passage ascending from lowest note to highest. This produced extraordinarily dramatic effect.

Impressions of Beatles. McCartney: friendly, outward-going, uncomplicated. Lennon: sharp, sardonic (to engineer who offered a helpful suggestion – 'Nobody likes a smart-arse'). Harrison: brooding, reserved. Starr: affable. Asked after Keith.

Atmosphere in studio euphoric. Rounds of applause. Girls dancing. Carnival feeling. Depressed to think that we are so far behind in terms of creative accomplishment, technical knowhow, sheer panache.

3 March 1967

Came back to Egerton Gardens Mews to find a note on the door from the photographer at No. 4 asking me round for a drink as he had 'something to tell me'. As I had nothing better to do, I went over immediately. The photographer is called Dougal Mackintosh: late twenties, acne-ravaged. Wall of his sitting room choc-a-bloc with portraits: Shrimpton, Twiggy and so on. The girl who opened the door to me that time sat cross-legged on the carpet blinking at the *Standard* and didn't look up.

'She's called Alexandra,' Mackintosh said, half-apologetically, as he showed me into the kitchen. 'You could probably have her if you tried hard enough. She's very amenable.'

'And still at school, I gather.'

'Doing her A levels at Godolphin and Latymer. She likes coming round to look at the models' pictures. Do you want ice in this? Actually' – he lowered his voice as he bent over the spirit bottles in the cabinet – 'she's a bit much for me. One of those nymphomaniac types who're always pestering you and don't seem to enjoy it when they get it.'

Outside in the Mews I could see Mrs Manningham labouring back with a wheeled shopping basket. I wonder what she would make of nymphomaniac types who don't enjoy it when they get it. In the sitting room, Alexandra had given up on the *Standard* and had switched on the early evening news. I could hear the announcer talking about nuclear tests in Nevada and what Mr Callaghan thought about the balance of payments.

Mackintosh turns out to be a public school boy from the Home Counties trying desperately to camouflage his origins with a *faux-*cockney accent. A bit star-struck by the world he has finessed his way into. Talks self-consciously about 'Jean' (Shrimpton) and 'Ossie' (Clark). Says the big money isn't in selling pictures to magazines but getting your prints onto agency files. 'Listen,' he said, 'do you know a chap called Shard? Donald Shard? I was taking some shots of him the other day – his idea, not mine – and your name came up.' He took a folder out from under the pile of newspapers on the kitchen table and showed me three or four black-and-white photos of a big man with a bald head and crazy Father Christmas eyebrows brooding over a desk strewn with legal papers. 'Between you and me, I was glad to get out of the place. Didn't like the atmosphere. Or him either. Do you know him? He's in your line of business.'

Do I know Don Shard? The Don Shard who was reported to have dangled a rival operator over a Wardour Street balcony by his ankles, the quicker to conclude a business transaction on which they were both engaged? The Don Shard of whom Ainslie had once cravenly remarked: 'If I heard Don wanted to see me I'd take Kenny and that Mad Ernie with me, and I'd tell fookin' Cyril the exact time I was going in there and to phone the police if I didn't come out within twenty minutes. That's what I'd do.' There are plenty of pantomime villains wandering around the record companies at the moment, barging their ingrate way through the hippy flotsam, but Don here is the real thing.

'Well, he admires your work – his exact words,' Mackintosh said. He was on his third vodka-tonic and there were some little white pills in a bottle on the table's edge that caught my eye. 'And he'd like to meet you to discuss – what was it? – "a mutually beneficial proposition".'

As he handed over the business card there was a stirring in the doorway and Alexandra marched into the room. Still wearing her school blazer, she looked more waif-like than ever but at the same time oddly formidable: a tough baby come to exact her due.

'It's time we went out to dinner.'

'Not yet surely?' Mackintosh demurred. 'It's only seven o'clock.'

'A girl's got to eat. And I've got my homework to do.'

'I don't think I'm especially hungry at the moment.' All trace of Mackintosh's cockney accent had gone. He sounded like Little Lord Fauntleroy addressing his valet. 'Why don't you have something to drink?'

'I don't want anything to fucking drink. I want you to take me out to dinner.'

After that the party broke up. I stowed the business card in my wallet where it lay incriminatingly among the cheque stubs and the clubland memberships.

'How much will you be charging for those photographs?' I asked as we stood on the doorstep.

'Oh, I don't think there'll be any question of a fee,' Mackintosh said grimly.

17 March 1967

Last night, working late at Berwick Street, I found a brown envelope marked 'Provisional Accounts 66/7', presumably left out for Ainslie by the accountant. For some reason the envelope was unsealed and I decided to open it.

The accounts aren't at all easy to interpret. But it looks as if Ainslie, trading as APD Productions – his second name is, of all things, Ptolemy – has made a profit of several thousand pounds in the past tax year. There is no indication as to what Ainslie has been allowing himself – as a director of Helium Kids Enterprises Ltd he is entitled to a sixth of everything the boys make, not to mention his other clients. On the other hand, even I can see that Norma has, until the week of her departure, been paid twice and that one of her salaries has been stealthily remitted back to her employer. Other salient items include a £1000 a year retainer to Clive for 'clerical services', a £500 payoff to Bernadette back in Cork and a list of expenses that seems to include the refurbishment of Ainslie's domicile in Sunbury-on-Thames.

All this is, of course, corrupt, but not *outstandingly* corrupt – some managers are buying themselves mansions in Surrey on the strength of royalties their charges never see and diddling them out of overseas income they never knew existed. And what does one do with this information having acquired it? I decide to sit tight, in the certainty that at some point – probably sooner rather than later – it will come in useful.

2 April 1967

Queer moment in the Mews. Like a breath of wind from a vanished age. Old Mrs Manningham and I are now on nodding terms. In fact, our acquaintance has prospered to the point where, on the way home from Berwick Street, and knowing her scatterbrain's tendency to run out of milk, I very often buy her an extra pint. These attentions are always graciously received. Coming back last night, milk carton in hand, I found a chauffeur-driven Daimler outside No. 3 and a guest bidding her farewell on the doorstep. I was about to retire discreetly to my own quarters when Mrs M., with one of those roguish old-lady smiles of hers, said: 'Your Royal Highness, may I present my friend

Mr Du Pont?' and I found myself shaking the tremulous hand of a spruce old gentleman with what had once been butter-coloured hair and wrinkles running in odd, chevron grooves down the sides of his face.

'Du Pont, did you say?'

'That's right, sir.'

'A French name, I take it?'

'That's what they tell me, sir.'

'Any relation to the banknote people?'

'I don't think so, sir.'

'Well, very good to have met you. *À bientôt*, Fanny.' And Mrs Manningham – Fanny – and I watched in silence as what could only be the Duke of Windsor stepped into the waiting car and was borne away.

8 April 1967

Tense atmosphere at Berwick Street. Apparently the album isn't going well. Several sessions have been cancelled. Sophie, the new secretary, is from Cheltenham Ladies' College, winces whenever anyone in the office swears, frankly despises Ainslie and occupies time not spent at the typewriter in being taken out to lunch by men with names like Piers and Hector. Without anything from the Helium Kids to promote, I end up escorting one of Ainslie's newer acquisitions – a girl group called the Cockney Sparrows – down to Margate for the day with a journalist from *Fabulous 208*. It is a complete disaster. One of the girls drinks three glasses of Babycham at lunch and spends the rest of the afternoon being sick. Another one forgets her story – the Cockney Sparrows are supposed to be cousins from the East End – and starts talking about her father's estate in Perthshire.

14 April 1967

Don Shard's office. Anonymous set of rooms in Maddox Street, full of bruisers in suits. One to open the door. Another to escort you into the great man's presence. A third to stand next to him in a vaguely menacing manner while he talks to you. Secretaries, typing cheerfully on in hutch next door, seem not to notice sinister atmosphere in which they labour. Don, as he likes to remind you, is an ex-professional wrestler – a picture of him in the ring hangs on the wall above his head. Other ornaments include various groups managed by Don, plus photo of tarty-looking teenage daughter Belinda, on whom he is reckoned to dote.

Conversation brisk and business-like. Do I like working for Ainslie ('the old *cunt*,' Don adds, making it sound like the choicest endearment)? Do I have a contract? Do I feel that my opportunities are limited in the current set-up? The burly sidekick, summoned every so often to ferry away teacups or extend his cigarette lighter, wears a look halfway between deference and contempt, as if to say that he's seen all this before, that I'm a poor sap who'll be lucky if Don doesn't throw me out of the window. There is no definite job offer, merely a gruff assurance of goodwill. In fact, most of Don's questions give me the distinct impression that he is quite as interested in the boys themselves. The dense hummocks of Belinda's cleavage rear up at me, desperate to escape the gauzy dress-front that restrains them. I am glad to get out of the place.

I decide not to tell Ainslie about the visit to Maddox Street. Once again, this is information that may be useful in the future.

Evening. Despatched by Ainslie, who has seen the posters, to the 'Technicolor Dream' at Alexandra Palace to find out – his words – 'what the fook is going on'. Arrived there to find several thousand kids, most of them high as kites, watching the Move, Tomorrow and, sometime in the small hours, the Soft Machine and Pink Floyd.

Dozens of people climbing the insides of the building, hanging off scaffolding, etc. Useless to pretend that I don't get a kick out of this – as sheer spectacle, if nothing else – without having the faintest desire to actively participate.

Meanwhile, the old world runs on without the least idea that the new world even exists. Thus, this morning in Berwick Street.

CYRIL: 'Ow was your weekend, Sophie, may ai enquire?

SOPHIE: Very enjoyable, thank you. We went to a cocktail party at the Guards' Club and then to watch the tennis at Hurlingham.

15 May 1967

Taking stock. Assets: £2000 in building society account; Dine drawing; Hockney sketch I bought at John Dunbar's gallery; mint copy of 'I Feel Fine', signed by all four Beatles. Really, I can leave Ainslie whenever I choose. In an ideal world I should start my own agency, but this will take time and capital I don't possess.

Beatles album apparently finished. People who have heard early pressings say it is unlike anything anyone else has ever done: 'like talking to God'.

19 May 1967

Airmail letter with Maine postal frank, sent sometime in April and forwarded on from different addresses.

Dear Son,

Pining as ever for news of you – your latter-day endeavours, present schemes – I venture to send a small budget of my own. I am now residing on the eastern seaboard, in sight of the wild waves – Nantucket is but a step away – hunkered down, biding my time, older, balder, wiser. The force of destiny still pulls me on, but less violently. There is plenty of news of England in the papers. I can see you there now, a man amongst men. What are you? A business person? A star of track and field? Some humbler yet providential trade? Right now we are raising chickens and watching the barometer, for surely there are STORMS AHEAD. A line to reassure me of your continuing filial regard would mightily oblige.

Your ever-loving father,

Maurice Du Pont

It is quite a masterpiece in its way. I am about to stow it in the manila envelope – where it will join the photo of some rusting agricultural machinery sent at Christmas 1965 from Cheyenne, Wyoming, a letter from Butte County, California, advising me of the imminent purchase of a fruit farm previously owned by one of the Three Stooges and a set of postcards sent at two-month intervals from locations along the north-western seaboard, each with the message AND NOW WE ARE HERE – when I notice that, unprecedentedly, there is a phone number. Not quite knowing why I do it – the force of destiny, perhaps – I dial the operator and instruct her to place a call.

'I'm not having much luck,' she says after a couple of minutes. 'Want me to try again?'

'Please.'

There is a longish pause. 'Number disconnected, I'm afraid.'

22 May 1967

This evening at about 7.30 there is a knock at the door. Open it to find Alexandra, school bag flung over her shoulder, face contorted with fury.

'Can I come in? Dougal's gone out somewhere and hasn't left the bloody key.'

'Be my guest. Would you like something to drink?'

'You can get me some gin if you want.'

'Do your parents mind you drinking gin?'

She follows me into the kitchen, throwing the school bag into a corner and giving a little snort of derision. 'As if they cared about anything like that.'

'What do they do?'

'Daddy's an orthodontist.' Pulling teeth is clearly the most disreputable profession a man can follow. 'Mummy pretends she's running an art gallery in Dulwich. But if there's one thing I *can't stand* it's people asking me questions.'

Close up Alexandra is less frail than when briefly inspected in Mackintosh's sitting room, pinker skinned and somehow sturdier. The blonde hair falls away from the sides of her face in dense, Pre-Raphaelite clusters. Here the resemblance to one of Mackintosh's studio portraits ends, as the knuckle joints of her right hand are blotched with ink and there is what looks like the beginning of a shopping list scrawled on the palm.

'How did you meet Dougal?' I ask, forgetting the prohibition on questions.

'He's one of Daddy's patients. Mummy and Daddy asked him to dinner – they're the kind of people who like sucking up to anyone who gets in the newspapers – and I happened to be there.'

'What do your parents think about . . .'

Alexandra gives another little snort. 'They don't have the foggiest. They think I'm at my friend Felicity's discussing the Schleswig-Holstein question. Or at the school debating society. Something like that.'

She is interested in the house, spares a glance for the Hockney drawing and stares for several seconds at the Jim Dine.

'I like your place,' she says. 'You've put everything very nicely together. Dougal couldn't design his way out of a paper bag.' Then, abruptly, her tone changes. 'Look, it's very kind of you to let me in. I don't want to annoy you. Would you like me to cook some food or something?'

'That would be nice.'

She fries us bacon and eggs with surprising skill, wholly absorbed in the task. We eat in the sitting room, cross-legged on the sofa in front of the TV. There is no sign of Dougal.

5 June 1967

Over the past fortnight a routine has set in. Every two or three evenings a tattoo beats on the front door and there she is again: sullen, unsmiling, blue-blazered, school bag in hand. Dougal is never mentioned, and might as well not exist. Does she come round when I'm not here? There is no way of telling. Curiously, or not so curiously, I get a keen thrill of anticipation ahead of her visits. Part of this is to do with sheer unpredictability. There is simply no knowing what she might say or do. I get the impression that, if crossed, she would stop at absolutely nothing. She says she once threw an ashtray at Dougal that hit him on the forehead and knocked him cold. On the other hand, the take-no-prisoners stuff is balanced by straightforward ingenuousness.

'I'm not interested in pop music,' she says once. 'I don't see the point of it.'

'What are your interests then?'

There is the hint of a blush. 'I want to be a model.'

'Why do you want to be a model? Apart from the obvious reasons.'

'There's nothing wrong with the obvious reasons. Apart from anything else, it would be worth doing just to annoy my mother. She'd be insanely jealous.'

She talks about her parents a lot: not uncritically, but in the style of an anthropologist bringing back news of some benighted tribe newly discovered in the Amazonian rainforest. Bizarre routines and customs crackle through the air. 'They live in Chelsea. You know, in one of those done-up houses with potted shrubs and hanging baskets all over the terrace. Breton tableware that somebody brought back from Quimper because everyone else is bringing it back. They're the kind of people who try terribly hard to keep up with everything and go to the latest films and wear the latest clothes – Mummy bought a skirt from Mr Fish the other day – but really find it all a bit of a strain. I mean, somebody got Daddy to smoke a joint at a dinner party the other week and he was sick all over the tablecloth.'

9 June 1967

Sgt. Pepper out for a week or so. It can be heard everywhere – drifting over the rooftops from open skylights, on building-site radios, whistled in the street. Descending the steps to Knightsbridge Underground the other morning, I heard a middle-aged woman softly humming 'She's Leaving Home' to herself as she strapped a child into its pushchair.

Conversation this evening in Egerton Gardens Mews. Alexandra, shoeless, in school blazer and skirt, is lying full-length on the sofa.

'Don't you find me attractive?'

'Extremely.'

'You ought to do something about it.'

'You're seventeen years old.'

'You must be a pansy.'

'A very hospitable one, though.'

She tumbles off the sofa, slips on her shoes and is out of the door so briskly that I don't have time to remonstrate – not exactly in a fit of pique, but with a kind of terminal exasperation, as if the one last ally she had in life has let her down. The school bag lies abandoned on the carpet. I can't stop myself looking at the contents, but there is nothing incriminating – just a stack of exercise books, with the teacher's name stencilled on the front (her English mistress is called Miss Anstruther-Ripley), each harbouring long, intricate essays written in a fussy, feminine hand. I leave the bag on the doorstep. When I look out of the window a couple of hours later it is gone.

I assume this is the last I shall see of Alexandra. But no, two evenings later, there she is again, slouching on the doorstep with a Sky Ray lolly sticking out of her mouth and another in her hand for me. This I take to be a peace offering.

She won't be coming any time again soon, she volunteers, as A levels are about to start. For the first time in our acquaintance she seems faintly embarrassed. The question of why she might want to come again, and what she might expect to find here, hangs in the air.

15 June 1967

Turning into the Mews I catch sight of a tall, spare, middle-aged man in a pinstripe suit shuffling his feet on the doorstep of No. 2. Any slight doubt as to his identity vanishes as he turns to confront me, for here in the face of a 45-year-old orthodontist are Alexandra's mad blue eyes.

'Is your name Du Pont?'

'I think you probably know it is.'

'I have reason to believe you are sleeping with my daughter.'

'If she told you that, I'm afraid she's lying.'

'Jesus *Christ*,' he says, in a kind of sibilant hiss, like air coming out of a bellows. 'I'll fucking kill you.' He is at least three inches taller than me. Worse, there are hints of bygone expertise in the way he squares up, swings one leg back to brace himself and then launches the other forward. But I am driven, too, by the thought of having behaved a whole lot better than might have been expected here in the free-and-easy Age of Aquarius, and left the forbidden fruit untasted. And so we scuffle for a moment or two, bat each other around the doorstep, swear and clinch, until the routines picked up in some unarmed combat session twenty years ago finally elude him and I manage to hit him quite hard in the chest, at which point he goes down on all fours and starts retching in the gutter.

'Is everything all right, Mr Du Pont?'

It turns out that Mrs Manningham has been calmly surveying the scene from the open window of her drawing room.

'Perfectly all right, thank you, Mrs Manningham.'

'Should you like me to telephone the police?'

'It's very kind of you, but I think we're more or less finished here.'

There is an odd look in Mrs Manningham's eye, a suspicion of past life resurrected. Who knows? Perhaps forty years ago Evelyn Waugh fought for her favours? The Duke of Windsor even? Nothing would surprise me about the world I currently inhabit.

Mid-July

At high summer a change comes over the West End. The dust lies piled up on the Soho pavements, the paralysing light turns the house-fronts more leprous by the moment and the people sitting outside the cafés wilt in the sun. In Meard Street the tarts have stopped parading in their finery and sit exhaustedly on their doorsteps guzzling ice-creams. Yesterday a drunk toppled over in Berwick Street and lay there fast asleep for half an hour until a police van rolled up to carry him away. The tourists are discontented. You can see they think there ought to be more to Swinging London than snoozing inebriates and fat women selling themselves at thirty bob a time.

Business item one: the album is finished and being mixed some-where, amid – or so the rumour goes – endless disagreements. A recording engineer is supposed to have been hit on the head with a microphone. Business item two: Don Shard has been in touch again.

Business item three: there is talk of a new BBC pop station once the Marine Offences Act has swept the pirate ships out of the sea, but no one is holding their breath. I am sitting alone in the office – Ainslie is off on one of his fanciful holidays – cooling myself beneath the winnowing fan when the phone rings. A woman's voice, with a high-pitched, adenoidal, south-west to Gulf of Texas twang.

'Nicko, is that you? This is Rozzie Knowland.'

The name means nothing. But the voice returns me instantly to that lost world of desert heat, eight-lane Arizona freeways, hygienic funeral parlours and call me Al.

'Do you remember? I think you used to know me as Rosalind Duchesne. Back in Phoenix.'

All this is so unfathomable that I can barely grasp it. Surrounding paraphernalia – the record on the turntable, the press releases on the desk – slide effortlessly away. It turns out that Rosalind is in London ('Can you believe that?'), staying at the Basil Street Hotel ('It's full of Americans, like the embassy started an annex') and keen to meet up.

'How did you know where to find me?'

'Marty reckoned you worked in music. I guess he made some calls.'

We arrange to meet for lunch the following day. A few moments after I put the phone down a motorcycle messenger brings a package. It is the artwork for *Paisley Patterns'* cover. In normal circumstances this would be a matter of pressing concern, enough to roust Ainslie out of his chalet at Menton or wherever this lackey of the Beautiful People has fetched up. Now, with the memory of Rosalind's voice to warm me, I can scarcely be bothered to open it. In any case, something tells me it will be the most awful piece of shit.

I make a point of arriving ten minutes early at the restaurant in Dean Street and taking a pavement table. This is done with the sole aim of watching her arrive. Everything around me seems extraordinarily charged and vivid: the red-faced drinkers spilling out of the Nellie

Dean; a man who looks exactly like Fred Flintstone goading a barrow of vegetables towards the market; the knotted foulard scarf around my neck; the pack of Kent cigarettes, chosen deliberately as a memento of past time, on the table before me. Predictably, when she looms into view – from the Oxford Street end, as I foresaw – I almost fail to recognise her. Like most of the American girls you see in London she looks older than she is: hair turned up at the corners like the women on the imported East Coast sitcoms; two-piece costume with the skirt extending to her kneecaps; ribbed grey stockings. She is what? All of twenty-four.

'Nick,' she says, when the introductions are over, 'I wouldn't have known you. Well, maybe I would. It's the hair.'

'Is it so very bad?'

'I guess not. In fact, it almost suits you. Marty still has a regular cut. But they're kind of particular at the brokerage. Wait though,' she says. 'You never knew I married Marty. Not that I was ever not going to, of course.'

It turns out that she and Marty tied the knot two years ago, six months after Marty fixed his job – old Mr Knowland gallantly finessing – at the brokerage. Rosalind, meanwhile, is an under-buyer at Macy's, here on a reconnaissance trip.

'I guess Marty would prefer it if I didn't work. They're pretty strict about that at Costa and Fishlawn. But I don't want to be cooped up in the house all day reading *Homes and Gardens*. Wow,' she says suddenly, her gaze shifting from my state-of-the-art *coiffeur* (collar-length hair with Victorian prize-fighter sideburns) to the sight of a genuine Soho hippy cortege (two men in kaftans, a tired-looking girl in what looks like a couple of lengths of curtain material with a baby lashed to her back) going mournfully by. 'Will you look at them?'

'Surely you must have people like that in New York?'

'Oh, we have *freaks*, for sure. But they keep to the Village. You don't tend to see them around so much.' Her eye follows what it now occurs to me may well be three-quarters of the Incredible String Band as they head off in the direction of Shaftesbury Avenue before returning to settle on my polka-dot jacket bought last week at Granny Takes a Trip. 'Are they the kind of people you work with? I mean, what sort of music do they play? Are they like . . .' – she searches through what I deduce is a fairly limited inventory of transatlantic talent – '. . . I mean, are they like Jefferson Airplane?'

'More like the Lovin' Spoonful.'

'OK. I guess I've heard of them. *Not* the kind of thing we have on at home. I mean, Marty's still listening to Sinatra.'

And for the second time in five minutes I detect a tiny pulse of resentment. Marty's berth at the brokerage; Marty's time-lagged crew-cut; Marty's old-world musical tastes. All sailing down the Gila River, ladies and gentlemen, to be engulfed by the big wide ocean beyond. Al, it transpires, is a yet more gargantuan Republican bigwig than he was before, a Grand Old Party panjandrum regularly summoned to the governor's mansion at Sacramento to advise Ron Reagan on protocol. Dolores was fired a year ago after her brother was caught siphoning gas from the Duchesnes' station wagon. It got so hot in Phoenix last summer that the tarmac actually melted. There is one conspicuous absentee from this roll-call of the folks back home.

'And how's your mother?'

'Momma?' Rosalind mints a seraphic smile that wouldn't fool Tiny Tim. 'I guess she's just fine. Right now she's staying with Aunt Laverne down in Tallahassee.' Aunt Laverne is one of the six sisters of the Ziegfeld wedding snap, and no doubt a dab hand at tidying away empty gin bottles. 'I guess she's not so interested in the political side of things these days.'

The lunch lasts an hour, and is an interesting clash of transatlantic styles. Unlike the wasp-waisted English chickaroos, Rosalind eats everything that is put before her. Here in the bright sunshine there are beads of perspiration on her forehead. She also smokes at least a dozen cigarettes. Unobtrusively fishing for detail, I discover that she and Marty have an apartment on East Seventy-Fourth Street, week-end on Fire Island, warmly approve of Mayor Lindsay and are deeply worried by some of the sinister influences working to undermine the morale of America's young people. Ten feet away, the Dean Street irregulars course by: Italian delicatessen owners with giant salamis borne against their shoulders like rifles; priests from the French church in Soho Square; off-duty Maltese cooks in jackets the colour of Neapolitan ice-creams; and what seems to be Soho's particular speciality this summer: spruced-up Jack the Lads in ten-guinea suits and co-respondent's shoes with adoring, moist-eyed girls clamped to their arms.

'You know,' Rosalind says, as one of these happy pairs toils giggling by, 'I never did buy that line in "She's Leaving Home".'

'Which line in particular?'

'The one about the girl going off to meet the man from the motor trade and having fun.'

'Why? What do you think would happen?'

'I think it would just be squalid. That she'd end up in a terrible hotel room with some gorilla and then go back home a fortnight later and find she was pregnant. Not much fun in that.'

Curiously enough, I have a feeling she may be right about this.

'It's been good to see you, Nick,' she says earnestly. 'I mean that. But if I stay any later I'll miss my next appointment.'

'Where at?'

She makes a pretence of studying her pocketbook. 'It's somewhere in the King's Road. To be honest, the buyer would have a fit if I bought any of that stuff back. But I thought I ought to take a look. Like Dr Livingstone searching for the source of the Nile.'

'You should go to Biba and buy a frock.'

'And see the look on Marty's face when I put it on? Thanks a lot.'

I watch her march off towards Oxford Street with that intent, purposeful stride I remember so well from the Phoenix sidewalks: the girl with the kaleidoscope eyes.

Ainslie back from Menton. Customary shutters dragged down over anything he might have done there. No hint of a suntan. Running around fixing publicity for the record, while knowing that my heart isn't in it. Undercurrent of tension at the office magnified by studio scuttlebutt. Ainslie: 'Do you know, in the end they mixed it twice? No, that's not true. Turns out Garth went back in there one night with the engineer and had another go at the master. God knows what the fookin' thing sounds like now.'

Another lunch with Rosalind. Her idea. Afterwards we walk down to the Embankment and then east in the direction of the Tower. R amused by the sights – exclaims at the Beefeaters – but not (I can tell this) truly interested. Preoccupied about something. When asked how she got on in the King's Road, shakes her head and says something non-committal.

Impressions. Extraordinarily beautiful. Far more so than when I last saw her. Her mother's trick of gazing off into the middle distance, as if enraptured by something nobody else can see. A deep-down irritation with something I can't yet locate that manifests itself in sarcastic remarks about everything from the dolly-birds on the street corners to the lack of air-conditioning. New York sophistication a veneer, with the old Phoenix habits regularly poking through. Says 'I'd admire to' and 'It don't matter a *da-yem*' like a waitress.

Keen on talking about her childhood, which she now seems to see as a mistake, full of missed opportunities, slammed doors and disintegration, with Al presiding over it like a goblin king. Lucille mentioned only in passing ('That was the time Momma wasn't well . . . That was the time Momma was visiting with Aunt Alma . . .'). Once she says: 'You have no idea what it was like growing up in Phoenix. None at all.

I didn't use to think it was so bad. Only then you go to the east and you realise it's another world you never knew anything about, even when you read about it in magazines.'

'And do you like New York?'

'It's kind of different,' Rosalind says, extracting the last cigarette from a packet that was full when we set out, and meaning, I take it, 'No.'

Paisley Patterns released. No chart-rigging this time, as Ainslie reckons it's too risky. A dozen copies delivered to Broadcasting House by a pearly king and queen on a brewer's dray. I have no idea why. A dozen more ferried out to the pirate boats, none of whom, we infer, will be here for very much longer. Promo film on Hampstead Heath with shots of the boys flying kites, marching up and down with mannequins hired from a dress shop, an idea Ainslie stole from Pink Floyd. Morning of regional press interviews, with Garth, Florian and Dale lined up before a bank of phones in Berwick Street answering questions from *Northern Eco*, *Eastern Daily Press*, etc. ('What do you think of the new album, Garth?' 'It's out of sight.' 'Have you a message for the fans?' 'Tell them we love them, they're beautiful and we hope to see them soon.') Ian and Keith, purposely excluded from these interrogations, skulk in Ainslie's office over a bottle of calvados. Carefully fabricated rumour that Dale is about to announce his engagement to Lulu makes page three of the *Standard* and is angrily denied. Profile of Garth in *International Times* ('We meet the sorcerer of Pop') in which he declares that 'the essence of the all is the godhead of the true'. The record goes to No. 5. I am thought to have done – Ainslie's words – 'a fookin' good job'.

Late morning in the office. Cyril asleep with his head on the desk. Sophie making haughty phone calls. The boys are out getting slaughtered with Ainslie at one of his clubs. On impulse I ring Rosalind at the Basil Street Hotel and ask her if she wants to go to Oxford for the afternoon. I can tell instantly from the lilt in her voice that this is a good thing to have proposed. We meet at Paddington and take the train westward through Reading and Didcot, past Thames Valley verdure and shimmering inflexions of the river. Here in the depths of the long vacation Oxford is nearly empty. Just a handful of tourists on the steps of the Sheldonian or prospecting through Tom Quad. The botanical gardens are fabulously overgrown, like jungle. Rosalind impressed for once, charmed by the old-world teashop to which I take her, the college porters at their lodge gates, the butterflies hazily adrift in Christ Church meadow.

On the train coming back, scarlet-faced from the sun, she says: 'You know, Nick, I have a confession to make.'

It turns out that she is the process of divorcing Marty Knowland. Not on any of the standard grounds – adultery, ill-treatment, neglect and so on – but because he's basically a big stiff from Phoenix with dollar signs for eyebrows whom she can't stand anymore. Moreover – something I had half-deduced already – the under-buyer's job at Macy's is fictitious. In fact, the trip to England has been funded by a providential legacy from another of her aunts.

The train rattles on through Radley, Pangbourne and Goring-on-Thames, past station platforms where men in dark suits stand reading the evening papers, alongside horsey-looking buccaneers in linden tweeds on their way back from the races. When she has finished we sit and stare at each other, like Tom Thumb and Hunca Munca, alone in the tenantless doll's house, the world laid out before them, inviting and unguarded, theirs to despoil, if so they choose.

Postscript 2007

According to Philip Ziegler's *Edward VIII: The Official Biography* (1990), the Hon. Mrs Fenella Manningham (formerly Fortescue-Jones) was indeed part of the then Duke of Windsor's 'early 1930s circle'.

Quite by chance, I came across Alexandra again in the mid-1970s at a party given by a booking agent somewhere in north London. She was then in her mid-twenties and working for a small feminist publishing house. She remembered the evenings in the Knightsbridge mews without enthusiasm: 'A real man would have fucked me.'

THE HELIUM KIDS – *PAISLEY PATTERNS* (DECCA)

Tracks: Carousel Ride (Dangerfield-Halliwell); Autumn Leaves (Hamilton); Footloose and Fancy-free (Dangerfield-Halliwell); Cosmic Dancer (Dangerfield-Shankley-Walker); Magic Carpet Ride (Halliwell); Bride of the Downlands (Dangerfield); As Dew Drops Drop (Shankley-Walker); Summerdawn (Halliwell); Castles in the Mist (Dangerfield-Halliwell); Astral Planes (Dangerfield-Halliwell), Kaleidoscope (Hamilton). Running time: 37 minutes.

If the times they are a-changing, then a hell of a lot of people are clearly desperate to be seen a-changing with them. *Paisley Patterns*, in fact, is a perfect example of a band trying to get with it, without having quite worked out what 'it' is in the first place. Gone are the Farfisa organ swirls and the top-heavy bass lines that distinguished last year's Mod concerto *Smiley Daze*, and in come quavery mellotrons, reverb-soaked guitar solos and a clutch of lyrics that could have been written by Edward Lear's ghost after something very unusual had been dropped in his tea. It's the same with the state of the art Janner and Curwen cover where the boys, once habitual *tenues* of the mohair jacket, the Sta-Prest jeans and the Crombie coat, have opted for the full Granny Takes a Trip/King's Road cornucopia of kaftans, bells, striped boutique blazers and unfeasibly flared khalzoons. If I say that Florian Shankley-Walker is not only sporting a ruff above a military tunic that seems to have been pilfered from some Waterloo veteran's corpse but is *actually seeming to like it*, you'll get some idea of the distance travelled. Oh dear, oh my.

As for that distance travelled, the Kids have come quite a way in the past three years, when they used to do a pretty good approximation of the Dave Clark Five on such young persons' TV shows as would have them (and also, it must be said, play exquisite R & B covers on the rare occasions they were allowed this licence). In that time they, or at any rate the Dangerfield/Halliwell part of the equation, found out about songwriting, expensive producers and the inestimable value of publicity. On the other hand, they probably haven't got their heads around the salutary story of the Expanding Man. The Expanding Man, in case you don't remember the dude, was one of Marvell Comics' second division characters, not up there with the Hulk or Spider-Man but good for a run-out when these two titans were otherwise engaged. The Expanding Man's particular skill was shape-shifting. Throw him in a river and he'd assume the properties of running water. Give him any kind of physical task and he'd pretty soon bend that ton of steel and concrete to his will. But while the Expanding Man was a good guy to have on your side in a crisis, there was one unignorable drawback, which was that for all his ability to calm raging torrents or put out fires he had no real identity of his own.

And so the Helium Kids, in their latest incarnation, put me horribly in mind of the Expanding Man. Opener 'Carousel Ride' is a pleasant enough noise, but it sounds way too much like 'Strawberry Fields', and who in their right mind would settle for Dangerfield and Halliwell when they could have Lennon and McCartney? 'Autumn Leaves' boasts every Flower Power cliché known to contemporary pop, not to mention some truly awful lyrics ('The chill wind in your garden/won't stop to beg your pardon', indeed), while 'Magic Carpet Ride' is one of those tripped-out hippy-dippy travelogues we have come to know so well in which everyone is zooming out across the skies to Marrakech or somewhere, getting off every so often to dance on the clouds – as if we were bloody Moomins or something. No, it won't do, it really won't, and neither will the shimmery haze of 'Summerdawn', which for all Garth Dangerfield's anguished expostulations about the Great God Pan and what he might be getting up to in the water meadows wouldn't have been given houseroom on that Pink Floyd album everyone was talking so excitedly about just the other day.

The exceptions to this rule are Side Two's clangorous opener 'Bride of the Downlands' and the equally rocked up 'Astral Planes', which goes on for eight minutes, has a ridiculous change of time-signature halfway through and some mighty drums courtesy of the hitherto somewhat underused stick-wielder Keith Shields. Both tracks are guitar-driven, allowing Dangerfield to sound much less prissy than he does on most of Side One, and in neither of them does Shankley-Walker seem to feature *at all*. This may or may not be significant. But the rest of *Paisley Patterns*, from the whimsical hey-nonny-nonnying of 'Footloose and Fancy-free' to the Tudor arpeggios of 'As Dew Drops Drop', can be straightaway filed under 'phase'.

Gandalf's Garden, Summer 1967

9. BEAUTIFUL PEOPLE

Let's take a walk in the clouds this morning
Let's take a stroll in the sky
Let's take a bath in the sunshine glow
Let's take a magic carpet ride

'Magic Carpet Ride'

The inner hallway of Ainslie's house had been painted up in bright, primary colours: blues, reds and yellows in charmless profusion. Worse than this, on the stretch of wall beneath the staircase someone had been encouraged to design a kind of collage, made up of seashells, newspaper photographs, record sleeves, squashed together under coats of varnish. All this made it resemble an outsize playroom, ready for a horde of noisy children to start making trouble, where the grandfather clock and the coat-stand would probably double up as goalposts.

'It really is terribly nice to see you both,' said Clive, Ainslie's gentleman friend, which was what you called the male attachments of other men in the months after the decriminalisation of homosexuality. He brought one stiff hand up to the level of his shoulder like a flipper and pointed coyly in the direction of a half-open glass door, diaphanously aglow with dense, autumnal light. 'They're all in the garden.'

It was about half-past two in the afternoon. Behind our heads, beyond the gravel drive and the leylandii hedge, the noise of Sunbury-on-Thames was starting to recede. Motorbikes; children's voices; ice-cream vans: all this was an illusion. It was only Ainslie's vestibule and its preening chatelaine that were real. Or rather anything but real, for the further you pressed inside the more the place took on the air of a never-never land, quaint and sequestered, where life had been expressly ordered to run slightly out of kilter. The grandfather clock and the collage gave way to a miniature harmonium, an empty bird-cage covered in glistening white dust and a bass guitar with only one string. On the far wall, next to the gleaming doorway, were pictures of Edwardian girls playing tennis and riding tricycles. 'We kept some of the original features,' Clive said, even more diffidently than before. 'Ainslie said his early life might just as well have taken place in the Edwardian era and it was nice to be reminded of it every so often.'

What would the Edwardian girls, who had never had the chance to listen to Jimi Hendrix, paint flowers on their cheeks or go to the UFO club in the Tottenham Court Road, have made of Ainslie and his houseguests? Well, they would probably have approved of Clive, who, to add to the plum-coloured frockcoat drawn tight across his chest, was wearing a pair of what looked like cellophane anklets.

'Are they *spats*, Clive?'

'Oh, do you like them?' For once Clive looked properly animated, brought into focus. 'I got them at Antonio's in Camden Market. Thirty shillings he charges for them, the old *Jew*.'

There was music playing on the other side of the half-open door.

I'm just sitting watching flowers in the rain. Feel the power of the rain, making the garden grow.

'Does this make me one of the Beautiful People?' Rosalind had asked, three or four hours ago, as she pulled on the frothy, pink-and-white coloured dress with huge leg-of-lamb sleeves in which now, a bit self-consciously, she appeared in Ainslie's hallway.

'It certainly makes you a beautiful person.'

'I guess that will have to do.'

Ainslie's kitchen, painted in white and aquamarine and full of champagne glasses and bowls of popcorn, was easier on the eye than the hall. There was a strong, sweetish smell, which grew worse as we headed out onto the terrace.

'I do hope none of the neighbours calls the police,' Clive said wistfully.

There were some people who said that Ainslie's garden looked its best in winter, ideally under snow, which disguised some of the imperfections of its landscaping. But there were other people who maintained that only spring could do justice to its long, rolling lawns and irregular treelines. Here in early autumn, with the grass grown up two feet high round the flowerbeds and the hedges untrimmed, it had a wholly fantastic look. The feeling that you had walked into a fairy-tale and might not easily walk out of it again was exaggerated by the nearness of the river, where ships' masts stuck up from under the bank, and also by the fact that someone had set up a long wooden dining table complete with candelabras in the middle of the grass.

'It's just like *Alice*,' Rosalind said delightedly.

There were other ways in which Ainslie's back garden, down the river in Sunbury-on-Thames, on a warmish Sunday afternoon in mid-September, was like *Alice in Wonderland*. One of them was the people – seventy or eighty of them at least – some of them dressed in the fashions of the day, others emphatically not, but all of them simultaneously nonchalant, incongruous and expectant. The other was the terrific air of tension, the hint that there were secret patterns working their way out here, huge extraneous forces poised to strike that neither Ainslie nor the Helium Kids nor anyone connected to them had the faintest chance of controlling. Tatterdemalion throng; distant quinqueremes gliding down the glassy river; autumn sunshine glinting on the foliage. All this combined to produce the one true sensation that I brought away from the sixties – the feeling that, for better or worse, you were living in a piece of performance art.

Ainslie was standing at the top of some steps at the edge of the terrace next to a row of deckchairs on which a trio of girls lazily reclined. He looked horribly out of sorts, but pulled himself together as we drew near.

'This is January, Summer and Melody,' he said, as if there was nothing at all odd in being named after a month, a season and an abstract noun.

'Take my tip,' one of the girls volunteered, 'and don't touch the Pimm's.'

'What's the matter with the Pimm's?' Rosalind said, who had clearly never been to a party where anyone had tampered with the drinks.

'It was all right,' one of the other girls said slyly, 'until *she* put something in it.'

Some hosts would have been alarmed by this news. But Ainslie had obviously gone way beyond the stage where he was prepared to worry about what somebody might have put in the Pimm's. Acknowledging by the merest inclination of his forehead that Rosalind existed, that she was with me, that she was welcome at his house, might even ornament it by her looks and dress, he tugged at my sleeve and manoeuvred me a yard or two to one side.

'I need to talk to you.'

('I like your frock,' Melody was saying to Rosalind, with a certain amount of patronage. 'But where do you put your fags? Down the front?')

'Go on then.'

'It's about that Garth. Well, mostly.'

I was used to Garth's exploits. 'What's he done this time? Burgled No. 10 and stolen the Prime Minister's pipe?'

There was another cavalcade of girls approaching – five or six of them, attendant children scampering at their heels – in Red Indian gear. Ainslie stared at them suspiciously.

'Look,' he said, after an immense pause. 'This is fookin' serious, this one. Can't discuss it now. I mean' – he glanced at the buckskin armada as it floated past – 'this lot are probably about to re-create Wounded Knee. Come and see me later on.'

I wandered off across the terrace, where more people were gathered round a white plastic table piled high with bottles and pitchers of lemonade. Here the atmosphere was a lot less like *Alice in Wonderland* and a lot more like parties of Ainslie's I had been to before: full of music people talking business; middle-aged women rather thrilled by their headlong descent into bohemia; hard cases downing glasses in one. Tatterdemalion throng. Distant quinque-remes gliding down the glassy river. Lined up in a ragged ellipse, the girls had begun to sing in high, keening voices. They were in their element. All this made you wonder why Ainslie had decided to sponsor this expensive entertainment here in the month of September, with the first autumn leaves drifting across the lawn and the hippy girls in sad chorale, for his attitude to hospitality was strictly utilitarian. He gave parties to impress people, to finesse business deals, to rub out obligations, not because he liked his fellow men and women, wanted to bring his friends together or had any sentimental attachment to them, and was once supposed, at two o'clock in the morning on a hired pleasure cruiser moored by Westminster Bridge, to have handed a glass of brandy to a record company executive with the words, 'I'll take an extra two and a half per cent on sales over one hundred thousand and you can have an option to renegotiate at six months.' Oddly enough, hardly any of the guests assembled on his lawn, now mostly inching out of earshot of the Indian girls, fitted this bill, for they seemed to come from every stage and compartment of his professional career. There were midget singers he had booked onto the thronged package tours of the early sixties, long-forgotten stars of the Beat era who had burned brightly for a season or two and then tumbled out of the firmament, a job lot of Liverpool poets who, back in the days of the Mersey boom, had been commissioned to make a spoken-word album called *Knotty Ash Eclogues*; Sandie Shaw; four members of the Dave Clark Five; half of Procol Harum. There was a symbolism about this, a sense of orchestration, as if the whole thing was a backdrop to an episode of *This Is Your Life*, and at any moment Eamonn Andrews would leap out from behind one of the potted shrubs to reunite Ainslie with his old Scout Master.

Still more people were flowing in across the terrace. Twenty yards away smoke from a barbecue rose into the still air. Rosalind had gone off to inspect the lawn, and I was left with Cyril, Ainslie's *aide de camp*, who came stumping across the flagstones with one hand flapping at a wasp that buzzed over his low, knobby forehead.

'What's the matter with Ainslie?'

'Ains?' Cyril would never have dared use this diminutive in Ainslie's presence, but he enjoyed pretending they were on man-to-man terms. 'I don't know. Probably on account of having his mother here. Reckons she might cramp his style.'

'Where is she?'

Cyril made a series of elaborate gestures with his hands, like a policeman directing traffic, and pointed out a small, intent-looking woman in a mackintosh who, careless of the throng of partygoers, was dead-heading some of the summer's roses.

'I didn't know Ainslie had a mother.'

'Neither did I. But she turned up this morning. Came in a taxi from the station and made Ains pay the fare. *Fucking* cross he was. But that's not why he's got the hump. Fact is, we had a visitor at the office Friday afternoon.'

'Not the Revenue again?'

Mrs Duncan had stopped snapping at the roses and was standing stock-still with the secateurs clutched in her fist, as if she was quite prepared to stab anyone who got in her way.

'You was out somewhere. Seeing that bloke from *Queen*. You know, the one who wanted to photograph them in that gentleman's club in morning suits, like they was lords of the fucking manor. Anyway, we were just about to close up and go down the Nellie Dean when' – he lowered his voice – 'Don Shard puts his head round the door.'

'What did he want?'

'You know,' Cyril said impressively, as if he were part of a TV panel invited to pass judgement on the personalities of the era, 'I think people *exaggerate* about Don. I mean, he's always been perfectly all right to me. Bethnal boys and all that. We don't forget where people come from down our way.' The myth had shifted now. They were two Mongol chieftains, blood brothers since birth, waving to each other from either side of the Samarkand trail. He paused. 'Scared Ainslie stiff, of course.'

'Then what happened?'

'Wish I could tell you, Nicko.' There were times when Cyril managed to rise above the situations in which he found himself and hint at powerful inner resources, and there were times when he looked what he was, which was a bit too old and a lot too fat for this game. Just now he was wriggling uncomfortably in the bright blue suit he had thought appropriate for one of Ainslie's parties. Mrs Duncan, who had now switched her attention to some long-dead daffodils, seemed far more at home. 'There's me and Ains staring at each other as if the Creature from the Black Lagoon had just walked in off the street and Don looks at me and says, "Go on, Cy, fuck off out of it." And the next thing I know I'm out on the stairs with the door shut in my face. That's one thing I will say about Don. Forgets his manners sometimes. His old mum would have something to say about that. When I came back half an hour later they'd both of them gone. Office door hadn't been locked either. Didn't see Ains again until this morning.'

'And he hasn't said anything about it?'

'Not a word. Sent me straight off to collect a couple of fucking hanging baskets from a garden supplier.'

'You ought to ring Don up and ask what's going on. As one Bethnal boy to another. I thought he came from Manchester.'

'You don't know anythink about it,' Cyril said, with a look that was meant to be man-of-the-worldish but ended up somewhere near hangdog. 'For Christ's sake' – this as the Red Indian chorale reached some kind of crescendo – 'can't those tarts put a sock in it?'

'Who are they?'

'They're called the Handmaidens of Pocahontas. Ainslie's got them on *Pop Scene* or something.'

It was mid-afternoon now, still warm but with a breeze blowing in stealthily from the river to stir the overgrown grass and play havoc with Ainslie's flowerbeds. Two or three gardens away, someone was burning leaves: pearl-grey smoke drifted upwards a puff at a time, as if a second Indian tribe, drawn by the singing, was trying to get in touch with the Handmaidens of Pocahontas. Two years into working for Ainslie, I was used to all this: the placid English backdrops; the superimposed weirdness; the Beautiful People; and blue-suited Cyril, who looked as if he had just walked in off the set of a *Carry On* film. Ten yards away, taking no interest in any of the guests who swarmed around her, Ainslie's mother was marching up towards the terrace.

'I bet she was a terror in her day,' Cyril said admiringly.

In fact, Mrs Duncan looked a terror now, like the red queen, disturbed by intruders, executioner in tow. As well as the mackintosh, she was wearing brown button boots. No breeze that ever blew could have disturbed her grey-white sausage curls. All this was another very common sight in the sixties: the older generation out to make trouble, not about to go quietly.

'Hello there, missus,' Cyril said, as she strode into view.

Mrs Duncan ignored him. It was me she was after. Her fists, plunged deep into the pockets of her coat, bulged ominously: knuckle-dustered, waiting to pounce.

'Are you a friend of my son's?'

'I'm his press officer.'

Mrs Duncan looked slightly less cross. Perhaps, after all, violence wouldn't be necessary, and the knuckle-dusters could stay where they were.

'You ought to tell him to do something about his garden then. Them roses need better treatment than they're getting. You'd think he'd have a proper gardener, the amount of money he makes, but the only thing I could find in the potting shed was these secateurs. And they could do with a good sharpening.'

'I'll tell Ainslie – Mr Duncan.'

Perhaps the fact that someone had called her son 'Mr Duncan' – a feat Ainslie was rarely able to bring off – accounted for the slight shift in Mrs Duncan's attitude. She stared at me critically for a moment or so.

'You seem a nice young man. Not like some of the people my son employs.' There was a pause. The Handmaidens of Pocahontas had stopped singing and brought out a kind of tepee which they were erecting on the lawn. 'Tell me, what do you make of this pop music business? I always thought the Beatles were nice-looking lads, but it's the *noise* I can't bear.'

'Will you have something to drink, missus?' Cyril asked. He had clearly taken the reference to the people Ainslie employed to heart.

'You mind your own business,' Mrs Duncan said with undisguised savagery. 'Butting in when nobody asked you.' You got the impression that if she came any closer to Cyril she would have torn him limb from limb. There was a disturbance near at hand, and Ainslie loomed into view.

'Oh there you are, Moother. I'd thought you were indoors having a cup of tea.' In Mrs Duncan's presence Ainslie's accent straightaway went up a couple of notches. 'Clive will be happy to make you one if you'd like.'

'That boy couldn't turn on a tap,' Mrs Duncan said. There was clearly a whole lot more to be said about the neglected roses, about Clive's shortcomings, the people her son employed, all kinds of deficiencies on which her eye had fallen, but for the moment she contented herself with clawing at his sleeve. Her fingers were gnarled little talons, full of remorseless vigour. 'Isn't that little girl over there from the television? Lulu is her name? Her legs'll get cold if she goes round dressed in that pocket handkerchief.'

'Why don't you come and sit down, Moother, and tek the weight off your feet?'

It was not, I decided, that Ainslie was cowed or oppressed by his mother – though he was definitely both those things – just that in his forty-something years on the planet he hadn't managed to work out a way of dealing with her. There was no game-plan, and whatever rubbish she came up with had to be addressed the moment it happened.

'What are those folk over there drinking?' Mrs Duncan now demanded. All the comparative good humour she had shown when talking to me had gone. 'I'll have some of that.'

Cyril fetched her a glass of Pimm's and she allowed herself to be shepherded away past the row of deckchairs. It was getting cooler now, and January, Summer and Melody had disappeared. Rosalind came up the terrace steps, stopped a yard or so away and made a little mock-curtsey.

'Who was that old lady?'

'She's Ainslie's mother.'

'What was she so cross about?'

'All kinds of everything. Are you enjoying yourself?'

'Sure I am. Nick, I've been thinking.'

Mrs Duncan, Ainslie, Cyril and their problems; Garth, Don Shard and whatever he was plotting all ceased to exist. It was only Rosalind who was real.

'What about?'

'I'm not going back to the States. Well, not immediately. I'll have to sometime, to sign the papers. I understand that. But what I really want to do right now is to stay here.'

I was surprised to find how little I was bothered by what Marty Knowland might make of this. Marty was a busted flush, a snuffed candle, out of the running from the start. But there was another factor in the equation, the potential violence of whose reaction couldn't be discounted.

'What's your father going to say when he finds out?'

'Daddy? I don't care,' Rosalind said, which was the equivalent, in Duchesne family circles, of a Dixiecrat senator from Alabam declaring that they could build one of those newly desegregated high schools on his front lawn tomorrow if they had a mind to and the time to bring our boys home from 'Nam was now. 'Why should I anyhow? And why should he? Listen, Nick. I don't know what you thought we were like when you were there that time, that time in Pheeny, but whatever it was has all gone. I mean, Daddy just does politics these days. Momma's up in Tallahassee, drying . . . well, sorting herself out, and I'm about to be divorced. Mrs Marty Knowland, who went to the big city and couldn't get the hang of it.'

What had I thought of them all that time in Pheeny? It was impossible to separate out what I knew or suspected then from what I knew or suspected now, to distinguish mythical chaff from real-life wheat. On the other hand, a deeply dysfunctional hutch-full of misfits featuring a fairy princess being simultaneously bossed about and ignored by an arch-manipulator and a drunk while sly old Dolores rifled the fridge and the traffic whizzed by in the Deer Valley beyond would have been pretty near the mark.

'You'd better excuse me for a minute, Nick.' Rosalind still had what I had come to realise was an authentic American habit of addressing you by name, irrespective of circumstance or the number of other people present. I watched her saunter off across the lawn and bury herself amid the hippy flotsam. The Handmaidens of Pocahontas had disappeared inside their tepee, although puffs of smoke continued to rise from the neighbouring garden. Ainslie stuck a plump, knuckle-less hand on my shoulder.

'Nice girl.' He had a trick of making the most innocent association sound thoroughly disreputable.

'You're right about that.'

'You want to watch those Americans, though.'

'I promise I'll be careful.'

The terrace was almost empty of people now. They were congregated on the lawn, sitting at the long dining table, stretched out by the water's edge looking at the river. Ainslie stared at them unhappily, as if he found all human behaviour mystifying and bound to lead to trouble. Cyril lurked a couple of yards away, his Brylcreemed head bobbing up and down slightly, like a greyhound in the slips.

'There's a problem with Garth,' he began.

'What sort of a problem?'

'Let me put it another way,' Ainslie said. Cyril jerked his head again, as if he expected his employer to lob a stick onto the lawn which he could have the pleasure of retrieving. 'When was the last time you saw him?'

It was a good question. Garth hadn't attended Florian's funeral. Neither had he kept an appointment to appear on *Juke Box Jury* two or three days afterwards. As the person who had had to deal with an angry producer, I was still cross about this.

'About three weeks ago.'

'That's about right,' Ainslie said. 'Though he was playing up before that, fook knows. The thing is, Nick' – Ainslie sounded nonplussed, as if he balked at attributing seriousness to something that might turn out to be completely trivial – 'the thing is, Nick, that … Well, you heard about what happened before Florian died, all that stoof at the meeting? Garth thought it was all his fault. Well, some of it.'

'You mean he blames himself for Florian dying?'

Ainslie whirled his fists up in front of his face, like a goalkeeper startled by a close-range shot. 'I wouldn't put it quite as strong as that. I mean, Garth's a fookin' funny bloke. He is, though. You remember that girl as wrote to the fan club saying she was dying of leukaemia? Well, Garth *brooded* about that. Sent her I don't know how many bunches of flowers. In the end, the parents had to tell him to stop. Anyway, a couple of days afterwards he said, "Ains, it was me goading him that did it. If I hadn't gone and mixed all those keyboard parts down on the record he'd still be alive today."'

Guilt. Brooding. Existential angst. These were new sides to Garth, who had previously got by on petulance, spite and rampant extroversion.

'Do you think that's true?'

'I dunno,' Ainslie said wearily. 'Actually, Nicko, now you come to mention it I don't. You want to know what I really think? I think Florian was just the kind of bloke to top himself. At any rate do something stupid. You can always tell. I had a singer once – Paul Ramon. You won't remember him. Nobody does. Slit his throat in the dressing room backstage at the Glasgow Kelvin Hall ten minutes before the Saturday matinee, and you could see it coming a mile off. The point is, Garth felt *responsible*. Thought he had to take some of the blame. Not to mention leave the scene of the crime, so to speak.'

'Where's he gone?'

'Tangier, so they say.'

I had a sudden vision of eastern minarets, muezzin bells, a white-robed Garth picking his way through dusty backstreets as beggars plucked at his skirts.

'"They" being?'

'Norman and Marianne and that lot down at the Speakeasy. Somebody had a postcard or summat.'

'Why would he want to go to Tangier?'

'Come on, Nicko. You've seen the stuff in the Sunday supplements. You know the kind of books he reads,' Ainslie said, failing to counter the suspicion that he knew them and had read them too. 'It's even fookin' money he thought he'd be spending his time in some caff with Paul Bowles and Bill Burroughs. Whereas if I know Garth he'll be out of his head on kif in his hotel room and just about ready for a trip to the clap clinic. Anyway, that's all very well. A bloke's allowed a holiday. But there are those Swedish dates coming up, not to mention Decca wanting a new single. So it's high time he came home. I want you to go out there and get him.'

'Why me?'

'You know how Garth respects you.'

'I hadn't noticed it.'

'Well, he does. He always says so,' said Ainslie, with no conviction at all. 'Always going on about how much he wishes he'd had your advantages.'

I was supremely bored with Ainslie going on about my advantages.

'When do I have to go?'

'Tomorrow. You can get a visa on the Spanish border. No need for you to be held up. None at all.'

I thought about what Ainslie had just said. As nearly always happened with the Helium Kids, the lure of travel collided head-on with its likely consequences. Solitary hotel rooms. Garth. Tedious negotiations. Garth. The trip home. Garth. It was not much of a job.

'You can have a really good talk with him on the way back,' Ainslie added, as if this were the last rich diadem that clinched the deal. 'See what's on his fookin' mind.' He stared out again across the lawn, where the breeze had begun to make inroads into the knots of partygoers and one or two people were looking for shelter, and turned suddenly melancholic.

'Fookin' shame about Brian,' he said suddenly.

'Isn't it?' Brian Epstein had died a fortnight ago, a day or so after Florian's funeral.

'You know, I never really saw why they made such a fuss about Brian,' Ainslie said peevishly – Ainslie, who of all Brian Epstein's contemporaries had revered him the most, and who would probably have sunk to his knees in worship had he unexpectedly strolled out onto the terrace. 'But stoof like that makes you think.'

Six months before, Ainslie would not have said a thing like this. But already we were settling down into the long afternoon of the sixties. Soon the Beatles would start to bicker away their remaining time together in the big studio at Twickenham; the acid casualties would be frying their brains in Chelsea flats; everywhere satanic majesties were on the prowl. One of them had prowled off to Tangier and would now have to be brought back.

'Jesus,' Ainslie said through his teeth. 'Why don't they all go home?'

The record duration for one of Ainslie's parties was thirty-seven hours. This was unless you counted a weekend in a borrowed country house in Wiltshire that had lasted from the Friday afternoon to some-time after lunch on the Tuesday and been complicated by some of the guests going away and then coming back again. But that had been before Florian had died, before Don Shard had turned up at his office, and Garth had fled to Morocco. Rosalind came back from her walk around the garden with her arms folded across her chest.

'It's getting colder,' she said.

There was a wind coming in from across the river. Gradually it began to increase in force, rushed over the tall grass, blew the smoke from the barbecue into billowing spirals, sent the tepee listing danger-ously onto one side, confounded the Handmaidens of Pocahontas.

Stirred into action, plastic plates bent and flattened in their hands, the tribes of hippy girls and their peacock-jacketed escorts started to move off, like troops from a battlefield. There was a commotion back inside the house, and Mrs Duncan suddenly appeared among them. Clive trailed behind her, semaphoring wildly.

'Are you all right, Moother?' Ainslie asked.

It was hard to say what was wrong with Mrs Duncan. Her eyes were wide open but she seemed not to see any of the people who stood in her path, and her fingers, more talon-like than ever, were drumming restlessly against the buttons of her mackintosh.

'Look at the angels,' she said. 'Nobody told me there were going to be angels.'

'Spiked,' somebody explained.

Soon afterwards it began to rain. Later on – much later on – walking hand-in-hand down to the station, we found Melody and Summer sitting in a bus shelter, cross-legged and demure, for all the world like a pair of ordinary teenage girls on their way back to prosperous bourgeois homes after a party in the suburbs. Which, when you came to think about it, is exactly what they were.

10. AUTUMN ALMANAC

Rising from the turbid deeps
The mermaid-haunted waters
Agamemnon's mighty sword ...

'Agamemnon's Mighty Sword'

In those days you got to Tangier by way of Gibraltar and then via ferry from Algeciras, which meant travelling through three separate jurisdictions with passport stamps to match. 'Don't worry about the money,' Ainslie had said, in faint mitigation for the trouble he was putting me to, and I decided to take him at his word. Ainslie, I told myself, as the taxi lurched off to Heathrow through the grey September dawn, would get an expenses claim like no other he had ever received. In this non-temporising spirit I took a first-class flight to Gibraltar, booked myself into the Majestic, on the grounds that it was the most expensive of the four hotels on offer, made a thirty-minute phone call home to Rosalind, plundered the minibar and ate a five-course meal I did not really want. Ainslie, I assured myself, would suffer for this inconvenience; and he would suffer still more for the vagueness with which the task had been framed. In particular, there had been a conversation which went: 'Where's he staying, Ainslie?' 'I told you. In Tangier.' 'But where exactly in Tangier?' 'It's not a big place, Nicko.

Well, not if you're white. You'll find him. Ask around a bit.' Meanwhile, Gibraltar stank of sewage and the waves lapping at the stony beach by the Hotel Majestic's swimming pool were the colour of gravy. Worse, it was only a week since the Sovereignty referendum; the Spanish government was making threatening noises and there was a frigate at anchor in the bay.

Next morning, out on the hydrofoil, things improved. The Mediterranean coursed beneath us like an undulating sheet of glass. In the distance, blue-grey mountains loomed over the Barbary shore. Great white seabirds hung in the thermals like scraps of paper. There were one or two Beautiful People lounging about on the upper deck – King's Road exquisites with wavy blond hair and carpet bags for luggage – but I kept clear of them. Only inside information would do, courtesy of old Tangier hands. In the end, after several false starts, I homed in on a middle-aged man in a linen jacket and an MCC tie poised winsomely over a Lawrence Durrell novel who consented to be bought a gin-and-tonic at the bar.

'Of course, the place isn't what it was,' he said, disposing of the gin-and-tonic in a couple of gracious swigs. 'Like everywhere else in this world, I'm afraid. You find somewhere halfway civilised and then authority steps in and starts *interfering* with everything. Not like the old days.' He gave me a nod, and the vision of those phantasmagorical old days – Allen Ginsberg reading his poems at the Café de Paris, obliging Berber boys at $3 a time – leapt into the air between us. 'The British Post Office has closed, Saccone & Speed have shut their branch and they've cut down the trees in the Zoco Gardens to make space for some wretched car park. Still, it has the edge on poor old Blighty. What do you make of this Wilson fellow?'

'He has his admirers.'

'He was the year below me at Jesus. Never heard him make an original remark. Then again, not really my type, you understand.'

I understood. The mountains loomed nearer. Closer up they looked like outsize lumps of Plasticine.

'If you wanted to experience the spirit of the old Tangier, where would you go?'

'All a question of resources, dear boy. I believe the Hotel Velasquez still has something to be said for it. That's where my friend Alec Waugh used to put up. But if you're feeling the pinch you might want to try somewhere in the Old Town. I say, you haven't got any English cigarettes, have you?'

'Only American, I'm afraid.' I gave him a packet of the Kents I bought in honour of Rosalind and he turned them over doubtfully in his hand.

'Never tried these,' he said. 'But they can't be any worse than the local brands. The people say they're made of powdered horse dung. Anyway, I'm obliged to you.'

Twenty minutes later, after we had docked at the harbour, I watched him being borne away by a Moroccan servant to a spot on the kerb where, guarded by three deferential policemen, an ancient Rolls-Royce lay in wait. The Beautiful People were met by a campervan with a coil of sunflowers painted on the side. The rest of the passengers – nondescript Spaniards carrying suitcases, a party of nuns with freshly laundered habits that sparkled in the sun – drifted away, and I took a taxi through the drab, dusty streets, where limbless beggars squatted in the dirt, livestock spilled squawking out into the road and the smell of spice drifted paralysingly through the open window, to the hotel. Here, in contrast to the teeming thoroughfares beyond, all was seemly decorum. A group of American tourists stood in the lobby under the winnowing fans proudly disputing their bar bill and there were far too many porters for the luggage. The rooms at the Hotel Velasquez began at $25 a night. Still irked by Ainslie's vagueness, I booked a suite, enquired about the best way to send a telegram, found a two-day-old copy of the continental *Daily Telegraph* printed on paper so thin that the fans took it and whirled it high above my head and went off to think about where Garth might be hiding. Oddly enough, my spirits had risen since the previous day in Gib, and the Lawrence Durrell fan on the ferry had put me in a good humour. Garth might be a needle in a haystack, I told myself, but he was a bright shiny needle and I intended to find him, to listen to what he had to say and drag him unresisting back.

There were several places, I soon discovered, where the Tangier expats hung out, and a wide variety of English haunts and homes. Over the next few days I tried them all. I sauntered in the Boulevard Pasteur, next to the Velasquez; I downed cups of bitter coffee sweetened with saccharine tablets at the Petit Socco at the Place de France; I had dinner at the Grillon, whose bill Ainslie would have a fit over when I presented it to him; I even chartered a taxi up to the Mountain, the big hill half a mile outside the city limits, lush with autumn greenery, where the cream of local society sequestered itself; but it was no good. The gossip was all about Joe Orton and Kenneth Halliwell – two more summer casualties to add to Florian and Brian Epstein, who had been there in June, scandalising the American tourists by saying 'fuck' very loudly in the hotel lobbies and annoying the local queens. No one had come across Garth. On the afternoon of the fourth day, thinking that Ainslie ought to have some return on the very considerable sums he was spending, I had my hair trimmed by the hotel barber and called on the Deputy Consul at his office on the Avenue Marrakech. He was a young man of about my age who shook his head over the questions I put to him.

'Fellow called Dangerfield, you say. Should I have heard of him?'

'He's quite well known back in England.'

'That doesn't mean anyone will take much notice of him here.' A breath of wind flicked in through the open window and he jumped up to secure the papers on his desk. 'What does he do, exactly?'

Here in sight of the Mediterranean, deep in the wreckage of the ancient world, what Garth did for a living sounded horribly inadequate. 'He plays in a pop group called the Helium Kids. They're quite . . .' I hesitated. What exactly were the Helium Kids? Successful? Celebrated? Culturally significant? 'Their records do rather well,' I concluded.

None of this cut any ice with the Deputy Consul. 'Between you and me, those pop people are the limit,' he said. 'They sit in the bars smoking kif and upsetting the locals, or they decide to drive to Marrakech and break down halfway across the desert and we have to bring them back. That's when they're not being blackmailed for sodomy.' There was a tiny lizard, no bigger than a sardine, clinging to the shiny surface of the wall next to his desk, and I watched it start to climb. 'Is your friend interested in that kind of thing?'

'I don't think so. We just need to know he's OK.'

'Well, we'll keep an eye out for him,' the Deputy Consul said. There was an Old Salopians Cricket Club fixture card on the desk next to the piles of paper. 'But I don't mind telling you that if I had a five-pound note for every time I've said that I shouldn't be working *here*.'

That night the hotel was invaded by a gang of American business-men come to inspect a construction project, who whooped and skipped through the corridors, threw bread rolls at each other and kept the party up till 3 a.m. I would give Ainslie another day, I decided, before catching the ferry back to Algeciras. And then, quite unexpect-edly, I had a lucky break. It came the following morning at breakfast, when a man who looked like a fleshed-out version of Alec Guinness playing Fagin in *Oliver Twist* sat down at the table next to me, ordered a double brandy to go with his toast and marmalade, and in doing so revealed himself as Simon O'Dell, the manager of a middling success-ful group of art school drop-outs called the Deadwoods.

'What are you doing here?'

'Oh, you know,' Simon said. It would never have occurred to him that there was anything odd in meeting someone you knew in a hotel in Morocco. 'Crispin' – Crispin was the Deadwoods' guitar player

– 'came here in the summer and heard a load of Berber tribesmen playing their drums in the casbah. Now he reckons he wants to make a record with them. I told him the record company won't stand it, but when does the Honourable Crispin Merryweather ever listen to anything I tell him?' Something struck him and he tapped a thumbnail against the rim of the brandy glass. The white-clad hotel servants stared impassively on. 'Are you looking for Garth?'

'In a manner of speaking.'

'Well, you only just missed him. He was staying under this very roof until three or four days ago.'

There was no point in letting Simon in on the secret of Garth's flight to North Africa. It would be all over Denmark Street in a week.

'Did he seem all right?'

'I'll say he did. He was with some bint. They were virtually having each other on the banquette.'

'Where's he staying now?'

'Somewhere near Dutch Tony's,' Simon said. When I looked blank he added: 'Native quarter.'

Towards lunchtime I engaged one of the hotel porters and had myself taken down to the Old Town. Here the streets grew narrower and the beggars more docile. Grit, blown in from the desert, crackled underfoot. The porter spoke perfectly accented English and said that it was his ambition to study at the University of Cambridge, preferably at the college of Trinity. Dutch Tony's turned out to be a kind of bohemian rooming house: red-faced European drunks sat outside on canebacked chairs, getting up every so often to stagger through the doors of the street cafés. The porter went off to confer with one of the waiters.

'He says your friend is living in a house not far from here.'

We set off again, less confidently, down another street where a small child stood urinating into the gutter. At the far end was a whitepainted building, less shabby than the others, with high, shuttered windows.

'That is the place, sir.'

There was no one about, so I stepped through the half-open door into a room that could have come straight out of *The Thousand and One Nights*: oriental screens; flung-about cushions; a yellow songbird in a cage. A blonde girl in a dressing gown who was sitting on a divan bed in the corner reading a copy of *Siddhartha* looked up unconcernedly, almost as if she had been waiting for me to arrive.

'Do you know where I can find Garth Dangerfield?'

'He's not here,' she said. 'He must have gone out when I was asleep. He does that sometimes.' She waved an arm vaguely around the room, implying that I was welcome to search the premises, turn out the cupboards, that whatever I did there was nothing to her. 'Or maybe he's gone out with his friend. I don't know.'

'Which friend would that be?'

'How should I know? He comes here sometimes. They're always talking.'

She would have been about Alexandra's age: thin to the point of needing medical attention, with splotched eye makeup and dirty feet; just the kind of girl whose life Garth liked to fuck up when he had the chance. Her heroic abstractedness, I decided, was down to genuine detachment rather than drugs, although you could never tell. Meanwhile, there were other things lying around the room that made it look less like the scented boudoir of Harun al-Rashid and more like a pop star's crash-pad: a twelve-string Gretsch guitar neatly positioned on a stand; an ancient box-cabinet reel-to-reel; several paperback books with titles like *Glimpses of the Infinite*.

'My name's Nick Du Pont. I'm Garth's publicist. Could you tell him that I'm very anxious to see him and that I'll call back later?'

'You'd better write it down so I don't forget. Don't you find,' she said, 'that you can't remember anything these days? I know I do.'

There was no paper anywhere. In the end I tore off the top of a cigarette packet, smoothed out the cardboard and wrote *Called but you were out. Back later. Nick Du P.* The girl looked on interestedly, as if she had never seen writing done before and wondered where it might lead to. I gave her the strip of card and she hid it in the pocket of her dressing gown.

'He'll probably be out for ages,' she said. 'He usually is. Not at all reliable. Have you got any money?'

'What do you want it for?'

'There's never any food here. I need to buy something to eat.'

I gave her a £5 note and she stared at it eagerly, mouth half-open, like a girl in a Pre-Raphaelite painting. There was sun streaming in through the open window. The songbird was chittering sorrowfully to itself. The scrap of paper with my message to Garth fluttered out of its hidey-hole and she stowed it away again. The movement disturbed the folds of her dressing gown and a tiny, blue-veined breast popped briefly into view. Still clutching the £5 note she went back to the divan bed and began to read some more of *Siddhartha*.

The sixties, it had to be said, were jammed to the rafters with encounters of this kind, massively inconsequential get-togethers with people so doped or otherwise detached from the world around them that they could barely communicate with you, against backdrops so outlandish that they might have been filmsets. If nobody minded, it was because nobody noticed. You walked into an orgy or a mad-hatter's tea party without turning a hair, moral inquisitiveness left with your coat at the door. In normal circumstances – if there were any such thing – I might have stopped to wonder who the blonde girl was, and whether it might not be in her best interests to be holed up in the Arab Quarter of Tangier with occult-obsessed Garth Dangerfield. At the same time, there were more pressing questions to hand. What was Garth up to? Would he listen to what I had to say? Would he want to come back to England? Who was the anonymous friend who came and went? The blonde girl, like all those other blonde girls who had flounced through history, would have to look out for herself.

Back at the Hotel Velasquez, the American businessmen, sober now and chalk-faced, were being packed into a minibus, and there was an urgent message from Ainslie. Putting the call through took several minutes. By the time the connection was established, Ainslie was incandescent with rage.

'Where the fook have you been?'

'It's all right, Ainslie, I've found him.' I explained about the house in the Arab Quarter, the blonde girl and Simon O'Dell.

'*That* fookin' lush,' Ainslie said. 'Wonder he can stand upright these days. I did hear the Deadwoods were being dropped off the label . . . But look, the thing is I've had a letter.'

'From Garth?'

'No, the Duke of fookin' Edinburgh.' Ainslie's voice faded away a bit and then loomed remorselessly back into focus. 'You never saw anything like it. All about how he wants to make some record where he recites poems and plays stuff on an acoustic. With the Swingle Singers or someone on backing vocals.'

'What poems exactly?'

'I don't know. *Leaves of Grass* for all I care,' Ainslie said, once again betraying the fact that he was much better educated than he liked to let on. 'Jesus. This call must be costing me a fortune. Look, you go back to wherever he's staying, pay off the tart' – Ainslie was fond of tough-sounding phrases like 'pay off the tart' – 'give her, I dunno, give her fifty quid, and get him back here within forty-eight hours.'

'What if he won't come?'

'Tell him I wash my hands of him,' said Ainslie, who I knew had never willingly washed his hands of any client still contracted to a major record label. 'Well, no. Don't tell him that . . . Tell him there's things we need to discuss. And that the boys are worried about him.'

Even after I had put the phone down I could still hear Ainslie's voice echoing in the air around me. Twenty feet away from the Perspex booth in which I had made the call, an extremely old woman, dressed in the fashions of the 1920s, her shuffling feet encased in a pair of gold lamé slippers, was being escorted to a chair by the hotel manager. Four porters carrying a rolled-up carpet laboured in their wake. It seemed a million miles from Berwick Street.

By the time I set off for the Old Town again there were muezzins calling the faithful to prayer and a breeze blowing up to deposit what seemed like half the sand of the Atlas Mountains in little heaps on the uneven flagstones. The drunks outside Dutch Tony's had all gone away. The door of the shuttered white house was open. As I drew level with the lintel a voice said: 'You'd better come in.'

In the three hours since my last visit someone had radically reorganised the contents of the room. The divan bed had been pushed back to the far wall and most of the cushions thrown on top of it. The space freed up was now filled by a wooden armchair that had not been there before and a mattress laid at right angles to it. Some kind of incense with a sour, sickly smell burned on a plate nearby. Garth, much thinner than when I had last seen him and dressed in a tie-dye T-shirt and jeans, sat in the chair. The blonde girl, still in her dressing gown, lay flat on her back on the mattress, motionless but with her eyes wide open. Meanwhile, in a second room to the back, behind a bead curtain, someone was moving about with restless, heavy footsteps, breathing stertorously as he went. The overall effect – the girl flat out on the floor, Garth in his chair, the reek of the incense, the phantom presence behind the curtain – was desperately sinister, so sinister that it was all I could do not to walk out into the street again.

'It's nice to see you, Nick,' Garth said. 'Flattering, as well. I was thinking it was going to be Cyril, but it turns out to be you.'

'I don't suppose Cyril's ever been out of England in his life.'

'And what if he's not?' About three-quarters of Garth's friendliness vanished on the instant. 'He might not like foreigners. Nothing wrong with that, is there?'

The blonde girl stirred slightly, closed one eye and then opened it again.

'Is she all right?'

'Julie? I should think so. Can't remember if she took two or three of those things of hers. If it was two she'll probably wake up in a bit.'

It was at this point, as opposed to all the previous points along the way, that the absurdity of the task Ainslie had given me struck home. There was no way of telling what state Garth was in, what he had been up to, what debts he owed to the blonde girl or she to him. Behind the curtain there was a noise of what sounded like water rising to boiling point and the rattle of china. Whoever lurked there was brewing himself a cup of tea.

'Ainslie said you were . . .' I gave up trying to put what Ainslie had said into words and settled for a head-on assault. 'That you were very upset about Florian.'

'Florian,' Garth said, chewing warily over the name and falling several degrees short of committing himself to ever having heard of it. 'I was sorry about Florian, Nick. Didn't behave very well. Regret it now. But Florian never lived by the will.'

'I don't suppose he did.'

'That's the most important thing you can do, don't you think? Live by the will.' He paused for a second, as if trying to remember a quotation. '*In conflict we find our destiny*. I don't think Florian understood that.'

There was no knowing what nonsense Garth was going to come out with next. By this stage nothing would have surprised me. I decided to press on.

'Ainslie needs you to come home. Everyone's worried about you.'

'Don't know why anyone should be worried about me,' Garth said, either genuinely mystified or doing a very good job of pretending to be. '*I'm* perfectly happy. Having a nice little holiday. Making plans for the future.'

'What sort of plans?'

Ten feet away the china cup rattled again and fell smack on the floor. There was a rending noise as the curtain parted and Don Shard stepped into the room.

'All kinds of plans. Isn't that right, Don?'

Don said nothing, but the little gesture he made with the clenched fist of his right hand confirmed that Garth's plans, whether or not sanctioned by the rest of the Helium Kids, would have no place in them for Ainslie Duncan. Six foot two or three, dressed in a dark suit, bald head gleaming in the light, he loomed menacingly over us.

'Don's been helping me with one or two things,' Garth suggested. There was something slightly patronising about this. But if Garth meant to imply by it that he regarded Don as some kind of hireling or higher grade factotum then he failed miserably. Merely by coming out of the kitchen Don had assumed power over us. It was as simple as that.

'Hello, Nick,' Don said, showing a line of ragged teeth. 'How's Ainslie?'

It was a good question. But however Ainslie was, however optimistic and future-facing a state he had coaxed himself into, he would be a whole lot worse when he found out about Garth's houseguest.

'He was all right when I last spoke to him.'

'Bit of a shock you finding me here, I daresay,' Don volunteered. He was hugely enjoying the effect he was having. 'Have a cup of tea now.'

We had a cup of tea. They were supermarket teabags, brought out from England, rank-smelling, like the scent of hobgoblins. What else did Don have in the kitchen, I wondered. Jars of Camp Coffee? Webbs' lettuces in Tupperware boxes? The blonde girl still lay at our feet.

'All this has got to fucking stop, anyhow,' Don said, as if he had only just noticed she was there. He turned towards me.

'You'll be working for me from now on,' he said. 'And don't you forget it.'

And so, in those two sentences, the transfer of power was complete. At some point, Ainslie would have to be told about it. At some other point, complex financial negotiations would have to be entered into, or perhaps, knowing Don, only very simple ones. But all the essential components were in place. Garth, I noticed, looked a bit wary, as if he hadn't bargained for the vigour of the genie he had just released from its lamp, and feared the consequences for himself and those around him.

It turned out that Don had one more trick up his sleeve. The reel-to-reel tape recorder I had noticed on my first visit lay a foot or two from Garth's chair. Don's eye fell on it and he knelt down and, with an odd, caressing gesture, flicked one of the spools.

'You listen to this,' he said, as music began to fill the room.

My first thought, as an up-tempo bass line gave way to clanging guitar chords, was that, unlike any previous Helium Kids song I had ever heard, there were no keyboards. It was as if Florian had never been. My second thought was that this must be the material Ainslie had talked about, taped on the day that Florian died. My third thought, rapidly cancelling out the other two, was that, against considerable odds, it was pretty good stuff, much better, for example, than any of the Beatle-ly approximations that had clogged up *Paisley Patterns*. At this precise moment the blonde girl – Julie – woke up with a start, made a kind of mewing noise, rolled over onto her side and began to be sick. This went on for some time. In the end Garth went to fetch a bucket. But still the music blared on. 'Agamemnon,' Don said gravely, when it was over, and here amid the stink of Moorish incense, Co-op teabags, the blonde girl's mauve-coloured vomit, another link in the Helium Kids' slow but inexorable rise snapped into place.

To the editors of *Melody Maker, New Musical Express, Disc, Record Mirror, Fabulous 208*

FOR IMMEDIATE RELEASE: 30 SEPTEMBER 1967

The members of the Helium Kids would like to announce that from 1 October 1967 their interests will be exclusively represented by Mr Donald Shard of Shard Enterprises Ltd. All enquiries regarding the group's future recordings and touring schedule should be directed to Mr Shard at his Maddox Street address.

Garth Dangerfield, the group's principal songwriter, commented: 'We should like to thank our former manager, Ainslie Duncan, for all the valuable work he has accomplished on our behalf. But we now feel that the time is right to move forward and reap maximum rewards from a potential that has not yet been fully tapped.'

Latest gen from our spies in Maddox Street is that loveable Flower Poppers the Helium Kids have junked long-term pilot AINSLIE DUNCAN from the cock-pit in favour of veteran scene mogul DON SHARD. The boys – still reeling from the death of ace keyboard player FLORIAN SHANKLEY-WALKER – whose *Paisley Patterns* was a summer smash, are expected to be back in the studio with a clutch of fresh Dangerfield/Halliwell compositions come November. Quoth Shard: 'I've been after these boys for some time – I think they have the potential to turn into something really significant.'

Ainslie Duncan was unavailable for comment.

New Musical Express, 5 October 1967

21 September 1967

Three days back from Morocco and still shaking the sand out of my trouser pockets. Rosalind solicitous. In my absence she has covered the chair and sofas with throws from the India boutique in Bond Street and Sellotaped a poster advertising the Monterey Pop Festival to the door of the fridge. This morning Derek Taylor calls. The Beatles are making some kind of film at an airfield in Kent. Would the boys like to tag along? Garth has gone to ground since the Tangier trip – not even Don knows where he is – but in the end Dale, Ian, Keith, Rosalind and I head down to Westerham in Dale's Daimler to see what all the fuss is about.

As might have been expected, everything horribly chaotic. Hundreds of people milling around. No script, nor much of an idea which order the scenes ought to be shot in. Several lectures from Paul on the virtues of improvisation: 'You've just got to be *spontaneous*. That's the only way we'll get anything done.' We spend the afternoon on set, during which time the Beatles, faces hidden by pigs' heads, mime to one of John's new songs and the tour bus which has brought them all up from the West Country is driven around at speed. God knows what the BBC, to whom Paul intends to sell the finished product, will make of it. Scenting the general air of licensed irresponsibility, the boys clown about, chat up unattached women and are eventually thrown off the bus. Rosalind spellbound at the idea of spending time in the English countryside with John, Paul, George and Ringo: 'I can't believe this is happening to me.'

It turns out that the invitation was Don's doing, the restitution of a debt owed him by the Beatles' management, such as it is. Don: 'You can do anything with them now Epstein's dead. Anything at all.'

15 October 1967

A white-label advance copy of 'Agamemnon's Mighty Sword' arrives in the office. It's been smartened up since I first heard it in the house in Tangier, with the blonde girl out cold on the mattress, the vocals double-tracked and the guitars heavily overdubbed. Light years better than anything they've produced before. As for the promotion, Don is fully prepared to bribe every disc jockey on the new Radio 1 station I can entice to lunch – there is already a pile of envelopes lying in the in-tray, each with two £50 notes inside – but I tell him there's no point. The single is strong enough to survive on its merits. Don approves: 'Well, at least you're not wasting my fucking money.'

Working for Don less of a trial than I had assumed. For one thing, he is rarely in the office. Tells me that as long as I do my job, he won't interfere.

16 October 1967

Six-thirty p.m. in Egerton Gardens Mews. Light fading over the Knightsbridge rooftops. Smell of lavender from Mrs Manningham's window-boxes coming in under the door. Rosalind drowsing on the sofa. Hard to convey quite how blissful this is. The silent room. The sleeping girl. The evening's promise. Meanwhile, there are airmail letters from Al Duchesne all over the kitchen table. Marty Knowland has written several times imploring her to come back. Individual sentences leap out and catch my eye. Al wants her to *reconsider this ill-judged step*. Marty alternates sentimental yearnings with stern injunctions *to stop being an asshole*.

'He has no idea,' Rosalind says. She has stopped wearing her dowdy New York matron's get-up and broken out into shot-silk culottes and King's Road romper-gear. 'No idea what it's like living with him. Watching him put on his suit every morning before he goes out to work at his fucking brokerage. Asking why I haven't put his pants in the press. Calling his secretary to tell her he'll be ten minutes late.'

Two views of Rosalind:

Objective: Spoiled ('Daddy let me have everything'). Brittle. Signs of a temper lurking beneath the kindly facade. The hint of trouble ahead. That Yankee fixity of purpose, applied to very trivial things

('Why move it when it looks better there?'). Low-level irritability. A dab hand at cunningly disguised emotional blackmail ('Well, if that's what you really want to do, honey'). Temperamental and impulsive, like Lucille. My mother, I think, would have been alarmed by her, but also impressed.

Subjective: Beautiful. Whimsically generous. Brings home extraordinary gifts from the West End shops (a cigar cutter, a soda siphon, a Guard's Club tie) – 'I thought you'd like them.' Apparently unmoved by the letters that descend on her head like so much confetti, the terrific stink awaiting her back home in Phoenix. The fact that I am completely obsessed with her.

A certain amount of talk about the old days back home:

'Why didn't you come on to me more?'

'Why didn't you?'

'I don't know. I suppose it was all too weird. I mean, you were like something from another planet. Never mind Daddy.'

'So what did he think of me?'

'Daddy? He said you were a little English creep.'

5 November 1967

'Agamemnon' in the singles chart at No. 13 and set to rise higher. But change is in the air. The band are still signed to Decca, who want another album, but Don – who won't even take their A & R man's phone calls – is already thought to be looking elsewhere. An advance of £12,000 from one potential suitor has already been turned down flat.

21 December 1967

Beatles' Christmas party at the Royal Lancaster Hotel. Everyone in fancy dress. Paul as a pearly king. John in Teddy-boy gear. At least three Charlie Chaplins. Rosalind in awe at the famous faces: 'Is that one of the Rolling Stones?'

26 December 1967

Boxing Day. Back at 3 a.m. from Simon Napier-Bell's Christmas party, Rosalind so exhausted that I almost have to carry her over the threshold. Later watch the Beatles film – now called *Magical Mystery Tour* – on BBC2. Generally agreed to be a disaster. No plot or structure to speak of. 'Jokes' horribly laboured. The boys barely appear, but there is a second or so when the camera lingers on Rosalind and me hand-in-hand on the back seat of the coach. 'Just think,' she says. 'Whenever anyone watches that movie in fifty years' time, they'll wonder who those two people are.'

Egerton Gardens Mews dissolving into shadow. A Rolls-Royce with what looks an ambassadorial pennant comes to fetch Mrs Manningham. R slightly sorrowful. I gather that this is the first Christmas she's ever spent away from the family hearth and snake-oil salesman Al.

'What happens in Phoenix at Christmas?'

'It's kind of weird. You know, we sing songs about chestnuts roasting on an open fire and then go out for a picnic.'

Happiness is turning me superstitious. Today I snipped an advert out of the newspaper and sent £20 to the Biafran orphans simply as a hedge against fate. Anything to stop God pulling the rug away from under my feet. Anything at all.

All through the later 1960s the letters from the old man came tumbling in. There was no pattern to their despatch – three in a month might be followed by none in a year – and no harmony to their tone. The information they conveyed could be flatly specific ('This is to inform you that Maurice Du Pont and Daphne Zygo are now resident at 24a Main Street, Pepin, Wisconsin') or whimsical to the point of delusion ('Dear Son, I am writing this – literally – on top of old Smokie . . .'). What united them was the bright, purposeful and increasingly manic scent of a mind stretching out to the end of its tether. That, and – as time went on – an odd and, to me, infinitely troubling hint of solicitude.

21 January 1968

Dear Son,

How pitilessly shines the noonday sun here in Nevada! How bleak the vista of endless rock and sand! A line to assure me of your health and happiness would be welcome . . .

19 November 1968

Dear Son,

Here in the great open spaces of the Panhandle I think of you often, wonder about your world and the triumphant march of your progress through it . . .

February 1969

I MAURICE CHESAPEAKE ALBUQUERQUE SEATTLE DU PONT LET IT BE KNOWN THAT I SEND MY SON MY LOVE

If the letter carried an address I wrote back to it, but there was never any indication that the replies had got through. No phone number quoted ever worked. Once, around the time of the Moon landings, I paid a private detective $2000 to spend a month trying to track him down. He got nowhere, unless you count an uninhabited shack on the shores of Lake Erie in which it was believed that the old man and his blushing consort had holed up for a few nights six months before. No federal authority knew anything about him; no bank ever seemed to have handled his cheques; no veterans' association had him on their roster. Like a pebble rolling off the highway he had slipped out of the known world into a secret space on its thorny margin, haunting me with his messages about the Nevada desert, the wide Texas Panhandle and the long-lost son to whom he sent his love.

[59]AGAMEMNON'S MIGHTY SWORD (*DANGERFIELD-HALLIWELL*)

Dangerfield – multi-tracked vocals, guitar, **Halliwell** – lead guitar, backing vocals, **Hamilton** – bass, backing vocals, **Shields** – drums, percussion, cowbell.

Recorded: 17 August 1967, Townhouse Studios; 19 August 1967, Townhouse Studios. Producer Shel Talmy

Widely – and justifiably – regarded as the overture to the Helium Kids' 'heavy' phase – an obsession with tonal dynamics that lasted as least as far as 1974's *Glorfindel* – the origins of this piece of highly amplified white blues rock can be dated to the February 1966 demos that were eventually to realise *Smiley Daze*. First envisaged as a keyboard piece (and in this primitive version available on the *Amen Corner* bootleg recordings), written by Shankley-Walker and already indebted to the staccato style then being pioneered by the Small Faces' Ian McLagan, *sans* middle eight and indeed most of the *sturm und drang* guitar effects added to the final recording, it appears to have lain in the can for nearly eighteen months, until rehearsals for a projected follow-up to *Paisley Patterns* had reached an advanced stage. At this point, with Shankley-Walker's status in the group in doubt – he was effectively sacked in August 1967, although this fact was not immediately communicated to the press – the track was apparently re-recorded in a more conventional rock styling, only the unusual C sharp key hinting at the original concept. Shankley-Walker's name is absent from the writing credits. He was certainly not present at the mid-August sessions – these took place shortly before his death – and may not even have known that they were scheduled.

Marked by Hamilton's distinctive walking bass – achieved using the upper register of a newly acquired Rickenbacker model – 'Agamemnon's Mighty Sword', despite its reliance on what were to become standard rock clichés, is a thoroughly idiosyncratic piece of work, and in its way a snapshot of the changing musical styles of 1967/8. Predicated on the customary 4/4 pattern, it swerves unexpectedly into 3/8 at 2.19 with any technical deficiencies overcome by the sheer vigour of the playing and the importation of several reverse tape-loops which, according to Halliwell (not always a reliable witness), consisted of Dangerfield and himself reciting The Lord's Prayer. Halliwell's solo at 3.23 is, too, an innovation for its time – not reverbed and multi-tracked according to the prevailing orthodoxy, but using a carillon style of descending chromatic scales. Despite a certain roughness to its edges (see Hamilton's fluffed bass notes at 1.03 and 2.14) the dynamism of the finished piece, though anticipating much of the sonic overkill of the later 1960s, makes it sound closer in spirit to a mid-period Beatles number – something McCartney acknowledged. In a December 1967 interview for *Rolling Stone*, a month after the track had reached No. 4 on the UK singles chart, he picked out 'Agamemnon' as 'a really superior piece of writing, something a lot of people could learn from if they wanted'.

Ian Macdonald, *The Helium Kids in the
Studio: A Song Chronology*, 1991

... But there were other acts, some of them from way down the sixties pecking order, who were poised to take advantage of the radically mutable conditions of the decade's end, the shift from single to album, the arrival of a more serious and appreciably more affluent 'adult' audience – that is, people in their mid-twenties rather than their late teens – and the massively inflated commercial rewards that were now available for playing live. The Helium Kids, for example, had been a rather ridiculous Flower Pop band, who enjoyed dressing up in kaftans and loon pants, until, late in 1967, in circumstances so murky that rock historians still puzzle themselves over the precise degree of skul-duggery and subterfuge involved, they were hoovered up by the legendary pop Svengali Don Shard. Shard, a bully, a braggart and a crook, who once persuaded another of the groups on his roster to sign away their US copyrights to a company he owned himself, was also a visionary, who saw that the future lay in playing to audiences in the newly built amphitheatres of the American Midwest rather than to a few hundred students in some campus sports hall in the English Midlands. He saw, too, that this emerging demographic required a new kind of music – more strident, less nuanced and made possible by new developments in amplification and stage technology.

The Helium Kids were hardly promising material for this kind of experiment. Their keyboard player had recently died in a drowning accident; their lead singer was a deeply unpleasant narcissist who was already displaying an unhealthy fascination with the occult; and their bass player barely spoke. What they needed, Shard deduced, who had worked earlier miracles in this line, was a *mystique*, some indefinable something that would set them apart from the swirly psychedelia merchants and the Age of Aquarians who were clogging up the charts at the end of 1967 and the beginning of 1968. He achieved this desirable end by pursuing a strategy that would become standard in the industry five years later, but here in the era of *Disraeli Gears* and *The White Album* – then being embarked upon at Abbey Road – was startlingly innovative. Rather than propelling them further into the glare of public scrutiny, he decided to withdraw them from it altogether. The devious buck-chasing of the mid-sixties had already made him a rich man, so he could afford to cancel their contract with Decca – a backward-looking label who were never going to appreciate the possibilities of rock's next conceptual forward leap – and underwrite an extended period of studio time while they got to work on a new record that was going to be much less winsome and much more heavy than anything they'd done in the past. When the tapes were finally available he had the clout and the bargaining skills to go to the major record companies and demand big advances. The £15,000 the Kids split between themselves early in 1968 – they had a virtuoso guitarist in by this time to replace the dead organ player – gave them each a lump sum equivalent to about twice the annual wage of the average UK clerical worker.

But this was only the start of Shard's transformation of the group's fortunes. By the late 1960s he had them near-permanently on tour in America, with a New York office making sure that they weren't able to stray too far from the path he'd mapped out for them. He also had them up their work rate, booking studio time to fill in gaps between the tour dates and ensuring that there was a constant stream of new product. No one was going to complain, because the money flowed in:

by 1971 the Kids were reported to be the third-largest grossing live act in the US behind Led Zeppelin and domestic contenders Grand Funk Railroad. When new albums appeared they were promoted less through the traditional channels of interviews and press pageants than by leaking advance tracks to sympathetic radio jocks. A *Rolling Stone* journalist who asked for an interview around the time of Woodstock – which they typically disdained to play – was told to call back in a year. Or maybe two.

None of this, naturally, made the Helium Kids popular in the business. Shard was too scary. The band themselves were seen as aloof and rather too obviously malleable, not exactly puppets – there were occasional stabs at solo albums and the burnishing up of individual identities – but essentially monkeys dancing to the organ grinder's tune. On the other hand, the mystique was working, and the strength of the band's live reputation allowed Shard to proceed with another business upgrade that he and one or two like-minded souls, such as Zeppelin's Peter Grant, had been working on for some time. This was nothing less than the reinvention of the concert industry. In the bad old days, promoters agreed a fee for a band's services and took their profits from the difference between fee and ticket sales, a piece of arithmetic which they themselves accounted for. Shard, knowing that he had a hot property, simply informed the promoter how much he would be allowed to keep out of the total proceeds. There was no need for anything much in the way of promotion – word of mouth and excited radio DJs usually meant that the tickets sold out within hours. On the other hand, Shard made sure that he kept the merchandising rights, so the profit on any T-shirts, baseball caps and facsimile guitar picks sold at the souvenir stands went straight back to the band. All this had a transformative effect on the way rock was perceived in the entertainment world between 1968 and 1973, turned it corporate, streamlined and efficient (it was no less corrupt, of course) and increased its potential from one month to the next. When Gary

Pasarolo, the lead guitarist, rang a friend in London to tell him that the Helium Kids were booked to appear at Madison Square Garden, the friend initially refused to believe him: pop groups simply didn't play at venues that big . . .

Extract from David Hepworth, *Rock's Golden Years*, 2005

PART THREE
Imperial Phases

Take me on a roller-coaster, take me on an airplane ride . . .

11. STATION TO STATION

Who is this that wakes from slumber
Here in Abaddon's blackened pit?
Mr Crowley, I see your features
Grinning through the visor's slit.

'Who is This that
Wakes from Slumber?'

'I'm thinking that you might like me to leave you some supper,' said
Selma, the black help, which was what you called young women of
Afro-Caribbean extraction who came in to clean three mornings a
week here on the eastern seaboard in the fall of 1971, especially if,
like Selma, they had a degree in comparative literature from a
liberal arts college in Pennsylvania. 'A fish pie maybe, or a clam
chow*dah*.'

Outside, limpid early morning sun fell across the squirrel-haunted
lawn and its drift of maple leaves. 'Has Ros . . . Has Mrs Du Pont said
anything about that?'

'Mrs Du Pont has not so far communicated with me, sir.' Of all
Selma's attributes, her courtesy was the most ominous. 'All I can say
from my inspection of the refrigerator is that you're all out of liquor.
You want me to fetch in some more?'

'That would be great.' I was always highly enthusiastic around Selma, far more enthusiastic than the relationship between us ever warranted. 'There's money on the kitchen table.'

'Sure. I saw it when I came in,' said Selma, who despite being an inch under six feet, high-heeled and looking like one of the high-fashion Aphrodites you saw modelling in the Fifth Avenue clothes stores, was not above a little atavistic field-hand banter. As the light sparkled through the sitting-room window, Selma gave me one of her mystifying half-smiles, which I always took to mean that as I was English she forgave me for at least some of the indignities visited on her race in the past quarter-millennium, and made a lightning flounce of a half-turn which revealed the copy of Fred Exley's *A Fan's Notes* sticking out of the pocket of her overalls. I passed reluctantly on into the hallway, with its clutter of album covers and golf clubs, wicker baskets and realtors' brochures, and up the over-carpeted staircase to the master bedroom where, even now, at 8.15 on a Monday morning, after a shakedown that had begun at nine on the previous night, Rosalind still lay feigning sleep.

Westchester County, Connecticut in the fall of 1971. The Richard Yates country, I later discovered, full of regular, or sometimes painfully irregular, guys called Pete and Shep and Arnie in seersucker suits or plaid lumberjack shirts for homely weekend wear winding down the windows of their Chrysler Saloons and short-finned Pontiacs to say hi and howdy and how-you-doing, of earnest provincial Democrats, heads down over the barbecue griddles and the picnic hotplates as they discussed whether McGovern had the balls – this was not the word they used in front of their wives, preferring instead 'gumption' or 'spunk' – to take on Nixon next year, of flower-arranging sororities and amateur theatre groups (Yates had been bang right about that) and Vassar-educated housewives driven mad with ennui going out of their heads on Valium, codeine, Librium (for the real space-cases) or anything else they could lay their claws on. Up in the master bedroom the curtains which I had tentatively opened at 7.15 had been ostentatiously pulled shut again and the gleams of light bouncing off the dressing table gave it the look of a vast aquarium tank, as if there were monstrous fish lurking in shoals by the wardrobe alongside white-armed sirens munching on the bones of drowned mariners. In the silence, otherwise broken only by the noise of the squirrels rampaging over the roof, I could hear Rosalind breathing – that overpitched, formal breath, long known to me now, of one who simulates slumber to make a moral point.

'Are you OK, honey?'

There was a long pause, long enough for one of the great battles of the ancient world to shift decisively to one side, Ozymandias be toppled from his throne, a Nobel laureate begin on some new and vital work. 'What time is it?'

'Time I left for the train.' Down in the kitchen, spoon in one hand and Exley's novel in the other, Selma would be breakfasting off a plate of stewed apples and raisins, as the public radio channel pulsed edifyingly on at her side. 'Can you make it to the party tonight?'

'What party is that?' Rosalind wrote down all our engagements on a flowery wallchart and committed them to memory the day they were received.

'The one A&M are throwing for Karen Carpenter.'

The body in the bed stirred in irritation. 'Nicky, honey, you *know* Monday is my art appreciation class . . .' The art appreciation class, at which the Vassar pill-poppers predominated, met at a nearby community centre, or sometimes in its members' homes, where martinis could be more conveniently provided, and judging by the literature that came home with them had got stuck at pointillism. 'Oh God,' she said suddenly, all thought of Sisley, Seurat and Bonnard gone. 'I meant to tell you. Momma called last night.'

The squirrels were still foraging over the roof. They were resourceful animals, hard to subdue. 'What did Momma have to say?'

'She's not too good. She says Aunt Wilma's out to get her. She says Aunt Wilma's putting poison in her coffee.'

The senior Duchesnes drifted in and out of our lives, like smoke blowing from a motorway pile-up. Al, the Reagan big-shot, Scorpion Al the Phoenix grifter, I hadn't seen in months. The terrifying pretence that Lucille was a perfectly ordinary middle-aged woman, if somewhat troubled by nerves, who enjoyed spending time with her sisters in various out-of-the-way locations, was still being strenuously kept up.

'I have to go,' I said. Stefano would already be at the office. Over at the Rockefeller Plaza Hotel they would be setting up for the press conference. Cabs would be in transit, shrimp mayonnaise in preparation. 'I'm sorry about last night.'

'So am I.'

The least you could say about the bedroom, I thought, as I gratefully quitted it, eyes now acclimatised to the murky light, was that it didn't look as if a major marital disagreement had taken place in it a dozen hours ago. The displaced objects had all been returned to their plinths and arbours. The only sign of upset was the smashed ashtray jammed in the doorframe. The absurd thing was that I could barely remember what had been argued about. On the other hand, it undoubtedly had something to do with that curious hinterland – half geographic, half spiritual – in which we found ourselves moving: the guy who travelled into New York each day to party with the longhairs in the music business, but spent his weekends in out-of-town bourgeois slumber; the woman who supported him in this questionable endeavour but never missed out on a charity bake-in. By rights we should have been living in a loft in the Village or an apartment in Manhattan, but Rosalind liked Westchester, liked the Sunday morning cocktail parties and the Coke and pizza orgies on child-scuffed lawns. Set against these gratifying entertainments the life she had known in Phoenix was the merest mocking preliminary. Meantime, that faint relish of bohemia she had displayed in London was entirely gone. There was no harmony between the life I lived in the office on Fiftieth Street and the life we pursued here beneath the Connecticut maples, and it showed.

I went downstairs two at a time, leaving the big fish to glide through the aquarium on their own. On Selma's transistor radio a self-confident but somehow traumatised-sounding Jewish voice that could have been Norman Mailer's was loudly declaring that the American novel was decadent, as decadent as the American political system, which was itself as decadent as the society it administered. There was a flurry of static as Selma flicked the dial – she was the kind of girl who would have strong views about Norman Mailer – and an odd, mellifluous and, I had been led to believe by the man who had engineered it, multi-tracked voice could be heard soaring above jaunty strings:

The two of us together . . . We've only just begun.

'Bye now, Selma.'

'Bye, Mistah Du Pont,' Selma said, who was clearly in one of her whitey-baiting moods. Later, I knew, she would steal up to the bedroom with a cup of coffee and a plate of cinnamon fudge-cakes and censoriously attend to whatever it was that Rosalind wanted to tell her about me.

To step onto the front porch, newspaper flapping on its topmost step, bird-life crazily erupting in the tree surround, was to experience an instant lifting of spirits: oh yes indeed. Up they went. Up and away. Smashed ashtrays; lurking fish; Big Norm – all of them hastily receded, to be replaced by the row of white-painted, timber-frame houses and manicured lawns, all the glistering promise of the day. In a dozen hours, all things being equal, I would be talking to Karen Carpenter – how weird and elfin, for all her Hymettus-honey soprano – in someone's penthouse flat. Out on the road, traffic was speeding by: Dodge Sedans and flatbed trucks, little-old-lady Fords and school buses trundling back empty to the depot. There was deep country not far away – that serene Sabbath tourist's world of endless meadows and bluebell woods. Even now we could have been settlers, hunkered down under the sheltering trees with the silence of the forest pressing up against our cabin door. Briefcase on the passenger seat, FM Radio on the dial (Grand Funk Railroad, Three Dog Night, Quicksilver Messenger Service), I urged the Chevrolet the half-mile to the station, found the last space in the lot, made the 8.42 just as they were sealing the doors and bounded along the carriages as the train juddered back into life in search of my regular berth in the restaurant car.

Here Marlboro-smoking company trusties in squashed trilby hats and button-down raincoats were telling each other that the firm was sending them to *Check*ago, that nope, Joanie wasn't none too good after her thyroidectomy and that these here computers were liable to put the adding machine concerns out of business, yes sir indeedy, and one or two of the more intellectual types were ostentatiously thumbing through the *Washington Post* and the *Hartford Sentinel*, but Christopherson, Auger and Maxwell, the boys in the poker school – they worked in lowly capacities for agencies on Madison, but basked vicariously in their employers' glory – greeted me with their customary Monday-morning fervour. They'd been playing since two stops back on the line and the Formica tabletop was already littered with dollar bills and one of the famously improvident Maxwell's IOUs, scrawled on the back of a Kleenex tissue. Sometimes I took a hand out of sheer curiosity, for the 8.42 poker school was the most exacting you ever saw, far worse than the one ceremoniously conducted in the basement of Atlantic Records on Friday nights or the closed-door, members-only hoedown at the Troubadour in Cincinnati – supposedly a mob joint – from which I once saw Don emerge victorious with a profit of $17,000. But this particular morning, as the cigarette smoke hung high above the trio of bowed heads and the train rattled through the Connecticut verdure and on into the New York suburbs and the stiffs in the raincoats talked lugubriously about how Grand Rapids was a great place for a vacation only they wuz letting in the shines something offal, and where could a man go in this country that wuz still his own, I said no, for tucked in the briefcase, amid the papers for the morning's press conference and the formal statements I had drafted for the boys, was something I especially, but especially, wanted to read.

The book, sent by registered post and bearing the frank of Don's London lawyers, had been delivered to the office on Friday morning. 'Believe me, Nick, it is the most awful piece of shit,' Stefano had prissily remarked in handing it over – he could never quite disguise the fact that he had been to Winchester – 'and we're probably going to sue the fucker. But you might just read it and tell me what you think.'

'What does Don think?' I asked, which was of course the central question in any issue regarding the Helium Kids.

'Don?' Stefano mused, in that permanently puzzled way of his. 'You know Don. He'll either ignore it or he'll have the bollocks kicked off whoever wrote it. So if you can just put down your Westchester fucking martini for an hour or so come Sunday afternoon' – it was a source of endless amusement to the people in the office that I lived in Connecticut – 'we'd all be ever so much obliged.'

The poker school was winding down now. Dollar bills were being regretfully stowed away in wallets, stray cards scooped negligently up into the pack. The train rumbled on, keeling over so far onto one side that it seemed to risk coming off the track, and then righted itself to surge through a stretch of market gardens, factory car parks that lay in the shadow of giant cooling towers, then long, low lakes with rich autumnal fog hanging over their furthermost shores. Even now, two years since I had come here, there was still something terrifying about American landscapes: the suburban sprawls that went on for twenty miles; the dazzling shifts in alignment and perspective; the alien throng. The book, I realised – it was called *Death of a Pop Star* and had

Florian's face peering from the cover, more greenish and seahorse-like
than ever – did not belong here. It was a memento of older days, afternoons in English gardens, summer sun, Ainslie's office in Berwick
Street, people who even now seemed to be fading from memory,
ghosts on the edge of time. Billed as a record of the last month of
Florian's life, with occasional forays backwards, it had not, so far, told
me very much that I didn't already know. There were some extracts
from a telegraphic diary Florian had kept (one of the entries brought
me up with a start, for it read *Saw Nick Du Pont, who I always like, in
Goodge Street*), a hint that the week before his death had been clouded
by a dispute with a builder to whom he either owed, or was owed,
money, details of the absolutely phenomenal amount of drugs he had
managed to consume in the summer of 1967. Uppers and downers,
leapers and creepers, barbiturates and antidepressants – Florian had
cheerfully, or perhaps not so cheerfully, swallowed them all.

As for the rest, a skim through the index (*'Dangerfield, Garth . . .
contemptuous attitude to F.S.-W. . . . belittles musical contributions of
F.S.-W. . . . Sabotages Lowrey organ of F.S.-W. . . . Pours beer over head of
F.S.-W. . . .*) confirmed that Garth was the villain of the piece. Dale,
Florian seemed rather to have liked. There were some wounding
remarks about Keith's dimness. For all the hypothesising about
Florian's last night on earth, it was difficult not to believe that the
version of events peddled at the time hadn't nailed the case. There had
been some kind of impromptu party at the farmhouse in Sussex, from
which the guests had gradually trooped away, leaving only the host
and a girl called Miggie (a famous figure around sixties Soho, who
was supposed to like having fried eggs eaten off her stomach). It was,
extant meteorological records insist, a warmish evening. Florian, who
had had a colossal amount to drink, depressed by the events of the
past fortnight and with all manner of pharmaceuticals sizzling in his
bloodstream, had gone for a late-night dip and passed out in the
water. There Miggie, who by her own account had fallen asleep on the

sofa, had discovered him three hours later. The only mystery concerned a visitor who might, Miggie thought, have been on the premises shortly before she lost consciousness but who was certainly not there when she came round. A neighbour had heard a car departing at speed in the small hours. There was a faint suspicion – so faint as to be well-nigh buried in a riot of conditional clauses – that this hurtling escapee might have been Garth.

Outside the windows there were tenement houses, parking lots, asphalt sports pitches all looming sharply into focus as the train stuttered into Grand Central Station. Florian has been dead four years. A whole lot has happened in that time. The Beatles have split. Lennon has gone off to make a fool of himself with Kamikaze Kate, the Yellow Peril. The Stones are in narcotic tax exile somewhere. Hendrix is dead, along with Brian Jones, Janis Joplin and countless lesser lights whose names have already been forgotten. Also dead, according to *Rolling Stone*, is the quintessential spirit of the sixties, whatever that is. Meanwhile, the thirteen-year-olds to whom record companies sold singles in 1966 have given way to their elder brothers and sisters, to whom record companies are now selling, and in greater quantities, vastly more lucrative and 'serious' albums. There is talk of 'mature markets' and 'popular art'. The big things right now are heavy rock – Led Zeppelin are making a fortune on the tour circuit – and wispily importuning singer-songwriters, although England has lately broken out in a distressing rash of bubblegum bands in sequin suits and braces. The crowds are getting bigger and, thanks to Mr Marshall, the amplification louder, and one of the biggest things of all right now, and right here, are the Helium Kids. You don't believe me? It is, everyone agrees – let us be clear about this – *amazing* what Don does with the Kids, how he fattens up their sound, cannily replaces keyboard-playing Florian with another guitar-player and finesses a deal with EMI. *Cabinet of Curiosities* sells three million copies worldwide, and the one after twice that. The big money, Don decides, is in America, and so, apart from the odd, preening ramble around Blighty, this is where the Kids spend most of their time. Late in 1970 they play three sold-out nights at Madison Square Garden. I happen to be in the same room as Gary, the new guitarist, when he phones home to tell a friend what's going down and also to supply the juicy tidbit that there are approximately three dozen women, ages ranging from fourteen to fifty, queuing moistly beyond the stage door from which this ever-salacious chancer can take his pick. The friend, a veteran of those be-suited sixties beat combos, of playing fifth on the bill at the Ipswich Gaumont on a Sunday night in February, of the classified pages of the *New Musical Express* ('bassist, good-looking, own amp, seeks to expand repertoire in hot new act. Cabaret no objection'), doesn't believe him.

How has Don done this? Or rather, what has Don done? (Naturally, mistakes have been made. We miss out on Woodstock for the simple reason that the $15,000 handed out to the Who is, in Don's humble opinion, chicken-feed.) These are questions that, cruising noncha-lantly into some mic-festooned press conference or poring over the *Billboard* charts, in whose lower reaches *Low Blows in High Times* still intermittently resurfaces eighteen months after its release, I frequently ask myself. Part of it, naturally, is sheer situational happenstance. The world for some reason wants bands of English longhairs playing heavily amplified blues rock with psychedelic garnishes in stadia newly built for the purpose all across America, and the Helium Kids fit the bill. Another part of it, though, lies in managerial design, in the converting of these five – let us be honest – not terribly talented or good-looking or even averagely personable young people into a collec-tive entity greater than the sum of its individual parts, and by throw-ing the traditional processes of this conversion into reverse. It is a fact, for example, that being the Helium Kids' publicist is tantamount to being their *non*-publicist or in some cases even their *anti*-publicist, in keeping them out of the papers as much as keeping them in. Don doesn't like journalists, infallibly stigmatised as 'nosy cunts'. Neither does he like TV interviews, colour supplement profiles or music magazine 'Meet the Stars' features. In fact, he abhors pretty much all the paraphernalia with which pop careers are customarily bedecked. What he does like, on the other hand, is mystery, subterfuge, collusion, unheralded announcements of one-off concerts on syndicated college radio shows, clamorous pre-dawn queues outside record stores and double lines of cops holding back the ticketless tide. The songs, meanwhile, are a mixture of tight, riffy little shuffles and extended orgies of bombast, with frequent mention of Aleister Crowley, Eliphas Levi and the sacrificing of goats. On the fall 1970 tour (seventeen states, thirty-one concerts, takings estimated at $3 million gross), the National Guard has to be called out in Oklahoma City and three of the gigs descend into riot, after which Don, disdaining suggestions that the band's onstage taunting of their audience may be responsible, sues the promoters for providing inadequate security. He is quite a genius in his way.

And I, too, have my life transformed. I have it transformed professionally, personally and, I fear, perhaps even morally. I abandon old ways and learn new tricks. I discover, for example, that the record pluggers on the FM stations are considerably more important than Mr Ralph J. Gleason of *Rolling Stone*, and I deduce that a press conference at which the band fails to show is sometimes more effective than one at which they boozily turn up. I become adept at circulating outrageous rumours, which it is then my painful duty to deny, at getting compromising photographs suppressed, at having bail money arrive in the nick of time, at smoothing things down or bristling things up as the situation demands. In my way, around my circle, among my *convives*, I am a famous figure. All the major-league publicists have their nicknames. Zeppelin's hobbity chancer B. P. Fallon's is 'Beep'. Mine, for some reason, is 'Nickola'. Is this because it rhymes with 'payola'? I don't care to ask.

It is the fall of 1971, and I have been legally resident here – this is down to the old man and my dual nationality – for two years. I stare from the windows of private jets as they head out over the silent, night-girt ocean and the band stir uneasily in their pharma dreams. I mingle discreetly among the raucous crowds at stadium concerts, with the upper-register bass notes thumping in my chest like an extra heartbeat. I prowl through white-painted and magnolia-scented California mansions in the dense half-hour before dawn, making sure that everybody is happy, well accommodated and, most important of all, alive. North Park seems very far away now, quite lost and submerged in the shiny, expedient universe that has grown up to replace it. I earn £8000 a year in English money, I have a timber-frame house in Westchester, Connecticut, and a wife who lies miserably in bed most days until twelve and whose bedroom carpet is patterned with smashed glass.

At Grand Central the poker school reluctantly dispersed to their offices on Madison. I bought a take-away coffee in a Styrofoam cup and, skinny tie flip-flapping in the wind, headed east along Fiftieth to the Rockefeller Plaza. Here, three years before, from a vantage point high up in the RCA building, Stefano claimed to have watched Jefferson Airplane give their celebrated concert on the roof of the Schuyler Hotel. 'You never saw anything like it, man. They were so stoned they could barely play. That chick singer they have could hardly stand up. I stuck my head out of the window and shouted: "Turn off that fucking hippy crap."' There was no hippy crap in New York now, dear me no. Over to the south-west, a helicopter was descending like a metallic dragonfly onto the Pan-Am building. To right and left, girls who looked like Edie Sedgwick and Jane Fonda, with swept-back hair, bolero jackets and stack-heel shoes, were hurrying by, and the breeze blowing in off the Hudson beat against the calves of my suit pants.

Shard Enterprises' office was halfway up a small block in the Plaza's considerable shadow. The only exterior clue as to the business conducted inside was a framed gold disc hanging up in the lobby. Otherwise we could have been dealing in fertiliser or marine insurance. There were five of us on the strength: Stefano and his assistant Jerry, Bernie the accountant, and a deeply unprepossessing girl called Angie who staffed the reception desk. As I muscled my way through the unresisting plate-glass door, inched past the couple of hundred shiny tour programmes that someone had dumped in a heap by the Coke dispenser (*Shard Enterprises in association with Platinum Productions Inc. presents* THE HELIUM KIDS: SAVOY BROWN: JO JO GUNNE – FALL TOUR '71) and registered the fact that someone had also dropped what looked like several lumps of cannabis resin on the luxuriant ochre carpet, she came slinking out from behind her counter, snaggle teeth gleaming, corkscrew-curled head tilted warily on one side.

'Nicky. Nickola. You want a 'lude?'

'No thanks, Angie.'

'Thought you might need one on a day like today.' She gave an impossibly foxy leer, far worse than the way people leered in films or on the TV. 'You want me to suck your dick?'

'Nor that either, actually.'

There were people, inside the office and outside it, who said that Angie could not possibly be as slovenly, as sexually voracious and as impulsively confiding as she appeared, and that the way she comported herself here on the reception desk in her tight little jackets and buck-skin-fringed maxi-skirts was simply an ingenious piece of camou-flage. On the other hand, there were those who urged that Angie was exactly what she implied she was, an altogether exceptional specimen of her kind, doling out sexual favours wherever and whenever she wanted to. All this raised the thought that there must surely be people, breezily importuned in the ochre-carpeted lobby, who were incapable of resisting these overtures, who said yes, had themselves shanghaied off to empty offices and wardrobes and were set energetically to work beneath Angie's hard grey eyes. In other respects, she was a dutiful girl who went home every night to her mother in Yonkers and had once stopped the president of Elektra Records from entering the premises on the plausible grounds that he 'looked like some fucking bum off the street'.

'What on earth's that noise?'

'Oh that? I guess it's Stefano bawling someone out on the phone . . . Hey, you better go in there, actually. He said he wanted to see you as soon as you came in.'

The shouting was getting louder by the moment. 'Even when he's bawling someone out on the phone?'

'I guess you better had.' Angie's rare moments of animation tended to come when she was being ordered around by Stefano. 'Hey Nicholas . . .' As I turned towards her, several things happened at once: a small vial of pills tumbled out of Angie's hand onto the carpet; a motorcycle messenger with an outsize parcel for signature came striding through the plate-glass doors; and several astonishingly loud noises, which I recognised as the sound of Stefano hurling the telephone against the door of his office, burst like a series of gunshots through the air. Angie turned out to be equal to them all. In what seemed like a single extended movement, she swept the pill bottle up off the floor in such a way as to prevent me seeing its contents, plucked a felt-tip out of her jacket pocket and scrawled her name incomprehensibly on the message pad, dumped the parcel on the desk and shrugged her shoulders.

'Jeez. Last time Stefano did that he pulled a fuckin' fingernail . . . The thing is, Nick, do you believe in alien life-forms?'

'What kind? Little green men? All that Roswell stuff? Area 51?'

'Not them. No. I mean, do you think there are actually extra-terrestrials, uh, living among us only we don't know who they are?'

'It doesn't sound very likely.'

'Only I read this article in the *National Enquirer* about a guy they found dead on the interstate run over by this truck or something, and when they cut him up for the autopsy or whatever there were a dozen, you know, egg sacs growing in his lungs.'

Down along the corridor, past the hutch where meek, whey-faced Bernie sat opening the morning's mail, the noise had started up again. Let no one tell you that those Bakelite telephones weren't sturdily made. Still bawling into a receiver that seemed to have lost one of its earpieces, weighing up the cradle in his other hand as if it were a bowling ball, Stefano waved me inside.

'... And I'm telling you that when we touch down in Denver there will be six limos waiting at the airport. One each for individual members of the band and one for me and my immediate entourage ... That's right, *entourage*. If you don't know what it means, look it up in the fucking dictionary. The vehicle sent to collect Mr Dangerfield is to have a Caucasian driver ... No, he doesn't have anything against black people. He is *superstitious*, and I surely hope you appreciate the distinction ... The limousines will take us to the Intercontinental Hotel for 7.30. Should we arrive later than the stated time, then I add $1000 per ten-minute delay to the expenses sheet ... I don't care if they're digging up the freeway. I don't care if you have to hire a fucking helicopter. I don't care, Chip, or Shit, or Cleatus, or whatever your fucking name is, if we never play Denver again, because the fact is there are easier ways of making money. Now, do I make myself clear, Chip, old buddy, old pal, you old Colorado *cunt*, do I make myself clear?'

Stefano's voice was slowing down now, which wasn't necessarily a good sign. Of all the different kinds of people he enjoyed insulting over the phone, the category he liked best was promoters.

'And rest assured, Chip,' he concluded, 'that if any of the arrangements fail to match up to my own or my clients' expectations of them, if a single flunkey should fail to genuflect when one of us walks by, if a single champagne flute should be missing from the tray with which I expect you to greet us on our return from the gig, then I will personally hang you up by your boots from a hook in the hotel foyer and set about you with a tyre-iron.'

There were those – mostly outside the office – who maintained that, like Angie in her tenancy of the reception desk, Stefano's telephone manner was pretty much a performance, and that the people at the other end of the receiver played up to and even took pleasure in it. Alternatively, there were others – I was one of them – who believed that when he threatened to hang someone up by his heels or remove their teeth molar by molar with a pair of pliers, he meant every word he said. He was a tall, burly, bulb-headed man in his early thirties, with dark tufts of hair sprouting from the backs of his hands who could happily have played a werewolf in a film alongside Lon Chaney Jr. The strain of constantly having to conceal things – his English accent, his intelligence and very often his whereabouts – left him slightly exhausted and liable to forget himself. He had once confessed to me that he had spent the night in a police cell in Wisconsin reading a novel by William Styron.

'Who was that on the phone?'

'I don't know.' Stefano – the sign on whose desk read 'Steven Bennington-Smyth' – stared at the shattered equipment with a slightly forlorn air. Outside, a brace of police helicopters chased each other through pale, unwelcoming sky. 'Some promoter or other.' He was calming down now, and remembering, with pleasure, both that he liked me (reasons stated varying from being good at my job to 'not being like these American cunts') and that he had tasks to hand that would seriously inconvenience me in their doing. 'Look, when you see Angie ask her if she's got any Tuinal.'

'Why do you want to go to sleep?'

'They're not for now, you cunt,' Stefano said, straightforwardly affable again. 'Need them for the tour. Anyway, first things first. Good work on the press pack and the tour programme. I even had that fucking Garth on the phone telling me he liked it.'

'He's always telling me to concentrate on his intellectual side.'

'Frightful load of bollocks, those books he pretends to read . . . Just one thing, though' – Stefano prided himself on his grasp of detail – 'why did you say Keith was looking forward to going back to Philadelphia?'

'There's a factory just outside manufactures die-cast aero-models. He always goes to see it.'

Of all the Helium Kids, the one Stefano had the most trouble keeping his temper with was Keith. 'Doesn't it worry you,' he had once asked, 'that a bloke who might think himself lucky being paid to pick up litter in the street is earning two hundred thousand a year banging a fucking drum?'

'Well, never mind that,' he said now. 'How many have we got coming this morning?'

'About thirty. Angie's hired some girls from an agency to come and fill the rest of the seats, and there'll be more outside. Where is everybody at the moment?'

Stefano looked at his watch with the same forlorn expression that he had stared at the smashed telephone. Music people on the point of being introduced to him for the first time, and scared out of their wits at the prospect, often asked what he was 'like', and the answer was, once the willed high spirits and the company raucousness had been stripped away, an essentially comfortless man. You suspected that deep in his werewolf's heart he wanted to be on a planet far away from the Helium Kids and their impossible demands, from Don's telegrams and the news desk of *Rolling Stone*, talking of abstract things.

'Don?' Stefano's brow furrowed over, like a strip of corrugated cardboard, as if this information had been laboriously memorised by rote. 'Don's at the Hilton meeting a gentleman called Mr Alfonso

Castiglione, whose name may suggest to you the nature of the organisation he represents. Don't even dream of telling him I told you.
Correction. Don't even dream of having that dream where you tell
him. But he'll be there. Don,' said Stefano impressively, strewing
phantom capitals as he went, 'Has Never Missed A Press Conference.
There's cabs picking up the boys just about now from whichever
scum-topped goldfish bowl Angie booked them into.'

'We'd better be off.'

'Yeah, yeah. Hang on. Hang on. Was something else that I . . . I
mean . . . What did you think of that fucking book they sent over?'

'I can't see that's it going to do any damage.'

'That's what I thought. All water under the bridge, isn't it?' Stefano
said with perhaps slightly less assurance than he intended. 'And
nobody there except some fucking tart who's Mandied out of her
head and wakes up to find lover boy drowned in the cosmic soup. You
think Garth had anything to do with it?'

'Doesn't seem very likely.'

'And neither did the Allman Brothers getting a recording contract,
but they did all the same. The thing is, in normal circumstances Garth
would be jumping up and down like a six-year-old robbed of his
pocket money. But I've not heard a word out of him. Not one.'

We were out in the corridor now, Stefano bent and round-shoul-
dered, making curious tugging notions with his brawny forearms as if
he were threshing corn or operating a hawser on an antique sailboat.
'Hang on,' he said, throwing open a door. 'Need to talk to Bern.'

Bernie's mild chipmunk face bobbed up from behind his hedge of
box-files. 'What is it, Stef?'

'How much were you aiming to bill that character in Denver for
limo hire?'

'I'll have to check. Don't we usually say a hundred dollars a
vehicle?'

'Well, double it. No, triple it. And no fucking about.'

'Always happy to help, Stef.'

Back at reception I warily negotiated Stefano's medicinal require-ments. 'Tuinal, huh?' Angie mused – she was always more circumspect when the contents of her desktop pharmacopeia were in question. 'Well, that's going to cost the fucker. What's he want them all for?'

'To get through the tour, he says.'

'He'll need more than Tuinal.' Angie's pocked goblin face tilted crazily. The whites of her eyes were a kind of peach colour. 'That's twenty dollars, tell him.'

Gradually, like some Viking raiding party, some provender-toting settler band, some hawk-eyed slaver's snatch-squad, the press confer-ence cortege assembled in the foyer – Stefano ape-like and uncom-fortable in his dark suit; Jerry, his deferential assistant, weighed down by half-a-dozen bottles of Dom Perignon in a portable cooler; yours truly with the press packs in a cardboard box; Angie clutching the belt of her leopardskin coat tight over her parched yet twitching flanks.

'Have the boys been told what to say if anyone asks about the free concert in Louisiana?'

'They've been told to keep their fucking traps shut … Actually,' Stefano said, with slightly more emollience, or slightly less contempt, 'the official line is that we're working to … uh, resolve the consider-able logistical difficulties that threaten to obstruct the actualisation of this worthy project. Which is another way of saying Over My Dead Body.'

Outside on Fiftieth the mid-morning traffic went sailing by. The sky was oozing yellow streaks, as if a very pale egg yolk had been dragged across it and then left to congeal. The police helicopters had disappeared to tail bootleggers in the Bowery or pursue escaping speedboats down the Hudson. 'Are you fucking mad?' Stefano demanded, when I attempted to stroll off along the sidewalk, and I remembered that this was a man who had once summoned a cab to ferry him from one side of a Manhattan street to the other. And so we stood in a defiant, counter-cultural elitists' huddle on the gum-flecked pavement as the fur-coated, poodle-walking women flounced by – the big man straightening up now from his orang-utan shamble; the smaller man at his side brisk and quizzical and looking – I sometimes flattered myself in those days – not unlike Peter Fonda in *Easy Rider*, Jerry cowed and silent; Angie capering between us like some malevolent sprite from the depths of the woods intent on sowing poison in the hedgerows – waiting for the limo that would take us the 300 yards to the Plaza Hotel, where the Helium Kids would proudly inaugurate their seventh US tour, and whose considerable expense would probably be charged up to the record company or the promoter in Texas or, as Stefano had once put it, any other fucker who might conceivably be browbeaten into paying for it.

Press conferences. Press conferences. Press conferences in luxury yachts out on the Hudson; in Tiffany's breakfast hall; on a mountain in the Adirondacks, whose 'vibes' a Native American who had momentarily attracted Garth's patronage had commended; on a Pullman coach, once, whirring through the Dakota Hills with the cocktail waitresses dressed as Calamity Jane and assorted bordello babes. Three years into the game, this kind of thing was losing its savour. Here in the ballroom of the Plaza Hotel, podium-bound, aloof and stony-faced before the throng of admiring journalists, the boys marked time. The three years had not, it had to be acknowledged, done them any favours. They looked grey and vampiric, creatures of the shadows massively discountenanced by the dazzle of light and the popping cameras, their spirits drained, their choreography gone. Sometimes all five of them would try to answer a question at the same time; sometimes there was an uneasy collective silence. Don, a late arrival from his meeting with Mr Castiglione, stood at the back, hands twitching, as if only deep reservoirs of self-possession hindered him from leaping on stage and conducting the business himself. Stefano

and I lurked to one side, poised to intervene if anyone veered dangerously off limits. The questions, too, had lost their zing.

JOURNALIST: Garth. I just wondered how your writing was going
at the moment. Is it, uh, progressing?

GARTH: Yeah. It's, uh, doing all right. Really, no, it is ... sort of ... I
mean, you know this cat W. H. Auden? I've been really, uh, getting
off on some of his stuff, and it's ... y'know ... having, uh, a beneficial effect.

('Is he on something?' Stefano demanded, far too loudly for
comfort, while this was going on. 'I bloody told him he had to
shape up for this one.')

JOURNALIST: Gary. You said a couple of years ago that it was an
interesting technical challenge adapting your style to the rest of the
band. Do you think you've settled in?

GARY: Yes.

JOURNALIST: Anything to add to that?

GARY: No.

(Gary, by the way, was a cherubic twenty-two-year-old guitar
virtuoso recruited three years previously from a moribund blues
combo whose manager owed Don money. His ambition, so far
unrealised, was to see his substantial contribution to the Helium
Kids' repertoire dignified by the courtesy of a songwriting credit,
but he was a polite boy and rather overawed by the company he
kept.)

JOURNALIST: Gary. Will you be writing any songs for the new
album?

GARY (*looks wildly at Stefano: latter shakes his head*): I'm quite happy
just playing my guitar, thanks.

DALE: I'd just like to say that we really value Gary's input, OK?

GARTH (*sardonically*): Yeah, let's hear for Gary.

JOURNALIST: Could I ask Keith if he's made any good kits lately?

GARTH: Go on Keith, mate.

KEITH: Well, last week I made an Avro 504 trainer. And then one of those Great War RE8s. Only they're tricky because of the struts.

IAN: You should see Keith nail those fucking struts, man. (*Laughter*)

JOURNALIST: What about this free festival in Louisiana the underground press have been talking about?

DALE: We'd really like to do it. We'd really love to be there. We really regretted not bein' at Woodstock and, uh, Altamont. But unfortunately there are an awful lot of ... things to be settled before we can, uh, turn up. Transport, accommodation, security ...

GARTH: ... Money. Nah, I'm joking. Seriously, we'd love to do it and we hope to be there to play to all you good people.

Out of interest – no, out of boredom – I decided to itemise what the boys were wearing. The garments were these:

Garth: Top hat with Stars and Bars scarf wound the brim (the latter a blatant plagiarism of Mick Jagger's headgear on the Stones' US tour of two years previously.) Green turtleneck with Uncle Sam motif. Purple frockcoat with elaborately flounced sleeves. Lavender gloves. Bell-bottomed denim jeans. Snakeskin boots, one of them heel-less.

Dale: Black leather jacket with stencilled skull and crossbones. Dark, wraparound sunglasses. Off-white T-shirt. Torn black jeans with imitation cartridge belt. Black sneakers.

Ian: Three-piece Savile Row pinstripe, with watch and chain attachment. Tasselled black Oxford loafers.

Keith: White boiler suit. Crimson braces. Black bowler hat. Tan work boots.

Gary: Denim shirt, jacket and jeans. White gym shoes.

'Ow's your old lady?' Stefano asked in his patented mock-cockney, as another journalist loudly demanded of Ian how many suits he owned. 'Ow's she faring?'

How was my old lady? How was she faring? It was a good question. I thought about the stricken figure in the king-size bed, the murky chamber, the smashed ashtray on the white carpet. The problem about the life I led – the advantage, if you came at it from another angle – was that its intensity cancelled out the domestic elements that ran alongside. There was no getting away from this. You could spend a week planning a tour, listening to Stefano throwing telephones at his office door, watching Angie stuffing packets of Quaaludes into her bra, attending to Bernie's complaints about the expenses claims he was daily urged to falsify, and forget that you had a wife, a Bank of America mortgage, a white timber-frame house in Westchester, Connecticut, and a curious obligation to play bridge every Saturday night with an excruciatingly blasé couple named Raymond and Lurleen Whitaker. Something had gone wrong between us, and I had no idea what it was. I was always trying to fix something I had no recollection of breaking. And what about me? How was I feeling? Not too badly in the circumstances, I thought. Not too badly. There were rocks and rapids to negotiate, sirens calling from afar, Scylla and Charybdis hailing me from the whirlpool's edge, but on the whole not too badly, thank you.

'Not too badly, thank you. She's thinking we ought to buy one of those extended sofas they have in Macy's now.'

'Couple of bourgeois cunts,' Stefano said.

It was getting towards lunchtime now, and the pink-patterned mayonnaise dumped over the tureens of Maine lobster on the side tables was beginning to reek. Infinitely bored waiters were artlessly uncorking champagne bottles. A posse of girls in bikinis and five-inch heels came out of the lift behind the glass double doors and tottered into view. It was instructive at these times to watch the faces of those present in a supervisory capacity: Don's impassive; Stefano's quietly furious, as if only the duty he owed his employer stopped him from springing into the audience and rending some of the people in it into mangled shreds; Angie's mouth hanging open as if the gates of heaven had just swung apart before her. And I thought, as I so often thought in those days, what it would be like to be a ghost stealing back here thirty years later, alone in the great, dusty ballroom, picking up some long-discarded button badge that said HELIUM KIDS: FALL OF 71 and hearing the long-dead laughter of the bikini babes.

The press conference began to wind down. The boys were lolling back in their chairs, arms stretched above their heads. Mysterious black-clad factotums emerged, as if from nowhere, to usher one or two of the more favoured journalists into Don's bleak presence and tell the others – longhairs from the underground press, showbiz-gossip hounds – to be on their way. Pretty girls were milling about. Several of these, armed with tour programmes and banners, now advanced on the raised platform where the band reposed.

'Good job you did, Ange, getting those girls in,' Stefano said approvingly. 'Anyone would think they were fans.'

'I never fucking booked them,' Angie said. 'They ain't nothing to do with me.'

The suspicion that something was up came over us gradually. Without warning one of the girls starting swearing in a high-pitched voice. Another one hit Jerry, who happened to be standing nearby, over the head with a plastic Coke bottle. The banner, now half-unravelled, turned out to read JUSTICE FOR FLORIAN. Garth, scenting trouble, backed away, but not before one of the girls – a tough-looking proposition in a biker jacket – had leapt up on the stage and aimed a couple of kicks at him. 'No, man, no,' Dale was saying vaguely. The journalists surged forward to see what was happening. Somebody further back in the crowd yelled the single word 'Murderer!'

One of Stefano's greatest skills, instantly acknowledged by anyone who had anything to do with the Helium Kids, was that he was good in a crisis. Half-a-dozen incidents in the band's recent history attested to this fact. Singlehandedly he had broken up barfights, hauled lifeless fans over crush-barriers at concerts and, on one occasion, seized the wheel of an out-of-control tour bus when the driver had an analeptic attack. Now, unperturbed, or perhaps only giving a good impression of a man performing a rather mundane chore, he lunged forward, grabbed the girl who was kicking Garth round the waist and handed her over to one of the black-clad assistants, tugged at the banner that said JUSTICE FOR FLORIAN from its moorings and tore it in half, and pulled a notebook from the hands of the man from the *Washington Post* who was recording details and ripped out the topmost page.

Gradually the situation began to resolve itself. Garth coughed a couple of times and began ostentatiously to massage a knee that might just have been caught by the leather-jacketed girl's boot. Stefano stared angrily at the clumps of journalists, keen to weed out anyone else who might want to cause trouble. Oddly, of all the people inconvenienced in one way or another, it was Angie who seemed the crossest.

'You want to watch what you're fucking doing, *sister*,' she told the girl in the leather jacket. 'You and your protest banners. If this was Ohio State you'd get a fucking bullhorn up your ass.'

There was mellow autumn sunshine streaming through the plate-glass windows, molten and reassuring – even to people who had left bitter wives in darkened bedrooms five hours before. Against overwhelming odds, nature was doing its best. The leather-jacketed girl was borne unconsolably away. It was only at times like this – fleetingly, so quickly gathered up that you could miss the moment passing – that the rock-and-roll lifestyle turned elegiac. Just now the bikini-clad girls were dipping their fingers in the mayonnaise and shearing off chunks of lobster. The waiters, tidying away ashtrays, swabbing patches on the parquet floor where things had been dropped, looked weary and ground down, as if their professional world was tinted with a sepia curtain that only they could see. Ian was running a forefinger languorously down the crease of his Savile Row suit, and you could tell from the care he put into the gesture that it meant more to him than any human utterance served up in the previous half hour. The people who had dutifully filed in dutifully filed out again. Garth, who had recovered his nerve to the extent of saying something to the woman from the *New York Times*, was told to go and fuck himself. The band disappeared to their limos, there to be transported to orgies, crap games in Atlantic City, pool tables in Little Italy – who could tell? Don and his henchmen simply dematerialised, one moment there, the next gone, so that you almost expected to see puffs of smoke rising from the spots where their feet had been planted. Five minutes later, Stefano, Angie and I were standing in an otherwise deserted lift.

'Well, that went well I thought,' Stefano said, sounding like an Oxford don on his way out of an examiners' meeting.

There were times, in the course of our working life together, when you could tell Stefano the truth, or a version of it, or a humorous redaction of it, and there were times when only the grossest dissimulation would do. For some reason I forgot all the provisos that normally had to be employed if I thought he was talking rubbish.

'You have to be kidding.'

Stefano bobbed his head. The fracas had put him in a good mood. He liked throwing people about. 'You don't want to worry about that. Half of them didn't see it. The other half will have got the nod from Don. Might be a few from the longhair press want to make trouble. *I'm* not losing any sleep.'

'Where did Don vanish to? I thought he was coming back with us.'

'I expect Mr Castiglione is showing him the sights of Forty-Second Street, don't you?'

'*Ah woant larf at yew when yew boo-hoo-hoo curz ah lurve yew,*' Angie warbled quietly to herself. It was the big English autumn hit, copies of which had come in on the plane last week. Angie had odd tastes in music.

Back at the office it was as if mid-to-late twentieth-century Manhattan had ceased to exist. In its place was a quaint world of fairy-tale, hastily rolled into view once the original tenants had been called urgently away. The reception area was crowded out by a couple of life-size Santa Clauses and a giant wooden sleigh. This, it transpired, was for a promo for a Christmas single by the Toblerone Set, another of Don's English groups, of whom Stefano already privately despaired. Barbette, the girl from the floor below whom Angie sometimes hired to take messages when she was away, was asleep face down on the reception desk, a tawny tide of hair almost covering her outstretched arms. Extracting the notepad from a spot under her left ear, I discovered that someone had phoned to say that the A&M party for Karen Carpenter had been cancelled. It would be an early night.

'Well, I'm off to the Warthog,' Stefano said, naming a bar patronised by music industry types even more louche and disreputable than he himself. 'Remember, the Oblivion Express leaves at three tomorrow.'

There were always two or three joke phrases doing the round of the office. 'Arkansas pool party' – now a bit outdated – referred to defective plumbing on the tour bus. 'Rockefeller wedding' meant too few canapés on the backstage rider. The 'Oblivion Express' was Stefano's name for the private jet. To watch him bounce off through the doorway, like an India-rubber ball cannoning off the surfaces that got in his way, was to appreciate just how much New York had changed since I'd first seen it in 1964. There had been yelling basket-cases on the subway back then; there had been surly Italians picking fights in bars; but there had never been anyone like Stefano. It was the same with the bachelor girls, who had stopped being Bobbie Gentry lookalikes in mini-skirts, ribbed stockings and patent-leather shoes and turned into jezebels like Angie more or less overnight

'What am I supposed to do with Barb?' Angie wondered. 'Throw a bucket of water over the bitch's head?'

'Just having a fucking nap is all,' Barbette complained, coming awake and flinging out her arms, so that a pile of press packs brought back from the Plaza went skittering over the floor.

It was barely three o'clock, but the afternoon, like so many afternoons here beneath the strung-out Manhattan skyline, already seemed to be fading away, drifting downriver on a slack tide. Great events might be in train, but it was near enough to the starting-gun for most of the tension to have drained away. A week ago, Stefano had been firing people and then re-hiring them, had himself been fired – by telegram from London – and taken back on again in the space of an afternoon. Now he was tying one on at the Warthog. The arrangements had all been made. Whatever would happen would happen. It was as simple as that. Back in his cubby hole, Bernie would, I knew, be going through Stefano's restaurant receipts for the past two months and assigning them to plausible sponsors. Jerry, to whom disagreeable tasks of this kind naturally devolved, would be telephoning hotels in Dayton, Chicago, Sioux City and Baton Rouge to relay requests – mostly from Garth – for suites that were furbished up in particular kinds of ways, with particular kinds of floral arrangements on their side tables, and particular kinds of room service arriving at particular intervals with particular kinds of people providing it. Somewhere in Stefano's files there existed a typed memorandum headed *Garth Dangerfield: to be avoided.* Of the dozen or so forbidden items, the ones I remembered were *niggers, redheads, fried eggs, café au lait* and *opening the curtains.*

Back in my room, I rang five or six of the journalists who had attended the press conference, but it was all exactly as Stefano had predicted. No one was interested in the lofted banner, the girl who had kicked Garth or Justice for Florian. *Death of a Pop Star* sat on the desktop as I talked, and I thought about that far-off day in Goodge Street and the newspaper taxis barrelling on through the late-afternoon sun. A couple of times I phoned home to Westchester, but no one answered. Rosalind would be in some supportive friend's chintzy kitchen by now, making notes about Klimt, hearing tales of marital oppression or seeing what the reading circle had made of *Diary of a*

Mad Housewife, as the red Connecticut leaves piled up against the doorframe. Selma, disapproving yet conscientious, would have left supper in the oven and coolly departed for the tarpapered bungalow by the rail-track she shared with her mother, a thousand books and a pair of cats named Eldridge Cleaver and Stokely Carmichael. At five o'clock I tidied my desk, transferred the half-dozen useful phone numbers the day had thrown up to a notebook, gave Angie the post-restante addresses to which mail could be forwarded in the next four-and-a-half weeks and went home.

There wasn't anyone I knew on the Westchester train. It was early for the poker school, for Christopherson, Auger and Maxwell, who would still be in client presentations on Madison. Instead the carriages were full of shopped-out Connecticut housewives. Coming back from the station, through clear, cool air and blown-about leaves, I began to wonder what might be waiting beyond the doorstep. Sometimes at the day's end we had conversations that were so representative of the Westchester world we inhabited that they might have been invented by a sitcom writer out to skewer the suburban lifestyle. Sometimes we embarked on deeply serious attempts to capture some of the demons that oppressed us. Other times we just sat and sulked. There was no sign of Rosalind's car in the drive, but a Pontiac with out-of-state plates and an insecurely fastened bonnet was parked at a forty-five-degree angle across the carport. As I stood in the hallway, trying to work out where the smell of smoke might be coming from – kitchen and sitting room were both strong candidates – a shrill yet wildly unfocused female voice said from a vantage point ten or twenty feet above my head, 'Nick. Nicko. Is that you?' There was a pause, sound-tracked by three or four lolloping, crab-crawl footsteps, and then – not absolutely to my surprise, it had to be said – Lucille Duchesne materialised at the top of the stairs.

The trick with Lucille, I had decided, since coming across her again three years back, was to keep things on the level. Had she descended by rope ladder from a helicopter onto the back lawn accompanied by a snatch squad of Navy SEALs, the safe response would have been to remark how well the flowers were coming on here in the east. Anything else was liable to fluster her, and as Rosalind had several times observed, the great thing was that Momma shouldn't be allowed to get herself into a tizzy.

'It's good to see you, Lucille. I'm afraid no one told me you were coming.'

'Aren't you the politest boy?' Lucille said, from halfway down the stairs, and sounding like a Southern belle in a stage play being offered a mint julep. She was holding an empty wineglass at the level of her shoulder and darting anguished glances at the rim, as if she couldn't quite decide where the liquid that should have been inside it might have gone. 'Actually I owe you an apology, Nick. You see, I didn't know I was coming here myself until last night. And then I just took off. Figured I might come and look you up. After all, it's not so very far.'

Aunt Wilma lived on the western side of Indiana – about 500 miles, say.

'Onna *whee-im*,' Lucille said, touching up the Mason–Dixon line lilt in her voice.

She was at the foot of the staircase now. The clock in the hall showed 6.30 p.m. Out along the Westchester back lanes, the Petes and the Sheps and the Arnies would be stomping into their brightly lit hallways, hurling briefcases onto tables and calling for their corn-haired children. I was alone in my house with a drunken mother-in-law and a smell of burning.

'Is there something on fire?'

'Oh *that*,' Lucille said. 'I'm awfully afraid I had a little accident with an ashtray. No need to look so disapproving, Nick. It's nothing we can't fix. We'll just have to put a brave face on it and do the best we can. But you really are staring at me rather a lot, Nick. What must I look like?'

What did she look like? A few preliminary observations might have been: a little gaunt, a little flushed, a little capillary-shot, a little frayed around the edges, a little too juvenile in her costume for one who must now have been in her early fifties; otherwise not greatly changed. The other Duchesnes always reckoned that if you kept Lucille busy, under the watchful stare of someone who knew her little ways, then serious disaster could usually be avoided. Clearly, Aunt Wilma had overplayed her hand. Or perhaps she had simply got bored. Most of Lucille's lapses occurred when members of her family rebelled against the unbelievable tedium of having her on the premises. It seemed impossible that we had ever sailed past Barry Goldwater in the foyer of the Phoenix Hotel, driven to New York together and done those things that made me bite my lip whenever I looked at her. Meanwhile, there were more pressing problems to hand.

'Where's Rosalind?'

Lucille sat down dramatically – collapsed wasn't quite the right word – on the bottom step. 'That's a very good question, Nick. Do you know, I can't answer it? She certainly wasn't here when I arrived. Perhaps she came and looked at me through the window and then went away. *I* don't know. The coloured girl let me in and fixed me a cup of coffee, which was very kind of her. But of Rosalind, my only daughter, Al's particular pride and joy, as he keeps on reminding me on the rare occasions when we meet, there wasn't the faintest sign. It's all very mysterious.'

The things I needed to do could not be accomplished with Lucille in tow. 'You'll have to excuse me while I get changed.'

'You do that,' Lucille said comfortably. There were times when I thought she must have forgotten we had once slept together. 'And when you're done, I can fix us a cosy supper.'

Left alone in a house – something her relatives tried to avoid – Lucille tended to prowl capriciously around it, exploring odd nooks and crannies that probably would not have occurred to more conventional guests. This time she had been having fun upstairs. There was an outsize suitcase thrown on the bed in the spare room. The burning smell turned out to come from a cigarette left smouldering in the bathroom soap dish. Here, additionally, Lucille had rolled up two bath towels into a kind of Gordian knot and left a lipstick hieroglyph on the mirror. Assessing the damage as minimal – this was a woman who had once let a tub overflow for two hours while she took a nap in it – I tracked on into the master bedroom, where the curtains were open, the bed made and the glass swept up. Aunt Wilma, found at home, plainly livid, but not unwilling to be plucked from her bridge table, confirmed that Lucille had left at eleven the previous night and there was not the slightest point in her coming back. As I attended to this considerable harangue, I made an inventory of the room, discovered that Rosalind had taken a few clothes, but not many, and a solitary pair of shoes, and that my pyjamas had been arranged on the pillow with more than usual care. (*'And would ya believe,'* Aunt Wilma was saying in her sassy drawl, *'she hyad the ahfrontahree ta suggest that ah wuz poisonin' her korfey?'*)

I came downstairs with a put-down that Rosalind had administered a week or two before ringing in my head. 'You,' she had said, looking up from the meticulous rearrangement of a supper table set for eight people I barely knew, 'need to woo me all over again.' It was impossible to work out what she meant by this. It was as meaningless in its way as the banner unfurled that morning in the ballroom of the Plaza Hotel. How could you have justice for Florian? Florian was dead. And what did justice for Florian mean? Itemising the precise circumstances of his passing? Lining up all the people who had been unkind to him, disparaged him or mocked him while he lived and giving them marks out of ten? In the same way, telling someone that they had to woo you all over again – a line that in any case looked as if it had been robbed wholesale from Hollywood – suggested that you could reduce to a formula something whose success depended on it not being formulaic, freeze a gesture in mid-frame and sell it on the open market.

Outside, the wind was buffeting the Westchester Bespoke Window Co.'s double glazing and the dusk was stealing in. The squirrels would be hunkered down in their nests, marshalling their resources for the dawn. I found Lucille in the kitchen, rootling around in the cupboard and – a new development – feigning girlishness.

'It turns out I don't have to make you a cosy supper after all, Nick. I'd quite forgotten the coloured girl fixed us something to eat. Still, I thought you might like to have a can of peaches for dessert.' She beat two of the tins together, like a doughty five-year-old invited to supply percussive noises to the reception class band. 'Looks like there's a storm coming.'

The eastern seaboard had a weather system that was all its own. Rain-heads blew in unheralded off the Atlantic. Pitched climatic battles that had taken place over Lake Erie played out their last, desultory skirmishes in the skies over Westchester. Snow punched up from Delaware on its way out to sea. It was one of those places where anything could happen.

'You know, there are times when I almost miss Arizona,' Lucille said unexpectedly. 'The Lord knows why, but there it is. I can be driving along in my car minding my own business, or listening to Wilma encouraging that half-witted nephew of mine who can't keep his tongue in his mouth however hard he tries, and then all of a sudden I can see Al coming in to tell me there's a turtle chewing up the lawn or there's another dozen black people he's managed to exclude from the voting roll. Do you know, I can even get nostalgic about Al? Now, who would have thought that?'

Selma had left us one of her chow*dahs*, with enough pepper in it to stop a mountain lion in its tracks. The rain lashed against the windows as we ate and drummed on the roofs of the cars in the driveway.

'And now you're off on tour, the coloured girl tells me,' Lucille went on. 'I can't imagine what my daughter thought she was doing, disappearing somewhere on her husband's last night at home. On the other hand, I had a perfect genius for doing that to Al. Tell me, Nick, tell me, Nicko, do you think this is a case of heredity working itself out? That old heredity. Or is it more serious than that?'

'Probably more serious.'

'Well then, I'm sorry, Nick. Very sorry to hear it. Not surprised, but sorry. You see, I did tell you this. Granted it was a long time ago, and no doubt I was in a highly emotional state. You could ask yourself: when was I not in a highly emotional state? But I did tell you. You see, Rosalind is her daddy's daughter. And when they made the world, well, take it from me, they made it for the Duchesnes. Which is a pity for you and me and for anyone else who fetches up alongside them, but that's how it is. How long will you be gone?'

'A month. Five weeks perhaps.'

'You'd better let me stay here. Me and the coloured girl will do fine, just as long as she doesn't put too much salt in the chowdah. And then when Rosalind shows up again, I can tell her just how disappointed I am about all this heredity working itself out.'

Later she fell catatonically asleep in a chair in the middle of *All in the Family*. I went upstairs to pack for the morrow. It was then that I found the note Rosalind had left. Not in any of the conventional places. Not on a pillow, or provocatively arranged on the bedside table or stuck accusingly to a mirror, but propped against a tooth-mug in the bathroom. Three words, and not one of them applicable to the situation I found myself in.

Your father called.

12. REAL COOL TIME

Wrap your lovin' arms around me baby
Squeeze my lemon till it bursts

'Lovin' Arms'

Here on the Oblivion Express, a moment or so before take-off, the atmosphere is unexpectedly subdued. Well, maybe not subdued, *subdued* not being a word we use much around here, along with *discreet* and *unavailable*. Let us just say that the willed raucousness that immemorially distinguishes Helium Kids tours has yet to kick in and that right now a highly individual kind of unresolved tension is the order of the day. There are about twenty of us: the band, their entourage, a few, a very few, favoured journalists, me, Stefano, Jerry and for some reason Angie who has earlier this morning been elevated to the post of assistant tour manager but is, I deduce, present in certain other private capacities. Outside the window there are plump grey clouds scudding feverishly by. Helicopters buzz in the middle distance. The stewardesses – rangy Amazonian foxes with whom you wouldn't wish to tangle, and who look as if they're promoting lingerie catalogues or dream homes in the west, prowl disdainfully by. They have names like Rhoda-Joe and Stacey-Jane, are on furlough from adult films or the Playboy Mansion, or so Stefano knowledgably insists, and have a tendency to forget drinks orders. Sixteen hours have passed since I discovered the note saying that the old man called: sixteen fraught yet oddly unmemorable hours; seven of them spent failing to sleep in the king-sized bed in Westchester; one passed breakfasting and negotiating with Lucille; and three drinking Alabama slammers with Stefano at a basement bar called the King Farouk Lounge at Fifty-Third and Third. The rest I don't recall. Stefano, jerking nervously back and forth in the seat next to me, is dressed in his customary touring apparel of Hawaiian shirt, khaki rat-catchers and outsize lime-green sneakers with purple laces. The Gladstone bag balanced on his fat thigh contains – I know this for a fact – not much under $40,000 in $20 bills. Also hidden there are half-a-dozen blank prescription forms tailed with the signature of a sympathetic doctor of Stefano's acquaintance on Staten Island and a notebook with the phone numbers of two dozen leading provincial law firms, one for each of the cities that the Helium Kids will be visiting in the next five weeks. Stefano may look like a Yugoslav tourist fetched up in Times Square, but that doesn't mean he wants to leave anything to chance.

'You know something?' he says, Gladstone bag now violently a-judder on his kneecap. 'You know something? I'm worried about Garth.' I steal a glance back down the aisle, where the object of this solicitude is staring intently at a book called *Occult Reich* while a platinum-haired girl in black fishnets and a combat jacket, tongue hanging out of her mouth in a meaty curlicue, rests an exhausted head on his shoulder. He looks more Dickensian than ever: you could imagine him in a Whitechapel garret feeding gin-soaked bread-crusts to Grip the raven.

'Why are you worried about Garth?' I inquire, omitting a further sentence that would occur to most people who know him: apart from the usual reasons? The plane is jerking into life beneath us now, and the foxiest of the Amazonian stewardesses is suggesting that we should put our fuckin' seat belts on, y'know, and be cool.

'Oh, I dunno . . .' Stefano, a martyr to travel-sickness and pre-flight hysteria, has to my knowledge consumed two Librium tablets prior to departure as well as the half-dozen Alabama slammers at the King Farouk Lounge: a certain amount of vagueness can be allowed him. 'It's just that . . . Jesus . . . Do you ever see that fuckin' stuff he has in his rooms . . .? I mean, someone told me that greatcoat he wears belonged to some Nazi general. Then there's . . . then there's . . .' – Stefano's voice is becoming more doleful than ever, as if a deputation from the IRS auditing department is waiting eagerly on the tarmac for us to touch down in Columbus – ' . . . those women he has in there. I mean, some guy who was delivering room service went in his suite once and saw a pair of fuckin' *manacles*.' The roar of the plane's ascent starts to drown out his voice and he puts his head so close to mine that I can smell his curacao-tainted breath, like the reek of the tomb. 'But, but, what's really worrying me is, Don was saying that . . .' We are airborne now. The stewardesses, hanging on to the headrests of vacant seats, look massively discontented, beyond cross. 'Jesus . . . Will you go find Angie, Nicko, and tell her I need to . . . need to see her?'

But Angie, vulpine and narrow-eyed, is already hovering at his shoulder. 'Actually,' the tiny, dark-haired man alongside us who has been quietly attending to all of this now strikes up, 'I've enjoyed several conversations with Mr Dangerfield and he strikes me as remarkably well-informed.'

'Does he now?' Stefano returns, calmed by whatever prophylactic Angie has palmed him in her flattened hand. 'Well, you can fuck off for a start . . . Only joking, son' – for the dark-haired man's look of faint condescension has been replaced by one of outright horror. 'Nicko, this is Irv I told you about. The guy Don wants to write a book about the tour.'

'Irving Kantner. Pleased to meet you, gentlemen,' says the dark-haired man, who I now recall from a wary memorandum sent over from London, freelances for *Esquire*, or *Playboy*, has written a novel called *Bitch-pack Confidential*, variously described as 'provocative' and 'unrelenting', and clearly has no idea what a month on the road, and in the air, with the Helium Kids will entail for his moral salubrity. 'But what I really need is someone to sign my letter of authorisation.'

'Oh yeah,' Stefano says, all interest gone. 'Well, I can't sign it. No fucking way can I sign it. You better ask the boys.'

'Well, I wouldn't want to distract them,' Kantner says, doubtfully. 'Not right now.'

'You go and distract them,' Stefano tells him, the boredom rising from him in invisible spirals. 'Stop them getting blown, or high, or something. Do us all a favour.'

We watch Kantner gumshoe off down the aisle, past the foxiest of the stewardesses and a journalist from one of the longhair magazines who is being sick into a paper bag cupped in the palms of his trembling hands.

'Those *books*,' Stefano says, as if anxious to initiate some high-flown philosophical discussion about literary culture's role in the modern world, 'they're never any good, are they?'

'This one might be,' I say, not because I like the look of Kantner, or think a record of the Helium Kids Fall of '71 US tour will do anything for their reputation, or mine, or Stefano's, or the music business in general, but out of a vague, contrarian feeling that literature ought to be defended.

'Fucking won't,' Stefano says. Whatever Angie has fed him has given him a semblance of cool rationality, a hankering for debate. 'He'll either write, uh, exactly what he sees – you know, Garth and his swastika bedspreads and Dale fucking everything that moves – or he'll ...' – Stefano searches for the *mot juste* – '... he'll fucking *romanticise* it, and write a load of bollocks about Dionysius and Apollo and Nietzsche or whatever. Look,' Stefano says, 'I got to say something. Instructions from Don.' He hauls himself to his feet, steadies himself against the motion of the plane, claps his hands and says loudly but before anyone has a chance to focus their attention on him: 'Ladies and gentlemen. I'd like to welcome you to the Helium Kids Fall of '71 North American tour. It's going to be a great ride. It surely is. Indubitably. And I hope very much that in the words of the song, we're gonna have a real cool time together. But what I really want to say is that there's going to be no dope on this tour, and that anyone who gets busted is on their own. Do I make myself clear? Well, thank you very much. Thanks a bunch.' There is a smattering of deeply ironical applause and Stefano flops back into his seat, his duty done.

Kantner trails forlornly back down the aisle towards us. 'They won't sign,' he says, holding up the sheet of typewritten paper for me to inspect. 'They won't sign. They say they don't know anything about it.'

'Leave it to me,' I volunteer, taking up the sheet, arranging it on the upturned copy of *Rolling Stone* with Neil Young on the cover and scrawling plausible approximations of the signatures of Garth Dangerfield, Dale Halliwell, Gary Pasarolo and Ian Hamilton. Then, which is cruel of me, I put an 'X' and write next to it, 'Keith Shields, his mark.' Kantner watches me with a kind of puzzled reverence, as if forging someone's signature on a self-produced letter of authorisation for a book which – I know – has at least a 90 per cent chance of not being published is both the worst thing anyone can do and a gesture of God-like munificence on my part.

The plane shakes, like a giant refrigerator about to rattle out a dozen chunks of ice, climbs again and settles grudgingly on the level. Two or three yards away a couple of the stewardesses are punctiliously rearranging their clothing and unselfconsciously talking hip-speak, that curious sub-celebrity language whose constantly replenished lexicon has colonised our world in the past five years, where things are rilly far out and there are heavy people on the prowl, you dig, ready to kick out the jams.

'Hey,' Stefano says, 'guess how much we're going to gross on this tour? Guess how much?' In fact, I already know the answer, having glanced over documentation from London that Stefano doesn't know I see, but I prudently shake my head. 'Three million dollars,' Stefano says proudly, as if one of his children has won a tap-dancing competition. 'Three and a half, maybe. Led Zeppelin didn't do that, last time they were out. Three million dollars. That's if nobody fucks up.'

'Will anyone fuck up?'

The foxiest of the stewardesses is telling her friend that Jack fuckin' Nicholson has problems like you wouldn't fuckin' believe and don't get her started on Warren Beatty.

'Who's to tell?' Stefano wonders, with one of those I-do-my-job-will-anyone-else-do-theirs gestures of which he is so extravagantly fond.

I wonder where Rosalind is, where the car has taken her, what Lucille is doing in the empty house in Westchester with only Selma and the scent of chowdah for company. Outside there is rain pattering on the airplane window in tiny pointilliste swirls. I glance down the aisle to where the band – by far the likeliest of the twenty people around us to fuck up – are ensconced, and am struck by how the years have aged them. Here in the artificial light of the Oblivion Express they look like grey ghosts winched up from the vault. These are men of twenty-six or twenty-seven and they seem a dozen years older, shrivelled and ancient before their time. 'Christ,' Stefano says, his eye falling too on Dale's profound facial pallor, his rotting fangs, his woad-stained gums. 'They look fucking terrible. All of them. What the fuck have they been doing to *get* like that?' The Latin tag that springs to mind, memorised a dozen years ago at the City of Norwich School, is *si monumentum requiris, circumspice*, but I decide to keep it to myself. What have the boys been doing to get like this? The short answer is taking too many drugs, chasing too many women, reading too many books with titles like *Occult Reich*, buying too many Savile

Row suits, making too many Airfix kits, living immoderately and damning the consequences.

'Three and a half million dollars,' Stefano says, having decided that what the Helium Kids get up to after sundown is their affair. 'Don would have pushed the ticket prices higher, only there's been fucking complaints.'

'Is that so? Who's been complaining?' This is a superfluous enquiry. People are *always* complaining about the Helium Kids: about the length of their hair; about their language; about Garth's paeans to Aleister Crowley; all kinds of things.

'Fucking longhair papers have. *West Coast Wanker. Smeg Sunday.*' Stefano grandly improvises. 'Actually, I blame Jefferson Airplane' – and here he names a particularly fashionable symbol of San Francisco freak-dom. 'All this *counter-cultural* malarkey. I mean, one month it's all peace and love and buckskin trousers and listen to the music, and then all of a sudden anyone who plays in a band is supposed to be some kind of fucking revolutionary and sticking it to the man every time they go on stage. Well, let me tell you, the Kids wouldn't know what the counter-culture was if it fell on their heads from off of a lamppost. You know, they were in England last time they had a general election? Well, let me tell you how they voted. Let me tell you, Nicko, how they exercised their, uh, *democratic prerogative*. OK, here goes. Garth and Dale voted Conservative. Ian voted Labour, cos he's a sentimental old cunt and his dad used to drive Nye Bevan to rallies or something. Gary voted for some retired brigadier who said he wanted to bring back the death penalty.'

'What about Keith?'

'Between you and me, I don't think Keith knew there was a general election on, or what they were having it for in the first place.'

'And so' – there is a phrase forming in my head from a recent interview with John Lennon – 'none of them has any revolutionary consciousness whatever?'

'None at all,' Stefano confirms. His fingers are still twitching at the Gladstone bag, as if minute electrical currents are somehow coursing through the leather. 'But you see, they're soft. Soon as anyone starts talking about a free concert they think they have to do something about it because it's for the kids and maybe Nixon wouldn't like it, man. You know what I think? I think there's nothing in the whole of Western civilisation quite so perfectly embodies the spirit of, uh, global capitalism as rock and roll. But try telling that to a bunch of longhairs in Asswipe, Louisiana, who think Garth Dangerfield is third cousin to Billy the Kid.'

'So you think there'll be a free concert?'

'Bound to be,' Stefano insists. 'And even money says they won't want the cops on account of we're all such radical little fuckers and look what happened at Ohio State. So, a hundred thousand kids will turn up in some fucking swamp – because no one who ever planned a free festival had the slightest clue how it ought to be done – with no proper security, and there'll be retards busting each other's heads in with hammers and hippy chicks giving birth in the backs of trucks, and it'll all be our fucking fault. My fucking fault, actually. So, no, I'm *not keen*, and neither is Don, but Garth and Dale – who, as you doubtless know, are the ones on that stage whose opinions properly count – will say yes because some student paper in Bullshit County, California, reckons it's their fucking civic duty.'

The sky outside looks as if it's gearing up for a storm, but miraculously the weather holds. At Columbus security decides that it wants to search the band, which, as Stefano says, is cool as anything remotely compromising secreted on their persons has been transferred to Angie's rucksack prior to departure. Angie, demure and innocuous and apparently not connected to this bunch of scrofulous leather boys *at all*, thank you officer, sails through unmolested. Here in Ohio it is still light, with great billowing tawny clouds burning off the distant horizon, and so we climb into the six limousines ostentatiously

assembled beyond the terminal and are driven off in a stately bohemian cavalcade past gas stations and roadside diners and used-car lots
where sit old, incurious black men who have taken no interest in this
thing they call rock and roll since the white boys appropriated Arthur
Crudup and Jackie Wilson for commercial purposes in the early fifties
and wouldn't recognise the Helium Kids if they plugged into a generator in the lot next door and started playing 'Bayou Girl', which they
know, and I know, and several dozen music journalists know, is a
straight steal from an old Willie Dixon song for which Mr Dixon's
heirs have received no royalties at all.

'Hicksville,' adjudges Stefano, with whom I am sharing transport,
and to whom all cities short of London, New York and Los Angeles
are no more than agglomerated swamps. Between us Irving Kantner,
to whom Angie has administered what she maintains is 'just some
mild trank, y'know', has fallen palely asleep. The gas stations and the
used-car lots give way to Columbus proper – the Roth country, I
remind myself – with its gleaming clumps of real estate, its polished
chromium fenders a-jostle in the four-lane highways, and Stefano,
hectic and livid from the flight, cheers up.

'What sort of place is this?' I enquire, as the limo swings round into
the hotel lot, and Stefano volunteers that, like the airport security, it's
cool, meaning that the management is accustomed to rock stars and
that randomly discharged fire-extinguishers, wanton damage and $800
room service tabs are all in the day's work. As we hit the foyer, where
sumptuous carpeting extends on all sides and deferential bellhops leap
to attention, there is a swirl of skirts and a furious clatter of four-inch
heels on parquet flooring and three flint-eyed but buxom women are
standing before us dropping mock curtseys. These are the GTOs –
Miss Pamela, Miss Mercy and (I think) Miss Cynderella – and it's a
mark of the Kids' paralysing celebrity that these ladies are at least two-
thousand miles away from their natural habitat in LA, the Valley and
Laurel Canyon, where they prowl Sunset Strip, hang out with Zappa

and – it is alleged – make plaster casts of celebrity genitalia. GTOs, by the way, stands for 'Girls Together Outrageously', or 'Girls Together Orally' or maybe even 'Girls Together Onomatopoeically'. Stefano whistles through his teeth, like the US marshal in the cowboy film whose attention has been drawn to a swarm of coyotes and plummeting vultures a quarter of a mile down the trail. 'Jesus,' he says. 'I fucked one of them once. Not one for the memoirs.'

'No?'

'I couldn't begin to tell you,' Stefano says mournfully, 'what she did to me.' There is a pause. 'Or what I did to her.'

Five minutes later I am alone in my suite, far away from Miss Mercy and Miss Cynderella, their carmined talons and their incriminating plaster of Paris, where proof of how unprecedentedly cool the establishment is can be found in a photocopied note from someone signing himself 'Captain Preemo' and stating that supplies of Afghanistan hash, Peruvian flake cocaine, Colombian marijuana, Thai sticks and seedless California sinsemilla are readily available on the number listed below. Beyond the window the last streaks of tawny twilight are disappearing into a purple surround. Faint notes of bird-song mingle with the traffic, and there is work to be done. I phone the local FM station to assure myself that the hippest of its three hip DJs has tickets for tomorrow. I contact the Mayor's office, where the switchboard is still open, and leave a message inviting that dignitary – also supposed to be cool – to the after-gig party. Next, I call Westchester where, after what seems like an eternity, while the very last streaks of tawny night fade into purple nothingness, the receiver is picked up by, of all people, Selma, who sounds coy, embarrassed and in possession of some mighty secret whose exact nature it would be impolitic to reveal. 'You're working very late, Selma,' I propose and Selma confirms that yeah-heah, that certainly is the case, Mr Du Pont, but that Mrs Duchesne has turned poorly and taken to her bed, and that she, Selma, has been tending to her.

'What's the matter with her?' I demand.

'Well, Mr Du Pont, I guess she's just plum tuckered out,' Selma says, giving a little squeal of what might be derision or sympathy or some other hybrid emotion caught halfway between. 'Or else she thinks it's something she ate.'

'You ought to go home, Selma. I'm sure she's perfectly capable of looking after herself.'

'Oh, it's no trouble, Mr Du Pont,' Selma says, who is clearly extracting huge amusement from playing the part of a dumb negro maid on the telephone, and the scent of complicity whistles down the wire, as if Selma and Lucille, forswearing race and social position, are suddenly in this together, busy devising some mutually beneficial strategy I can't begin to comprehend.

'Has Rosalind – has Mrs Du Pont been back?' I wonder, and Selma abandons her impersonation from *Gone with the Wind* to tell me that she has had no communication from that quarter, although several phone calls have been fielded by Lucille, to which she, Selma, has not been privy.

The receiver is only twenty seconds back in its cradle, and I have barely begun to contemplate the spectacle of what must be going on in Westchester, when Stefano looms titanically in the open doorway. 'You busy?' he asks, the look as he surveys the premises conveying bleak disappointment that Miss Pamela and Miss Cynderella and a rollicking crowd of fourteen-year-olds they managed to procure on the way upstairs aren't shackled naked to the bed.

'Not so much. What's happening?'

'The usual thing,' Stefano says with brisk disgust. 'Garth's just got room service to send up two bottles of Dom Perignon and as much caviar as they can find in the chiller. Dale's playing pool with the maître d'. Ian just asked where he could get three of those suits of his dry-cleaned. Thing is, though,' Stefano says, arms akimbo and one dropsical leg coiling anaconda-like round the other. 'Thing is that

John Lee Hooker' – he pronounces it *uker* – 'is playing some blues joint down in the boondocks. Got Little Walter with him on harp, somebody said.'

'Little Walter's dead, Stefano.'

'I can't keep up with the mortality rate in this business,' Stefano says brusquely, 'specially not with the spades. One moment it's Chess Records retrospectives, the next they're dead in a drainage ditch someplace. Anyway, you want to come? It can't be any worse than sitting listening to Garth telling us that Martin Bormann was a very misunderstood guy.'

Rosalind. Lucille. The old man. Two dozen stopovers in two dozen of America's finest hotels. Suddenly the prospect of John Lee Hooker hollering into the Ohio night has an undeniable savour. 'Might make a good press story, too,' Stefano airily pronounces, but here I have to shake my head, for the relationship between the Helium Kids and the old Afro-American blues masters from whom they derived – no, pilfered – the greater part of their repertoire is as poisoned as the muddy waters – no pun intended – of the Ganges. In theory, the boys tread a plateau of mutual interracial esteem alongside Chuck, 'the Wolf' and other notables. In practice their biannual sojourn in the States is an excuse for plagiarism suits to descend on their heads like so much wedding confetti. For what is 'Uptown Strut' off *Low Blows in High Times* if not a more cacophonous version of 'Sweet Little Sixteen'? And what is 'Hot Lemon Boogie', *Cabinet of Curiosities*' rousing finale, if not Bo Diddley's 'Pretty Thing' with a couple of chord changes and some vocal histrionics? I was present once backstage at a gig in Chicago when Garth and Dale attempted to pay court to Chuck Berry and the great man kept the door of his dressing room proudly shut for an hour and a half. John Lee Hooker, I tell myself, waving Stefano out of the room and jotting notes on a sheet of paper for Angie to add to tomorrow's schedule, will surely have all this information at his dusky fingertips.

Outside the window, the Ohio night is settling in. A geometrid patterning of car headlights runs off into the distance. Beyond that the sky is as black as pitch.

Rosalind. Lucille. The old man. Downstairs the hotel lobby has a winded feel, as if marauding tribes or armies of occupation have passed through it, pillaging as they went. Miss Mercy, shoeless, braless and arrayed in what looks like the costume of a Roman slave girl, lurks in a chair by the row of telephone kiosks drinking an arsenical-coloured cocktail. The regular guests – middle-aged men in business suits and their dowdy womenfolk – pass wanly by. There are five takers for John Lee Hooker: Stefano, myself, Dale, Ian and Kantner, the latter still half-asleep.

'Have you any idea what that woman gave me?' he asks, to general amusement. 'No, I mean it,' he goes on, eyes staring out of his pale, chipmunk's face. 'Have you any idea what that woman gave me?'

'Don't give me any of that crap,' Stefano says, not unsympathetically. 'You're still standing, aren't you? This is Lester,' he says, gesturing with a wave of his hand to an elderly black man who has been waiting humbly at the foyer's outer edge. 'He's going to drive us to – whatever's the name of the fucking place? The Blues Bunker?'

Lester says that he don't mind, but we ought to know that the establishment we're heading to is no-how select, and presently, with the lights of the hotel slowly dissolving behind us like a palace floating away into the watery night, we are packed into Lester's equally elderly Dodge Sedan and hustled off into a landscape of tangled backstreets, billboards for products no one has ever heard of, chicken joints and project housing where black girls in track pants cluster under the lamps and there are sinister-looking old men playing checkers in the glow of flickering porch lights. Lester, meanwhile, has the dial turned to some local gospel station, and the air is full of whoops and God-dangs and Oh-mah-Lawdies. His face, fixed on the road, is quite impassive, monumentally detached.

'You know,' Ian says, of all the Helium Kids the one most consistently interested in the blues and their native exponents, 'this is a great
honour. I can't think why the others don't want to come. I mean, I'd
sooner see John Lee Hooker than – I don't know – go to Buckingham
Palace and shake hands with the Queen.' Ian, I notice, is wearing
about £300-worth of Savile Row's finest grey pinstripe. This in sharp
contrast to Dale, who appears to be got up like Lord Byron attending
a *fête champêtre*.

The spectres of Rosalind, Lucille and the old man are receding a
little now, clamouring a little less emphatically in my head. Meanwhile,
the road is starting to give out – there are fields looming up through
the mist and the spectral shapes of farm animals – the bump and
judder of music is coming from somewhere close at hand, and Lester
brings the Dodge dramatically to a halt between a couple of fenceposts, says that this heahyah's the Blues Bunker to which the gentlemen are kindly welcome and he'll take $5 for his trouble now if we
don't mind and the rest later.

Beyond the comfort of the Dodge, the air has turned cold, the
ground underfoot is simultaneously wet and gritty and Stefano is
explaining to the two giant custodians of the vestibule, one of whom
has a baseball bat tucked under his elbow, that he has a party come to
see his good friend Johnny Lee here if that's cool. 'Is this place *safe*?'
Ian wonders. 'Great to see you cats,' Stefano is telling the guy with the
baseball bat, not a whit abashed, 'and do you know, I'd be really grateful if someone could keep an eye on our driver.' Unbelievably, this
stratagem works. The doormen wave us sternly through, a drunk who
is weaving around the vicinity is ordered to fuck off *outta* here right
now, and five seconds later we are admiring the Blues Bunker's dark
and sweaty interior, where about seventy people, young, old, middle-
aged but exclusively black, are watching a disdainful ancient in a
check suit with a three-piece band solidly a-chug behind him, declaring that he loves the way ya strut and, *whoah*, he likes it like that.

'The trick in these places,' Stefano loudly announces, 'is not to take any crap. You simply need to tell the people what you want and make sure they give it to you. That way they respect you. Am I wrong? Hey, you,' he says to a man who looks like Sammy Davis Jr but would appear to be one of the establishment's bar staff, 'table near the front, OK?' Again the stratagem works, and half a minute later we are seated a yard or two away from John Lee's tapping left heel, while Stefano, $20 bill extended between thumb and forefinger, is asking Sammy Davis Jr whether they have any Kentucky bourbon, or 'failing that' a bottle of Rebel Yell. There is no Kentucky bourbon, or any Rebel Yell, and we have to make do with some local hooch that tastes like double-strength paraffin residue sweetened with lumps of molasses. Kantner takes a sip from his tumbler and instantly goes to sleep with his head on the table.

Meanwhile, Dale and Ian are appraising the performance. ''E ain't exactly at his best,' Dale opines. 'In fact, half the time 'e's missing the fucking changes, but then every so often . . .'

'Band's tight, though,' Ian acknowledges. 'Wish fucking Keith could play like that.'

'Ah, but Keith, man . . .' Dale counters, and I get an odd whiff of the solidarity that envelops the Helium Kids at these times, that glosses over their technical shortcomings and led the man from the *New Musical Express* to acclaim them as 'a workable musical street gang'.

The song lurches to an end and the band bob up and down uneasily while their kingpin blinks at the single row of bulbs of which the stage lighting consists.

'What I like about the cat,' Dale is saying seriously, 'is that 'e's always *pissed off.*'

'Would you care for anything to eat?' Stefano wonders, in the same lordly tone of voice he adopts in the Savoy Grill. 'Let's see if they run to a menu . . . Play "Crawling King Snake",' he shouts. This request is ignored.

Sammy Davis Jr, grown grandly proprietorial, brings bowls of potato chips and some pieces of chicken bone to which a few fragments of meat tenuously adhere. Two of the bulbs pop and go dead.

'You know something, man,' Dale says to me in a comradely tone, while Stefano is paying for the food, 'I worry about this tour.'

'Why in particular?'

'Well, wouldn't you? I'm not saying we 'aven't rehearsed. Or that Keith's off his head most of the time, which to be perfickly honest, 'e is. Or that Mr Fucking Superman' – he means Garth – 'is back in his room summoning up the Devil or whatever. It's just that' – he pulls up short and examines Kantner's recumbent form with a puzzled frown – 'I thought this geezer was supposed to be writing a book about the tour? 'E's not going to write anything if he's asleep all the time.'

'I'll wake him,' Stefano says, jerking the cigarette out of the corner of Dale's mouth and brushing the smouldering tip over the back of Kantner's outstretched hand.

'*Fuck* was that?' Kantner yelps, rising instantly back into consciousness.

Hooker plays 'Goodbye Blues' to sporadic applause and then marches off. 'Fucking *legend*,' Stefano says proudly. 'Now, that's the kind of cat we ought to have playing support on the tour. Not Savoy fucking Brown or whoever. Let's go and see the man. Let's go and pay our respects to this . . . *genius*.'

With the music fallen silent, the house lights up, the band stowing away their gear and the crowd stirring in their seats, our skin-tone is perhaps more of an issue. Undeterred, Stefano presses on round the side of the stage to a door behind which can be heard the sound of the main attraction demanding of his bass player what the fuck he think he's doing turning up his amp so loud ya hear me, Cornell, during the final number. For some reason Stefano's courage fails him. 'You do the honours, Nick,' he intones, and it is left to me to negotiate our entry into a room the size of a suburban dining table, where John Lee, the sweat glistening on his bald old head, shirt sleeves rolled up over his brawny old forearms, three sheepish sidekicks giving him as wide a berth as the space allows, is upending a bottle of Rolling Rock into his twisted old mouth. Here in the expedition's vanguard, only I get to hear him ask who the hell these white motherfuckers are.

'John,' Stefano says effusively, who to my certain knowledge has never met Hooker in his life. 'Johnny boy. Good to see you, man. These cats here' – by this time Dale, Ian and Kantner are crowded into the doorway – 'are just dying to shake your hand.'

There is a terrible, yawning silence, in which about a century and a half of interracial disharmony and musical expropriation seems to be gathered up. The bottle slides out of Hooker's fist and rattles on the concrete floor.

'Mr Hooker,' Ian says, bony white hand gingerly extended. 'Could I say what an honour it is to see you and how much I've enjoyed listening to your music?'

Hooker gives a little flick of his fingers. His shoulders twitch. 'Appreciate what you're saying, boy,' he says. 'Appreciate it.'

Five minutes later we are back outside in the parking lot, where Lester has fallen bleakly asleep in the Dodge's front seat and a couple of dull-eyed teenage hoods are fishing round the hubcaps.

'Come on,' Stefano says, placing himself by the rear wheel, monstrous, vindicated and unanswerable. 'Fuck off out of it.' Meekly the boys comply.

Ten hours later I wake to find the sour Ohio sky threatening rain and a rumpled Xerox from Angie outlining the day's activities in a precision-timed schedule (*3.34 p.m. Band assembles in hotel foyer; 3.36 p.m. Band leaves for sound-check*). Like most things connected to the Helium Kids, it is notional to a degree. Downstairs the breakfast bar is all but empty. The businessmen and their loaf-haired wives have been and gone, off to salesmen's conventions in Akron and Toledo, the waiters are busy clearing away smeary plates that once bore eggs over easy and hash browns, and there are only Ian and his wife June eating a modest refection of brown toast and English marmalade. Of all the Helium Kids and their partners, long-term or here for the ride, Ian and June are the most workaday, the ones most naturally tethered to some kind of observable reality.

'Enjoying yourselves?' I enquire.

'That's right,' Ian says. 'We'd have gone for a walk before breakfast, only they don't seem to like pedestrians round here, do they, love?'

'Silly, isn't it, a place not having proper pavements?' June says guilelessly.

Pretty soon they are telling me about their house in Surrey ('Banstead way'), its all-weather tennis courts ('The balls keep getting stuck in the hedge,' June explains. 'I have to buy a new packet every week') and how Ian would like to do the garden himself if he went there more often.

Back in the foyer, Stefano is deep in conversation with the hotel manager. The Gladstone bag dangles at his side. Miss Pamela, Miss Mercy and Miss Cynderella, having wreaked God knows what small-hours havoc, have disappeared somewhere. Garth's room-service tariff for the previous night is a comparatively modest $219.

Slowly the long day waxes and wanes. Come noon I shepherd Dale, Keith and Gary to an interview at the local radio station, where each agrees with a white-pant-suited lunatic named Morty the Wolfman just how much he is looking forward to tonight's concert, how pleasant and inspiring it is to be back in Ohio ('Where exactly are we?' Gary wonders as we troop into the studio) and how thrilled he is at the prospect of the new album. At two, I ride shotgun on Garth, a sulky guest of the local TV channel, as he deals out a theory or two about Roswell and Area 51, defends polygamy ('The cats on those Pacific islands or wherever are into it. It's cool') and volunteers the information that he intends to be cryogenically frozen after his death.

Rain falls intermittently on the drab Ohio plain. By four we are sound-checking at the venue, a big old 20,000-seater on the outskirts of town that used to be a baseball stadium and where the Beatles played on their 1965 tour.

'Fuck the Beatles,' Garth retorts, when this fact is brought to his attention. 'Fuck them, man.'

'And just where would you be without the Beatles?' Dale asks him.

'I'd be getting by,' Garth tells him. 'So would you.'

While the engineers are tinkering with the balance, he perches on one of the monitors reading a book called *Nazi Goldhunters*. From the back of the hall, where I stand coolly surveying the proceedings, the sound seems alternately tinny and gargantuan, a jingle of faintly amplified strings followed by a Wagnerian decibel rush. And still the equipment is trundling into place: half-a-dozen Marshall stacks, their dials artfully customised to display an '11' setting; two stout cabinets for Ian's thunderous bass; all the exotic paraphernalia – cow bells, timpani, Rank movie gongs – with which Keith likes to surround his industrial-strength drumkit. Angie, dressed in a leopardskin jumpsuit and crimson sneakers, is hectoring her attendant dogsbodies about the backstage rider, its numberless beer cans, its shrimp salads, its high-end amalgams of guava and passionfruit. Miss Mercy appears from nowhere and jitterbugs across the stage as Gary and Dale run through the guitar parts to 'Agamemnon's Mighty Sword', is told to fuck off will you darling by Stefano and does so.

Slowly the long day waxes, wanes, waxes, wanes and is mysteriously renewed. Tea, taken en masse at the hotel and meticulously pre-ordered, is a quaintly English affair: a choice of pekoe or Earl Grey; crumpets; boudoir sandwiches. 'They haven't sliced the cucumber thin enough,' Ian complains.

Afterwards I sneak up to my room to phone Westchester, and once again get Selma, who tells me that Mrs Duchesne is just fine but taking her bath right now. Of Mrs Du Pont there is no word. Twenty minutes later the cortege of limos steams off again to the concert hall where, in our absence, twenty thousand young Ohioans have been working themselves up into frenzy. Laminated security pass around my neck, the band safely established in their underground lair thirty feet under the stage, I wander out to inspect them. Jo Jo Gunne, the first of the two support acts, are finishing their set of anonymous scattergun boogie, and the kids – the wide-eyed girls with bangs hanging over their eyes, the canvas-jacketed high school footballers and their dates – are turning restive. There are dense clouds of cigarette smoke gathering under the roof and a paralysing smell of cooking oil from the burger and French-fry stands. Jo Jo Gunne go off to no applause at all and are replaced by Savoy Brown, more properly the Savoy Brown Blues Band, a leathery-faced assemblage of gnarled blues rockers whom the band have known since way back and of whose ferocious twelve-bar chug-a-lug-a-ding-dong they mildly approve. The sound, by this time, is preposterously loud and the balconies built at the top of the arena above what once were bleachers are vibrating up and down.

Back in the winding corridors, from whose ceilings condensation drips in king-size blobs, on my way to the dressing room I pass a pack of youngish men in white T-shirts and laminated security passes who, instinct assures me, are unconnected to the promoter and his staff.

'Who are all the guys with security passes?' I ask Stefano, who is leaning wearily against a breeze-blocked concrete wall while Angie itemises a list of the venue's inadequacies, how the dressing-room toilets are already blocked with paper and there's kids at the back trying to jump over the fuckin' wall for Chrissake.

'Dealers,' Stefano says. 'What can you do? Garth's been handing them out like invites to his wedding.'

The band, by this stage in the proceedings, are curiously elusive. There is no sign of them in the dressing room. The wide vestibule, decorated with pictures of basketball stars and football heroes, is empty of their spoor. Eventually I track them down to a kind of culvert, deep below the surface, like miners awaiting the cage that will return them to the pithead. Above our heads Savoy Brown are still flailing grimly away. At this depth the sound is wholly undifferentiated. *A-wharamalamala, a-wharamalalala, chug-a-lug-a-lug-a-lug. B'doing, b'doing.* 'They're no fucking good, are they?' Dale says sadly. He is wearing a kind of string vest over a green shirt with a portrait of Bobby Charlton on the front. Keith, slouching alongside him in white boiler suit and bowler hat, a drumstick clutched in each hand, stares fixedly into space.

It is nearing 10 p.m. The band will play for two hours, maybe three, depending on how they feel. And how do they feel? Garth looks stricken, Dale composed, Gary eager, Ian detached, Keith bemused. Somebody puts their head around the culvert wall and says, 'Five.' The band stir like troubled dreamers. Destiny is calling. It is calling, destiny is. There are back-slappings and rump-bumpings, all that willed raucousness that has replaced the effervescent satisfaction of the early days, when it was enough merely to play. 'Fucking *get* in there.' 'You fucking *know* it, man.'

I give them the thumbs up and trail back along the serpentine corridors to a door that leads to the media pen, slantwise to the stage, where two dozen or so journalists, hangers on and members of the promoter's family are craning forward for a better view of the elderly desperado in white tuxedo, bootlace tie, gardenia buttonhole and Stetson hat (where do they get these emcees? Where do they get them?) who, amid a gathering tornado of whoops and hollers, is declaring that *ladeez 'n' gentlemin*, it's his *grey-hate pie-leisure ta intra-dooce from Enger-land, the grate-assed rock 'n' roll band in the whirr-hurled, ladeez 'n' gentlemin, the Helium Kids* . . . And, all of a sudden, as if by magic, there they are, five diminutive figures loping shyly on stage into a lightstorm of ricocheting lasers and billowing dry ice. The bass starts up, like some gross seismic disturbance from beneath the crust of the world, and I can hear Garth ponderously intone the open-ing lines of 'Avalon Bound'.

For I am bound for Avalon . . . mystic city far across the astral plain . . .

As ever on these occasions, objectivity is thrust aside by spectacle, what the highbrow critic in *Recorded Sound* once called 'the visual oomph of the mimesis'. Every aesthetic instinct I possess counsels that each individual part of this cacophony – Garth's screech, Dale and Gary's guitar trade-offs, Ian's whomping bass lines, Keith's route-march 4/4 – is the most frightful bollocks. And yet the girl alongside me is already in tears, with one hand raised above her head in Pentecostal fervour, while the boy next to her has adopted the stance peculiar to male Helium Kids fans – a kind of bug-eyed crouch with clenched fists windmilling the empty air. *These are dark times*, Garth informs us, *but we will guide you to the light*, and the two hundred crazies nearest to the front surge forward to smash upon the security line braced against the stage front. In an intensely competitive busi-ness, how do we rate the Helium Kids? I'd say that, if not quite equal to the Stones, they are every bit as good as Led Zeppelin and about a thousand times better than Grand Funk Railroad. They do 'Chronos Wakes', one of Garth's paeans to the occult, by which time the girl next to me has her hand down the front of her jeans and is moaning quietly. A frail, dervish-like figure comes gyrating past, whirling at such a speed that it knocks a cigarette out of the mouth of a woman standing nearby. This turns out to be Angie, who yanks my arm, brings her face to within an inch of my ear so that I can smell her hot, sugary breath and murmurs, 'Isn't this terrific, Nicko? Rilly terrific.' And it *is* terrific. For we are in the imperial phase, where the Kids can do no wrong, where no summit is beyond their grasp, where Garth could run for president, were he eligible, where everything they touch is irradiated by the bright sheen of romanticism, that mythical compact between group and audience, on which all popular music ultimately depends.

Later the boys will return to their hotel, where, with the exception of Ian, who likes an early night and dines frugally in his room, they will party, score drugs, have sex, gratuitously insult the wife of the Mayor of Columbus, and run up a damages bill of $10,483.15.

The tour proceeds without incident. Well, more or less. Columbus, Ohio. Chicago, Illinois. Duluth, Minnesota. A dart back to New York for two long-sold-out nights at Madison Square Garden, and then a whistle-stop peregrination around the southern states. St Louis, Atlanta, Birmingham. At New Orleans, a confederacy of local Baptist churches pickets the gig to protest at Garth's 'Satanist' lyrics. At Little Rock, a stack of vinyl records is ceremonially incinerated by the Klan. At Austin, Keith is narrowly prevented from driving a purloined coupé into the hotel swimming pool. There is an anxious moment as the plane touches down at Galveston, where Dale is found to be suffering from a surfeit of fast white powders (Stefano, an expert in these affairs, manages to revive him on the tarmac without the need for medical assistance) and a mild frisson of excitement when the entourage is joined by Genevieve Le Strange, who, in addition to being the most celebrated groupie that the West Coast has to offer, is a young lady of only fifteen years of age. When not engaged on her professional duties, Miss Le Strange can be seen in the hotel foyers eating striped candy out of a paper bag. The reviews, meanwhile, with the exception of Ralph J. Gleason in *Rolling Stone* ('a dismal and discordant confection of over-heated blues rock, devoid of lyrical grace and musical intelligence') are good-to-excellent. On the strength of these endorsements, *Got Live with the Helium Kids* peaks at No. 3 on the *Billboard* chart. Don, communicating by telegram from London, is reported to be very pleased.

Meanwhile, there are letters following me west. A stack of them at Sioux City. Another mighty clump waiting at Sacramento. From

Lucille, a note written in bilious green biro on a lettercard adorned with 'Scenes from Old Massachusetts' that reads *Dear Nick, You will be pleased, I am sure, to know that I am having a splendid time here in 'the East' and can think of no earthly reason to leave it. Selma's help is, of course, greatly appreciated. But where is my daughter? Yrs L. D.* From a law firm called Cladding, Grunewald and Niedermeyer, documents pertaining to a divorce petition filed by Mrs Rosalind Lafayette Du Pont, of Westchester, Connecticut, on grounds of unreasonable behaviour and then some. I read this down by the hotel pool, in whose turbid shallows Garth, Genevieve and Miss Cynderella are lobbing beach balls at each other, marvelling not only at the misery it is possible for one person to inflict on another but at the incongruity of the two lives I so unharmoniously lead. Miss Cynderella surfaces from one of her athletic handstands, gives me a negligent wave and handfuls of chlorinated water fitfully descend over Messrs Cladding, Grunewald and Niedermeyer's letter. And then, too, there is this, dated a fortnight ago but sent on from Westchester, written in a hand so wavery that it takes several minutes to decipher.

The House of Peace, Love and Serenity, Echo Beach, Oregon

My dear, dear Boy,

How long is it since last we spoke? Three years? Four? I contend that the fault is undoubtedly mine, but that there are REASONS for this to which you should be made party. I am hoping all is well with you and that the name of Du Pont is making its lustre shine wherever you go. I have fetched up here in Oregon with some YOUNG PEOPLE whose company I savour – again for reasons to which you should be made party. In short, son, I invite – no, I instruct – you to visit me as soon as you conveniently can, for the flesh grows weak and may soon be extinguished altogether. The

dust flows forward and the dust flows back. Telephone me on this
number, which is sometimes answered, on other occasions not.

Your ever-loving father,

Maurice Du Pont

'You know what I think?' says Angie, who reads this over my shoulder, with one jelly-fish breast pressed into the centre of my back. 'I
think he ain't well.'

'What makes you say that?'

'Had an uncle who used to write weird letters like that. And then
not long after he died.'

And here is something else. I seem to have developed this thing
with Angie. I have, though. It all began on the night of the Columbus
concert, in its moist afterglow, when she sidled back to my room to
help me assemble the next day's schedule and was still there at dawn.
Who knows how these things happen? She can't weigh seven stone,
and her hipbones stick out of her pelvis like cleaver blades, but she is
at heart, I discover, a homely girl. Coming back from breakfast on that
first morning, I find her, kimono-clad, on the phone earnestly enquiring about the welfare of various oddly named male acquaintances. 'So
who are Donovan and Jimi?' I enquire – not exactly jealous, but nonetheless hungry for detail. 'They're my fuckin' *cats*,' Angie explains. 'You
want a 'lude?' Angie is solicitous of my welfare. She has room service
bring me glasses of milk at all hours, folds up my clothes and places
them fondly over chairbacks and keeps me au fait with gossip that a
less-seasoned observer might miss. It is Angie, for instance, who files
the disquieting intelligence that Dale owes $3000 to one of his dealers
('And Dale had better fuckin' wise up, cos the guy is, y'know, connected'),
and offers details of the rivalry between Genevieve Le Strange and the
GTOs, a sordid inter-generational conflict whose blue touch-paper
was lit in a hotel bar in Galveston where Miss Le Strange lightly
demanded to know who all these fucking old women were.

It is Angie, too, who makes me telephone the number on the old man's letter and shakes her head when there is no one there. As for me, milk glass in hand, clothes tidied away, scuttlebutt pouring into my ears, I am clearly cracking up. I stare out of the hotel window at the Iowa cornfields, at the California desert's edge, but my mind is a couple of thousand miles away back in Westchester, in a curtained room with broken ashtrays scrunching underfoot, the wind buffeting the high windows and the squirrels marauding over the roofs. Meanwhile, all the incidental scenery of a Helium Kids tour is being wheeled into place. Don's parchment-skinned English lawyer flies in to Chicago, locks himself into a hotel suite with Stefano for an hour, and then goes away again. The once reliable and tractable turn erratic and dangerous. At Sioux City a roadie appears in the hotel restaurant where the band are at dinner waving a loaded pistol: he is eventually pacified and subdued. Afterwards Stefano flings the pistol down a waste-disposal chute. At breakfast, over flagons of black coffee and tall glasses of frosted orange juice, people compare notes. They decide that the kids are less amenable now, security more edgy, the cops more scared, the local authorities less indulgent. The damages bill climbs to $21,000. *Got Live with the Helium Kids* is still hovering around the top five.

Three weeks gone, the tour rolls into LA, where five days furlough is in prospect prior to six or seven West Coast stadium shows, to which the boys, or so I inform the local media on their behalf, 'are greatly looking forward'. In fact, everyone is exhausted. The band hole up in a big house on Mulholland, from which address they are chauffeured to fancy restaurants, the Playboy Mansion, a surreptitious session or two – no work permits for recording have been issued – and, in Keith's case, aeronautical museums. Garth celebrates this intermission by going to sleep for thirty-six hours and then staging a party at which – I only have Stefano's word for this – the cabaret is provided by a chorus line of naked dwarfs. LA, meanwhile, is not looking its best. The smog hangs over Mulholland in a dense orange groundsheet and Laurel Canyon, where the hippy ladies sit over their embroidery and tend their bean curd, is thick with fog. Absolved of her usual duties, with only the band's limos to book and the chef to chivvy, Angie turns steadily more confiding. Like many of the denizens of this queer, sequestered world of ours, she has ambitions that prodigiously transcend it.

'Do you know what I'd like to do one day?' she demands one morning in the bedroom under the roof on Mulholland Drive, half-dressed and turning away from me so that the principal image in view is the snake tattoo disappearing into the cleft in her buttocks.

The divorce papers and the letter from the old man are staring at me from the desk. 'No. Tell me.'

'I'd like to study literature someplace.' She looks at me closely. 'At some arts college.'

'What sort of literature do you like?'

'Well, I sort of like John Updike,' Angie says, looking more vulpine than ever. 'Only it's not, uh . . . It's not what I'd call *realistic*.'

All around us can be heard the sound of Mulholland Drive getting into its collective stride. Away down the corridor someone is strumming – badly – the opening chords to 'Jumping Jack Flash'. There is a splutter or two and a slither of lightly shod feet as Miss Mercy and Miss Pamela or whoever go chirruping down the staircase. Outside, the sun is a pale yellow disc behind lurching clouds.

'Angie,' I say, cheered by the talk of John Updike, the naked back and the snake tattoo. 'You ought to come to England with me. Come to London and see the sights.'

'I'd like that,' Angie says, uncorking from its vial something that has hitherto been in short supply on the tour – a feeling of unalloyed sincerity. Down in the communal dining room, where Filipina maids with imperturbable expressions are bringing in trays of exotic fruit and a massive cabinet TV has shots of Nixon stepping warily out of a limousine, there is an air of barely suppressed excitement. Jerry, greeting us in the hallway, puts a finger to his lips and gestures at the figures of Stefano and Don's English lawyer bent over a squawk box and clearly in the middle of a conference call. The voices rasp back and forth and, after a sentence or two, I deduce that the subject under discussion is the free concert in Louisiana.

'What you must understand, Mr Tirpitz,' Stefano regally informs the speaker, 'what you must understand, is that I cannot cut you a deal. I can listen to what you have to say and I may approve of it, but I cannot cut you a deal. Only Mr Shard in London can do that. I have Mr Shard's legal representative beside me and he can confirm this. He can also convey proposals to Mr Shard. Isn't that right, Mr Palamountain?'

'That is correct,' Mr Palamountain uneasily concurs, who would much rather be in his chambers in Lincoln's Inn Fields watching the English rain than here with the freaks in smog-bound LA.

'All I want to know, Mr Tirpitz,' Stefano goes on, 'and what Mr Shard and Mr Palamountain want to know, before the negotiations proceed any further, is, to be perfectly frank, how much money we can expect to get paid for this.'

There is a prolonged detonation from the squawk box ending with the words 'free' and 'concert'.

'Now I really think we ought to be a little more grown up about this,' Stefano says, somewhat less regally than before. Miss Mercy, traversing the room with a joint the size of a carrot in her hand, comes suddenly to a halt and whips up the top of her jerkin for him to admire the dense, honey-coloured protrusions beneath. 'You can call it anything you want, and my associate Mr Du Pont will be happy to prepare any publicity material you wish to distribute. But the fucking Who got $15,000 for Woodstock and my boys don't go anywhere for less than twenty-five.'

There is another tremor or two from the squawk box.

'And no, I am not paying for the fucking light show, Mr Tirpitz. And there had better be a helicopter to take us to the site.'

Angie has disappeared somewhere. The letter from the old man is in my fist. I walk through into the cubby hole, beyond the dining room, which Stefano is using as a makeshift office. Here there are numberless hotel receipts, a DA's letter relating to an unspecified but compromising incident in Sioux City, a cheque made out to Shard Enterprises for $85,000 and a Bakelite telephone. Against all expectation, the number is answered on the second ring.

'This is the House of Peace, Love and Serenity. How may I help?'

It's the usual blissed-out male hippy voice, but with an odd, scholarly overlay, as if Poindexter had been induced to sample some Indian hemp.

'Would it be possible to speak to Maurice Du Pont?'

'Is that his son? We've been waiting to hear from you, man,' the voice solemnly intones. A dozen feet away, behind the boxwood partition, Stefano is issuing a series of complicated threats and instructions about cash payments, support acts and security details. 'Where are you right now?'

'Outside of Los Angeles.'

'That's groovy. Well, you better get here as soon as you can if you want to see him.'

'Why's that?'

'He's dying, man.'

Somehow the news that the old man is dying seems less important than his actual whereabouts.

'What's the House of Peace, Love and Serenity?'

'It's a self-sustaining community of like-minded liberal individuals working for the common good,' says the voice with evident pride.

'How do I get there?'

'We're about a half hour out of Salem.'

Further particulars follow. Curiously, the $85,000 cheque that lies a foot away from the phone cradle is unsigned. The dining room, when I return to it ten minutes later, is empty save for Stefano, red-faced and peevish, to whom a Filipina maid is administering coffee.

'Jesus,' Stefano says. 'That fucking girl has got to go. Shoving her tits in Mr Palamountain's face like that. What's the matter with you, Nick?'

We look at each other across the wine-stained carpet and its fruit-laden tables, baffled and exhausted by the world in which we have had the misfortune to fetch up. Outside the traffic snorts and concertinas on Mulholland and the smog hangs lower.

'You want a 'lude?' Angie asks, shortly afterwards.

'Anything you got,' I tell her, gratefully.

'GROOVIN' WITH THE BAND' – THE MEMOIRS OF MISS LEONIE CREEMCHEEZE

You know, I think the public seriously misunderstands the groupie lifestyle. Sure, there are girls who just want to sleep with rock stars, but that's only an animal thing. Really, it's a lot more complicated. I always think of myself as a social worker. You know, the guys are in this alien place, and it's like: are the natives friendly? Where can I get my jeans fixed? Is there a washing machine around here? And we sort stuff out for them, put them in touch with people who can help them. Yes, there's sex involved, but usually it's much more maternal . . .

The Helium Kids? Well, really they were just the sweetest kind of guys. Well, mostly. I remember when Dale showed up the first time in here, straight off the plane, no shows for a couple of days, in this city he's only ever seen in the movies and on TV, and he's like 'I really need some food, some English food I can eat. Can anyone get me some Earl Grey tea?' And some Gentleman's Relish, which is this weird kind of anchovy paste. And believe me, this kind of stuff isn't easy to find on a Sunday afternoon in LA, but we did our best, and he really appreciated that . . .

. . . Naturally, I was very excited to meet Garth. Groovy Garth Dangerfield, we used to call him. And when somebody said, 'Garth

Dangerfield is in town and he really wants to meet you,' I was just like this dippy teenager who's got a date to the prom. But do you know, it wasn't at all like I expected. I mean, I got to his room at the Marmont and there are all these black curtains hanging over the window and incense burning and a copy of the *Tibetan Book of the Dead* on the table. And, I mean, I've been in some heavy scenes in my time. But then Garth turns out to be this real gentleman. Always sending flowers up to my apartment. I introduced him to my mother, which is not something I generally do, on account of my mother *not really approving* of my lifestyle, and she said: 'Honey, if I were you I would head on back to England and *chain myself to the gates of his country estate* or wherever it is he lives.' And I had to tell her that while there are a lot of women in Garth's life, he knows I'll always be there for him ...

... Ian I didn't know so well, which is probably on account of him being a loner and then getting married and all. A very serious, thoughtful guy. But there was one time when he said 'Leo' – the guys all used to call me Leo – 'you have to do something for me.' And I said, 'Sure, Ian, what's that?' – not really thinking about it because, you know, we get a lot of unusual requests in this business. And he said, 'You have to read to me.' 'What exactly do I have to read?' I asked. 'Saul Bellow or Norman Mailer or someone?' And he said no, that wasn't what he wanted. And so we got a cab and went to this children's bookstore, and he bought a copy of Laura Ingalls Wilder's *Little House on the Prairie*, and had me come back to the hotel and read it to him, which I am proud to say that I did ...

... Keith I never had much conversation with. Not the most sociable guy. I think he missed his wife and his kids back in England. He was always sending them postcards or calling them from his room and not realising about the time difference. And then he'd start ordering drinks from room service, and crying a little, and it was the saddest thing ...

... The one I really *hated* was the road manager. Stefano. Nobody liked Stefano. I don't know what he did because I always kept apart from him myself – I'm a very fastidious kind of person – but there were girls on the LA scene who'd just *vomit* if you told them Stefano was having a party and he wanted them to come ...

13. ECHO BEACH

West Coast baby always wins the race
West Coast baby always on my case . . .

'West Coast Baby'

There was a hippy girl with rat's tail hair at the wheel of a flatbed pick-up truck to meet me at the airport. She looked thoroughly bored, so profoundly disillusioned with the Age of Aquarius that bets could have been taken on her readiness to expire on the dashboard next to the packets of soap and the hanks of paper tissues. The road wandered south through a wasteland of car parks and service stations and breakers' yards filled with twenty-foot-high piles of teetering scrap, and the truck floundered on its uneven surface, sending the farm tools in the back racketing every which way. For a mile or two the girl kept her eye on the tarmac. Then, as the metal yards gave way to back lanes leading out to the coast, she perked up a little, announced that her name was Lindy and made self-conscious efforts to start a conversation.

'Richard said you were in the music business. Is that right?'

'More or less.'

'Richard doesn't let us have a record player or nothing. He says it's bad for morale. But there's a radio in the kitchen we can listen to when we do the chores.'

Pale, ochre light swept in from the west. Lindy's hands gripped the steering wheel so rigidly that the knuckles had turned white. Her fingers were unfeasibly small, like crab bones winking up from the ocean floor. She would have been about twenty-one.

'Who's Richard?'

'Oh, I don't know. He's the guy who's kind of in charge of us. I mean' – she briskly corrected herself – 'nobody's actually in *charge* of anyone. We all have our, uh, individual autonomy. But there are some basic rules and Richard kind of says what they ought to be.'

By now we were moving rapidly through empty backroads with high grass verges, past villages of straggling white houses, community centres made of breeze blocks, all the quaint paraphernalia of north-west Oregon. The ocean, looming ever nearer, seemed grey and constricted. Lindy had got the hang of the truck now, and there were fewer jolts.

'Do you know my father? Maurice Du Pont?'

'Oh yeah, Maurice.' She looked uneasy for a moment, as if admitting to knowing someone was something else that 'Richard' might not approve of, and took a right onto a dirt-track so that the farm tools clattered again in the back. 'He's a sweet old man. But he don't come out of his cabin much these days.'

'Is there a woman called Daphne with him?'

Lindy gave a little high-pitched giggle, showing a line of variegated teeth, as if the mention of Daphne's name conjured up the memory of all manner of comic interludes here on the Pacific shore, high-grade dissipation from a happier time. 'Not any more. She left a while back.' The truck slithered on, through patches of mossy greensward, bumped over a root or two, sent various specimens of poultry fluttering into the undergrowth and then came to rest in a clearing boxed in by tall trees. Here a table had been propped up vertical against an oil can and covered with a sheet on which someone who had trouble forming their 'e's had stencilled the words *The*

House of Peace, Love and Serenity. Welcome. 'I guess this is it,' Lindy said.

Like everyone else in America, I had seen footage of the hippy communes – their news value a bit diminished by now – on the cine-reels and read about them in the *New York Times*. The band had even spent a week in one as a publicity stunt – a $50-a-day celebrity cara-vanserai modelled on Rishikesh, with morning prayer sessions led by a Maharishi lookalike known as the Mighty Bhagwan, and gourmet cookery. The images served up for public consumption were always the same: lissom girls in see-through summer frocks with flowers in their hair romping in the sun; singalongs to limping acoustic guitar; long lines of what looked like romantic poets bringing in the hay. The House of Peace, Love and Serenity was a much more down-to-earth version of this ideal. A dozen or so nondescript huts had been erected by the clearing's edge, gathered around a long, low barn. Closer to where Lindy had parked the truck, a patch of grass had been stamped flat. Here a few chickens pattered feebly back and forth, and a group of women dressed in shapeless frocks – two of them in the last stages of pregnancy – were grimly disputing whose turn it was to work a handpump. These activities were being keenly supervised by a dark-haired man with a big, jutting chin who stood in a Napoleonic atti-tude with one foot planted squarely in front of the other on a mound of raised turf.

'That's Rick,' Lindy said, showing more interest than usual. 'He's really cool.'

Fetched up in the clearing, luggage still in my hand, I felt suddenly ill at ease. There was a sharp wind coming in off the sea and the drag-gled sisterhood tugging at the pump handle shivered as they worked. Looking for signs of civilisation – aerials, electricity, storehouses – I turned up nothing but a telephone line snaking in across the treetops. For a moment it seemed perfectly possible that the women might each produce a hatchet out of their robes, truss me up with ropes and drag me off for sacrifice at some lynching point in the woods. Richard, stumping across from the raised mound with the toes of his boots carefully angled against the mud, did nothing at all to allay these qualms. He looked suspicious, beady-eyed, cross at being interrupted in all the outstandingly important tasks he had planned. As he came near he drew himself up and announced formally:

'Welcome to the House of Peace, Love and Serenity.'

'It's good to be here.'

'A sanctum where the traveller finds respite and the seeker after truth receives enlightenment.'

A pig had now appeared among the chickens and was gobbling up the ears of corn they had left behind.

'I'm sure they do.'

Here again the newsreels had failed us. The men you saw in the *Time* magazine photospreads, flanked by their bright-eyed women-folk, were rangy, leonine types. Richard, alternatively, was short and running – no, hurtling – to fat, so tubbily diminutive in fact that he should have been hanging around Bag End with Frodo and the boys. Having got the stuff about serenity and enlightenment off his chest, he seemed to relax slightly. Perhaps, after all, there was a life beyond livestock and handpumps.

'A tall Englishman,' he said, not so much to me or Lindy but to a vast, unseen audience that had clearly congregated beyond the clearing's edge. 'I guess I was just about right.'

'Right about what?'

'I'm *psychic*,' Richard said matter-of-factly, as if he were explaining that he was left-handed or took sugar in his coffee. 'I can tell what people look like, and what they're thinking. It's quite a gift. I can recommend it. For example, I can tell that when you look at those pregnant women over by the pump you're wondering whether I'm the father. A reasonable assumption, but in this particular instance wrong.'

Smiling at this, I turned to Lindy to see if she felt like sharing the joke, but her face was absolutely impassive. Meekly, almost cringing as she spoke the words, she said: 'Can I go and get dinner now?'

'Did you fetch my prescription from the pharmacy?'

'Oh my God. I forgot.' Lindy's features contorted in anguish. 'I'm so sorry, Rick. Truly I am. Can you forgive me?'

'We'll talk about it later,' Richard said, a bit too gratified by the effect he was having on his acolyte for comfort. 'And now, Mr . . .?'

'Du Pont. Nick Du Pont.'

'Yeah. Du Pont.' On the instant, he became more business-like, like a headmaster showing prospective parents around a school. 'I expect you'll want to know something about our set-up here.' The women, who had finished whatever they were doing at the pump, stared at him invitingly, as if eager to be given something else to do. Richard ignored them, and instead marched me off towards the row of huts. 'There's about twenty of us. Nineteen, maybe. You'll see that we're pretty much self-sustaining. Grow most of our food. We haven't found a way of making our clothes just yet – the cotton don't take too well here – but we're working on it. You'd better let me show you around.'

There wasn't a great deal to see. The huts were sparsely furnished, with tarpaper tacked over the windows. In the barn, three silent men in thick pullovers sat darning blankets. The storeroom, stoutly padlocked, turned out to contain several hundred packets of pasta and some tins of pilchards. The wind blew in off the sea with increasing force, crazing the branches of the trees.

'As for your dad,' Richard said, surveying the pasta bags with a look that suggested it was a wonder so much of God's bounty could be concentrated in a single spot, 'I don't know how far you're aware of his, uh, involvement with us?'

Outside the storeroom there was a pile of what looked suspiciously like human excrement. 'Hardly at all. When exactly did he arrive?'

'Let me see. We have a pretty high turnover here. Sometimes the people aren't what you'd call committed.' He gave a little sniff of contempt at all this human frailty. 'It's not always easy to keep track. Two years. Or maybe three. There was a woman called Daphne with him at first – bit of a peculiar piece, that one – but she didn't stay too long. Had trouble getting used to our' – Richard cast about for a phrase that would do justice to the complex administrative arrangements he had in mind – 'our little ways. Now, at first your dad – Brother Maurice, we like to call him – played a, let me see, highly active part in the life of the community. Fixed us some lobster creels at one point. That was very much appreciated. But these last few months he hasn't been so well.'

It was definitely human excrement by the storeroom door. 'What's the matter with him?'

'It's his lungs,' Richard said, suddenly abandoning all pretence of suavity. 'He can't hardly breathe half the time.'

'Has he been getting medical attention?'

'There's a doctor comes over from Cimino to see him once a week. Dr Fargas, his name is. Quite a groovy guy. He sympathises with what I'm trying to do. You have to understand that we're not used to dealing with illness here. Usually people just go the emergency room in town. Don't mind me being frank, Mr Du Pont, but all this has cost me a hell of a lot of money.'

'Where is he right now?'

'Brother Maurice is in there.' Richard gravely indicated the furthermost of the line of huts. 'You've got to excuse me. I have to give those women something to do. If you don't keep them occupied there's no knowing what they mightn't get up to. One time they broke into the storehouse with some of the art supplies and started making collages out of the pasta.' The pale, stubby face with its jutting jaw creased over in irritation. 'Look. Don't think I'm bullshitting you. He's really sick, man. Really. You hear what I'm saying?'

He strode over to the waiting women and began lecturing them in his high, earnest voice. Mutely attentive, they crowded round.

The door of the hut was slightly ajar. Its surface was soft and yielding, balsa-frail. Inside, thin, low-level light glowed eerily around the window frames. There was a suspicion of mice skittering away into silence and a faint, susurrating burble that turned out to be coming from a kerosene heater so ancient that Aunt Em had probably fixed it up for Dorothy back home in Kansas before the tornado struck. Oddly enough, the second object that caught my eye was an elaborately framed, peach-hued poster from the summer of 1967 advertising the Grateful Dead, Quicksilver Messenger Service and New Riders of the Purple Sage at the Winterland, back in the days when Haight-Ashbury had been an Elysian Field rather than a needle-run. God knows what I had expected, but there he was, eyes gleaming, cadaverous and glum, propped up against oatmeal-coloured pillows, breathing hard. The sound ran in counterpoint to the hiss of the kerosene heater. The wind rushed in suddenly, slamming the door back onto its hinges, and I pushed it to.

'How are you doing?'

How was I doing? There was absolutely no way of answering this. Did I tell him about the emotional wrecking ball back in Westchester? The extravagances of Mulholland Drive? Angie's naked back in the LA dawn? 'I'm doing OK,' I said, searching the room for signs of just how much Richard had been neglecting him, but finding only water carafes, little mounds of pills in saucers, neatly folded blankets and laundry heaps. 'How are you doing?'

The old man thought about this, as if it was a question he'd never really considered before, concealing some highly abstruse code that needed to be cracked before he could answer. 'Not good,' he said eventually. 'Not so good at all. You get my letter?'

'I got *a* letter. The one where you talked about the young people whose company you savoured.'

All the time I was trying to work out how I felt about being here on the west coast of Oregon on an increasingly chilly day in December, in a hippy commune sickbay. In fact, there were three emotions that could be separated out. The first was a terrifying sadness at finding him here, alone and in pain, in the devitalising company of a dozen or two simple-lifers who thought that some end could be served by calling him Brother Maurice. And the second was the usual anger at the hurt done to my mother and to me, the humiliations of childhood, the cardboard box in the attic – all that old North Park stuff which was as vivid to me here in the Oregon boondocks as it had ever been in the world outside. But the third was a feeling of incongruity, the thought that while Richard drilled his attendant nutjobs on their muddy parade ground and the old man lay gasping for breath on his oatmeal pillows, there was another world boiling chaotically away beyond them, the world of palatial hotels and smuggled pharmacopeia, Angie's hipbone bumping against mine in the tangy king-size bed.

And then, all of a sudden, it got worse. A whole lot worse.

'Where's your mother?' enquired the old man, his powerful, wide-eyed glare sweeping the room. 'Didn't she come too?'

Oh Christ, I thought. *He's only lost his marbles as well.* After which all thought of reparation vanished into the ether, and I sat and stared at him. Father and son. Son and father. Here in the House of Peace, Love and Serenity, which Richard, I now remembered, pronounced peace, *lurve* and sereni*tee*. In the west Oregon cabin with the wind surging in through the gaps in the slats and melancholy late-afternoon darkness duelling with the glow from the kerosene heater and the mice frisking in the shadows.

'Why the hell you crying for, anyhow?' the old man wondered.

Why was I crying? Again, there was no way of answering. After a few moments' highly desultory conversation, during which the old man once again queried the absence of his wife, I excused myself and stumbled off into the twilight. The clearing was empty, but occasional glints of light broke out from under the doors of the huts. On a hunch I selected the largest one, which additionally had a primitive artist's representation of the sun painted on the door, and stepped inside. Here, desk illuminated by a storm lantern, rapt, eager face like an intelligent rodent, Richard was arranging shards of coloured glass into a complex, symbolic pattern.

'You didn't tell me his mind had gone.'

'Brother Maurice is a little ... confused,' Richard said, non-committally. 'But really, you know, perfectly lucid most of the time.'

'I need to call an ambulance.'

'The line's down,' Richard said, waving a bunch of white, prehensile fingers. 'Why not wait until morning and then Lindy can drive you over in the truck?' He examined the shards of glass rather sorrowfully, as if, like the people who lacked commitment, they had somehow let him down. 'Anyhow, it's late. Come and have something to eat.'

We had supper – it was mostly beans – in the barn where the men had been darning blankets. A fire burned into a defective chimney, sending clouds of smoke rolling hazily round the room. If the people you saw in the *Time* magazine stories about hippy communes all seemed to be cut from the same distinctive pattern, then the denizens of the House of Peace, Love and Serenity, found here partaking of their evening meal, were all running heterogeneously amok. The oldest would have been about seventy; the youngest was pale, flustered Lindy. The food was eaten in silence, broken only by the clang of cutlery against plate, the crackle of the fire, occasional coughing (the fault of the smoke) and the sound made by Richard's high, corn-crake voice as he read to them some improving remarks about the need to strive for unity between man and nature. When he had finished, one of the pregnant women brought him a bowl of soup. I glanced at the book's cover. It was a paperback edition of *Walden*. After this Richard clambered to his feet to declare that the toilet rolls were running low and that three of the chickens had disappeared, and bawled out an elderly man in a ponytail who had failed in some unspecified domestic task. Nobody in the audience stirred.

All through the meal, I could hear a far-off booming noise mingling with the thump of the wind as it drove in against the treetops. It was only when Richard had finished upbraiding the man in the ponytail and a shock-haired under-strapper in a dress the size of a bell tent named Sister Marigold began complaining about the sanitary arrangements that I realised it was the sea. Leaving Sister Marigold to continue her harangue about the tampons that were clogging up the portable toilets, I checked on the old man (asleep) and then followed a path that led from the clearing's edge through rows of great high birch trees that shone in the moonlight and over to the long spar of the beach. Here the sky had turned blue-black, and the tide was coming in: rolling white breakers that crashed endlessly onto the briny sand as if there were phantom horses cavorting in the swell. The air was heavy with spray. Time was moving on, I thought, like black hounds under the moon, moving on for the old man, moving on for Stefano, Angie and the others down on Mulholland Drive, moving on for Don in his Mayfair office suite, moving on for Lucille, three thousand miles away in Westchester, moving on for Rosalind, wherever in the world she was, and moving on for me. Moving on so rapidly that before I knew it I would be able to look back and fix its constituent parts – the white hair of the waves combed back, the tumbling wind, the old man in his cot, the poster of the Grateful Dead at Winterland – in a trajectory whose arc could only be guessed at.

Back in the hut the old man had woken up and was scrabbling timidly at the covers. Someone had brought him a storm lantern, in whose cylinder the light flickered and gambolled, to add to the glow of the kerosene lamp.

'Where you been?'

'Down to the sea.'

'I used to go down there sometimes awhile.' He made it sound like a camping trip to the Bayou, trekking in the Ozarks. 'You stopping long?'

'In the morning I'll get an ambulance and we'll take you away from here.'

'I'm just fine,' the old man said, looking at me without precisely seeing me. 'Nice bunch of folks.'

'You need proper care and attention.'

He muttered something I couldn't catch. A weird, eldritch noise started up from the barn, which turned out to be community singing. *Puff the Magic Dragon, lived by the sea*, the voices chorused. *And frolicked in the autumn mists, in a land called Honna Lee* ... Cognoscenti always maintained that this was a paean to dope-smoking. I wasn't so sure.

'Richard, now,' the old man said wearily, addressing a space somewhere between the tarpaper wall and the back of my head. 'He's an educated man. Taught psychology at Duke or someplace.'

The counter-culture was full of 'educated men'.

'So what's he doing here?'

'Bringing enlightenment to the world, I guess.' *Little Jackie Paper loved that rascal Puff/And brought him strings and sealing wax and other fancy stuff* ... As sung by Peter, Paul and Mary on the TV hootenannies, this had always seemed a rather fanciful nursery rhyme. Now it sounded like 'The Battle Hymn of the Republic'.

'Nice, *educated* guy,' the old man said, flinging his hands out in front of him as if conducting the distant choir.

He talked a lot that night, fervent and impatient, on into the small hours. Puff the Magic Dragon flew in under the door to hear him and little Jackie Paper sat wide-eyed at the bedhead with his strings and sealing wax, and on he talked. Occasionally he spoke to me direct, but most of the time the audience were phantoms, gathered up in the shadows, somewhere between wall and heater, between Puff and Jackie, and, as it turned out, this world and the next. Most of it I barely understood, although Daphne's name recurred, but sometimes the mists rolled back, revealing landscapes I could wander with him, and there was a terrible moment when he said: 'Where's Nick? Nick ought to be here.' Shortly after this I checked his pulse, and found it was 120. The hippy singalong had long since died away. There was a mattress propped against the far wall of the hut and I manoeuvred it onto the floor, lay down on it and listened to the noise of the Oregon night: wind, rain, wild animals rampaging through the undergrowth, Richard's voice calling out once or twice, high and querulous, like someone directing traffic, and always the sound of the old man chuntering excitably to himself. Several times I got up to look at him – once I went so far as to smooth his forehead – and his face, mouth moving restlessly back and forth, had a mad, faraway look as if its animating spirit had long since checked out.

When I woke up, far into the dawn, the noise of the old man talking had stopped. In its place I could hear what sounded like someone pulverising pieces of wood into tiny fragments. He was quite dead. I stretched the blanket over his head – it caught, I remember, on the tomahawk tip of his nose – pulled open the door of the hut and strode out along the path to the beach. Here the sea had receded and there were jellyfish washed up on the strand. I walked up and down for half-an-hour or so, in among the brothers and sisters who were out prospecting for driftwood, seeing the old man's face in each jellyfish that I passed, the back garden at North Park, my mother's shadow in the doorway.

When I got back to the hut, Richard was lurking in the doorway with a curiously excited look on his face.

'How are you, man? Tough one to take. I timed it at 4.35 a.m.'

'What do you mean?'

'I told you before. I can foresee these events. I have the gift. I woke up at half-past four and said to myself: *There is a soul about to leave us.* But look, there's something here you ought to see.'

The sheet of off-white paper was stamped with the address of a Portland hotel. Halfway down it, in his unmistakable, looping, faculty-scrambled scrawl, the old man had written:

I, Maurice Chesapeake Albuquerque Seattle Du Pont, being of sound mind, and in full possession of my faculties, do solemnly and irrevocably swear, on this the eleventh day of November, Year of our Lord Nineteen Hundred and Seventy, that should I have occasion to die while resident on these premises, I hereby instruct those present and such of my heirs as may be contactable to expedite my passing from this world in accordance with the rituals and practices of a community where I have spent so many happy and profitable hours.

It sounded no worse than anything else that went on at the House of Peace, Love and Serenity. 'What are the rituals and practices?'

For the first time in our brief relationship, Richard looked uncomfortable. The goods were suspect and he knew it. His face was more gopher-like than ever. 'I'll be straight with you. This never happened before. It's the first time anyone died here. But we always said that if they did there should be a set way of doing things. Something that relates to the principles of how we live. It's our aim to return our . . . children to the cosmic soup they came from. Basically, we burn them up.'

'Cremation?'

'No. Incineration. We got half-a-dozen canoes down on the beach. We always said that if anyone died on us, we'd launch them out to sea on a burning boat. Die like a Viking. You understand what I'm saying?'

'Is that legal?'

'Nobody knows he's here, man. Excepting the doc. Not a letter in two years. You're the only person who's been to see him since Daphne left. Are there kin that need to be told?'

I thought about this. Somewhere across America, on obscure landing stages in the Everglades, in hunting lodges on the Great Plains, in Brooklyn speakeasies, in maple-syrup manufactories in Wisconsin, there might be people who could acknowledge the old man as cousin, great-uncle, maybe even father. God knew what agglomeration of humanity he had left behind him. But there was no way of bringing them together at short notice for his funeral. What was I supposed to do with him? Richard, interested in my dilemma, his usual ecstasy of self-absorption set to one side, had furled the sheet of paper into a cylinder and was tapping it against his chin.

'We could do it this afternoon. When the sun goes down. It could be a very moving ceremony. Floating out to sea on the tide. Returned to the water whence he came. Are you a religious person, Nick?'

'Not very.'

'It's something I think about a *lot*. We're an experimental community. We have no commonly agreed spiritual practices. All of us try to find our way to . . . wherever it is we need to go. But this could be an affirmation of our belief in the value of the individual soul.'

'I'm sure you're right.'

'Look at it this way, man. What have you got to lose?'

I thought about it. What had I got to lose? To judge from the life he had led, or the life he had led that I knew about, being sent out of the world like Leif Erikson would have appealed to the old man. Besides, I seemed to be living in a time where anything was possible and where no sort of ordinary standards applied, other than the duty to see him decently despatched from the planet. It was hard to think of anything else I owed him.

'How would we do it?'

Richard's eyes keeled crazily in their sockets. For a split-second he looked as mad as the old man in the hours before his death. 'Wasn't he a veteran? I heard him talk about it once. There's a Stars and Stripes somewhere. We'll wrap him up in it and douse the whole shebang in kerosene. I've seen it done in India.'

There was weak sunshine coming in over the clearing. Here and there the women of the House of Peace, Love and Serenity went stoically about their work. It wasn't a bad day for December. Five hundred miles away in Mulholland Drive, Angie would be ordering up a dinner of fried ribeye steak for seventeen persons, chartering the limo fleet to see a baseball game or getting Dale an appointment with a venereologist. I had an idea that the thing with Angie could not last very much longer.

'Let's do it,' I said.

'Oh man,' Richard said faintly. 'This is going to be *immense*.'

I was beginning to get the hang of the path down to the beach. The false trails that led perilously away to concealed clifftops and thickets of unnavigable bracken and pine held no terrors for me. I knew where to go. As the bier carrying the old man's corpse reached a sand-strewn defile where fir trees hung low over the track, I was ready to reach out and claw the branches aside. The body sewn up in the flag seemed worryingly small, like a child's. To watch the file of mourners in wary descent was to remember a certain kind of continental war film: partisans coming down the mountainside with their dead comrade; the *maquis* silently reconnoitring their territory. Richard went before me, making sweeping movements with his hands, as if scattering seed. Sometimes he stopped to let the cortege pass by, only to shake his head and skip in front again. The heels of his sandals left marks in the soil. Behind the four men carrying the bier – knocked up that morning out of a couple of packing cases – the others walked in single file. Lindy and the two pregnant women brought up the rear.

'We'll have a simple service,' Richard had said. 'Say a few words. Pay our respects. Commend him to the mighty deep.' By the water's edge a canoe lay turned over on one side. It stank horribly of marijuana. The tide was in sharp retreat, so sharp that each slap of the waves left the canoe further away. There were white birds sailing noisily overhead. The surf boomed in my ears. After some manoeuvring, the pall bearers lowered their burden onto the sand and we gathered round it.

'We're here,' Richard began, almost shouting the words into the wind, 'to mark the passing of our dear friend Maurice Du Pont. The House of Peace, Love and Serenity mourns him. Truly it does. He was a man who dwelt among us, and now he is gone. But he shared our ideals, and our hopes for betterment, and we mourn him. He came from that great infinity and now he returns there, and the ... the mystical presence who ordained his going will surely receive him.' ('We got all sorts here,' Richard had said. 'Baptists. Presbyterians. Maybe even a Mormon. I'll make it ecumenical.') 'He leaves the earth, and he will hasten away from it through fire and water. Does anyone have anything to say?'

Nobody had anything to say. Richard's face, as he posed the question, wore a look of absolute exaltation.

'What about you?' Richard said, turning to me. 'You were his son. Do you have anything to say?'

The faces stared incuriously. Lindy had her knuckles in her mouth. The body lay at my feet.

'He was my father,' I said. 'I hardly knew him. I wish I had. He kept his life away from me. I wish he hadn't. It's difficult to forgive him for that. I wish I could.'

'Amen,' someone – one of the Baptists or Presbyterians, presumably – chipped in.

'And now,' Richard said sonorously, 'he shall sail forth. Sail forth to the destiny that awaits him.'

Someone produced a couple of oil cans. Instantly the marijuana smell was overlaid by the reek of kerosene. 'No way,' Richard was saying, and giving a faint impression of having done this before. 'You really need to soak the wood. Throw it all on.' He took the second can and, with a quick, excitable movement, as if he were trying to trap some washed-up creature of the sea that was trying to scuttle out of reach, lodged it in the prow of the canoe. 'That'll fix it,' he said. Then, the funeral pyre complete, he hesitated.

'Hey. You really want to do this?'

'No point in stopping now.'

'I guess not. You're not going to get mad at me afterwards or anything?'

'No.'

He reached forward and pushed the canoe into the water, motioned to one of his helpers to secure the stern, pulled a cigarette lighter out of the pocket of his jeans and applied it to the edge of the kerosene-soaked flag.

'There she blows.'

The flames rose gently at first. Then, as the current took the canoe and propelled it out to sea, they took hold with a vengeance. Interested in what was going on, the gulls swooped low. The strong, sweet smell came back on the wind. Twenty or thirty yards out, the canoe juddered a little in the swell and then righted itself. It was well ablaze now, and releasing a plume of grey-black smoke.

'Any time,' Richard said.

Just as he spoke the second kerosene tin caught fire and exploded. There was an almighty bang, like the end of the world, and the canoe went up, scattering debris as far as the shore. The gulls screeched and tracked away. To add to the excitement, one of the pregnant women clutched her stomach with a trembling hand and promptly went into labour.

After that, we went back to the clearing.

Afterwards, tidying up in the cabin, I found a box-file with the initials *M. Du P.* on the spine. Inside were three or four uncashed social security cheques dating from the mid-1960s, a dozen or so excitable letters from people I had never heard of relating to matters I had never heard of (*Mo – you're bullshitting me, right? $50 gets you in and not a cent less*), a copy of the citation, signed 'Dwight D. Eisenhower', distributed to Allied troops on the eve of the invasion of Europe, and, unexpectedly, a tiny black-and-white photograph of my mother. The picture of my mother I kept. The rest I threw away.

Early the next morning, Lindy drove me back to the airport. We were barely out of sight of the clearing when she swerved the truck up onto the verge, beat the steering wheel with her fists, and said: 'You've got to get me out of here.'

'I thought you said Richard was cool?'

'He's a mad fuck,' Lindy said bitterly. 'A mad fuck. *Totally* deranged. Uppers. Downers. Everything you ever heard of and then some. Plus, he treats all the women like he owns them. I can't take it any more. You got to get me out of here. I'll do anything you want. Anything.'

There was no doubt, from the way in which Lindy pumped out her meagre chest, what 'anything' meant.

'Have you got any money?'

'Thirty dollars I kept back. We're supposed to turn everything over to the community, but I figured: why should Richard just get to spend it on Percodan?'

'Where do you need to go?'

'Springfield, Illinois.'

At the airport I bought her a one-way ticket to Chicago. Greyhound buses could do the rest. 'You're a good man,' she said, hanging her arms around my neck and pressing her head into my shoulder. From it rose the scent of patchouli. 'I'll never forget that you did this.' I left her in the departure lounge, next to the doughy Oregon farmers' wives, off to see their married daughters in Helena, Montana, and the college kids flying home for the vacation, a small, solitary figure, hunched over an apple and copy of *Newsweek* that advertised a flaring article about Chairman Mao.

Back in LA, the big rented house on Mulholland was eerily deserted. The only person I could find there, tripping down the magenta-carpeted staircase, clipboard under her leather-jacketed arm, foxy eyes a-glint, was Angie.

'Where is everybody?'

'Gone to the fuckin' circus or somepin.'

'What's been happening?'

'Not much.' I noticed that certain changes had occurred to Angie's get-up. The shadows under her eyes had been picked out with kohl and she had what looked like an Iron Cross shaved into the side of her scalp. 'The Coliseum gig went off good, only they think Keith sprained his ankle falling over a cable. I rang the guy at WKD like you said. The free concert's scheduled for next week, but they can't find a crappy enough support act.' She ticked these great events off on her fingers, one by one. 'Garth's been acting kinda weird.'

'How weird?'

'Sitting in his room with that Genevieve or whatever her fuckin' name is' – Angie's hatred of Genevieve Le Strange was practically fathomless – 'making voodoo dolls. Oh, and that Kantner – the guy that's writing the book – got beat up.'

'Who beat him up?'

'Stefano,' said Angie exasperatedly, as if I had asked her who currently sat in the White House. 'They had an argument about whether he could bring his tape recorder to some dinner. Stef said he was a louse and he was going to beat his brains out. Hey,' she fondly continued, 'why don't we go up to your room?'

'Angie. This can't go on.'

'Can't it?'

'No. Do you mind?'

Angie stared hard at her clipboard. The two words visible at the top of the sheet were *fucking Stevie*.

'I guess I can live with it,' she said cautiously. 'Hey ... There's one of the lighting guys been hitting on me real strong. Would you mind?'

'Not really.'

'That's OK then.' From beyond the window came the sound of car doors slamming and peevish English voices raised in recrimination. 'Hey,' she said, 'I was really sorry about your dad.'

'Yes,' I said. 'So was I.'

14. DOWN SOUTH, JUKIN'

All of these demons in my head
All of these people want me dead
Running through a world that's upside down
Trying to find a friend in Schizoid Town

'Schizoid Town'

Dipping under the low clouds, the helicopter came in at an angle over the hill and then veered up sharply so that the crowds swarming on its surface fell out of focus again, and the tents and the ragged banners they carried diminished into tiny points of colour. Pieces of luggage spilled haphazardly out of the overhead lockers; two or three people fell forwards out of their seats; the girl from the *New York Times* who was covering the concert, and whose nerves, as she had earlier confessed, were already shot to ribbons, clamped her knuckles to her mouth and said, 'Oh my, oh my,' six or seven times, beneath the roar of the rotor blades; and then the chopper, an ageing Sikorsky which had seen service in 'Nam and still had recesses in the fuselage where ammunition crates could be stored, somehow righted itself and swooped away towards the low, level terrain beyond. All this you can see in *Burning Skies*, which those two dullard siblings from Saratoga had been busy filming for the past week and a half. What you don't see, alternatively, is Stefano ingesting a line of amphetamine sulphate off the back of his wrist, there being no upturned mirror or tabletop conveniently to hand, a green-about-the-gills Kantner throwing up into his denimed lap, and the notoriously weak-bladdered Ian getting up to urinate daintily into a bucket. 'It's just like Woodstock,' somebody – possibly the girl from the *New York Times* – remarked in wonder as we sailed in low across the boiling multitudes towards the acre of burned-off turf that was someone's idea of a landing pad. This, too, failed to make the Juniper brothers' final cut, for the scene that stretched out for at least a couple of miles beyond the helicopter's undercarriage was not like Woodstock. Not at all. It may have been like the last pitched battle between two warring armies, each bent on wiping the other from the earth, it may have been like larvae seething in some underground cocoon or like your worst imagining of Mordor in the years of the Dark Lord's rise, but it was not like Woodstock. I was at both, and I can tell you that whereas Woodstock – officially at any rate – was about peace, love and understanding, Ogdenville was about greed, indifference and incomprehension. Oh, and narcissism. As we scuttled out of the chopper's winnowing arc towards the waiting truck that would take us up to the encampment, and the bouncy rumble of the music blew back from the main stage, Garth fell in behind me – the fronds of his buckskin jacket fell over the guitar case he carried in one hand – just as a giant clod of earth, coming in from such a distance that it might have been flung by a medieval catapult, landed in the space between our feet. 'What the *fuck*,' he wearily demanded, 'is all this about?'

At this point in the proceedings – four hours before the Helium Kids were due to take to the stage – I knew only slightly more about Ogdenville than the band, which is to say only the things that Stefano had told me with strict instructions not to forward them to anyone else. It was only later, watching the rough-cut of *Burning Skies* and reading the newspaper accounts, that I was able to appreciate the full enormity of the mistakes that had been made. The first problem, naturally, was the promoter. In those days the old-style provincial music moguls we had dealt with in the sixties were on the way out, winded by the advent of spreading corporatism and sharp-eyed accountants from New York City, but Pa and Ma Proudfoot, genial sponsors of the Ogdenville Free Festival, as it was now called, were genuine throwbacks to a vanished age. Basically, Pa Proudfoot – a Pickwickian figure of eighteen stone, who liked dressing up in red-and-white striped shirts like the trumpet player in a vaudeville band – was a Louisiana turkey farmer who had read about this heah rock and roll in an article in *Newsweek* and was determined to chase some of the bucks that were clearly available to those who cracked its code. To this end, he and Ma – a terrifying gorgon whose features appeared on their boxed poultry dinners under the caption MA PROUDFOOT'S TALKING TURKEY – leased a debased eighty-acre plot off some local landowner, chainsawed down its remaining trees, dumped a make-shift stage at the further end and declared that they were open for business.

If there was a drawback to this scheme of creating a concert arena down in the Louisiana boondocks, it lay in the fact that half the site was still mostly undrained swamp, that the nearest rail station was fifteen miles away and the nearest bus depot a further five. To give Pa Proudfoot his due, he was a sharp operator in his way and although he was supposed to be holding a free festival (nobody knew about the $25,000 the band was getting) he expected to recover two or three times his outlay by selling the movie rights and catering to visitors nonplussed by the absence of shops, bars and, it was alleged, anything other than a solitary water tap concealed behind a tree at the arena's furthermost edge. The advertising was top whack, too, which meant that by the time the State Governor found out about the event – a bare three days before it was due to commence – there were 200,000 kids in shambling transit across east Louisiana and the whole thing was beyond cancelling. The federal authorities had been alerted and the National Guard put on standby, but the numbers were too great and the rumour going round the site was that law and order had pretty much broken down.

The second problem was the support acts. The original idea had been that the Kids, having got the public on their side by announcing that they intended to appear *gratis*, would cement this reputation for free-handed counter-cultural benevolence by hiring some raw and upcoming talent to assist. Names mentioned included Alice Cooper and Fat Mattress. It was left to Stefano, always a realist in these matters, and who had attended one of Cooper's early gigs, to suggest that he would probably blow the headliners off the stage and was therefore better avoided. Instead, led by Garth, then in one of his 'political' moods, the Kids had opted for a clutch of radical bands, street rats out of Detroit and Ann Arbor such as the MC5 and the Stooges. Now, the Stooges were just a bunch of doped-up, superannuated high-school kids and supposedly imploding, but the MC5 had White Panther connections and were, additionally, managed by John Sinclair, which meant that, unbeknown to us all, the FBI had begun to take an interest. Matters were made perhaps slightly worse by the Stooges announcing that, while they intended to fulfil their contractual obligations, they regarded the Helium Kids as 'corporate whores'. Meanwhile, as I later learned, it had been raining torrentially for three days, there had been an outbreak of food poisoning, upwards of four-hundred people had gone down with influenza and were being accommodated in a makeshift field hospital, and the Red Cross were about to declare the place an Emergency Zone.

The truck sped upward through the mud towards a gypsy encampment of tents and trailers somewhere at the back of the stage, and the people surged around. All the old solidarity seemed to have gone.

There were the usual hippy girls in Indian prints and swirling dimity frocks with po-faced bearded men in dungarees trailing dutifully in their wake, but alongside them were biker gangs with San Francisco and Oakland colours, short-haired local kids in sawn-off jeans gawping at these emissaries from the big world who had ended up on their doorstep, together with moustachioed city hipsters come to see the fun. You could tell that nobody among these representative factions of contemporary youth culture much liked each other. Meanwhile, the National Guardsmen, in knee-high boots and jodhpurs, were keeping out of the way and the mud, as far as I could see, was rising higher by the moment.

At the truck-halt, where there was a fenced-off enclosure and the usual crowd of hangers on in sycophantic attendance, I buttonholed Morrie Estrada, one of Stefano's associates, a lugubrious character in army surplus battle fatigues and aviator glasses, who had come on twenty-four hours ahead of us to spy out the land.

'What's been happening?'

'Place is jest about ready to blow, I should say. Last thing I saw there wuz seven-hundred people in the line for one burger stand.'

'What have the bands been like?'

'Man, those Stooges are *baad*. They done two numbers and then Iggy says he's kind of bored, and gets his cock out, and a Louisiana state marshal jumps up and arrests him right there on the stage. They were still collecting up the busted bottles twenty minutes later.'

'Any more light relief?'

It occurred to me that Morrie was about as narcotically challenged as it was possible to be while still remaining on your feet.

'Ol' Pa Proudfoot's giving an interview over in the tent if you want to listen.'

I ploughed on through the mud, whose surface was clogged with cigarette packets, beer cans, discarded Band Aids and the like, to a bell tent struck between two of the trailers, and came upon Odgenville's onlie begetter, sou'wester cocked above his big, pineapple head, booted feet sinking into the ooze, bellowing into a radio mic, held up to the purple crease of his mouth by a girl in a bright red mackintosh, that, yessir, there'd been a few teethin' troubles, and them boys outta Michigan wouldn't evah be let back on his land, no way, and he was a-wishin' the goddamn rain would leave off, but basically everyone was havin' one helluva time, wasn't they just. Ma Proudfoot, identifiable by her waves of carefully primped yellow hair and lantern jaw, lolled on a sofa reading a copy of the *National Probe*. From somewhere overhead there came a blast of thunder. The noise from the stage, which had stopped briefly as the truck surged up the hill, throbbed menacingly back into life. It was about five o'clock in the afternoon and the dusk was fast coming on. Two lean-looking men, as unlike the rest of the people standing by in dress and deportment as could possibly be imagined, stepped out of the throng silently appraising Pa and Ma Proudfoot as they treated with the media. One of them tapped me lightly on the shoulder.

'You with the – what is it – the Helium Kids?'

'That's right.'

'Is Mr Dangerfield anywhere on the site?'

'I don't think he's arrived yet. I believe there's another helicopter coming in a while or so.'

'Well, thanks for that.'

As I was hastening away I heard the one who hadn't spoken say, 'I told you we should have done this in LA.'

Stefano was sitting on his own in the smaller of the two trailers given over to the Kids and their entourage for what were known as recreational purposes.

'There's two plainclothes guys over the way asking for Garth.'

'Shit! What do they want him for? It's not about that stuff in Sioux City, is it?'

'They didn't say. I told them he wasn't here yet. You'd better tell him to stay inside.'

'That shouldn't be difficult. He's scared shitless. Don't know what he was expecting in a swamp in Louisiana, but it wasn't this. Jesus,' Stefano said, 'I asked one of the Proudfoots' goons – hang on, though, shouldn't that be *Proudfeet* ...? I asked one of the Proudfoots' goons who was handling the security and he said there was a couple of water-bailiffs with a rowboat in case anyone fell in the river.'

'We should have brought some of our people.'

'We should never have come here in the fucking first place. But there was all that crap in the papers about the ticket prices. You wrote the press release, Nick.' He quoted in a sing-song voice: '*A gesture of appreciation to our wonderful fans, for whose support we are eternally grateful*. Sometimes you have to do these things.'

'Sometimes you do. Have you got the money?'

'That's another thing,' Stefano gloomily confided. The effects of the amphetamine sulphate were wearing off. Thrown back on his own resources, he looked suddenly baffled by the enormity of the task before him. 'Look. I've got to ... I've got to ...' Not even Stefano, even here in a trailer in Louisiana with the rain drumming on the tin roof and the noise of 200,000 people baying in our ears, could admit that his most urgent need was *to go out and score some drugs from the first person he could find who was dealing them*. 'There's things I need to do,' he ended up lamely. 'Let's see if the boys are settled in.'

Outside the rain was falling in torrents. The helicopter had taken off again and was lumbering back to the airport, like a gigantic scarab beetle. The Kids' trailer was a more grandiose affair than the one in which Stefano and I had found ourselves. It ran to a collapsed sofa and a long, low, plastic table on which reposed a carton of milk, two packets of Cheerios and some bottles of root beer.

'So, how are you boys doing?' Stefano enquired, making it abundantly clear that he had no interest at all in any answer, and whether they lived or died barely concerned him.

Here in their tornado years, at the tip of the rocket's scintillating parabola, the Kids had evolved a kind of collective choreography for their public appearances. Usually it meant that Garth, Dale and occasionally Gary took centre stage, while the others occupied subsidiary positions on the flanks. This arrangement generally held unless Keith had decided to go on one of his jags, in which case the others peeled unobtrusively away, happy to defer to a talent for raw exhibitionism that, when indulged, was undoubtedly greater than their own. Just now Garth, Dale and Gary were seated abreast on the collapsing sofa while Ian and Keith perched symmetrically on the armrests. Their stage costumes – Garth was wearing a Harlequin coat, Gary a lime-green jumpsuit – looked horribly incongruous. In the corner of the trailer, what was either a very large mouse or a very small rat came slinking out of one hidey-hole in the wall, streaked out across the carpet and disappeared into another.

'Is there TV?' somebody asked.

'Fuck off,' Stefano said. It was the first time I had ever seen him lose his temper with anyone in the band. 'What do you think this is? Madison Fucking Square Garden?'

'Well then' – it was Ian, he of the weak bladder – 'is there a khazi?'

'For Christ's sake, go and find a fucking tree to piss behind. I daresay that's what everyone else is doing. Listen' – his manner softened a little and he became aware once more both of his responsibilities to the boys and of what Don might say if reports of this indiscretion ever got back to him in Maddox Street – 'there's a couple of hundred thousand maniacs out there, including a biker gang from Fresno who are supposed to be the very worst motherfuckers on the planet, no security to speak of and a typhoon blowing. Just sit tight, will you, and keep your heads down? If you want anything, Nick here will go and try to get it. Anything within reason, that is. And . . . Will you just *fuck off.*'

The door of the trailer swung open and the smaller of the two Juniper brothers could be seen hauling a tripod camera up the steps.

'Sorry and all that,' Stefano said, recalling the importance Don was known to attach to the *Burning Skies* project. 'Now, perhaps someone would like to say something amusing for this gentleman and his fucking camera?'

But the boys had already grown tired of saying amusing things for the camera. Outside, the darkness was properly coming on. Over from the stage the sound of a furious, high-octane shuffle suggested that the MC5 were on and playing 'Sister Anne'. The Juniper brother was stalking the room, filming whoever caught his eye from unusual angles. There would be nothing happening for an hour or two. Thinking that it had been a long day, which could only get longer – might not even end, in fact, until several hours into the day booked to follow – I went back into the second trailer, empty now except for an anonymous hippy girl who had gone to sleep under a blanket in the corner, sat on the single chair and reviewed the events of the past few days, and the succession of failures that seemed to lie at their core. My father was dead. Rosalind was gone. Why hadn't I been able to establish a satisfactory relationship with either of them? The answer seemed to be that the old man hadn't wanted a relationship at all, or, if so, only on his own, highly specialised terms, and that Rosalind, who had wanted a relationship, hadn't found it satisfactory. There was no getting away from this, I decided, as in the distance the MC5 launched into the manic stop-start of 'Kick Out the Jams' (*'Yoo gotta decide, uh, bruthas and sisters . . . if yoo pardof the prawblem or . . . uh . . . pardof the solooshun'*), and the problem was that both of them had been in pursuit of some mythological ideal that I either couldn't, or wouldn't, be a part of myself. But what had they wanted? The old man, I was pretty sure, simply had a vision of himself as some vagrant, mercurial spirit cruising the world and deluding himself into believing that the value it put on him was identical to the one he put on himself. Everyone else – myself, my mother, even Daphne, presumably, and the happy campers of Echo Beach – was merely caught up in his slipstream, collateral, not so much ignored or abandoned but having come to the point where they had ceased to serve any useful purpose. And what had Rosalind wanted? She, too, I realised, had a vision of herself, which grew out of the house in Connecticut and the big trees in the garden and the Sunday brunches with the orthodontists and the realtors and their wives and the Simon and Garfunkel records playing on the stereo. The old man's myth, clearly, wasn't permeable to anyone who didn't happen to be him – there was just no way through the door; even blood relations were excluded – but Rosalind's, equally clearly, was. If I had been failed by one, then I myself had failed the other. During the twenty-second earthquake of drum flourishes, power chords and rhythmic collisions in which 'Kick Out the Jams' motored to a halt, the hippy girl groaned in her sleep and there came a gentle tap at the door. It was, of all people, Irving Kantner.

'Mind if I come in?'

'Be my guest.'

'Who's the chick?'

'Could be anyone. Grace Slick. Janis Joplin. Who knows?'

'Janis Joplin is dead.'

'So she is. How are you feeling?'

Always pale-complexioned, Kantner had now turned wallpaper-white. His leather jacket was splashed with mud and he was making little circular movements with his thumbs. It was difficult to know if the look he shot the hippy girl indicated hunger or disdain.

'I need to ask you something,' he said. 'This is a free concert, right? So how come the band is getting paid?'

'Who said the band is getting paid?'

'A guy I just talked to who works for Proudfoot.'

'I can't answer questions like this. I'm just the PR. Why don't you try Stefano?'

'I can't.'

'Why not?' I knew exactly why not, but it seemed a good idea to establish in just what way Stefano had struck terror into Kantner's craven heart.

'He said if I ever asked him a question about money he'd cram my head down the toilet.' Kantner paused, interested despite his terror. 'Do you think he'd do that?'

'Sure to.' There was no harm in reassuring Kantner on this point. 'But you can relax. The band isn't getting paid.'

'Thirty thousand dollars is what I heard.'

'If you mean the expenses guaranteed in the original contract, then yes, I suppose thirty thousand might cover it.'

'Thirty thousand dollars just for *expenses*?'

'Flights. Helicopter hire. Insurance. New raincoats all round.' The last item was a joke. 'These things add up.'

Kantner looked uncertain. Self-righteous, but also scared, and, as he would have acknowledged, a long way from home, he had to be careful not to overplay his hand.

'Listen, Nicko,' he said. 'You've always been straight with me, and I appreciate that. Do you know something? I never could understand why you hang out with those guys. No, really.'

I knew what he meant, but such complexities could not be gone into. Not here. Not now. 'It's a living.'

'Sure it's a living. But . . .' Suddenly his voice had the fervour of a revivalist preacher denouncing the Whore of Babylon. 'I've worked with music people, and I know. They're scum, man. They are. That Garth treats people like dirt, just because his album's in the *Billboard* top five.'

'So why write a book about them? What is this? Some kind of morality tale for our time? That won't sell many copies.'

It occurred to me as I said this that I had been sitting in the trailer for a good two hours, and that the music, which had stopped with the MC5, hadn't restarted. Just as I was assembling these thoughts, while Kantner stared at me even more doubtfully, transfixed by the suspicion that, like the Pheeny girls who went skinny-dipping in the Gila River, he had gone too far, there was another knock at the trailer door and Ian Hamilton stepped inside.

'Quite a party,' he said, looking from me to Kantner, at the hippy girl – now snoring loudly – and back again. 'You'd better come ... No, mate,' he added, as Kantner made as if to follow us out of the room. 'Not you.'

Outside the rain had all but stopped. The ground beneath our feet allowed no purchase, threatened to slip away at any moment. It was quite dark, and there were people milling about, moving in and out of the shadows thrown by giant arc-lights.

'What's the matter?'

'There's been a bit of a row,' Ian said. Close up his face was dry and husky. He grinned faintly. 'A bit of a row' in the quiet, understated code by which he communicated could mean anything from a massed brawl to somebody being shot dead.

'What about?'

'It's that Garth,' Ian said, and I tried to recall the precise state of the finely calibrated roster of likes, dislikes, long-term treaties and temporary alliances that distinguished the Kids as an operating unit. At the last time of asking, Garth and Dale had been ganging up against Gary over the writing credits, while, in a separate manoeuvre, Dale and Gary had been in conflict with Garth over some injudiciously dropped remarks about professional competence in one of the music papers. On the other hand, Ian – who liked a quiet life – usually kept out of these disagreements.

'What's he done?'

'Getting on his high horse,' Ian said, in a way that suggested he had no objection to anyone, least of all Garth, getting on a high horse, but appreciated the damage that this kind of hauteur could inflict. 'There's a truck coming to take us up the road to the stage, right? Due to go on after the MC5. I liked the sound of the MC5,' Ian said, a bit regretfully. 'I'd have liked to see them. And then Garth decides to throw one of his wobblers. *You* know,' Ian said, summarising in two words the countless eruptions of temperament that we had witnessed in the past seven years. 'Said he wasn't being treated proper, he'd never been so insulted in his life, who did they reckon they were dealing with, and he wasn't going to go on.'

'What did Stefano do?'

'Well, that's the funny thing. You know how Stefano usually is with Garth? Tells him 'e's Christ come back to earth and they're all baying for him? Well, this time he just shuts him up with a wave of his hand and says, "Don't give me that shit. You're here to play and you'll play. And there's two hundred thousand kids ready to riot if you don't."'

'What did Garth say to that?'

'He just looked at Stefano – you know that poncey way Garth looks at people? – and says, "My people won't riot."'

'Then what happened?'

'Stef says, "They're not your fucking people, you cunt, and riot is exactly what they'll do unless you get off your fat arse and stop whining." So Garth says: "I won't be spoken to like that. You're fucking fired." And then Stef says: "You can't fire me." And hits him in the mouth. Quite hard, too.'

'How did he take that?'

'We're on in fifteen minutes.'

It was all the same to Ian, who liked old blues records, and Savile Row suits, and walking country lanes with his wife and Labrador, and who, I sometimes suspected, only stuck with the rest of the Helium

Kids because he'd been with them so long, and that this was the only
world he knew. In the chaos that followed, he was perhaps the only
one of us who seemed to be unmoved: bass held perpendicular to his
torso in that peculiar way he had; one weather eye on deeply unpredictable Keith; packet of biscuits within reach on his Marshall stack.
Take it from me, of all the qualifications brought to rock and roll by
those caught up in it, the one to prize above all is detachment.

Most of what happened in the next forty-five minutes you can catch,
if you've a mind, in *Burning Skies*, or read about in Kantner's book.
Not everything, though, for these are partial records, surface scratchings, the practised discriminations of a suspect art. The Junipers, for
example, had at their amateurish disposal only a couple of tripod
cameras at the back of the stage and an assistant with a hand-held
clinging to one of the gantries. As for Kantner, well I happen to know,
as I was standing next to him at the time, that halfway through the
proceedings Stefano ripped the reporter's notebook out of his hand,
tore it into pieces and threw the bits out over the heads of the crowd.
From the Junipers you obtain at least a sense of the vastness of it all
– the multitude stretching back as far as you can see, the endless
surface of bobbing heads seeming to ripple and sway according to
some collective impulse that nobody watching could hope to predict
or contain, the imploring faces of the people at the front as the wave
swept forward and lashed them into the front end of the stage. The
stage, just to compound these difficulties, was only six feet off the
ground. You get to see the band in nervy close-up, heels tapping to the
beat, anxious expressions whenever a beer can comes sailing out of the
darkness. Why, you even get to see me, hunkered down stage left, face
obscured by a baseball cap that a girl who thought I could introduce
her to Gary had boldly presented to me on the way up the hill.

What you don't get to see, or indeed hear, is the spectacle of Garth,
between songs, while the others are tuning up or lighting cigarettes or

registering just how very seriously things are getting out of hand, insulting the crowd. He did this in a gorgeously camp mock-American drawl and it would have been wildly amusing had the band been twenty feet above and twenty yards away from the crowd rather than six and one and the security detail consisted of several hundred riot police rather than a few dozen Louisiana deputy marshals who were more interested in keeping out of the rain.

'Well, uh, we just *lurve* coming down to – where is it? – Louisiana, because we think you kids are rilly where it's at. No, we rilly do. We just *lurve* all your faggot bikers in your leather gear lookin' like, uh, *Marlon Brando*. Yeah, it must be one long party in this wunnerful country of yours, with all you, uh, rilly beautiful people getting it on with each other . . .'

What happened? Kantner's book, overwritten in that quaint, mid-seventies rock journalist's way, portrays it as the apogee of Dionysian excess, a kind of immensely sinister pagan hoedown (with Nietzschean overtones) in which the last rites of the sixties were painfully enacted in a waterlogged field in Louisiana. The bare facts, as far as anyone ever made out, were that about halfway through 'Who is This that Wakes from Slumber?', enraged by Garth's mockery, the biker gang from Fresno attempted to rush the stage from the right-hand side. In the mass displacement of bodies that followed, one of the lighting towers went over, killing a local bank clerk and his fiancée who were sheltering beneath and injuring a dozen other people trapped by its near-instantaneous descent. Simultaneously, the power went off and someone exploded half-a-dozen magnesium flares. It was at this point that Stefano decided enough was enough. 'War-torn survivors from a battlefield of their own devising, blank-faced and ashen, as culpable in their own way as any hoodlum in the seething crowd, the Helium Kids ran – literally – for their lives' is Kantner's summary. All I remember is women's voices screaming, a real gunshot or two (this was state troopers firing over the heads of the crowd), the baseball cap tumbling away into the mud and a mad dash over oozing duckboards back to the truck. Then, in the helicopter, crammed with twice as many people as regulations allowed, Jerry leaning over to Stefano and saying importantly: 'Hey. You know they arrested Garth right after the gig?'

'What for?' I found I could sympathise with Stefano's complete lack of interest.

'Illegal transportation of a minor across the state line.'

'I give up,' Stefano said. 'Garth can talk his own way out of that one.'

Glancing down, I saw that darkness had fallen in over the Ogdenville site, with only the occasional flash of fire to illuminate the turmoil that presumably lay beneath. The rotor blades roared, the girl from the *New York Times*, supposing that normality had returned to our lives, bared her splendiferous teeth and asked if anybody had a bottle of water, and the helicopter tracked on through the soft Louisiana night.

Of the many preposterous things about Ogdenville, the most preposterous of all, it turned out, was the pretence, loudly insisted upon by Stefano, that life could go on as normal in its wake. As little as three days after the lighting rig had crashed down into the Louisiana swamp, with the newspapers – lachrymose and accusing by turns – still full of pictures of the teenagers who had died, and Don's lawyers attempting to extricate Garth from the penitentiary (it took a $50,000 bail bond to spring him, and the bribes to the state prosecutor's office to get charges dropped cost another $100,000), he had us back in New York at work on some two-year strategic plan that Don allegedly thought vital for the band's onward march. It was December now, and the light was already leaching out of the grimy uptown streets; no one was near to recovering from the devitalising effects of five weeks on the road; and as we sat languidly around the boardroom listening to Stefano talking about the two million in sales Don anticipated from the album that would straightaway be recorded once Garth had over-come his little difficulty, I remember looking round the assembled company and wondering where we might all be in two years' time. As I recollect, Angie would go off to work for a firm that manufactured paper drinking cups; Bernie was headhunted by RCA; while Stefano would be undergoing Don's patented shock treatment of any employee thought to need rehabilitation after a period of excessive drug use, which consisted of being locked in the attic of a house in Meard Street until such time as they felt able to face the world anew. Jerry, on the other hand, simply disappeared, vanished, wandered off into Manhattan one evening after work and was never seen again, not even dredged up three weeks later from the depths of the Hudson or found proselytising for a religious cult in New Mexico.

And then something else happened. I was sitting in my office later on in the afternoon, drafting a succinct paragraph or two about how Garth's spirits were being kept up by the good wishes of his fans, when Angie put her head round the door. The affair with the lighting engineer had not worked out. The iron cross was growing out of her hair and she looked uncharacteristically subdued.

'Hey,' she said. 'There's a guy in reception asking for you. Looks like Ed Sullivan's brother, too.'

Without ever having made the connection, I knew instantly who she meant.

'You'd better send him in.'

It was six months since I had last seen Al Duchesne. He looked not exactly wretched, but stricken in some private and mysterious way. Though no less expensively dressed than usual, he seemed not to have put on his clothes with any great attention. What remained of his faintly dishevelled hair was standing up on the top of his head, as if he had just walked down Fiftieth in a howling gale with wolverines tear-ing at his insteps. When he saw me, he hesitated for a moment and then stuck out his hand.

'Is this about Rosalind?'

Al looked surprised, taken off guard, as if it were simple madness to suppose that a man whose daughter was filing for divorce might want to discuss this fact with his son-in-law.

'No, it ain't. Rosalind is . . .' – for a terrible moment I thought he was going to say 'a fine young woman' – but he recovered himself and settled for 'as grown up as she'll ever get. She can marry who she likes.' It was whispered among the vast sorority of Rosalind's aunts that Al had never really 'got over' Marty Knowland. He lost the thread of his harangue, gave the office door a disapproving glance, stared at the portraits of Garth, Dale and the others as if only their absence from the room prevented him from tearing them to pieces on the spot, and said: 'You know a woman named Selma Reed?'

'Sure. She cleans the house three mornings a week.'

'You see her recently?'

'I only got back the other day. The place is empty.'

'Uh huh. Well read this.'

There was no cheaper stationery than the kind that Al now pushed across my desk. Pale blue and translucent, with a stencilled flower-stalk occupying the top-right corner, it had been bought at a gas station or pulled out of a dime-store bargain bin. On it Lucille had written that she and Selma were sharing a house together – no address supplied – were supremely happy in their new existence, and that no communication from Al was expected or desired.

'I haddem tracked,' Al said. As if suddenly aware of how out of sorts he looked, he had started patting at his coat pockets, fastening stray buttons, bending to fix an untied shoelace. Next time, the wolverines could watch out. 'Haddem tracked down. For sure. Living upstate, near Albany, in some shack. There's a nigger church they go to in the evening.' He sighed. 'You know anything about this?'

'No.'

'I got no quarrel with you, son.' It occurred to me that it was the second time in my life that Al had said this to me, and perhaps the first time that he meant it. 'Any idea why she might want to play a trick like this?'

'No.' It was true, as well. Why Lucille would want to run off to Albany with Selma, live in a house with her, go ecstatically to bed with her – this was the letter's implication – was completely beyond me. It had been the same seven years ago when she had wanted to light out for New York, sworn at Barry Goldwater and appeared in my hotel room.

'Me neither. You know,' Al said, suspiciously, 'you read about all this stuff in the papers and then it happens to you.' He put the letter hastily back in his pocket, as if the shame of exposing it to view was too much to bear, and then stood there a little uncertainly, rocking on his heels, eyeing up the wall of framed record sleeves and the collages of music press cuttings.

'Hey,' he said. 'Is it true about the women?'

'Is what true about the women?'

'You know.' He made a gesture that wasn't quite obscene but edged a fair way towards it.

'Oh yes,' I said. 'Absolutely. You know that guy from Spirit? Four girls inside an hour. I can swear to it.'

'Jesus,' Al said. 'Some age to be young. You hear anything about Lucille, you let me know, OK?'

'I'll do that,' I told him.

Not so very long after this, Stefano told me, coming out of the building at the close of a December day, he had been accosted by a woman who said that she was Genevieve Le Strange's mother. Not some pompadoured LA orthodontist's wife or West Coast supervixen of the kind you read about in *Cosmopolitan*, Stefano insisted, but a small, black-clad personage with red, over-scrubbed facial skin and a shuffling walk, who cornered him in the space where two other front-ages met and loudly accused him of helping to corrupt her daughter.

'Jesus. What did you do?'

'Well, what would you have done?' Stefano looked puzzled, mysti-fied as to why he might have been singled out in this way, or that there should be any doubt about his answer. 'I told her that if anyone had done any corrupting it was her Genevieve. Never seen such a dirty girl.'

PART FOUR
Traps for Troubadours

No Elvis, Beatles, Stones or the Helium Kids in 1977

The Clash, '1977'

HOW THEY THREW IT ALL AWAY

... And now to the big question that any chronicler of the Helium Kids has ultimately to answer. Where did it all go wrong? When did it all start slip-sliding away? 1972, I'd say. Or maybe 1973. This was the year the US office closed and I came back to England. *Definitely* by the time they made the prog album, stray copies of which may still be found in charity shops the world over. *Glorfindel* it was called: the studio jammed up with new-fangled Roland synthesisers; Jethro Tull's Ian Anderson guesting on flute; a male-voice choir brought in to augment the seventeen-minute closer 'Tom Bombadil's Lament'; and a poeticising vicar's wife from the West Country summoned to assist an increasingly strung-out Garth with the lyrics. It bombed so prodigiously ('Jejune in every sense of the word,' *Melody Maker* opined) that Don forbade all mention of it in his presence. Meantime, the band were busy falling apart, not liking each other, not liking the members of rival ensembles – a notorious spat with Led Zeppelin, a prolonged bout of juvenile name-calling with the Stones – not liking themselves. And then there were the side-projects, the artless collaborations, the solo misadventures, the aeronautical museum gamely financed by Keith in a disused hangar on the North York Moors, Dale's New Bond Street boutique, Garth's book of poems. Garth's book of poems . . . *Aristogeiton: A Harmony*, influenced, its author was keen to acknowledge, by Tolkien, Aleister Crowley, Eliphas Levi,

Swedenborg and Nietzsche, was eventually, after no little negotiation, brought out by Messrs Sidgwick & Jackson on the understanding that at least ten-thousand Helium Kids fans would rush out to purchase it. In the event, and despite an extensive advertising campaign, only 154 members of this constituency availed themselves of the opportunity. A fortnight after the volume had been published, to a resounding silence, an embittered Garth telephoned me to protest.

'Where are the reviews, man?'

It was quite early in the morning.

'What reviews?'

'The reviews of my book, you arsehole.'

'Haven't there been any?'

'The fuck there have. What I want to know is what are you going to do about it?'

In the end, after an *ex gratia* payment of £300 to a journalist I remembered from college, a two-paragraph notice appeared in the *Daily Telegraph*'s 'Poetry round-up' column, declaring that, if bereft of scansion and lyrical import, *Aristogeiton: A Harmony* was at any rate a tribute to its author's versatility. By this Garth professed himself satisfied.

And so it went on. The year after that they made, in alarmingly quick succession, what might just have masqueraded as a soul LP, had it not had five hairy white men leering from the sleeve, and then a covers album – competently done, everyone agreed, and breathing no little fugitive life into the hoary originals, but who wanted to hear a gang of thirty-year-olds hammering their way through 'Little Queenie' and 'Memphis, Tennessee' here in the glitter-spun and deeply ironical era of Sparks, Queen and Steely Dan? The European tour booked to support it was postponed in grounds of 'fatigue' (whose fatigue, exactly? Garth's? Dale's? The lighting engineer's?) and the dates were never rescheduled.

And yet, deep down, far below the surface embarrassments of cancelled concerts and TV no-shows and ludicrous books of poetry, something far worse was going on. What was going wrong was that, gradually yet irretrievably, Don had begun to lose interest. Meetings, which had once been day-long orgies of inconsequential banter and fond indulgence, with nude girls bringing in trays of lobster and *pâté de foie gras*, withered into terse interrogations, some of them not actually chaired by Don but left to the nit-picking supervision of his accountant, his lawyer or, on one deeply humiliating occasion, his secretary. The fanciful expenses claims that had once been waved through by complaisant minions were now queried, recalibrated and sent disputatiously back. An audit of a UK tour whose hotel bills Don's money man thought excessive resulted in Garth receiving an itemised invoice for £17,000. All this the band saw, and wondered at, but being essentially complacent and un-self-questioning never troubled to do anything about. They were Don's boys, and Don would see them through, even after the interview Don gave to the *New Musical Express* in which he described Keith as 'a bit mental really' and 'lucky not to be in a home', or the occasion on which Garth, cavalierly asking Don for the present of a vintage rosewood Gibson Les Paul with a sunburst finish, was told that he could fuck off, son, and learn to play the banjo.

What were the Kids up to in the mid-1970s? Taking drugs, I suppose, or hanging out with their old ladies – which was the standard music-press summary of time spent at leisure with wife or girlfriend – or footling about on vanity projects that never saw the light, or skiing at Gstaad, or travelling overland to the Orient and having to be rescued when the Land Rover broke down in the Gobi Desert. If I can't file a precise answer to this question it's because I didn't see so much of them, because Don, my employer, was less interested in carrion than fresh meat. Sure, there was still work to do, but it tended

to involve babysitting Keith as he stuttered his way through an interview with *Airfix Magazine* or *Aeromodeller*, or superintending a colour
supplement photomontage of Ian's suit collection, or penning a denial
of the age-old rumour that Garth was about to leave the band to form
a supergroup with ex-members of Traffic and Spooky Tooth. Press
releases, which had once been the proud harbingers of fifty-date
North American tours or vainglorious intimations of sold-out nights
at Madison Square Garden, dwindled away into subjunctives and
conditional clauses.

Dangerfield Hints at New Album 'Dale Halliwell and myself have
really been getting it together,' maintains Helium Kids frontman
Garth Dangerfield, last seen squiring Britt Ekland to Lady Bubbles
Rothermere's Watteau-themed *fête des Anglais* at St Tropez's yacht
club, 'and I don't think it's premature to say that studio time has been
booked for the spring.' (October 1975)

Helium Kids to Tour? *Melody Maker* can exclusively reveal that 'more
than tentative' plans are afoot for a Helium Kids tour of Europe in
support of their forthcoming album, the provisionally titled *Welcome
to the Apocalypse*. (February 1976)

Pasarolo 'very excited' by new album Gary Pasarolo tells *Sounds* why
his songwriting partnership with rock legends Garth Dangerfield and
Dale Halliwell is finally bearing fruit . . . (April 1976)

Did the Helium Kids tour Europe in 1976? Did they make an
album entitled *Welcome to the Apocalypse*? And was Gary Pasarolo
credited with any of the compositions? The answers, in case you don't
have the relevant compendia to hand, are no, no and no. Meanwhile,
I worked quietly yet industriously on the roster of wistful glam rock-
to-prog bands whom Don confidently expected to add to his bank

balance as the 1970s – that troubled and unpredictable musical decade – ground on. The Spangles. Dante's Inferno. Bicycles from Space. You may not remember them. Nobody much does.

Nick Du Pont, contribution to Allan Jones (ed.), *War Stories: Despatches from the Rock and Roll Front Line*, 1983

15. TALES FROM THE RIVERBANK

I'm not your Technicolor dreamboat, honey

I'm not the boy next door

'Street Assassin'

The knot of flies had stopped swarming around the half-lowered sash window and begun to drift haphazardly towards the middle of the ceiling. An advance party was already clinging onto the lower reaches of the chandelier. In the depths beneath us someone was playing a bass guitar through an amplifier so over-driven that you could hear the frets squeak. The Lytton Grange cat, docile up to now, suddenly reared in terror from the sofa and leapt for the door. All this gave the atmosphere in the room a sinister quality, as if someone were shooting a horror film on the premises. Any moment now a tide of green goo would erupt out of the parquet floor, or an ogre with an axe spring out of one of the cupboards and decapitate interviewer and interviewee on the spot. But there were no ogres and no tide of effervescing green goo, only Dale Halliwell and a fresh-faced youngster from *Melody Maker* enjoying what would later be billed as 'a no-holds-barred parley about what's really going down in the world of rock legends the Helium Kids'.

'So, Dale, what do you think of the new music?'

'The new music?' Dale's fingers, now found rolling a cigarette from which tobacco fragments cascaded onto the antique chaise-longue, were a curious plum-pudding colour. 'What kind of new music would that be?'

'Well, what do you think of Bowie's new one?'

'*Diamond Dogs?* The thing about . . . *David* is that you never know where you are with the cat. One moment 'e's wearing a dress, the next 'e's some fucking space alien or something. It'll be sea shanties with a trawlermen's choir in six months' time, you mark my words.'

The flies were intensely interested in the chandelier. Clearly none of them had seen anything like it before.

'Only the other day,' I volunteered, before Dale could seriously incriminate himself, 'Dale was saying to me that he thought Bowie was a pantomorphic chameleon. Isn't that right, Dale?'

'My exact words.'

It was about three o'clock in the afternoon – early by Lytton Grange standards. Downstairs in the oak-panelled refectory they would still be clearing away the breakfast plates. Beyond the window, on the lush, peacock-haunted lawn, two girls in their underwear were playing badminton. Perhaps a hundred yards behind them what looked like a hot-air balloon, secured by guy-ropes to a fan of metal staves, was having something done to its undercarriage. In the distance, dipping in and out of view behind the willow trees, a rowing eight hastened by. What had been a warm afternoon was turning seriously hot.

'Donald Fagen has said that the mystique of rock has started to fade, certainly as a cultural item. What do you think of that?'

Was the mystique of rock starting to fade? It was a good question. Had it ever had much of a mystique in the first place? The girls had stopped playing badminton and were running wildly over the grass in the direction of the blimp. Whatever Dale said in reply was lost in sensory overload: summer lawns; iridescent plumage; flying feet.

'Are you an admirer of Steely Dan's work, Dale?'

There was a silence. I thought about the various tasks I had booked for the rest of the day, which included ferrying Keith to an aeromodelling shop in Henley-on-Thames, ghosting a column called 'Dangerfield's Dalliances', which Garth was contracted to have written for him by one of the music weeklies, and generally helping to sustain an ambience in which, as Stefano had put it over dinner on the previous evening, 'these cunts can get off their arses and do some serious hard work'.

'Christ!' the man from *Melody Maker* now exclaimed, all deference thrown to the winds. 'The bugger's only gone and fallen asleep.'

Inevitably, there was a limit to what the rock PR could do for his charges. You could intervene if you thought your client was making a fool of himself. You could, if desperate, seize a tape recorder and throw it out of the window. In exceptional circumstances you could get Don to lean on the editor and have the piece pulled. But you could not stop the subject falling asleep, going out of his head or, as had happened on one occasion, threatening to dismember the interviewer with a samurai sword.

Silently we contemplated the exhausted figure on the chaise-longue.

'You'll have to forgive Dale,' I explained. 'He's on a very punishing schedule just at the moment.'

'The bloke who drove me here from the station said he hadn't done a hand's turn since he got here.'

The girls had satisfied their curiosity about the hot-air balloon and were scampering back.

'Well, look here . . . Andrew.'

'It's Allan, actually.'

'That's great . . . *Allan*. When you've gone I'm going to ring up my friend Ray at the office – how's his back these days, by the way? – and tell him what a wonderful job you're doing and how much we all like having you here. In the meantime, why don't you take a look around the Grange? Enjoy the facilities. I'm sure Piers would be happy to give you a tour. Or maybe you'd like to talk to Stefano? He's just outside in the hall.'

'No thanks very much,' Allan said hastily. He had clearly heard of Stefano. 'Tour of the palace would do just fine.'

And so we wandered out into the great baronial hallway, which sparkled in the refracted sunshine like an over-lit filmset, where once Sir Neville Lytton, the hero of Marston Moor, whose portrait by Lely hung above the staircase, had graciously received his tenantry. Later on in the seventies Lytton Grange would become notorious. At least three people would certifiably die here, and members of the Damned allegedly destroy £150,000-worth of state-of-the-art recording equipment. Just now it was merely an agreeable country house with a below-stairs studio whose owner, a piece of ex-hippy sixties jetsam named the Honourable Piers Cranston, let it out by the week to rock bands.

'How's Garth, anyway?' Allan from *Melody Maker* now wondered.

'Garth's fine.' There was a pause. 'You know Garth.'

'Somebody told me he spent four days in the studio trying to get the overdubs right on – what's that track with the male voice choir on it called? – "Tom Bombadil's Lament".'

'Garth's certainly a perfectionist about these things.'

I was getting tired of this, tired and suspicious. There was no know-ing how much Allan knew about Garth and his protracted stakeout among the overdubs or what bait might be required to drag him away. Happily, relief was at hand. Down at the far end of the hall, where a couple of deerhounds sprawled languidly in the sunshine, Stefano sat in a deckchair tipped so far back that his arms were at the level of his head, reading what looked like a paperback copy of *The French Lieutenant's Woman*. Allan, flinging up his arms in horror, disappeared into nowhere, gone so quickly that it was as if an invisible hand had scooped him up and carried him off into the ether. Stefano shot out a plump hand and, with elaborate, pasha-like gestures, beckoned me over.

'Who's that fat fuck?'

'Allan from the *Melody Maker*.'

'I've heard of him.' To his credit, Stefano had an encyclopaedic knowledge of music journalists and their foibles. 'Isn't he the one Keith Emerson beat up in the pub car park?'

'Well, he definitely knew about Garth.'

'Garth, Garth,' Stefano said sorrowfully, like a Shakespearean actor examining a skull winched up from the vault. 'Who gives a toss about Garth?' The thought that Stefano might be in one of his off-duty intellectual's moods was confirmed when he beat on the cover of *The French Lieutenant's Woman* with his fingers and handed it over to me for inspection.

'What do you think of John Fowles?'

'I wasn't convinced by the alternative endings.'

'So you're not one of these – what are they called? – fucking post-modernists?' There were thought to be two reasons for the state of profound dejection into which Stefano had sunk over the past week. The first was that he was off drugs. The second was that on our arrival at Lytton Grange, the Honourable Piers had greeted him with a cry of 'Hullo Benners, you old chiz!' ('What was he like at school?' I asked later. 'Oh, you know,' Stefano offered. 'He had the smoothest skin of anyone I've ever been in a rugger scrum with.') But experienced Stefano watchers, of whom I now counted as one, had diagnosed a third source of misery.

'How's Flora?'

'Floribunda . . . Well, she was still there when I phoned home last night.' Stefano, I noticed, had lost weight. Becalmed in the deckchair, he looked like a frail, elderly grasshopper. 'Jesus, Nick,' he went on. 'Have you ever noticed how *weird* women are these days?'

'Lots and lots.'

'I mean, I know we're living in an age of greater sexual equality and all that. I read the papers like anyone else. But whenever I get to fuck her – which, let me tell you Nick, is *not often* – it's as if she's doing me a favour. And then there's what she tells . . . what she tells her friends. It's just . . . I'm a tolerant guy. I don't mind people knowing I had her on the bonnet of a car down in Savernake Forest that time, but I do resent, I really do resent, Nick, a lot of *harpies* who look at me as if they'd like to reach for the castrating shears thinking I leave bogies on the bedsheets.'

Down below our feet, the sound of the bass guitar was turning more muffled. There were other noises – chirruping synthesisers, a percussive clang or two – moving in on its flank. All this returned us to more pressing problems.

'How's the album going?'

'You tell me. I've not been down there. Well I have,' Stefano said, pulling a ragged tennis ball out of his trouser pocket, throwing it into the air and missing its descent by about a foot and a half. 'Tripped over some fucking tape-loop that's hung over a speaker and Garth went off like I was trying to cut his throat. The *last time I looked*,' Stefano went on, the italics fizzing between his lips, 'he had one that went over the mixing desk, round the drumkit, up one wall, over the ceiling and down the other side.'

'What's on them anyway?'

'Christ knows. Flocks of seagulls played backwards. Tibetan monks chanting. There's one track called "At the Black Gates of Mordor" that he's been working on for three days now.'

'What does Don say?'

'Don' – Stefano gave the little twitch of dissatisfaction that for the last year or so had accompanied any mention of the great man's name – 'Don's in, I don't know, Berlin. Vaduz, maybe. In fact, now I come to think about it, definitely Vaduz. Said he'd told EMI they'd have the masters by the middle of next month and if they didn't someone would have his arse kicked. But speaking frankly, Nick,' Stefano said, as if the notion of free, uninterrupted discourse had only just occurred to him, were some wonderful panacea whose benefits ought to be urgently canvassed to the governments of the world, 'it's not Garth I'm worried about. It's fucking Keith.'

'I thought you said he'd calmed down a bit?'

'That's what we all thought,' Stefano gravely intoned, giving the impression that countless agencies regularly convened to ponder the question of Keith's well-being. 'Especially after they put him on – what's that stuff called? – Largactil and sent him back to his missus. Only then we found out he was seeing Rusty on the side.'

'Is that the model girl he brought to the Christmas party?'

'That's the one. Between you and me, "model" is doing her a favour. I mean, would you want to be knocking about with some foxy babe who has her fanny all over *Cunning Stunts* or whatever it's called?' Stefano said, altogether failing to disguise a suspicion that he knew exactly what it was called. 'Anyway, three days ago she gave him the heave-ho. Right here on the studio phone. In front of everyone.'

'What did he do?'

'Let's see now.' Itemising acts of wanton destruction was one of Stefano's specialisms. 'Well, first he trashed his drumkit. No big deal. I mean, everyone does that once in a while. Then he broke the neck off Gary's Stratocaster. There was a point when I thought he was going to set fire to one of those suits of Elizabethan clothes Piers has hanging up in the gallery, but we managed to stop him in time. After that, well . . . bit of glass got smashed over by the greenhouses. But take it from me it could have been a lot worse.'

'What's he doing now?'

'Between you and me I went over to Reading yesterday, found a toyshop and came back with the biggest model of a USAF World War Two Superfortress I could find. He's not stirred from his room since I gave it to him. But it won't last for ever. You have to remember that Keith,' Stefano said with an immense sober seriousness, 'is not like ordinary people when it comes to women … Actually, now you come to mention it, I'm worried about Garth.'

'Haven't they finished "At the Black Gates of Mordor" yet?'

'Oh, the album'll get done. No question about it. I reckon Garth's got another week of co-producing and then the record company'll fire everyone and take it back in-house. But he's definitely up to something.'

'What is it this time?'

'Wish I knew. Phone calls to the studio – and not dealers trying to sell him *Aleister Crowley's Guide to Goat Sacrifice.* He always brags about them. These ones he just mutters a bit and hangs up. Bikes bringing telegrams. The other day he says to Piers: would it be OK if a friend of his dropped by and parked his helicopter on the lawn?'

'What did Piers say to that?'

'Let's just say that *noblesse* did not *oblige* … So that's what's been happening while you've been up in town dining with Princess Margaret. Keith's in serious danger of going tonto, Garth's weirding out and the album's still not done. Look, what are you doing in the next four days?'

'What I always do. In this case, working on a non-existent album. And promoting those European dates which are coming up in August, in case you hadn't noticed.'

'Three to one says they'll get cancelled,' Stefano said morosely. In our six-year acquaintance it was the most despondent I had ever seen him. 'So just do me a favour, will you? Stick around for a bit. Tell Gary you're absolutely sure he'll get half-a-dozen writing credits on the album. Ask Ian if you can see the new suits he will undoubtedly have bought. See if Dale needs a lift to the appointments I happen to know he has fixed up at that clap doctor in Devonshire Street. Right now, I need all the moral support I can get.'

*　　*　　*

And here we were in the summer of 1974, with the glam-rock band-wagon rolling on past Oblivion Corner, the kids in the discos attending to the sanitised version of blue-eyed sixties soul known as the Sound of Philadelphia, sales of Pink Floyd's *The Dark Side of the Moon* climbing to ten million copies, and dark rumours starting to emanate from north London pub-land of hard-edged rhythm and blues bands with names like Ducks Deluxe and Dr Feelgood. None of which the members of the Helium Kids so much as noticed. As far as they were concerned, and despite mounting evidence to the contrary, it was still 1971, or maybe even 1969, with the pink faces of the hippy children mutely imploring from the festival crowds as far as the eye could see. As for that mounting evidence to the contrary, well let me tell you that the tax year 1973/4 was the first twelve months in which Helium Kids Ventures, an entity to be distinguished from the barrelling commercial juggernaut of Shard Enterprises, made a trading loss. And how had this happened? Some contributory factors might have included:

- a ruinously expensive 'Third World Tour', involving the transportation of thirteen tons of equipment in seven articulated lorries to what Garth, its instigator, described as 'some really groovy places where ordinary bands don't go to'. Venues included an ancient Cretan amphitheatre, the shadow of the Pyramids and a village in the foothills of the Atlas Mountains.
- 'Wotan Records', the independent label founded by Garth and Dale with the aim of 'signing all those new young bands that the majors won't touch'.
- the elaborate gatefold sleeve of *Street Assassins*, designed by a Celtic folk-artist Garth had met on a field-trip to Skibbereen, including runic inscriptions in embossed silver foil and a mock-medieval leather clasp.

Each of these interventions, alas, blew a gaping hole in the profit and loss account. The concert under the Atlas Mountains, with its half-hour firework display, its Moroccan banquet, its two-dozen journalists flown over from Gibraltar in a chartered jet and its audience of bewildered Berber tribesmen, produced gross receipts of a little over £8. EMI, though willing to license and distribute the Wotan Records catalogue, made sure that its start-up costs were charged back to the Helium Kids account, and there was a scandal when the label's initial signing, a band called Willy's Rats, discovered that a song called 'Spirit of the Necromancer' had been expropriated by Garth for his own private use. The production processes involved in manufacturing the gatefold sleeve were of such complexity that the customary economies of scale somehow failed to apply. Meanwhile, the boys were spending more time in the studio racking up production costs that were set against their advances, hiring limos to take them to the shops and staying at places like Lytton Grange; one of those wholly artificial environments, so common to the early 1970s, where the outside world never intruded and the only disturbance liable to afflict a sensitive, over-indulged soul was the sound of the foxes making a small-hours raid on the Honourable Piers's chicken coops.

But there were times when the external world could not be kept at bay. The Lytton Grange copy of *Melody Maker* arrived on Thursday morning, together with the *Poultry Farmer's Gazette* and the *Financial Times*, in which Piers monitored the performance of his share portfolio. Found reading it in the empty breakfast room, through whose mullioned windows the sun fell in a series of hexagon shapes, Stefano seemed unnaturally cheerful, like a small boy on whose undeserving head some unlooked-for treat had suddenly descended.

'Jesus, will you listen to this?' he crowed. '"Portrait of the artist as a narcolept. Allan Jones writes: "In my brief career as amanuensis to the stars, it has been my privilege to be sworn at, ignored, have an Alsatian set on me, dangled off a fire-escape and thumped by an enraged guitar-player who mistook me for this organ's news editor. But I have never – ever – had some bozo in a lavender-coloured cambric jacket fall asleep on me." Hey, you get a mention as well. "There is an hilarious moment when Nick, your man Halliwell's all-too attentive PR, tries to pass off a polysyllabic description of David Bowie as his dullard client's original thought."'

And here, it seemed to me, was another mark of Stefano's devitalised state. Two years ago he would have been straightaway round to the pub next to *Melody Maker's* offices in Fleet Street to pour a pint of Special Brew over our reporter's head and grind his ear into an ashtray.

'What does Don say?'

'Don?' Stefano folded the paper into the shape of a footpad's cudgel and placed it carefully in the back pocket of his jeans. 'Don won't even notice. Too busy on that deal the Spangles are getting with Chrysalis.'

'Is he taking twenty this time? Or twenty-five?'

'Twenty-eight,' Stefano said, with what might have been reluctant admiration. 'Don says it's time to stop pissing about ... Look, what are you doing for the rest of the day?'

'Phoning the *Mirror* about what Garth is supposed to have said about Enoch Powell.'

'*Fuck*. I'd forgotten about that.' One of the girls I had seen playing badminton in her underwear sat down at the table opposite and began primly to eat a boiled egg. 'What line will you be taking?'

'Well-meaning young man, deeply worried by the present political situation, feels that he has to speak out, regrets that some of his remarks may be open to misinterpretation.'

'Sounds good to me. Well, hang around until the afternoon. Piers has organised one of his balloon trips. Might be a story in it. Photo for the papers or something. You know: *Helium Kids take to the skies*.' He looked suddenly doleful, all the bright promise of the morning gone. The girl at the adjoining table snapped at her spoonful of egg and a stream of bright yellow liquid spurted out over her chin.

'Jesus,' Stefano said wretchedly. 'Someone ought to teach that chick how to eat.'

'How's Keith?'

'Keith . . .' Stefano looked puzzled, as if presented with a cipher it was beyond his ability to solve. 'Oh, *Keith*. Keith's fine. As good as gold. Piers gave him some . . . er, Nembutal or something and a bottle of tequila. Haven't had a peep out of the fucker for twenty-four hours.'

Afternoon sunshine, falling slantwise over the Lytton Grange lawns, enhanced their profound air of unreality. Time had stopped somewhere in the 1870s. It would never move forward. Piers, who could be seen grubbing around in the kitchen garden with an alpenstock, clad in a pair of mustard-coloured gaiters, was a Victorian squire. The girls who had been playing badminton in their underwear, now more conventionally dressed and roaming hand-in-hand through the arboretum, were Pre-Raphaelite beauties. Pretty soon Alma-Tadema would emerge from the summerhouse, set up his easel and start to paint them. Only the noises from the basement studio spoke of the mechanised hum of another age.

Slowly – infinitely slowly – the afternoon wore on. Dale and Ian played pool in the Lytton Grange billiard room, flanked by a bookcase which was found to contain a first edition of *Origin of Species*. Gary was thought to be in the basement laying down guitar parts. Of Keith, jilted, Superfortress-manufacturing Keith, there was, and had been, no sign. After a certain amount of negotiation, I brokered a deal with the *Mirror* whereby Garth's view of the immigration problem was exchanged for an exclusive interview with a girl group Don was interested in called the Velveteens.

Then, at about half-past five, I made my way across the lawn to the spot where the hot-air balloon lay awaiting its launch. Here were gathered a motley array of people, poised halfway between a garden fete and an exhibition of morris dancing: the Kids (minus Garth) and their sumptuous womenfolk; one or two of the Lytton Grange staff; children from the village come to see the fun. Piers, sporting a cavalryman's tunic that one of his ancestors had worn at Quatre Bras, and thought to enjoy these occasions, was at least three-parts drunk.

'It's all perfectly straightforward,' he was explaining. 'There's room for four. Plus the pilot, of course. You just drift around for half an hour or so, while we follow you in the van and pick you up wherever you come down. The best thing to do is draw lots. So just write your names down and put them in the hat.'

Writing my name on one of the slips of yellow paper that Piers produced from his cuirassier's jacket and placing it in the antique top hat that lay on a stool next to the balloon's square wicker basket, I felt a sudden pang of unease. Something was going to go wrong. The certainty that disaster threatened hung in the air above our heads. So strong was this presentiment of doom that for a moment I could have been back on the road to Jackson with Florian, the hills rolling away into winter sky and the buzzards perched on the picket-wire. The first three names drawn from the hat were Dale's, mine and the girl who had eaten the boiled egg at breakfast. Then, as Piers bent to select the fourth, a voice said: 'I'll go. Let me go.'

Until now I hadn't taken much notice of Keith, only registered the fact that he was there, and that Stefano's efforts at therapy might have been judged a success. Now I realised that one of those moments from the great age of Soviet cinema had hurtled up to confront us: the moment when a character once thought nondescript and anodyne suddenly declares himself, becomes in the space of a few seconds the person he was meant to be. Eyeing Keith up for what seemed the first time in years, I saw that he was even more weirdly dressed than ever. floral shirt, black tracksuit bottoms and a pair of pink sneakers had all fought their way clamorously out of the wardrobe for the privilege of adorning him. The fact that we were in the process of conducting a lottery, that chance rather than sheer effort of will would carry the day, scarcely seemed to have occurred to him.

'I'll go,' he said again, less to Piers than the crowd as a whole. 'Let me go, wontcha?'

'Keith, man,' Piers said, who had caught the scent of aggression but also the odd beseeching note. '*Keith*. I'm sure we can fix that. Sure we can.' He gave the faintest of nods in Stefano's direction but got nothing back. 'Why don't you step right up?'

The wicker basket was about five feet high. A step ladder rested against its side. As the three of us climbed gingerly up to the rim, Keith took a run-up, hurled himself over in the manner of an old-fashioned high-jumper performing the Eastern Cut-off and landed in a heap on some coils of rope. Dale, who in an indefinable way seemed to have taken charge of the flight, ignored him.

'What's your name then, darlin'?' he enquired companionably of the girl.

'Lynsey. Is your friend all right?'

'Search me. Keith, mate, are you all right?'

The moorings had been cut loose by now and the pilot, walkie-talkie pressed to his ear, was issuing instructions to a man on the ground. Slowly Keith got to his feet, placed both hands at a ninety-degree angle on the edge of the basket and peered over the side.

'Jesus,' he said.

'I'll have to ask you to stop moving around, sir,' the pilot offered. 'Might unbalance us.'

The Oxfordshire countryside was beginning to disappear beneath us. The crowd that had waved us off receded into ant-like insubstantiality. Fields, ponds, stretches of woodland, church spires were all on the point of blurring. Every so often, flickers of wind set the basket faintly astir.

'Jesus,' Keith said again. He took a half-bottle of vodka out of the back pocket of his tracksuit bottoms, looked as if he might be about to take a swig, but instead upended the contents over his head.

'All right then, Lynsey?' Dale was saying to the girl. He was hugely enjoying himself. 'What's your Zodiac sign?'

We were several hundred feet up now, and still rising steadily. Many of the songs of the 1960s had been about balloon trips: sailing through the sky; magic carpet rides to infinity. None of them had had anything to say about white-faced maniacs pouring bottles of vodka over their heads. Keith, I now registered, was making queer little chirruping noises.

'Keith, mate,' Dale said, breaking off his discussion of what passionate people Capricorns were, 'put a sock in it, OK?'

What happened next could only be reconstituted in fragments. Lynsey gave a yell. The wicker basket lurched violently from side to side. Keith, springing up on one leg, hooked the other over the rim, tried to get the trailing leg to follow but hung there, a slightly puzzled look on his face, suspended between earth and sky. Thrown back on my heels, I could only watch as Dale, not seeming especially put out, grabbed Keith by the scruff of his floral shirt and wrestled him back to the floor. As Keith struggled to his feet and the balloon tipped again, Dale hit him on the point of his chin and knocked him out cold.

'Shepperton Boys' Boxing Club,' he said, ruefully inspecting his knuckles. 'You never forget.'

The support truck returned us from the barley field on which we had gently descended twenty minutes later without further incident. Keith, his misadventure attributed to striking his head against his outstretched knee, lay dreamily across the three back seats. On arrival, he was taken off to Newbury hospital, diagnosed with mild concussion, and kept in overnight. By this time, Lytton Grange was sunk in torpor. The crowd had disappeared and the rolling lawn was empty. Two or three of the peacocks strutted across the gravel drive shrieking unhappily.

'All right, Nick?' Dale demanded. The events of the past half-hour had put him in an even better mood than usual. 'What you up to, man?'

'Carrying on with my long career of setting the record straight.'

'Uh huh. Well, why don't you come down to the studio for a while? 'Is Majesty wants some extra voices. For that closing track, isn't it? You know, the one about the elf-maiden or something. Reckons it'll make it sound like "Hey Jude".' Dale laughed. Deep in the innermost circles of the band, it was thought that he got over his regular annoyance with Garth – his constant scheming, the limitations of his songwriting, the excesses of his stage gear, his political opinions, the women he was seen with – by regarding him as, first and foremost, a source of amusement.

There were about a dozen people jammed into the studio. Some of them were veterans of the balloon launch. Ian sat in the corner tuning a Fender Jazz bass. Garth, who had not left his post for the past three days, bent over the mixing desk talking to one of the engineers. But for the bags under his eyes, he looked surprisingly well. Seeing that Dale and I had arrived, but not acknowledging our presence in any way, he straightened up and began on one of the long, self-important but not wholly humour-free monologues that an interviewer from the *New Musical Express* had once suggested would make a short book entitled *Why I am Right About Absolutely Fucking Everything*.

'... Want to get a kind of *mantra* effect ... Mostly in 4/4, but there's a bit in the middle where it goes into 6/4 ... Da-da-da-da-*dah*-da ... No, I don't need any bass, Ian ... Just *unsupported vocals* ... What we're going for is a kind of relentlessness, with the emphasis on the second syllable ... Ga*lad*riel. Like that ...'

Silently the line of faces – most of them respectful, a few contemptuous – composed themselves. This was going to take some time. The engineer produced a small blue pill and slipped it into the corner of his mouth. Just then the phone rang in the Perspex box that did service as a control room. Garth shook his head, as if to say that no message, not one from President, Prime Minister or the Chairman of EMI Records, could possibly compete with the vital work he had before him, but Dale, always on the lookout for diversion, strode into the booth and picked it up.

'Garth Dangerfield here,' he said. 'And 'ow may I have the pleasure of assisting you?'

It was generally agreed that Dale's impersonation of Garth was of a very high standard, and that it precisely reproduced the curious amalgam of self-regard and insinuation with which he addressed his fellow human beings. At any rate, it seemed to have worked here. There were three or four exchanges, Dale seeming pretty much to agree with whatever was suggested at the other end. 'Thanks very much,' he said eventually. 'That's very interesting. And thank Ritchie too, will you?' Outside the control room door there was a small table on which pieces of teamaking equipment – a kettle, two or three mugs, packets of sugar lumps – lay scattered about. Without warning, Dale seized the kettle by the spout, skipped across to Garth and poured the considerable amount of warmish water that was inside it over his head.

'You *cunt*,' he said sorrowfully.

Someone took Garth away to sponge him down. The rest of the session was cancelled. It was later established that the caller had been inviting Garth to join Deep Purple.

3 October 1974

Autumn here in Eccleston Square. Beech leaves drifting over the tennis courts in the railed-off gardens. Coaches from Victoria idling in the parking bays. 'Galadriel', the first single off the album, in at No.

37 in a chart whose first three places are occupied by Carl Douglas's
'Kung Fu Fighting', John Denver's 'Annie's Song' and Johnny Bristol's
'Hang On in There Baby'. Review in the *NME*, by Nick Kent, consists
of the two words '*Oh Jesus!*' Garth and Dale for some reason behaving
as if they've already scored a monster hit. Champagne party last night
in Soho to celebrate.

9 October 1974

Long day at the office. Conscious of breaking that unwritten PR's
rule about not chasing the coverage but letting it come to you. Don
involved in some kind of row with the record company (reasons
unspecified), which ends with the MD himself coming round in a
cab. Apparently there are problems in the States, which we could do
without in advance of next year's tour.

12 October 1974

'Galadriel' at No. 41. No *Top of the Pops*, despite much agitation from
Maddox Street. Coming back across the square at dusk I find a
middle-aged-to-elderly lady, carrier bag in hand, waiting on the doorstep. It takes a moment or two, and the sound of a high, nasal voice
enquiring my name, to establish that this is Daphne, the old man's
girlfriend, last seen that Christmas in Queens ten years ago.

Escorted up to the flat and settled in an armchair, Daphne seems
more solid, less liable to crumble into dust at the touch of a finger.
Her hair, the colour of barley sugar now, is piled up on top of her head
in a kind of pompadour. 'I got ya address out of the telephone book,'
she explains. 'Ya don't mind me coming round here or nuthin'?' It
turns out that Daphne, in London to visit relatives ('My sister lives in
Crouch End or someplace') was possessed of a sudden desire to look
me up. The incongruity of her presence in a Pimlico drawing room,

Macy's shopping bag balanced on her knees, doesn't seem to have occurred to her. She looks sharp, vigilant, perfectly able to take care of herself – in a Pimlico drawing room or anywhere else.

'Hey,' she says. 'Remember that time ya came round the house and I tolt ya forchewn? Did any of it work out?'

'A little, perhaps.'

'Yeah? I'm good with forchewns,' Daphne says complacently. 'Got the gift, ya dad useta say.'

Here in the shadow cast by the flaring streetlamps, Daphne fills in several of the gaps in the old man's late-sixties transit around the USA: fugitive days in upstate New York; time spent in Florida managing an orange plantation; the flight to Oregon. 'I never could stand the place, but Maurice kinda liked it. Guess he thought it was as good a life to settle down ta as any. A friend I had there – *not* that fuckin' Richard – wrote me when he died and I was gonna go out there and visit, but Mr McClintick – that's my husband – argued against it, and his vote counts. My friend said you burned him up out on the ocean. Now that musta been quite a sight.'

She stays for upwards of two hours. Impossible to work out whether she sees this as a courtesy call or some curious last rite in her relationship with the old man. When she gets up to go she says, a bit importantly, 'He used to talk about ya a lot. In fact, he'd talk about ya so much ya'd want him to talk about something else. No offence, ya understand?' As if for the first time, her eye falls on the décor of the room, the framed album sleeves and the Jim Dine drawing. 'Nice place ya got here,' she says. 'He'd have liked that. We mostly lived in crap holes.'

I take her back downstairs to the front door, where decades-old post lies in unclaimed piles and there are bicycles stacked against the wall. Outside the traffic zips and whirs.

'It's been nice talking to ya,' she says. 'Mr McClintick will like to know about it.' Her hand, briskly extended, is a small, bony fin. 'Listen.

I'm here the week. I got some stuff ya might like ta have. Nuthin' fancy. Just a few old things in a box. Call me at my hotel' – the bony fingers press a card into my hand – 'and we can fix ta hand them over.'

I watch her move off across the left-hand corner of the square towards the coach station, barley-sugar hair softly aglow in the naphtha horizon.

18 October 1974

Traces of Daphne's perfume – a paralysing odour of musk – still hanging in the air. 'Galadriel' down to No. 57. *Glorfindel* due in a week. Advance orders 'holding up', whatever that means.

Meeting at Maddox Street to discuss press for album. Boys – uncharacteristically subdued – agree to all suggestions. No sign of Don.

When I call Daphne's hotel, it's to be told that she checked out three days ago.

BAD VIBES IN TEXAS – ON THE ROAD WITH THE HELIUM KIDS

Nothing in life is certain, except North of Texas. And here your faithful correspondent is, set down by Gulf Airways (a big thankya to its nattily dressed pilots, its dinky stewardesses and a Tannoy I couldn't make head or tail of just *howevah* hard I tried) in the Lone Star State, specifically Austin, where everything is big and fat and fine, and sound-tracked by Texas Radio, which has a constitutional weakness for old blues shouters like Arthur Crudup and Pee Wee Scattergood, and even the cacti lining the roadside on the trip from the airport like a silent vegetable army puff out their chests as if to say that they're bigger than any goddamn succulent that Arizona and Kansas can offer, tracking those veteran rawk noise-makers the Helium Kids on their umpteenth tour of the dear ole US of A.

And whisper it not, gentle reader, but these are nervous times for the Kids, or perhaps I should say Kidz – that being how at least one of the local radio outlets has started spelling their name. The Austin Thunderdrome, where the boys are booked to play tomorrow, seats 10,000 and the word on the street is that the place is by no means sold out. It was the same at Houston and apparently at Baton Rouge, of which my informant, an immensely likeable jock on the local station with hair growing out of his ears and access to some of the *fahnest* weed that your dogged newshound has ever had the pleasure of sampling, remarked: 'Everyone, *but everyone*, sells out the Capitol Theatre. There's bluegrass fiddle bands from Kentucky could sell out the Capitol Theatre.' ZZ Top play three nights in a row there when they're around. Not the Kids, alas, who entertained a house one-third empty *even after* a week's saturation advertising and several of those send-in-a-letter-saying-why-you-and-your-friends-lurve-the-Helium-Kids-and-we'll-send-you-free-tickets promotions of which regional American TV channels are so fond. Nervous times, indeed.

It's the same at the Plaza Hotel, where your tenacious gumshoe has thankfully managed to score a bed and a closet for the pair of white C&A suits he reckoned appropriate for Texas in the month of August. A friend of mine travelled around the States with the Kids in '73 when *Street Assassins* was doing good business (not the *best* business but still good, ya unnerstand?) and reckoned it was complete screaming mayhem, with groupies crawling in through the hotel ventilator shafts and a $10,000 damages bill at one luckless establishment which the Kids' redoubtable manager Don Shard settled *in cash*, if you please. Keith Shields, the band's venturesome or maybe just halfway insane drummer, is supposed to have galloped a Harley Davidson motorcycle through the foyer of a Pittsburgh hotel without anyone so much as batting an eyelid. But the Plaza is just sunk in late-summer torpor, like one of those John Cheever novels in which the expectation that something might happen is cancelled out by the growing suspicion that it probably won't, with a bunch of Republican bigwigs just dying to draft Ronald Reagan or some other right-wing scumbag for next year's Presidential ticket (this is Republican territory and then some, and Watergate don't seem to matter a dime) and a women's club in the lounge listening to a middle-aged dude with processed hair talking about how spirit hands have touched him and only the sight of a couple of guitar cases in the lobby and a big old equipment truck parked out back to remind us all – 'us' being myself, the goofy girl from Radio KLM and a guy who claims that his byline once appeared in *Crawdaddy* or someplace – why it is we're here. Honest t'Christ, ladies and gentlemen, I never saw a place that looked less like a rock and roll band was staying in it.

Maybe this, ah, *disparity* is down to the fact that Don – big, bad Don, of whom even bug-eyed rips such as Zep's Peter Grant speak with reverential awe – ain't here yet. Where is Don? Nobody 'xactly seems to know. According to one rumour he's on some big shot's boat 1500 miles away in Key Largo. Another piece of scuttlebutt has it that he's holed up in Noo Yawk finessing a deal with Atlantic Records (this last bit, by the way, I find VERY HARD TO BELIEVE). Still, Don will be along presently, everyone assures me, the presumption being that a Helium Kids tour wouldn't be a Helium Kids tour in the absence of this vital piece of furniture, and that the sight of Don Shard puzzling the bartender with a request for some impossibly antiquated refreshment like a gin ricky while advising the terrified local promoter in precisely which stretch of the Mississippi River he can go and drown himself is worth any amount of empty seats and tour posters that spell his protégés' names with a 'z'. In his absence, an impressive solidarity pervades the premises. The Baton Rouge gig was a wowser, Nick the band's PR assures me, and took the roof off the place, while *Return to Base*, the rock and roll covers album which my friend Mr Kent reviewed in these pages only a couple of weeks ago, is doing very nicely thank you.

Meanwhile, everyone wants to know – well, I want to know, and so does the goofy girl from Radio KLM, who 'rilly wants to get down with Garth in a kind of interview situation', and even the guy whose byline may or may not have appeared in *Crawdaddy* or someplace – where the band is. And where is the band? Ian the bass player is at the bar drinking occasional vodka-tonics, but he's a quiet reflective soul and in half-a-dozen conversations with him spread out to fill nearly the same number of years your correspondent has wormed out of him not much more than that he likes the playing of Jaco Pastorius and

that his improbably small hands make it difficult to hammer the
bottom E of his Fender Precision with quite the vigour that he'd like.
I get the phone number of Dale Halliwell's room off Nick the obliging
PR ('Don't say I gave it to you') but there's no reply – he's off inspecting the venue, or eating some clam chowder, or getting laid, or doing
whatever touring rock stars do when they ain't actually playing – and
that leaves only Keith the drummer in plain sight, leaving me to have
one of those meat-and-potatoes exchanges that music journalists over
the years have tended to have with Keith. 'Enjoyed the album, Keith.'
'Yeah, it's good innit?' 'How did you get that drum sound on "Sweet
Little Sixteen"?' 'I dunno. Something the producer did.'

All of which makes as good a place as any to ask the question: what
is a concerned young person such as myself to think of the Helium
Kids halfway through their (research, in the form of Nick the PR,
confirms) seventh full-scale stumble around the Land of the Free?
Me, I always had a softish spot for Garth, Dale, Ian, Florian (RIP)
and co. ever since I used to watch their weedy beat-group approximations on *Ready Steady Go!* when I was jest a boy, as one of those old
Country and Western singers would put it. Sure, they were always six
months behind whatever the Fabs and the Stones were up to, but
Paisley Patterns (if you don't remember *Paisley Patterns* then just what
kind of sixties pot-head are you f'Chrissakes?) has worn a whole lot
better than, say, *Their Satanic Majesties Request*. Then, of course, came
the full-blooded, Gary Pasarolo-assisted power-quintet phase, but if
they were never quite as hot as the Zep or other subsidiary lice in the
locks of rock's pompadour, then boy did *Low Blows in High Times*
rock out. As for the recent stuff, *Glorfindel* is as big a turkey as ever got
served up for Thanksgiving dinner and someone should have told
Garth Dangerfield zillions of years before he sat down to tape the
vocals to *Feeling the Pressure* that he ain't a soul singer, never will be
and should leave this difficult art to the cats from Philly. Oh, and
Return to Base isn't bad, only, as ever, Lennon got in first with *Rock 'n'*

Roll and does these things with considerably more panache. But, as I say, I always liked 'em and even now, in what a more hard-bitten reporter than myself might want to call their decline, it's still a pleasure to be with them here in God's Own Country while wondering where the blazes Don is and why, if Garth has promised me an interview – which the faithful Nick assures me he has – the dude don't show.

And so time passes in the way it does down here on the Panhandle, with the big fat Pontiacs and Zephyr Sedans cruising down Main Street, with big fat Texans half asleep at their wheels and the saffron-coloured sun hanging in the air like a fried egg, enabling your reporter to relax poolside with a copy of Mailer's latest (not bad if you like that kind of thing) and shoot the breeze with Charysse, the goofy girl from KLM, who is 'rilly pleased' to be here while sensing a certain amount of 'negativity', with nary a glimpse of Don and only the sight of Garth's coat-tails (literally – I followed him into the bar in pursuit of our promised sit-down and then fruitlessly followed him out a whole thirty seconds later) to persuade me that the rock and roll circus was definitely in town. Finally, on the second night, we get to see them at the Thunderdrome, which is *no way* full, and where the PA makes the rhythm section sound like an ancient dinosaur crawling into its cave, or wherever dinosaurs hang out, to die. To the band's credit they ain't bad, stick resolutely to the mid-period stuff and have cut back on the dry-ice-and-lasers strategy that was such a disagreeable feature of their last whirl around the States, and the kids down the front – bullet-headed Texan teens with occasional longhair support – are clearly digging it.

Back at the Plaza, post-gig, Don – dear, loveable, dangerous Don – finally shows up from Key Largo or Manhattan or wherever he's been, and some vague attempts are made to get up a rock and roll *parteh* of the kind that, alas, your reporter is insufficiently old enough to remember. Various young ladies are introduced to the company;

Keith, always a scream, balances a chair on his extended forearm; and Charysse, who reckons the gig 'rilly impressive', drinks far more tequila than is good for her. Don, for the record, his moustachioes at well-nigh Fu Manchu length, is affable, but will not be drawn on his dealings with Atlantic, if such they are, and at one point tells the tour manager to be careful with the fire extinguisher he is so incontinently wielding. And yes, after what seems like hours of parlaying and cancelled introductions, I do get to talk to Garth Dangerfield. Garth thinks the concert went well ('We're not Jethro Tull, but we can still pull them in'), is pleased by the (relative) success of *Return to Base* and looks forward to getting back to the UK, where 'you know, we can go out there and play to our own people'. On the other hand, you have a suspicion that for Garth – hilariously got up, I have to say, in a kind of spangled romper suit – the real action is going on off camera. Or should I say on the damn thing. There is, for example, talk of a film project with no less an *auteur* than Michelangelo Antonioni, and a solo album which Glyn Johns ('He's a bit busy right now') may or may not produce. Let's be candid about this. Garth wants to talk about the last Joni Mitchell album ('I mean she's really good, even with all that jazz stuff'); he wants to talk about Bowie's excursions into soul and funk; but he sure as hell doesn't seem to want to talk about his band of brothers.

And so the evening grinds on. Charysse and Mr Halliwell, it must be said, are getting on *splendidly*. Don – dear, loveable, dangerous Don – grows more unsmiling by the minute. Your correspondent, too, drinks more tequila than is probably good for him and retires early with a headache and an old blues tape that Ian, an expert in these matters, has pressed upon him. Next day I wake up to find that the party's over and the cavalcade has moved on, leaving me with a wrecked hotel room – whaddya know, the buggers must have sneaked in and done it while I was asleep – and that *fahn*, chugging, bouncy beat of Texas radio. Oh, and the feeling that whereas once a tour with the Helium Kids used to be the epitome of rock and roll in all its ear-outraging, eye-catching, magnificent excess, now it's just another tour with the Helium Kids.

Charles Shaar Murray, *New Musical Express*, 3 September 1975

16. 1977 (I)

There in the verdant water meadows
My lady Goldberry did wander
Until the cruel orcs
Stole her away . . .

'Tom Bombadil's Lament'

'It'll all blow over in a year or two,' my friend Freddie pronounced.
'You mark my words.'

'You think so?'

'Bound to, dear. I mean, look' – he threw an elegant, dove-like hand
out into the Speakeasy's smoke-filled air that somehow managed to
encompass both the establishment's foetid décor and the hordes of
spotty boys in leather jackets milling around it – 'just *look* at them all.
I can't imagine many of them can read their recording contracts, much
less play their instruments. No dear, what will happen' – the fingers of
the hand which was still describing graceful arabesques above its
owner's lap had been touched up with black nail polish, I noticed – 'is
what *always* happens whenever a new artistic movement toddles
along. A few talented people will go on to make nice little careers for
themselves while the others return to the primeval swamp whence
they came. It was just the same with Dada.'

'And after that everything will go back to normal?'

'Oh I think so, don't you? I believe they're already selling bin-liner T-shirts in Woolworths. I saw a countess's daughter in a pair of bondage trousers only the other day. It's called the Revolt into Style.'

Cheered a little, I glanced up to see a Radio 1 disc jockey walk into the room, stare at the spotty boys – one or two stared menacingly back – and walk out again. For these were comforting words for the early part of 1977, emollient balm sent to heal the wounds of a world in which buzz-saw guitars and gabbling mock-cockney voices loomed very large. Once uttered, on the other hand, they seemed vaguely insubstantial, as open to mockery as the mauve smoking jacket that Freddie had negligently draped over his shoulders, hung wispily in the air like the drifts of smoke above the Speakeasy's banquette. Freddie looked round the room again, took a darting, humming-bird's sip from a giant-sized lavender-coloured cocktail that appeared to have a small shrub growing in its upper regions, and frowned.

'I'm not saying that it isn't all very upsetting, dear. I saw that nice man from Emerson, Lake & Palmer the other day – would his name be Greg? – and he said their accountant was last seen having a *fit* in the *lavatory* … Johnny Rotten, Howard Devoto, The Lurkers' – he pronounced this list of newly fashionable names with maximum petulance, like a prison governor hastening down the penitentiary roll – 'who are they? What do they want?'

By way of an answer, a tall boy in leathers and a pair of biker boots moved out of the crowd, shifted himself into the space before our table and waved his fist in the air. But Freddie was used to dealing with this sort of thing.

'Mr Ferocious!' he exclaimed. 'And how's the world treating you? Well, I hope. Now *that*, my dear,' he went on as the apparition lumbered away again, 'is a regular saucy boy. His, ah, *ensemble* were recording in the studio next to ours only the other week. I can't begin to tell you some of the things they got up to. Now, are you sure you aren't going to stay? You could be my Gandalf and defend me from all these goblins.'

'Can't, I'm afraid. Off to see Stefano.'

There was so much smoke rising over the crowd of eagerly conversing heads that the drinkers on the further side were hardly visible, just wraith-like shadows gathered up in gloom. 'Well, give him my love. I don't suppose he'll remember that heavenly party we went to in Montreux. People are so forgetful these days. Which reminds me, I saw your Mr Halliwell the other night. What was he doing? Coming down the steps of some two-bit sleazy dive, I think. But the point is he was *completely out of it*. Mandied out of his head, I believe the expression is.'

'I think he's feeling the strain.'

'Aren't we all, dear?' Freddie remarked, as a waitress approached with another of the shrubbery cocktails. 'You tell Stefano from me that he ever gets that lot on stage together again it'll be a small miracle.'

'I'll tell him.'

And so I said goodbye to Freddie, who I always liked and whose death I greatly regretted, jostled my way through the crowd of spotty boys, strode out into the balmy night of a Soho spring, fetched the car from its subterranean parking space and sped off through the dense, unhappy streets to what Stefano, in the telephone call confirming our meeting, had called 'a proper chat' about that horribly forbidding territory which lay before us, 'the future'.

It was a mark of quite how far we, or some of us, had fallen that Stefano, who had once pitched his tent in Knightsbridge, who had run up his standard on the battlements of Mayfair, should now, after several lightning removals, be living in a debased suburb on the wrong side of Barnes Common. As the car headed west over the oily glint of the Thames to the naphtha-drenched byways of SW13, I thought about the letter that had come two days ago, its grim imperatives, its sly ultimatums and its overwhelming scent of panic. Things were bad. They would probably get worse. That much was certain. Stefano's latest bolthole lay halfway along a terrace of identikit townhouses, whose white frontages gleamed in the moonlight. His immediate neighbours, he had explained, were a loss adjuster and a junior partner in the accountancy firm of Saffery Champness. ('They're incredibly straight, Nicko. They think I'm some kind of hippy gorilla.') The front curtains were undrawn, and as I approached I could see him standing a little way back in the bay with his great bulb of a head looming out of the shadows.

'Nice to see you, Nicko,' Annabel said, opening the door and pecking my cheek with all the enthusiasm of a shrike let loose on a gamekeeper's gibbet. 'You want a drop of sumfink?' Shrivelled and petite, with extraordinary little pipe-cleaner legs that dwindled away under her pelvis, Annabel was also a mark of quite how far we, or some of us, had fallen.

'No thanks.'

'Reely, it's no trouble' Annabel said cheerlessly. She lowered her voice. ''E's in the front room. The fucker.'

Annabel had days when she professed to quite enjoy being the girlfriend of the assistant manager of a rock band, and days when the sheer drudgery and uncertainty of this role were cruelly brought home to her. This seemed to be one of the second sort. I went on through a hallway obstructed by piled-up copies of the *Barnes and Richmond Gazette*, an unframed gold disc for *Low Blows in High Times* and a life-size cut-out of Garth that had once featured in a record-store promotion, turned right into the dining room and came upon Stefano standing in the window and looking uncannily like a photo I had once seen of Field Marshal Rommel inspecting his troops before the Battle of El Alamein.

'Look at me, Nicko,' he said as I appeared in front of him. 'Just look at me. Wouldn't you say – wouldn't you say I was . . . well, wouldn't you say I was the kind of man who kept himself in good shape?'

'I would, Stef. I'd definitely say that,' I said, ignoring the fact that the eye turned on me was the colour of the knotted apricot foulard scarf worn by Warren Beatty to attend one of the after-parties on the last-but-one US tour. 'You've got' – I remembered a phrase that Stefano had sometimes unabashedly used of himself in the old rois-ter-doistering days of forty-eight-hour cocaine jags and week-long bacchanals – 'the constitution of an ox.'

"E's been down the gym and all.' Annabel, who had stolen into the room like a shadow, seemed to have lost her former resentment. 'Working out on one of them machines.'

There was a desk five or six feet away under the light, covered with what looked like telexes from American promoters. 'What's all this about anyhow?'

'It's that Don,' said Annabel. 'The fucker. Reckons Stef's not up to it no more. Thinks he hasn't got the stamina.'

In this, as in all his judgements about the Helium Kids and the people he hired to smooth their progress through the world, Don was showing his usual astuteness. For Stefano, patently, had not got the stamina. In fact, he was a sixteen-stone recovering alcoholic, of whose last divorce settlement a highly placed legal friend he could not afford to employ had remarked, 'Well, they certainly took you to the cleaners and no mistake,' and left it at that.

'That's ridiculous,' I loyally offered. 'Don must be losing his grip.'

'No, no,' Stefano said huskily, waving a fat, admonitory hand in the patch of dense air before his mottled face. 'I won't hear . . . I won't hear a word against Don. But the fact is . . .' There was no doubt about it. He was in terrible shape. Annabel by this time had taken his arm – this had all the lumpy consistency of a glutted python – and was fondly massaging it. 'You see, we had one of our meetings last week.'

'You had one of your headaches, didn't you, darlin'?' Annabel said, still massaging away.

'In any case,' I wondered, 'what do you suddenly need all this stamina for?'

'All right,' Stefano said, pleased by the precision of this enquiry. '*All right.*' He looked more hapless than I had ever previously seen him, worse than the time the police had arrived to collect Garth at the airport, worse than the time a promoter in South Carolina he had summoned with a shout of 'Hey there, cracker' had brandished an assault rifle in his face. 'Go make us a pot of coffee will you, Bella? Look, the thing is, Nicko . . .' The python-bicep was coiled around my shoulder now, as he led me off in a fatherly fashion to the telex-strewn desk. 'You know what it's like out there now, right? I was talking to a bloke at RCA the other day and he said if you go in there wearing a pair of flares A&R won't see you. The thing is . . . the thing is Don's thinking of cutting his losses. He is though,' Stefano said, ever reverential in the presence of power. 'The boys don't know it, but they've got one last chance to turn it around.'

'Is that what all this is about?' I glanced at the sea of papers.

'I'll get to that. How are you fixed at the moment?'

How was I fixed? 'Not a lot happening. That Gravediggers single flopped, and Velvet Goldmine aren't touring until the summer.'

'Well, from now on you're working for me again full-time. Don agrees. Velvet Goldmine can fuck off.' From the kitchen I could hear the sound of Annabel warbling to herself as she brewed the coffee. *Chanson d'amour . . . Da-da-da-da-dah . . . Play ongcore.* Perhaps Don ought to fix her up with a recording contract. 'They're only a bunch of poofs anyway.'

'What have you got planned?'

'What have I got planned?' Stefano looked more animated now, conspiratorial, calculating. 'Jesus, I wish that bitch would turn the sound down . . .' In the kitchen, Annabel had moved discordantly on to 'Knowing Me, Knowing You'. Rain broke suddenly onto the uncurtained window, spilling haphazardly over the glass. 'OK, we're talking about a three-stage operation here. First, I want them on the *Old Grey Whistle Test* – not second billing, the main act – debuting some new material. And before you start' – I already had my mouth open to question the likelihood of this ever happening – 'Gary's written a new song.'

'*Gary's* written a new song?'

'That's what I said. It's not "Agamemnon's Mighty Sword" but it's better than anything on the last album. *Way* better. So we do the *Whistle Test*. We'll send that bearded spazz who fronts it a stripper with a case of champagne so he'll say he likes it. Then we do a comeback tour of the States. The paperwork's all here. Thirty, forty concerts. *Stadium* gigs, too. Not pissing about in high-school gyms. Madison Square Garden. That place in Philly we played in '73. The Winterland . . .'

'The Winterland's closed.'

'The fuck it has? Well, maybe not the Winterland then. And afterwards, when they get back to Blighty' – Stefano always called the United Kingdom 'Blighty' – 'instead of letting them get off their heads again we put them straight into a studio with Roy Baker or someone on the knobs – Don says he doesn't care how much it costs – and they do an album. Really stripped down and, er . . .' – Stefano struggled gamely for a word that could convey just how earth-shattering this new project was intended to be – '*contemporary*. No keys or mellotrons or anything. Just guitar, bass, drums and vocals. And nothing longer than three minutes. Bang, bang, bang and no messing. What do you think?'

What did I think? It wasn't important what I thought. What was important was what Bob Harris, and the tour promoters, and the UK record company, and the US record company, thought. And more crucial even than this line of notabilities was what Don, that arbiter of souls and fashioner of destinies, thought.

'What's Gary's new song called?'

'"Getting Down with the Crazy Ladies".'

'It doesn't sound very contemporary.'

'Jesus! It's got a two-note guitar solo, and the lyrics are all about hookers on the Strip. I don't think you could get more contemporary than that.'

'What do the US promoters say?'

'Nicko, they are mad for it.' Stefano spread his hands into a wide, fleshy fan, in a way that suggested a flock of doves was about to take shimmering flight beneath them. 'Well, most of them are. Apart from a few fuckers on the East Coast.'

The coffee came (*Knowing me, knowing yoo, uh–hurgh ...*) and we drank it, while Annabel fussed needlessly around the desk, straightened pieces of paper that did not need straightening, had another superfluous chafe at Stefano's arm and regarded me in a friendly manner.

'You want a Tunnock's teacake or sumfink, Nicko? There's a packet in the cupboard.'

'I'm fine, thank you.'

'And 'ow's that gel I saw you with the other week? That Polly?'

'Holly. She's very well, thanks.'

I saw that I had underestimated Annabel, that in a peculiar, roundabout way she was good for Stefano, that she calmed him down, soothed his discontents, furnished the finely calibrated atmosphere of guileless admiration and hard-headed realism in which he tended to flourish. Far more so than some of the Amanda-Janes and Felicity-Boos who had preceded her, you could see her still living with him thirty years later, the two of them burrowing companionably into the suburban compost, searching for lost electricity bills in the drift of paper by the door, being found by anxious neighbours dying side by side in their ancient bed. Once she had gone, the good humour stirred up in Stefano by the paper straightening and the arm massage vanished on the instant.

'So, what do you think?'

To be fair, it sounded about the best that anyone could have come up with in the circumstances. A prestige TV appearance to whet the appetite of the music press. A comeback tour to further stimulate these expectations. A new album to confirm them.

'It sounds great . . . Is it *viable*?'

'Of course it's viable. Why wouldn't it be . . . Why wouldn't it be viable? And if the US tour goes OK we'll get . . . we'll get an invite to play one of the summer festivals over here. Knebworth or somewhere. I'm not saying there aren't *problems*,' Stefano somewhat agitatedly concluded.

'What sort of problems?'

'Mr Garth fucking *Dangerfield*,' Stefano intoned, clearly still scandalised by the piece of information he was about to convey, 'has only gone and said that he wants a fucking *solo* spot, where he can sing some fucking folk songs he's written with some bloke from Steeleye Span that no one in this organisation has so much as fucking *heard* of.'

'The others won't let him get away with that, surely?'

'I'm not worried about Garth,' Stefano said. 'Because, frankly, Nicko, Don won't stand for it, and Garth's been terrified of Don ever since that business about the guitar. Which between you and me really put the frighteners on him. No, what I'm worried about is Keith.'

'What's Keith done?' I wondered, as Keith, for all his shortcomings and the regrettable incident in the hot-air balloon three years back, was one of the Helium Kids' few failsafe elements, always the last man standing at the after-party, the least likely to give trouble about studio schedules, a stranger to jealousy, resentment and pique.

'Keith now . . .' Stefano said, as if this was a subject to which he had given long and serious thought, might easily compose some monograph upon once the time was right. The rain slapped against the windows and the cars sailed by in the street. 'You know, I started off thinking Keith was . . .' – he searched for a word that would somehow combine the contempt he felt for Keith as a human being and the respect he was due as a full director of the organisation which employed him – 'y'know, *backward*. All that trouble he used to have with menus in restaurants. I mean, couldn't the fucker read or what? Now I just think he's . . .' – he searched again for a word that would do full justice to Keith's idiosyncrasies – '. . . *retarded*. You heard about the religious jag? No? Well, he got in with this lot who dressed up in sheets and lit fires up on Box Hill and thought the end of the world was coming. Now, I've got nothing against religion. You probably don't know, but my great-uncle was a Free Church Elder. But Keith got *really* wrapped up in it. Gave them a lot of money, too. And now . . . Well, right now he's going about again dressed like one of them – what were they called? – the guys in the Kubrick film who went around monstering people.'

'Droogs.'

'That's right. Last time I saw him he was wearing a white boiler suit, a bowler hat and a pair of bovver boots. Putting away a hell of lot of the sherbet, too. So, yes, since you ask, I'm worried about him. But hey,' Stefano said, slipping a cassette tape out of his pocket and jamming it into the music centre, 'listen to this.'

'What is it?'

'It's Gary's new track they're going to do on the *Whistle Test*.'

I cocked an ear, aware that the pulse of the rain was drifting in and out of the music, like the phasing effects you used to hear on psyche-delic records back in the Summer of Love. It was exactly the kind of thing that second-division rock bands, nervous of the way the future was shaping, had begun to put out here in 1977: full of chugging guitars, drenched in reverb, with an over-excited male vocalist yelling about foxy ladies and the price being right.

'What do you think?' Stefano demanded, even before the conclud-ing sound effects (smashed glass, police sirens, gunshots) had vanished into the night.

'That's not Garth's voice, surely?'

'Course not. It's Gary's fucking guide vocal. Garth'll sing it on TV.'

'The drums are way out.'

'Look, it's just a demo, right? Gary put it together in some studio in Marble Arch. I don't think the others were even there. What do you think?'

What did I think? Again, what I thought was less important than what Stefano thought. Or what Stefano had managed to convince himself that he thought.

'It's . . .' I hesitated. 'It's a bit like Bad Company.'

'That's just what I told Gary,' said Stefano, delightedly. '*Exactly* like Bad Company.'

There was a long, continuous disturbance in the corridor, sugges-tive of chairs being thrown about, plaster casts being toppled from their plinths, chaotic games of ten-pin bowling, and Annabel put her head round the door.

'You want something to eat?'

'What have you got?' Stefano asked, bearing the cassette tape triumphantly in his lofted fist.

'There's some oxtail soup left.'

We ate the soup under flickering lamplight in a tiny back room, on whose Regency wallpaper hung colour magazine portraits of the Kids from six or seven years ago. At this moment in time, the dress styles they then affected looked very nearly ridiculous. On the other hand, Stefano had cheered up. He was back in his favourite role: the head conspirator; the chief of the rebel army marshalling his resources. Promoters, journalists, TV executives, A&R men, the band – even Don – would be forced to bow to his all-encompassing will.

'All of this has to be in the press release,' he instructed. '*All* of it. New material. Forty-date tour. UK gigs to follow. Triumphant return. Album pending. You can put in any quotes you like and I'll clear it with the boys. Or maybe – maybe – I won't even fucking show it to them.'

This was dangerous territory. 'Won't Don want to see it?'

'I've got a free hand here, Nicko. Just trust me.'

On the doorstep I remembered the message I had been bidden to convey.

'I saw Freddie at the Speakeasy. He said to give you his love.'

'Freddie, eh?' said Stefano fervently. He had forgotten the record company shindig three years before when he had affected to mistake Freddie for one of the cocktail waiters. 'Well, that was kind of him.'

How far we had fallen. And yet how much further had we still to fall.

In those days I was living in a mansion flat by the river in Fulham, a location quite as mundane in its way as Stefano's bolthole in Barnes. When I got back the light was on in the front room, there was loud, unfamiliar music coming from the record player and Holly sat cross-legged on the carpet staring at a row of spreadsheets.

'Someone called Irv Kantner rang,' she said, without looking up. 'Says he needs to talk to you.'

'Did he say where he was staying?'

'The Basil Street Hotel.' She was a tall, graceful, dark-haired girl who, unusually for the time, worked as an accountant for one of the independent record companies, and regarded most of the arrangements contracted by the Helium Kids as dangerously out of date.

'What's that you're listening to?'

'They're called the Buzzers. No, the Buzzcocks. The label's thinking of signing them, only the singer's just left. That reminds me, I heard something about your lot the other night.'

'The Kids?'

'That's right. It was from a chap' – Holly had been educated by the Girls' Public Day School Trust and said 'chap' rather than 'guy' – 'who works at EMI.'

'What did he say?'

Holly rearranged the spreadsheets so that they formed the shape of a cross rather than a square. Her fine sable hair fell into her eyes. 'He said they were seriously in a hole over unrecouped advances. Something like half a million for the last three albums.'

'They'll recover that on the back catalogue.'

'You'd have thought so. But apparently it's part of the problem. He said they pressed another hundred thousand of *Greatest Hits Volume I* when *Greatest Hits Volume II* came out, and ninety-five thousand of them are still sitting in the warehouse.'

'There'll be a new album in the autumn.'

'They won't pay the recording costs. You'll see.'

There was an odd abstraction in the way that Holly dealt out these snippets of record-company gossip. The thought that I might be materially affected by what happened to the Helium Kids or the ninety-five thousand copies of *Greatest Hits Volume I* gathering dust in the warehouse scarcely occurred to her. This didn't make me like her any the less.

The spreadsheets were all gathered up now and returned to a bulky briefcase. 'Are you coming to bed?'

'Oh dear me, no.' I said. 'I've got work to do.'

For the last dozen years I had been at work writing press releases. I had scrawled them on the backs of envelopes in chilly, pre-dawn hotel rooms, in limousines on the way to godforsaken airports in the flyover states, dictated them to Angie in the big office looking out over the Manhattan skyline, brooded over them in stolen moments between sleep and waking in the clapboard house in Westchester County while Rosalind lay snoring at my side. I had written them to mark concert tours and album releases and court cases. I had written one to publicise Dale's marriage to the celebrated sixties supermodel Tammy Slade, and another twelve months later to acknowledge the filing of divorce papers on grounds of unreasonable behaviour. I had commemorated the christening of Ian's first child, Tallulah Persephone Goldilocks Hamilton. I had announced, with maximum ostentation, the unveiling of the Garth Dangerfield Charitable Foundation for Sick Children, in association with Great Ormond Street Hospital, and then disclosed, with maximum regret, nine months later, the Foundation's temporary suspension on grounds of financial irregularity. All this had made me as adept at my chosen form as any sonneteer mulling his Petrarchan stanzas. I knew when to tell the truth, and when to lie. I knew when to file an extravagant claim, and when to be humbly matter of fact. Like the defending counsel in a murder trial, I knew when to play on the credulity of my audience and when to throw myself on their mercy. But it took me four hours to write the fucking press release announcing that the Helium Kids were booked for a forty-date tour of North America. Neither triumphalism nor defensiveness, I realised, would do. What was needed was a nod to changing circumstances and shifting landscapes, together with a pious determination to make good.

FOR IMMEDIATE RELEASE

All good things come to those who wait. And so Shard Enterprises, in association with Atlantic Entertainments Inc., is proud to announce that the Helium Kids will be undertaking their first American tour for two years, with the prospect of several UK dates to follow. Opening at the Union Theatre, Baltimore, Maryland on 30 June, and concluding at . . . [*Stefano could fill this in*] the tour is scheduled to last approximately two months, giving the band a welcome opportunity to debut material from their forthcoming album, the thus far tentatively titled *Ladies of the Night*. Lead vocalist and principal songsmith Garth Dangerfield commented: 'The boys can't wait to get back on stage doing what they do best. We've been sitting on our butts for too long. Sure, there's some new kinds of music come along while we've been away, but we're out to prove that we can kick ass with the best of them, and we intend to rock till we drop.'

NOTE TO EDITORS: Owing to pressure of rehearsal schedules, the Kids will be doing only a very limited number of interviews. You are advised to reserve your place in the queue now. Rock and roll!

*   *   *

Readers of a certain age keen to dust down their old copies of *Cabinet of Curiosities* will no doubt be mildly gratified to hear that the Helium Kids – remember them? – are planning a forty-date summer tour of

North America and, potentially, Europe, with the prospect of a new LP to follow.

Melody Maker

Helium Kids to tour? Yawn. I mean, are these losers still alive?

New Musical Express

So, what is a concerned pop person to think about the Helium Kids in these tumultuous times? Well, I dug my copy of *Smiley Daze* out of the cupboard where such things repose at Peel Acres the other day – signed it was, too – and I can tell you that to my decrepit old ears it didn't sound half bad. Now, here's the new one by the Vibrators . . .

John Peel Show, Radio One, 17 April 1977

Yes, I know they're old dinosaurs. I know they hang out with Princess Margaret on Caribbean islands, have thousands of dollars-worth of prime Bolivian boo hanging out of their nostrils and probably crap into gold-plated toilets, but as one whose first sexual experience took place to the strains of 'Agamemnon's Mighty Sword' playing on his brother's Dansette, I can proudly say that I shall be at the front of the queue for tickets. If there is a queue.

Sounds

After a long period of inactivity, popular musical group the Helium Kids have announced that they intend to undertake a series of engagements in North America.

Daily Telegraph

'You did your best, Nick,' Stefano said. 'You did your best and I'm not complaining. Don says the same. Fucking great idea to limit the number of interviews. Who have we got?'

'I'm working on it,' I told him.

Among other tokens of his regard, Irving Kantner insisted on squiring me to lunch at a highly fashionable Vietnamese restaurant in Soho. He was less nervous and better dressed than I remembered him, and had clearly spent part of the past six years learning how to give waiters the hell of a time. One mark of this newfound confidence was his attitude to the presence of Mick Jagger, found quietly eating a bowl of noodles in the corner of the room, whom he greeted with the faintest of nods. His trip to Europe, he explained, was being financed by *Rolling Stone*, on whose behalf he had just interviewed David Bowie, and was shortly to bring off the all-but unprecedented coup of cross-questioning all four members of Led Zeppelin.

'I liked your book,' I said, as we began on the chilli-crayfish tails. This was, in fact, a lie. I hadn't liked Kantner's book. And neither, so far as I knew, had anyone else.

'Thanks,' he said, head lowered modestly over his seething plate. 'I thought it was, well . . . *sincere*.'

'What I really liked about it,' I continued, 'speaking objectively, of course, was that although you saw them as essentially grotesques, you were prepared to allow them human characteristics as well.'

'I guess I hadn't really thought about it like that. But now you mention it, I have to say I see what you mean.'

'Don't mind my asking, but how was it that Stefano didn't sue?'

'Signed statements,' Kantner said, slapping the pocket of his jeans as if he had several years' worth of incriminating paperwork stashed inside. 'Everything I said he did was corroborated by two witnesses. There was some noise about a writ to begin with, but we just sent him copies of three or four of the testimonies and that was the last we heard of it. Look,' he went on, calmly lowering his voice, although Jagger was in the middle of an argument with the maître d' about some vagrant bowl of soup, 'it's actually the Helium Kids I want to ask you about.'

'Ask away. They're going out on tour in the summer. You can come if you want. I daresay I could swing expenses.'

'You're very kind,' Kantner returned, with well-nigh Olympian grandeur. 'But I'm too old' – he was three years my junior – 'to go out on the road with a bunch of rock stars. I'll catch them when they come to New York. No, what I want to do' – the chipmunk face brimmed with enthusiasm – 'is write an anniversary piece.'

'The anniversary of what in particular?'

'Florian Shankley-Walker. It's ten years this August. Time for a retrospective, wouldn't you say?'

'I don't know that there's anything else can be said. I mean,' I improvised, 'you're probably too young' – this was a dig at the Olympian grandeur – 'to have seen them in the sixties. Take it from me, they weren't much good. And then he goes and drowns.'

'In highly suspicious circumstances. I take it you read the book that guy wrote? Surely the implication is that Dangerfield was there when it happened?'

'You know I can't comment on this. Have you talked to anyone?'

'I've tried. No one's interested. Dale won't talk. Ian won't talk. Keith won't talk. Curiously, Garth *will* talk, but only if I don't mention Florian. I've even tried' – for all his shiny leather jacket and his skinny black tie, Kantner was still a Princeton man at heart – 'Mr Shard.'

'Did you now?' I said, marvelling at this act of foolhardiness. 'And what did he have to say?'

'He said that if so much as a line about Florian Shankley-Walker appeared in the English press he'd call a friend of his at the embassy and get my visa cancelled on the spot,' Kantner explained, with that impeccable Yankee seriousness I could never get my head around. 'I couldn't tell if he was joking or not.'

'Oh, you know Don,' I said. 'But take it from me, there isn't a story.'

'Well, maybe you're right.' Outside the window the edgy Soho faces went by. Jagger and stopped complaining about the bowl of soup and consented to sign an autograph. 'Maybe I'd better stick to Led Zep. After all' – he gave a tiny, insinuating smile – 'they're where it's at right now.'

It could only have been as an act of revenge that, two months after this, on the very eve of the tour, and in the *New Musical Express*, which then had a circulation of a quarter of a million, Kantner printed his celebrated interview with Garth – a piece of journalism so legendary that it was instantly picked up by the broadsheet newspapers and syndicated across America, and even now is still periodically reproduced in anthologies of rock journalism. It is, lest you have forgotten, the interview in which Garth receives his guest from a throne carved out of imitation wooden skulls, invites him to inspect an autographed copy of *Mein Kampf*, confesses, with a modest gesture at his near-skeletal frame, that he is off solids, and talks about eugenics, immigration, racial purity, world peace, the 'faggot' Rolling Stones and his support for the South African government. Inevitably, there were repercussions. The student body of the University of Edinburgh, which, three years before, had elected him to their rectorship, hastily rescinded the appointment. Meanwhile, the protestors who marched on the Manchester branch of the Virgin Megastore to demand that Helium Kids records should be removed from the shelves laid down their banners when they discovered that none was actually in stock.

FIVE MINUTES
WITH GARTH DANGERFIELD

Q: Where are you right now?

A (*suspicious*): In my room.

Q: What are you doing there?

A: Reading.

Q: What exactly are you reading?

A (*more animated*): It's a book called *White Stains* by Aleister Crowley. Have you read it? It's very rare.

Q: Would you like to tell us what you're wearing?

A: No. You can use your imagination.

Q: What have you been doing today? (*It is about 3.30 p.m.*)

A: I don't know. Well, I suppose I do. First, I fed the animals. Then I took a walk around the estate. Then the guy came who sells me antiquarian books and we looked at some stuff.

Q: What can you see when you look out of the window?

A: On a good day, Wales. Right now, fog.

Q: How are the rest of the band?

A: I think they're doing what they do.

Q: What is that, exactly?

A: I don't know. We're not soulmates. We're just in a group together.

Q: When we last spoke to Dale [*Halliwell, Helium Kids guitarist*] he said you spent all your time sitting in a darkened chamber reading books about Satanism and never went out.

A: We all find different ways of attaining our destinies in the cosmos. I'm sure Dale would agree with that if you asked him.

Q: Are you writing at the moment?

A: There's a new track called 'Chronos and Abaddon' that we might be demo-ing. Beyond that I can't say.

Q: Have you seen any of the new bands?

A: What new bands are those?

Q: Come on, Garth. The Pistols. The Clash. Buzzcocks. The Jam. The music press has been full of them.

A: I don't read the music press.

Q: Thank you for your time.

A: Thank you for yours.

Sounds, 23 March 1977

17. 1977 (II)

Getting down with the crazy ladies
Turning heads on Sunset Strip . . .

'Getting Down with
the Crazy Ladies'

And so, with what feelings of pride, camaraderie, confidence and exhilaration did the Helium Kids and their entourage set out on their North American tour of 1977.

No, let's start that one again.

And so, with what feelings of dissatisfaction, lassitude, reluctance and shame did the Helium Kids and their entourage set out on their North American tour of 1977.

In actual fact the auguries were not, as they say, unpromising. The *Whistle Test* appearance, for example, was adjudged a modest success. The drums were, once again, way out, a cymbal went crashing over during the final chorus and Garth's choice of costume (Roger Daltrey-style cape, steeple hat, skin-tight Spandex trousers) was perhaps unfortunate, but at its close the bearded presenter, who had watched tolerantly from stage left, one hand clasping his bristly chin, was seen to turn to the camera and murmur words which, if you turned up the volume to ear-endangering levels, or could lipread, were assumed to be 'Great to have them back.' As if to swell this vote of confidence, there was a flutter in the tabloid press when the wall of the Cambridge college bed-sitting room occupied by a minor member of the Royal Family was found to display the multicoloured Roger Dean poster that, three years before, had advertised the release of *Glorfindel*. On the other hand, a hastily arranged but 'exclusive' warm-up gig at the Marquee in Wardour Street was attended by twenty-three people and a clerk from Westminster Council who had come to enquire about the venue's licensing arrangements.

Meanwhile, like a medieval siege machine grinding into gear, the logistical preparations rolled inexorably on. Several tons of equipment were flown out to the eastern seaboard. A fleet of charter planes (the Oblivion Express had been sold to Bachman–Turner Overdrive two years before) stood by, and Stefano and I took up residence in a tatty office on Tenth Street, the better to direct a publicity campaign that would, as Stefano, who had recovered some of his enthusiasm, put it, 'make these motherfuckers sit up and take notice'. There was plenty of money about – God knew where it had come from – fistfuls of fifties to pay off cabbies or be palmed discreetly into the hands of pluggers or DJs or to underwrite costly meals for a dozen scene-swellers and opinion-formers in the showbiz restaurants Stefano and I had discovered in the early seventies but were now, like the people who frequented them, beginning to show their age – and there were times, cruising along Fifth Avenue, say, as the sunset mellowed into dusk, watching the flocks of pink-faced joggers in football shirts and leg-warmers (this was a new thing – no one had ever gone running in New York before) heading back from Central Park, when it was possible to believe that everything was still as it had once been, that Nixon still reigned in the White House, that Grand Funk Railroad would be headlining tomorrow night at the Fillmore East, and that all the people you read about in the New York music papers – the Ramones, Patti Smith, Television – were somebody's private joke rather than disquieting evidence of the way the world had begun to turn.

The original plan had been for a two-month coast-to-coast tour taking in forty dates and half-a-dozen stadium shows, but within a week of Stefano and I establishing ourselves on Tenth Street this had been cut back to six weeks and thirty dates, and by the time the hootenanny had actually kicked off, in Baltimore at the end of June, it was down to five weeks and twenty-four. The curious thing was how irresistible this process became. You could not control it: it simply happened. A promoter who had offered a 10,000-seater amphitheatre would call up a fortnight before and downgrade you to a 3,000-seater college baseball park, or a club on the other side of town, or nothing at all, and the tour manager, a wisecracking butterball from out of Philadelphia named Larry Minhinnick whom Stefano and I had both decided we actively loathed, would shake his head, settle his neck more comfortably into his crimson starburst jacket, and say that at times like this you had to go with the flow.

Meanwhile, as no tour ever takes place in a vacuum, there was other stuff going on. 'Getting Down with the Crazy Ladies', hastily issued as a single, criminally over-produced by some lackwit associate of Don's and backed by a twanging Pasarolo instrumental on which the other four-fifths of the band had unhesitatingly refused to play, entered the *Billboard* chart at 193, rose to 157 and then sank into obscurity. Simultaneously – the itinerary had staggered on to Montgomery, Alabama, by now – there came dreadful rumours from the London office that EMI were about to pass on the contract-renewal option that was due later in the year.

And what did the band do? Well the band, ladies and gentlemen, played on: game, yet faintly bewildered, not liking the incontestable fact that when the house lights went up the bulk of the audience was clustered towards the front of the hall, leaving banks of sparsely populated shadow behind them, and necessarily compromised in their attack by Keith, who by the time the tour reached El Paso was having to be carried to his drum stool by a couple of roadies and carried back again at the show's end. Things improved in the Midwest, where popular taste lagged a comfortable half-decade behind the rest of America – there were still girls with bangs and boys with crew-cuts in Minnesota – but, all the same, something had gone. Not competence, or even enthusiasm, but the *dynamic*. I knew it from the moment I went into the audience at the start of the Baltimore show and heard them launch into 'Seventh Son of a Seventh Son'. All the essential elements were there – Garth's eldritch holler ('a voice like a cut-throat razor', *Melody Maker* had once remarked), the interlocked guitar lines, the lolloping hum of Ian's bass, the route-march drum patterns (albeit a half-beat off the pace) but they no longer wove together, so that you heard five individual noises rather than one collective sound.

But still, like the band, I went on doing my job. I called regional newspapers and organised free passes for Lurleen and Marty and Sally on the desk. I frowned over the day's media schedules, such as they were. I sat in on radio interviews where Garth and Dale, confronted with evidence of falling ticket sales and playlist exclusions, prattled steadfastly about reaching out to the core fanbase. I kept in touch with London, where the big excitement was the Royal Jubilee and the Sex Pistols' 'God Save the Queen', and 'Getting Down with the Crazy Ladies', released only after a personal visit paid by Don to the head of the EMI A&R department, and without my practised hand to guide it, had failed even to make the Radio 1 daytime roster and been confined to a few late-night spins on the specialist shows. I tried to call in favours from the old thrusters and chancers from the Westchester days who turned out to have reinvented themselves as creative realtors or Columbia journalism professors or scriptwriters for *Saturday Night Live*, and when not otherwise engaged I listened to the radio. The big AM hit that summer was *Rumours* – wistful little songs about your woman going off with your best friend, and not stopping thinking about tomorrow, and the rain washing you clean, and as far away from the Helium Kids as the surface of the moon.

Some memories of that tour: a few – a very few – delirious teenage girls in halter-tops and platforms parading through the arrivals lounge at Madison, Wisconsin, with a banner that said WE LOVE YOU HELIUM KIDS; the Hamiltons, husband and wife, materialising as if from nowhere in the hotel breakfast bar at 8.15 each morning to eat precisely the same meal of porridge, crust-free brown toast and English marmalade (when available, fuss made if not) and embark on precisely the same conversation about the weather and the news from home; a roadie approaching Keith's drum stool each night after the show was over to lay a plastic sheet under the kit and shake the cocaine residues off the cymbals; an outdoor concert in one of the prairie states with biker gangs hurling beer bottles at each other; the snow-capped tops of the Rocky Mountains white and gleaming beneath us, with condors idling in the thermals far below; an endless stream of American musicians, producers and record company executives stopping anxiously to enquire what we thought of this, uh, *new wave* music; Stefano haggling with the local promoters; June Hamilton telling me about her five-year-old, 'a very forward child', well advanced with his reading; noise, clamour, white powder, uproar in hotel corridors late at night; blue skies, the satisfying thud of the aircraft's wheel striking tarmac, all those indigo-tinted West Coast sunsets; all that disquiet, disillusionment and decline.

We became very close, Stefano and I, in those last days. How could it have been otherwise? There used to come a moment, in the closing stages of a tour – especially an unsuccessful tour – when the routines would begin to wind down, when tasks that once required the most exacting supervision mysteriously started to perform themselves. And so Stefano and I ended up spending time together. We hung out in deserted breakfast bars, dowsing cigarettes in abandoned cups of coffee, after the other early risers had drifted away. We sat by empty swimming pools as weary janitors skimmed their surfaces for fallen leaves. We sat up late over brandies and Benedictines while Stefano totted up per diems and wondered why Keith could possibly want another $500 to add to the $500 he'd been given the previous evening. And in this way, as the long mornings dragged into lunchtime, as the late nights crawled towards dawn, in the back seats of limousines, in subterranean corridors of the auditoria of the American Midwest, we became confidential.

'How did you get into this?' I asked one afternoon, as we were standing on the terrace of a hotel in Boise, Idaho, beyond whose picket-wire periphery the potato fields stretched out endlessly into the distance. 'I mean, how did you get into this business?'

Stefano, who had drunk a bottle and a half of red wine at lunch, while simultaneously digesting a telegram from London whose contents he hadn't yet deigned to impart, peered down at the potatoes and then up into the glossy Idaho sky.

'I was an old jazzer,' he said. 'No, *not* be-bop. Not Coltrane and all that racket. Fucking horrible noise. *Trad.* You remember trad? Blokes with mutton-chop whiskers in bowler hats and striped shirts playing "Bad Penny Blues". I loved all that stuff. Used to go along to Acker Bilk's club nights. And then when the bottom fell out of trad, I ran a blues joint in Dean Street. Eric Clapton played there once. After that, I fucked around a bit. I was married to that old scrubber Martina then. You remember her? Used to ring up the office about her alimony sounding like Princess Margaret. You've no idea how easy it was to make money in '64, '65, Nicko, when the Mod thing started. You could get your grandmother signed up to Immediate if you bobbed the old girl's hair and put her in a mini-skirt. I'd known Don from Dean Street, when he ... when I ... Well, anyway, one day Don rings up and says he's got some trouble with these cats who're basically fucking him over, and would I come and be his ...' – the operative word here was possibly 'bodyguard' or perhaps 'enforcer', but Stefano, no doubt mollified by the bountiful Idaho sun, settled for '. . . personal assistant. What about you?'

And so I explained about Phoenix, the trip to New York, Artie Semprini and the first American tour.

'Uh huh. So what makes an educated man like you' – there was no way of knowing whether this was meant ironically – 'spend the best years of his life telling lies for a bunch of retards who ought to be fitting tyres on the Great North Road? No offence or anything.'

'I've got my plans,' I told him, puckishly. 'I'm sure you've got yours.'

'Oh, I've got *plans*,' said Stefano bitterly. 'We've all of us got plans. Annabel's got them. Don's got them. Record companies have got them.' Which I gathered was his way of informing me that EMI had dropped the Kids from the label.

Being thrown together with Stefano in this way, I could not but become privy to certain of his secrets. Some of them, naturally, were to do with Don, and the terrible, scorched-earth trail the pair of them had blazed through Tin Pan Alley in the sixties ('So then Don picked the guy up, hung him over the balcony and . . . Told his wife that if she wanted to see her husband again she could . . . Set fire to . . . Picked up the sledgehammer and . . .'), but one or two of them were to do with the subterfuges of the here and now.

'What do you think I've got in this briefcase?' Stefano shyly enquired, one afternoon in Fresno, holding up the battered Gladstone bag that, for as long as I'd known him, accompanied him about the place.

'I don't know. A severed head? Half a dozen of Keith's Airfix kits?'

'No need to be sarcastic, man.'

Hoisting the Gladstone bag onto the bar table, and giving a shifty glance around the premises to assure himself that we were in no one's line of view, Stefano jerked open the clasps. Inside, bound up in plastic bands, were thirty or forty bundles of $100 notes.

'What's that? The per diems?'

'Fuck no. Mark' – Mark was the tour accountant – 'pays them out. No, this is a third of the take.'

'How much?'

'Two hundred thousand dollars last time I looked.'

'I thought the promoters – what's that clause in the contracts say? – "remitted all monies by check".'

'You're not wrong,' Stefano conceded, with something very close to graciousness. 'Quite a lot of it they do. But the rest they hand over to me in cash.'

'With what end in mind, exactly?'

'Like you were saying the other afternoon, Nicko, we've all got our plans.'

And then, finally, in the first week of August, with the temperature soaring into the nineties and the sun a molten disc in the pale sky, the tour crawled into Boulder, Colorado (5000-seater stadium, two-thirds of the tickets gone, torchlight protest threatened by a Baptist church alerted to Garth's occult fixation, everyone rather cheered by the whiff of controversy), for a two-night stay at the Century Canyon Hotel. And this, in its way, was another mark of how far we had fallen, for back on the tours of the early seventies, those gonzo cavalcades that were already the stuff of music journalists' legend, the Helium Kids had taken a pride in staying in hipster joints or mob caravanserais where management rather welcomed the publicity afforded by smashed-up suites and high-end electrical goods lobbed cavalierly out of windows. But this was 1977, an era of constraint and inhibition, and so we put up at regular places that otherwise played host to political conventions, salesmen's hoedowns, clubwomen's embroidery classes and ordinary Joes, and where the letting off of a fire extinguisher was a very serious business. The gypsy caravans of ancient days had moved on, and the rank grass where once their horses had grazed yielded up to the manicured lawns of a sober corporatism.

Up on the sixth floor of the Century Canyon, the air-conditioning had been turned full on: beyond the windows the giant palm trees in the hotel forecourt shimmered in the heat. Here in the early morning – it was about 9 a.m. – the janitors' carts were out. The day's schedule in hand – a radically attenuated document that read simply *10.30 Keith interview; 13.30 lunch; 17.00 soundcheck; 20.00 drive to gig. NB No bar tariff to exceed $35, this is an order* – I dodged between them, the soles of my deck shoes catching on the threadbare carpet, came eventually to the central area where stairs descended and elevator doors gaped, and ran smack into my first shock of the day. With brisk yet jittery movements, a venerable white-haired character, sprucely got up in a dark blue suit with bulging shirt-cuffs, was clambering out of the lift. He had one of those irritable but curiously inert faces, so characteristic of the southern American states, liked an embalmed jackrabbit lying glassy-eyed on the butcher's block, or a dental patient shot full of novocaine, and it wasn't until he turned sharp right, neatly furled copy of the *Washington Post* held out before him like a relay baton, that I realised who it was. But there was no mistaking him. Only the other day, I'd seen him on NBC chastising the incompetence, the vacillation and the all-round depravity of President Carter. Barry Goldwater.

I suppose I must have stared a moment too long, for Barry, button-down features still registering no emotion whatever, fixed a stony old eye on me and demanded: 'Did we ever meet someplace, son?'

Nothing loath, I explained about Phoenix, and the 1964 election, and the charming Republican family with whom I'd spent so much of my time, and the old monster – throwing out his wizened chest as if to demonstrate just how sappy and vigorous he was – listened with what might have been mild interest.

'Al Duchesne,' he said, when I had finished this recitation. 'Still doing fine work for the GOP. You'll be hearing from him when Ron Reagan gets in.'

I said I was pleased to hear it, and Goldwater shuffled his tasselled black Oxfords on the worn carpet, as if he were about to embark on a soft-shoe routine up and down the empty corridor, gave a reluctant but foxy smile – it was the first time I had seen any part of his face move – and murmured: 'Nice talking to you, son. You take care of yourself, d'ya hear?'

I promised I would do that, and stepped into the lift, where the powerful stench of Barry's cologne still lingered and a black member of the hotel janitoriat, clutching a mop, who clearly had strong views about the Republican Party and its tribunes regarded me with a look of serious displeasure.

'*Jesus,*' I said, putting an arm out against the mirror to steady myself, and noting – such was the effect of all these past associations brought unexpectedly to the surface – that the blood had drained out of my face. '*Jesus H. Christ.*'

'Now don't you blaspheme,' the janitor said, and as the cage descended its half-dozen flights we stood and stared at each other: black against white; denim overalls against seersucker suit; mop and pail against giant black clipboard; real life against its faggot fantasy projection. The ride lasted a minute and a half, but it felt like several hours.

Down in the breakfast bar the air-con was running full-tilt and a tableful of ancient gentlemen in sharp suits, of whom Barry had undoubtedly been the principal ornament, was loudly discussing budgetary constraints and mid-term prospects. Some Midwestern Republican caucus, I diagnosed, convening for its summer clambake. Despite the earliness of the hour, the corner where the tour party hung out was unusually full: its occupants included Garth and the latest protemporaneous Mrs Dangerfield, who needed only a shepherdess's crook to complete her resemblance to Little Bo Peep; the Hamiltons, already stoked on prime Earl Grey; Stefano's assistant; Angie's replacement Carrie-Ann, who stood no nonsense and had once, when a little light horseplay was proposed in some after-party rumpus-room, broken one of Dale's fingers. In fact, there was only one obvious absentee.

'Anyone seen Keith?'

'I don't think so,' Carrie-Ann said, with the seriousness she brought to every aspect of the day's activities, and beginning one of her pencil-waving headcounts. 'What do you want him for?'

'Interview with KL-67. I said we'd be there at 10.30 and it's a twenty-minute drive.'

'The cab's due at 10.10,' Carrie-Ann confirmed. 'He knows about it. I'm sure he'll be down.'

Keith, it had to be said, for a drummer, and given the bottom-scraping consistency of his early career, had now matured into rather a favourite among the radio interviewers. He was not Ringo, and he was not Keith Moon, but the speechlessness that he alter-nated with half-baked repartee was sometimes taken for dumb charm.

'I've just been talking to Barry Goldwater,' I announced to the room at large.

'Oh yes, and how was he?' Ian asked, who of all those present was perhaps the only one liable to know who Goldwater was. 'Here, have a cup of tea. Hot, ain't it?'

And so I had a cup of tea with Ian, who that morning was wearing a Gieves & Hawkes double-breasted pinstripe, and June, dressed in a white trouser-suit and floppy hat, smoked a cigarette and stared out of the window at the hotel forecourt, where burly men in singlets were throwing bales of laundry around and the sun reflected back off the fountain in a wall of searing white light. It was now about twenty to ten.

'Did Keith get the schedule?' I asked Carrie-Ann, who was adding up bar receipts with a pocket calculator while trying to adjust the plastic clip that corralled the furze-bush of her yellow hair.

'Went under the door last thing. You want me go get him?' Carrie-Ann's liking for economy extended even to infinitives.

'No. Let's give it another five. Anyone seen Stefano?'

'Manager's office, I think. Jesus. There are sixteen old-fashioneds on this tab. Who on earth can have drunk them all?'

'What have you good people got planned for this morning?' I asked Ian and June companionably.

'Round of golf,' Ian said. 'That is, if it's not too hot.'

'Getting my nails done at the salon.'

'Nothing like a spot of the high life.'

A few more minutes passed. The Republican caucus had got onto its chances in Colorado Congressional Districts 4, 5 and 7. Carrie-Ann finished her sums and snapped the calculator back into its plastic case.

'It's 9.50,' she said. 'Maybe I ought to go see where he's got.'

'You do that.'

There was a wide stretch of carpeting at the breakfast bar's further end that led to the elevators. As Carrie-Ann glided purposefully over this terrain she passed Stefano. He, too, was going at an extraordinary rate of knots. Whatever she said to him as she went by was ignored. As he sped up to our table, I saw that he was horribly distressed, but also – this was clear from the way he came to rest at the level of my shoulder – unwilling to share this disquiet with anyone else. When he could bring himself to speak – and this took several attempts – it was in a peculiar high-pitched voice.

'Come with me.'

'What's the matter?'

'A fucking disaster, that's all.' By this stage, with Stefano's pudgy hand to guide me, I was a yard or two away from the table.

'What sort of a disaster?'

'I just went to the manager's office and had him open up the safe. The bag's gone.'

Half of me was still rehearsing the questions that the KL-67 jock would probably put to Keith in thirty minutes' time.

'Which bag?'

'The bag with the money in it. I leave it in the hotel safe every night. Now the fucking thing is gone.'

'What's the manager say?'

'Doesn't have a clue. No one has a clue. Not the night staff. Not anybody.'

'Have the police been called?'

'The *police!* What makes you think I want to call the police?'

And instantly I saw Stefano's dilemma. It was not just that the money was gone. It was that its very existence was something he couldn't admit to. Whatever its intended destination, whether by way of a complicated series of laundering arrangements to Don, or, as seemed far more likely, into Stefano's own pocket, its presence in the bag was an admission of somebody's guilt.

'What are you going to do?'

Some of the colour was coming back into Stefano's face. 'Has to be an inside job. Nothing else is missing. The first thing to do is to get the boys together and go through everybody's rooms.'

'How are you going to do that? And what happens when they find out you've been wandering around Colorado with a third of the tour takings in a briefcase?'

'I don't know. I'll think of something. I'll fucking . . .'

As if summoning all the hotel staff positioned roundabout – managers, janitors, coffee waitresses, laundrymen – who could be enlisted in this pursuit, Stefano flung his arm out dramatically. Carrie-Ann, returning at speed from the foyer, managed to duck beneath it and came breathlessly to a halt. She, too, was seriously upset.

'You'd better come upstairs.'

'What's the matter?'

'It's Keith.'

'Oh, *Keith*,' said Stefano, instantly returned to weary matter-of-factness. 'Don't tell me. The fucker's dead or something.'

'He's breathing, I think. But I can't wake him up.'

'Christ. *Christ*. What state's the room in?'

'It's a mess. I mean . . .' – ever the model of prudence, Carrie-Ann lowered her voice – 'there's coke everywhere and he . . .'

'OK, OK,' Stefano said, straightaway sizing up the situation and determined to stamp his authority on it. 'Calm down, darling, and then we'll . . .'

'Don't you call me darling.' Carrie-Ann's voice rose to a shriek. 'You fucking fat *cunt*. Keith's up there with his eyes staring out of his head. He's . . . *soiled* himself too, if you're interested. And you're telling me to calm down.'

'OK. OK,' Stefano said again, ignoring her. 'Nick. Go up there and check it out. Whatever's lying around, chuck it down the khazi. Have them call the paramedics. Even money, he'll wake up in a minute or two . . . Fuck. Hang on, though. You stay here. I'll do it myself.'

It was now about 10.15. By degrees the band and their hangers on drifted through into the foyer, where they stood about talking. The Republican grandees passed by into their conference, scowling at us as they went. The manager came out of his office and tried to shake their hands. Shortly after this, sirens began to sound. There came a noise of wheels grinding up gravel on the forecourt.

And that was how it ended, there in the hotel foyer, in the sparkling Colorado sun, with the stretcher-bearers hoisting Keith's outsize and apparently paralysed form up in the ambulance, and June sniffing into a handkerchief, and the busboys gawping, and Stefano complaining to me that here was so much fast white powder to hand that he'd ended up sluicing most of it down the sink. There in that hotel foyer, the Helium Kids, they of the five certified platinum *Billboard* albums, they of the half-dozen No. 1 singles and the twenty-seven separate *Top of the Pops* appearances, those stalwart custodians of the *zeitgeist*, this raggle-taggle band of rock-and-roll gypsies, reached the end of the road. The party was over: it was time to go home.

Or so we thought.

And afterwards. What happened then?

Toxicology tests put the amount of cocaine in a 100-millilitre sample of Keith's urine at an almost unprecedented 55.7 milligrams. Experts concluded that his brain had effectively been sending messages to the rest of his body instructing it to shut down. He spent two weeks in a coma, later returned to the UK for six months' recuperation on a neurological ward and was, as they say, never the same again.

The media storm that blew up over Keith's demise had the welcome effect of distracting attention from the robbed safe. When finally acknowledged, the money's disappearance was presented as a straightforward theft, which it may well have been. The *New Musical Express*, which hinted that the whole affair was a tax scam, engineered by Stefano with Don's connivance, was threatened with legal action, after which the allegations were withdrawn. After several weeks' fruitless enquiry, a police investigation was abandoned.

The Helium Kids never played another concert. Neither did they record another album, although *Sky High: The Very Best of the Helium Kids*, the first of several buck-chasing compilations, reached No. 13 in the UK and No. 7 on the *Billboard* chart on its release in the autumn of 1979. Subsequently, an entity known as 'Helium Allstars', consisting of Dale, Ian and various sidemen, made modestly successful forays around the US in the early 1980s. An attempt to reunite the band for the Live Aid concerts of 1985 perished in a legal quagmire. It was suggested that, at this stage, no fewer than nine pieces of litigation in which members of the group featured either as plaintiff or defendant were currently awaiting judgment. The most notorious of these was *Pasarolo vs Enticing Visions Inc.*, the action brought by Gary against

Garth and Dale alleging the deliberate withholding of songwriting credits and consequent royalties. This was eventually settled out of court at a cost of £270,000 to the defendants.

Even before the disastrous final tour, Don Shard had been attempting to disassociate himself from the band. In the event, Shard Enterprises severed its ties with the Helium Kids, and coincidentally with Stefano, a mere twenty-four hours after their return to the UK. The news was conveyed by sealed letter delivered to each individual's private address. An attempt by Stefano to sue his former employer on grounds of wrongful dismissal was abandoned after a brief visit to the former's house by the latter's legal representative. Don continued to prosper in the music business and beyond it, and by the early 1980s was believed to have built up a commercial empire whose net worth was estimated at several million pounds. Retiring to his country estate in Sussex, he was frequently visited by music journalists in search of lurid recollections of what was already coming to be known as 'rock's golden age'. A martyr to his liver, and other afflictions, Don died in 2003.

Of the four functioning members of the Helium Kids, Garth and Dale seemed the most likely to profit from a career beyond it. In the half-decade following the band's demise Garth recorded two solo albums – *Crystal Mirror* (1979) and *Extra-terrestrial* (1982) – the latter reflecting his newfound interest in space travel. Neither was an unqualified success, although *Mirror* reached No. 23 in the UK and No. 17 on the *Billboard* chart. Much more of a commercial proposition was *Dangerfield–Halliwell*, an album cut with some top-level sessioneers, which made the top ten on both sides of the Atlantic in the summer of 1986. However, soon after this the pair fell out. The tapes of their final recording sessions were never commercially released. By the 1990s each could be found in the line-ups of various 'supergroups' containing the former members of such ensembles as the Electric Light Orchestra, Uriah Heep, Yes, Deep Purple and Emerson, Lake & Palmer.

Ian returned to his original love – the blues – and, with a number of amateur musicians remembered from his early days in Shepperton, recorded the album *Shadow of the Westway* (1981). He subsequently founded the Ian Hamilton Blues Orchestra, touring and recording successfully for nearly twenty years.

After recording a solo album, *Metal Present* (1980), and emerging victorious from his court case with Garth and Dale, Gary disappeared without trace. He was variously reported as having become a born-again Christian, working as a music technician at an arts college in Lincolnshire and, in the late 1990s, serving three years in HMP Maidstone for possession with intent to supply.

Whether or not Stefano had received any pay-off from Shard Enterprises was unclear, but he cut a surprisingly prosperous figure in the music scene of the late 1970s and early 1980s. As such, he was well placed to exploit the burgeoning 'Acid House' movement of the later eighties, owning several clubs and music venues in the Manchester area and putting up the money for the E-Type record label. 'These new drugs,' he told me in a telephone conversation around this time, 'are fucking *extraordinary*.'

Irving Kantner became a highly respected music critic and cultural historian, contributing to – among a raft of publications – *Rolling Stone*, *Melody Maker*, *Q*, *Mojo* and *Uncut*. Of his many books, the best-known are *Icons of American Song: Sinatra to Springsteen* (1981), *Cobain and I* (1996) and *Thirty Years of Punk Rock: A Study in Musical Phenomenology* (2000). I find his work preening, self-satisfied and concerned to promote his own mythologising at the expense of objective truth, but people seem to like it. He has sent me many a Christmas card.

Ainslie Duncan and I kept up in a small way. He continued to manage groups until well into the 1970s, and claimed credit for discovering the Clash, only to have the prize snatched from his grasp by Bernie Rhodes. By the early eighties he had drifted into concert promotion. When last heard of, he was working as a Butlin's Redcoat.

I last set eyes on Al Duchesne on TV in January 1981, in the fourth row of the dignitaries attending Ronald Reagan's inauguration on Capitol Hill. He would then have been in his early seventies. Two weeks later, under the headline 'SISTERS ARE DOING IT FOR THEM-SELVES' SAYS WIFE OF PRESIDENT'S MAN, a gossip magazine interviewed Lucille and Selma at the Massachusetts barn conversion in which they had established themselves. Al died in 1985.

Rosalind married for a third time to a Republican congressman from Indiana named Cyrus Bullitt, had two children and took an active part in Tipper Gore's campaign to affix 'Parental Advisory' stickers to records thought to harbour inflammatory content. All this she confessed to me during the course of an amicable lunch in the restaurant of the London hotel at which she was staying sometime in the early nineties while accompanying Representative Bullitt on a Congressional trade delegation to the Square Mile. She was plumper, staider, more conservative and a great deal happier than when I had known her. We agreed, over our second bottle of wine, that we had loved each other but couldn't get on.

After seeing my picture in a magazine, Lindy, the hippy girl from Echo Beach, wrote to me out of the blue in the late 1980s. She was by then lecturing in Experimental Psychology at a university in the Midwest. She confirmed that the experience had been 'a very weird time', and enclosed a photocopy of a press story from some years previously detailing Richard's arrest and subsequent imprisonment on charges of abducting and illegally detaining minors, neglect, the deliberate withholding of medical treatment and statutory rape.

As for myself, using the capital I had accumulated during the fat years with Don and Stefano, I set up a small independent label – Resurgam Records – which opened for business in modest premises in Shepherd's Bush during the latter part of 1978. Leaving nothing to chance, I did the A&R myself, hired producers with whom I had personal dealings back in the 1960s and persuaded Virgin to take on the distribution. Turnover in the first year barely reached seven figures, but we signed the Robin Redbreasts, the Delta Teens and Chloe and the Cupcakes, all of whom did good business, grew used to seeing our records in the lower reaches of the singles chart and were much approved of by the *New Musical Express* and John Peel. In 1986, tired of the high advances that managements seemed to be expecting and indeed the repertoire itself – the mid-1980s wasn't a good time for 'English music' – I sold the company to a major for a whisker under £2 million.

A CLOSE ENCOUNTER WITH THE DON

'Well, Don's really a recluse these days,' offers Melissa the PA, who kindly volunteers to ferry us from Haywards Heath station. 'There was a photographer came the other week from the *News of the World* and he wouldn't even let him in the house.' Chez Shard's location, deep in the Sussex arable, amid rambling lanes and beaten-down cart-tracks, would seem to bear this statement out. So do the towering cypress hedges and the six-foot-high security gates that surround Tintagel Grange, Don's ten-acre country pile. There is a certain amount of doubt as to whether our host will show ('He likes keeping people waiting,' Melissa nervously concedes), but in the end Mr Donald Aloysius Shard comes limping ostentatiously down the gravel drive ('My foot's fucked. Dunno how I did it.') with the aid of a Malacca cane, massive, ring-embossed hand extended, dressed in tweed suits and gaiters, and apparently as pleased to see *Mojo* as *Mojo* is to see him. The interview takes place in Don's study, a capacious sanctum hung with Helium Kids gold discs and a portrait of its owner that bears an uncomfortable resemblance to Olivier as Richard III.

How are you these days?

I'm good. I'm not getting any younger [*the reference books confirm that our man is approaching his sixty-sixth birthday*]. I have to swallow a dozen pills a day and I'm off the booze. Other than that, you can't complain.

Current level of engagement with the music industry?
Retired. Well, semi-retired maybe. There's a boxset coming out in the autumn [*Helium Kids: Dreams and Responsibilities 1964–1977*] and a load of film clips someone wants to make a DVD compilation out of. One's input was required.

Do you still see any members of the band?
Garth I never see. Don't know why. Fucker never phones. Simple as that. Keith has a trout farm a dozen miles away. We have a drink every now and then. I always liked Keith. A very thoughtful guy. Awful the state he's in, though. Awful. Ian and Dale I bump into every so often. What was the name of the other one? Gordon? Graham? [*Gary Pasarolo, guitarist 1968–77*] No idea what happened to him. Probably dead or something.

Did you read Garth's book?
I heard about it, yeah.

It suggested that you were quite a formidable proposition in your day.
I always think those stories about the sixties are exaggerated, don't you? It's like Keith Richards, who is a very good friend of mine, always says: people go on about the women and the drugs, but half the time if you were backstage with the Stones they'd be complaining there wasn't any Worcestershire sauce on the rider.

But didn't you actually hang a music journalist out of a window by his heels?
I may have done. I don't really recall. You've got to remember that I had my interests to protect. Besides, nobody got hurt. Nine times out

of ten, whatever happened on tour, or in the office, you'd laugh about it afterwards.

Do you bear any grudges?

One or two. There are always going to be grudges in a business like this.

Are there things the band should have done which you regret they didn't? And vice versa?

That prog album – what was it called? [*1974's* Glorfindel] was a mistake. Make that a horrible mistake. And we definitely should have done Woodstock – something for which I take full responsibility, I may add. But the way it was sold to us was a load of hippies playing bongos in some fucking field in upstate New York. So, you can see why I wasn't keen.

Going back to Garth's book, what did you think of all the occult stuff?

I thought it was bollocks. No, really. That Garth! Thinking he's Abaddon or Chronos out of the black pit when he's really just some hairy-arsed chancer from Shepperton who got lucky. On the other hand, there was always something weird about him. I remember one time on tour he was convinced 'e was possessed or something and we had to get a priest in to exorcise him.

What do you do with your time now?

You'd be surprised how many letters I get sent. People you met in the States in nineteen sixty what-fucking-ever who want to stay in touch. And just now I'm doing quite a bit of reading. Dickens isn't bad, but the geezer I really like is William Makepeace Thackeray. Ever heard of him?

Do you think the band will ever re-form?

I can't see it happening, can you? To the best of my recollection, Garth and Dale haven't spoken for five years. Last time I saw Ian 'e said he was going *deaf*. And Keith can't hardly take a crap on his own, let alone play the drums. No, the money would have to be top whack. And let's face it, they're not fucking U2, are they?

Mojo, October 1998

Shard, Donald Aloysius [ps of Harry Greenbaum] (1932–2003), rock music manager and impresario, was born on 25 August 1932, at 7 Brewer's Buildings, Prestwich, Manchester, the eldest son of Lazarus Ezekiel Greenbaum (?1898–1954) and his wife Hepzibah (?1899–1973). His parents were Lithuanian Jews, who worked in the Manchester garment-weaving trade. Though he venerated their memory, Shard did not talk much about his early life. Of limited formal education, he began his business career at the age of fourteen, selling cheap jewellery and trinkets from a barrow at street markets. By his late teens, he was working in the office of a variety-hall agent booking performers for music halls and concert parties in the north-west of England. The contacts made during this somewhat chaotic apprenticeship would later prove useful. As he succinctly put it: 'There are people who owe me favours and I know where to go when they're owing.' He changed his name to 'Donald Shard' by deed poll at Prestwich register office on 17 September 1950.

Shard's activities in the early 1950s are poorly documented. He certainly contrived to evade National Service, and may even have taken to the wrestling booths as 'Little Donny Shard', although corroborative evidence of these appearances is lacking. This *nom de guerre* can only have been a joke, as he was well over six feet in height and, at his considerable prime, weighed nearly seventeen stone. What

is known is that on 14 December 1951 he married Gladys May
Withrington, a circus acrobat, and in the following months established himself as an agent-cum-producer in his own right. These were
twilight years for the variety halls, whose audiences now preferred to
stay at home and watch television or engage in other leisure pursuits.
But Shard determined to take advantage of such opportunities as
were available. His forte was striptease or burlesque, often advertised
under eye-catching and/or alliterative slogans (*Shard's bacchanalian
beauties/Young, free and shirtless*) or masquerading as historical *tableaux
vivants* (*A Night in Cleopatra's Boudoir*, etc.). There was trouble with
watch committees and city fathers, but Shard proved surprisingly
adept at keeping his shows on the road. An attempt to combine his
customary fare with circus acts – *Beauties and the Beast* featured a line
of girls dancing inside a lion's cage – was less successful.

But popular entertainment had begun to change, not always, Shard
maintained – he was nostalgic for the pre-war era when, as he remembered, 'there wasn't any trouble and people behaved themselves' – for
the better. By the early 1960s, consequently, he moved south to
London, occupying offices in the Soho district, and relaunched
himself as a popular music impresario promoting concerts in the UK
by visiting American stars such as Gene Vincent, Bo Diddley and
Chuck Berry. Even at this stage, his reputation as a man who brooked
no opposition went before him. Reggie Kray (*q.v.*), for whom he
briefly worked in an unspecified capacity, is supposed to have remarked
that 'You didn't want to mess with old Donny.' Exasperated by the
behaviour of Vincent, who had lingered too long in the company of a
female companion in his dressing room, he is alleged to have picked
the performer up by the trouser legs and thrown him bodily onto the
stage. While the business prospered, the rewards offered by concert-
promoting were, at this point in the development of the music business, comparatively small beer. As well as arranging concerts and
taking his percentage, the always financially astute Shard determined

to find a group who suited his requirements, manage them and superintend the making of their records.

There were, inevitably, a number of false starts. The Kinks eluded him. The members of the Who were, supposedly, so wary of his personal manner that they refused to sign a proffered contract and left the building at which the meeting had been convened by a separate entrance. But in late 1967, Shard succeeded in his objectives, replacing, in somewhat mysterious circumstances, Ainslie Duncan as manager of the Helium Kids. Informed sources judged that by this stage in a career extending back to the early days of the sixties 'beat boom', the group were in low-ish water. Under Shard's tutelage, on the other hand, their fortunes dramatically improved. There were lucrative tours of the United States, bestselling albums and, stylistically, a move into the 'heavy sound' then being exploited by such ensembles as Led Zeppelin and Black Sabbath. Shard's attitude to his protégés was both avuncular and proprietorial. In surviving concert footage he can frequently be seen at the sides of the stage admonishing members of the road crew, inspecting equipment or taking photographs with an ancient Box Brownie camera. Curiously, or perhaps not so curiously, Shard took little interest in the music the group produced. It was 'just noise', he once informed a reporter from *Melody Maker*. His own preferred listening was the light operas of Gilbert & Sullivan.

No details of Shard's contract with the Helium Kids were ever vouchsafed. At the height of the group's success he was alleged to be receiving 30 per cent of gross receipts. In the field of concert performance he struck what were, by the standards of the day, astonishingly hard bargains, often restricting local promoters, especially on the burgeoning US circuit, to as little as 15 per cent of the proceeds. Though regularly rebuked for his overbearing manner and an absolute determination to get his own way, he was rarely worsted in any of the commercial or personal conflicts which his activities seemed to generate. A music journalist who had offended him was sent a succession of dead rats in the post. For his own part, Shard deplored efforts to portray him as 'some kind of monster', insisting that he was instead 'a pussy cat', whose sense of humour was sadly misunderstood.

After nearly a decade and a half in the business, the Helium Kids broke up in 1977 following a disastrous American tour. Thereafter, though continuing to manage other acts, Shard proved adept at exploiting their back catalogue. He became litigious, successfully suing a newspaper that claimed that he had profited from the 1985 Live Aid concerts, and seeing off a High Court challenge (*Dangerfield and Halliwell vs Shard Enterprises*) by members of the group who alleged that he had not only withheld songwriting royalties but in some cases tampered with documentation to make it appear that he had co-written certain compositions himself. Shard's private life at this period, and indeed before it, was obscure. He remained married to Gladys, who bore him three children. In his sixties he retired to an opulent country house in Sussex, living quietly and apparently untroubled by a hard-hitting Channel Four documentary, *Shard: Taking Care of Business* (1995). He died, of what were described as 'toxicological compilations', at St George's Hospital, Tooting, on 22 August 2003, three days before his seventy-first birthday, leaving a vainglorious autobiography (*The Don Speaks*), published a month after his death, to cement his reputation as one of the most rapacious musical Svengalis of his age.

Sources: *The Don Speaks*, 2003; 'Death of an Opportunist', *Guardian*, 23 August 2003; J. Hartley & P. Gissing (eds), *The Economics of Popular Music Management in the 1960s*, University of Lancaster Press, 1993; private information; personal knowledge.

Wealth at death: £3.5 million (probate 17 December 2003)

Oxford Dictionary of National Biography, 2005

PART FIVE

Bringing It All Back Home

They say that home is where the heart is
But I never get to find where my heart is . . .

18. 2007

(i) 5 July 2007

My house is on the large size for this part of Norwich: three-storeyed, with spacious attics to boot. The front garden, in a locale keen on boxy uniformity, stretches fifty feet to the road. According to my researches, it was built in 1901. Previous inhabitants have included Ralph Miniver, author of *Norfolk Days and Norfolk Ways*, the Home Fire Superintendent of the Norwich Union Insurance Society, a consultant paediatrician from the local hospital, and his widow, who was finally coaxed out of the premises at the age of ninety-eight. Back when Miniver was writing his essays about gypsy caravans and tithe barns this was the city's outermost limit, but in the past century the houses have marched another mile or two on to the south-west. Just now I look out on a confluence of four streets, a twenty-four-hour garage with mini-mart attached, an unpromising pub and a roundabout. Here on summer evenings the mad kids from the West Earlham estate exercise their equally mad cars.

As far as the mad kids are concerned, the roundabout has an historic significance. Fifty years ago, it was the frontier between respectable working-class Norwich and the Indian territory of the Bowthorpe and Larkman Lane. Just out of my line of vision, for example, is the once-celebrated thoroughfare of Cadge Road, in those days a row of seething stucco council houses from which, on Saturday nights, tough boys in Teddy-boy drapes would cruise out into the city with the aim of kicking the shit out of people like me. But time and the planners seem to have done for the tough boys. The stoat hutches in Cadge Road have given way to sheltered housing; the aisles of the mini-mart are clogged with Zimmer frames and students from the university buying flagons of sparkling water. If anything survives from this lost Arcadia it is the hard girls marching in from West Earlham on weekday mornings to the new academy school along the road. Oh, and the pub, which is a thieves' pub and, as such, raided by the police one Saturday night in three. I was coming back from the mini-mart the other morning when a couple of the hard girls went by. They had round, chalk-white faces, grotesque approximations of the school uniform and hennaed hair tied cruelly back in face-distending scallops. As they passed, one of them said to the other, in tones of quiet satisfaction: 'Jaylene's been doing Karl. But she didn't know he was doing Peppa and all. Now she's says she's gonna go round her owce and deck the cunt.' What would my mother have made of the hard girls from the Bowthorpe? I don't think she would have made anything at all. They are different people, sprung from a different world.

I have a routine around here. Oh yes, I have a routine. Rise at 7.30 in the bright post-dawn. Breakfast at eight, looking out over the viridian garden and the rotting summerhouse. Here, according to his autobiography, *A Scrivener's Tale*, Ralph Miniver liked to write his newspaper articles. I can imagine him there, goading his fountain pen over the white foolscap pages. At nine, once the traffic has calmed down, I head out to the mini-mart to buy the local paper. Like Cadge Road, this is not what it was. The lofty editorials about the City Hall Treasurer's Department and the school prizegiving reports have given way to pictures of terminally ill children ('Little Kayleigh's Smile of Hope') and overweight women jogging for charity. On the other hand, the announcements page is still full of people with names like Pilch and Allman and Chittick, all giving birth or celebrating their diamond wedding anniversaries or dying in the Norfolk & Norwich after a courageous fight against lymph cancer, to be remembered as fond gramps and doting nanas and urging that donations be sent to 'Big C' appeals and animal sanctuaries in their memory. And every so often there is a spread of archive photographs to stir the surface of past time. Children tobogganing on Mousehold during the freeze-up of 1963. Crowds queuing for tickets in the '59 Cup run. Prime ministerial visits from the 1970s. On the other hand, there is something intangible about the sight of Jim Callaghan shaking hands outside the Cathedral. Like the tough boys in their Teddy-boy drapes, he seems too far away to be brought back.

This particular morning, having dispensed with the local news ('Sad Triplets' Sunshine Journey'), I head for the computer. And what does cyberspace have to offer us on this languid forenoon in July? (Norwich is dead by the way, everyone is away at the Costessey Showground for the annual display of agricultural machinery and perambulating heifers known as the Royal Norfolk Show.) Well, Bush, Brown and Merkel are up to their usual and the Middle East is in cataclysm. Meanwhile, over on the celebrity sites, Paris Hilton has been disgracing herself again, there is news from former supermodel turned midlife feminist Kimberley Stanton (a blast from the past, this, as she was an occasional squeeze of Garth's in the mid-1970s, to the point where I once had to draft a press release denying their engagement) and her forthcoming autobiography *Manhole*, and a whole heap of stories about Opal. Do you know about Opal? Depending on where you get your cultural commentary, she is either a plucky waif from the backstreets of Haringey catapulted into stardom or a talentless know-nothing scooped arbitrarily from the gutter by the talons of the modern celebrity process. I only found out about her the other week, but it seems she has already appeared on a reality show where the contestants end up eating termites in the desert, married and then divorced a boyband alto named Tyler McLintock (there are two children called Caramel-Jo and Purple) and scored a couple of top-ten hits. Just now, though, the tabloids and *Celebslut* are very worried about Opal, who has been seen leaving a Harley Street clinic and whose last single barely scraped the Top 40. Tyler, needless to say, thinks she's made a dreadful mistake divorcing him.

This morning it turns out that cyberspace has more for me than George, Gordon, Angela, Kimberley, Opal and the man from Penge who has managed to tattoo 98 per cent of his total body area, eyelids and perineum included. For once, in fact, cyberspace is telling me something I want to know. For there, on one of the entertainment websites, at the very bottom of a file of music gossip (U2 are touring, Ozzie is out of rehab) comes news that the award-winning indie director Karl Ove Tanizaki is shortly to release his documentary *Take Me with You When You Die: The Lives and Times of the Helium Kids: A Romance*. There are at least three intriguing things about this announcement. The first is that the director, doubtless for the best artistic reasons, has taken his title from a single that, on its release in 1970, received next-to-no airplay on the incontestable grounds that it encouraged suicide pacts. The second is that tantalising suffix, 'a romance'. The third is its singularity. The last few years have been a lean time for the Helium Kids. The belated recognition, the crowded re-release schedules, the admiring retrospectives in the music mags accorded to Jethro Tull, ELP and Mott the Hoople have passed them by. The career-encompassing CD boxset (the eleven studio albums, plus out-takes, plus a live DVD shot in 16 mm at the Marquee Club in 1969) sank without a ripple. To plug their name into a search engine is, generally, only to emerge with an earnest exchange or two from the fan-sites over the lyrical content of *Paisley Patterns* and unflattering reviews of an autobiography that Garth wrote, or had written for him, back at the last century's end. Bush's troop movements; Kimberley's conversion to feminism; Opal's trip to Harley Street: all these will have to wait their turn. This is real news.

Curiously, corroboration arrives only a couple of hours later with the delivery of this month's copy of *Heritage Rock*. Do you know *Heritage Rock*, I wonder? It has a rising circulation, countless features about the Fabs, Mick, Keith, Bob, Zep and Brian Wilson, and reads as if the veins of everybody involved in it from commissioning editor to ad sales manager were shot through with embalming fluid. Karl Ove Tanizaki is pictured on one of the news pages. He is an odd-looking character with a Viking hairdo but deeply recessed oriental eyes like those of a Tartar horseman. Mr Tanizaki has apparently been listening to the Helium Kids 'since I was at High School'. *Take Me with You When You Die* is 'the fulfilment of a childhood dream'. He is also the proud beneficiary of an EU Arts Foundation grant, passed on by the University of Bergen. There is talk of previously unseen archive footage and a bonus CD of early recordings when the package makes it to DVD.

I take the copy of *Heritage Rock* out into the wild garden, intending to read it on the summerhouse veranda. Here, oddly enough, there are traces of Ralph Miniver. Clearing out some of the debris when I moved in, and rooting through a canvas satchel someone had left there, I found an unframed watercolour with the signature 'R. de L. M.' in its lower right-hand corner. The scene – a water meadow at sunrise – is one of the illustrations to *Norfolk Days and Norfolk Ways*. Apparently Miniver was known for his local landscapes. According to a dealer in Elm Hill, the painting is worth as much as £250.

I read disbelievingly on about Karl Ove, his childhood dreams, his relish for what he calls, with no discernible irony, 'the psychedelic heavy sound', the awards he has won for a film called *Oslo Night Train*, to an accompaniment of fruit dropping off the pear tree that lies beyond the summerhouse's eastern flank. The pear tree is not in good shape. The pears that tumble from it are not yet ripe. Once fallen, they give off an odd, sickly smell, like spilled chemicals. Wasps are diligently at work in their interior. From a long way off, deep inside the house, the telephone rings.

Over the years, Stefano's voice has turned steadily grander. These days he flattens out his 'a's to say *thet* instead of *that*, and drawls out *yes* as *yerse*. He also likes to talk about Winchester, the public school where he was educated. But then we nearly all of us return to base in the end. I am back here in Norwich watching the pears fall. Ralph Miniver spent the last years of his life in a rustic cottage at Hingham, a stone's throw from his father's rectory. Just now, Stefano inhabits a riverside development at Staines, from which his third and impossibly juvenile wife runs an interior design business.

'You know what it's like with these kids,' Stefano confidentially intones, as if we last spoke three days ago rather than three years. 'Always think they have to be doing something. She got a commission last week to embroider some fucking *curtains* for Robbie Williams. You never heard the end of it.' Stefano's new upper-bourgeois voice is somehow far more grating than his old *faux*-plebeian snarl. 'Listen, Nick. You heard about the film?'

'Not until an hour or two ago. What's it like?'

'Your guess is as good as mine. He interviewed me a couple of years ago, and then I forgot all about it, as you do,' Stefano says, implying that the path to his front door has been trodden to dirt by the steps of documentary-makers come to question him. 'Anyway, I had a bit of a ring-round. He's talked to one or two of the boys, of course. And he's definitely been digging around at EMI or whatever it's called now. One of the people in accounts told me.' It occurs to me that Stefano, for all his breeziness, is deeply irritated by this ransacking of a long-sealed vault. Are there private myths being tampered with here? It is difficult to tell.

There are screeching noises coming from the garden. A glance through the kitchen window confirms that a couple of jays have taken up residence on the summerhouse roof. Their plumage glints in the sunlight.

'How are the boys?' The boys have a collective age of something over three hundred – even youngster Gary is a ripe fifty-seven – but they are still the boys.

'Oh, you know . . .' Stefano's voice sounds as if it is coming from a long way off, random and disconnected. 'Dale's still got that place up in the Highlands. I think Ian's making an album, or else he's out on the road. Last I heard from Garth he'd fucked up big-time.'

'How come?'

'Well, you know he was supposed to be doing some stuff with that hippy folk-singer who won the Mercury? Alt-folk they call it these days. Martina Faye or whatever her name is? *Dangerfield Unplugged* or some fucking rubbish. I saw them on Jools Holland and I was, you know, screaming for someone to put an amplifier out there. Plus his voice is shot to ribbons these days. Cooking Vinyl or someone were supposed to be giving them a deal. Only then Garth goes and puts his hand up her dress or something and she calls the whole thing off there and then. I said to him: "Garth, mate, this is the twenty-first century, and you just can't do that any more. It's not like the sixties where they *expected* you to fuck them in the lift."'

'What about Keith?'

'Not good. Kelly rang me just the other day. Half the time he sits in his wheelchair and looks out of the window. The other half he goes and cleans the weed off his duck pond. That's all he does. Hey,' Stefano says – his voice is back in focus now – 'did you see there was some bloke on *Mastermind* the other week chose the Helium Kids as his special subject?'

'How did he get on?'

'Thirteen points. Only missed on two. Couldn't remember the track-listing of side one of *Low Blows in High Times*, and got Gary's date of birth a year out … Look, Nick,' Stefano says, 'you hear anything about this, I mean, if anyone gets in touch or anything, you let me know, all right?'

Copy of *Heritage Rock* once more in my lap, unripe pears continuing to plummet, it strikes me that Stefano has been fishing for information. Perhaps the breeze blowing in from the Thames at Staines is chillier than he represents it. Who can tell? One of the jays is perched on the summerhouse's rotting stanchions. Something pink and glistening hangs from its savage beak.

Later on, emboldened by the chat with Stefano, I take a bus into town to do a little market research. And just how are the Helium Kids faring here in a provincial English city thirty years after they ceased to function as an operational unit? Well, the Chapelfield Mall branch of HMV has a CD of *Paisley Patterns* marked down to £3.99. The second-hand vinyl shop in Magdalen Street offers dog-eared copies of *Cabinet of Curiosities* and *Greatest Hits Vol. I* at, respectively, £10 and £8. For purposes of comparison, a mint pressing of *Rubber Soul* is priced at £35. I do better in the music section of the Millennium Library, which runs to four CDs from the 1990s remastering series. It doesn't look as if a great many people have borrowed them. On the other hand, they turn up fairly regularly on some of the compilations: *Sixties Summer Breeze*; *Pop's Golden Age*; *A Walk in the Sky: The Best of British Psychedelia*. *Sixties Summer Breeze* even has a fingernail-size portrait of Garth on the back, in a collage otherwise ornamented by Jimi Hendrix, Arthur Lee and the members of Procol Harum. With his tan complexion and bristling side-whiskers, he looks like an orang-utan.

On the way back from the city centre, I make what is now getting to be a thrice-yearly pilgrimage to North Park. The house was long ago snatched from local authority control by some Thatcher-supporting council tenant, and serially refurbished. Right now, what was once white stucco has been supplanted by plum-coloured render. The over-grown hedge has several plastic bottles and a cigarette packet concealed in it. As I wander by a couple of pre-teen children scamper through the gate, which dangles drunkenly on its solitary hinge, and a bald goblin in tracksuit bottoms shambles into view.

'What are you looking at then?'

'I used to live here,' I tell him. 'Back in the 1950s.'

'What are you, a fucking nonce? Go on. Fuck off.'

Here in a less trusting age, it is a fair point. I fuck off.

(ii) 9 July 2007

Four days now since news of *Take Me with You When You Die* went public, and the fan websites are earnestly debating its prospects. The prognosis is mixed. *Psychfest* wonders whether Tanizaki – revealed to be in his late thirties – can do justice to an artform that was getting into its stride before he was born. *Metal Fury* suggests that he could have chosen a better subject. *Sturm und Drang* carries an interview with the man himself from the Berlin hotel where he is currently holed up prior to attending some continental film festival. This, Tanizaki insists – he is not, by all accounts, a modest man – will be 'a different kind of documentary', more realistic, less concerned with character than 'situation, atmosphere, responsibility'. I have no idea what he means by this.

Meanwhile, cyberspace continues to be worried about Opal. Not only is there the visit to the Harley Street clinic, but a CCTV system has been ransacked to supply pictures of her weaving through the aisles of a Morrisons near her home in Croydon. Later, she can be seen plunging headlong over a cache of disposable nappies while attempt-ing to load them into the boot of a 4 x 4. In the vengeful aftermath of this transgression, her ex-husband from the boyband has suggested that she 'may not be a good mum'. There is talk of her various product endorsement contracts – these include a range of hot-tubs and a downmarket fashion chain – being revoked. Further photos of Opal adorn the covers of the celeb magazines displayed in the mini-mart: a small, plump girl with the mouth of a recently landed trout. She looks bewildered but game, not sure why so many people hate her so much, but anxious to give value for money while the going is good.

The rain, which set in at dawn, persists until lunchtime. From the kitchen window, I can see it wreaking havoc on the half-collapsed roof of the summerhouse. The wildlife is keeping to its nests and burrows: the jays have disappeared. Later on, in fine, needlepoint drizzle, I trek across to the Black Rat to look up my friend Trevor. The Black Rat, like many of the local hostelries, has seen better days. Smoking is no longer allowed, of course – the addicts are hunched over their roll-ups out in the yard – but the ceilings and the badly distempered walls haven't yet been repainted, and the winded sofas are covered with burn marks. Trevor sits on one of these vantage points, half-full pint glass balanced on his knee, shaven head bent over the *Racing Post*. An autumnal leaf-drift of empty pork scratchings packets covers the floor.

'Hello, mate. How are you doing?' Trevor says enthusiastically, almost knocking over the pint in his eagerness to set it down.

'I'm good, mate,' I tell him. 'How are you?'

Trevor gives a little crafty-cockney grin, like one of the actors in *Only Fools and Horses*, the grin of one who has momentous news to impart. 'You missed a bit of fun here, mate. A right kerfuffle. Just before you came in.' Trevor, by the way, not only calls people 'mate' but does so repeatedly, like a Geiger counter. ('Hello, mate. Nice to see you, mate. Cheers, mate. Mind that door, mate.') His amiability is infectious.

'Oh yeah? What happened?' The Black Rat, I notice, is nearly empty, with only a haggard barmaid staring disgustedly at the row of taps and a couple of youngsters blowing the froth off their lagers at the pool table.

'Well, mate, you know that Ashley Dorling? Come in here with a bag of weed the size of a football.' The Black Rat, as well as being a thieves' pub, is also a drugs pub. 'Hadn't so much as sat down in his chair before the Old Bill turns up, on account of someone's tipped them off. Bad news for somebody, that is, mate.'

Hairless, chunky figure accentuated by his tight Top Man jacket, weird little goatee looking like a wisp of paintbrush glued to his chin, Trevor could be any age between forty and sixty. He is, I am led to believe, fifty-three. Since leaving school in 1969 he has been employed, successively, as an apprentice butcher, a painter and decorator, a taxi driver, an assistant groundsman, a gardener and a bailiff's right-hand man. Just now he does morning and evening deliveries for a news-agent in Cringleford, with occasional stints as doorman for a club in the Prince of Wales Road. The bouncing evenings, though, are getting more sporadic. ('Too many of these young cunts looking for trouble.') I have a feeling, too, that security work conflicts with his essential good nature. Mrs Trevor – they live in a house on Larkman Lane – is rarely mentioned save in terms of her virtues. ('She's a good woman, mate.')

Like Stefano, Trevor doesn't sound like the person he used to be. The old west Norwich accent he must have had as a child (*rarely* for 'really', *int* for 'isn't') has picked up traces of Estuarine from the TV. Or perhaps this is simply a result of his exposure to the wider world. On his own admission, Trevor has been about a bit. In the eighties, the painting and decorating took him on refurbishing jaunts to Marbella and Gran Canaria. When funds permit, he is not above holidaying in France. ('It's all right, mate, if you like that kind of thing.') On this particular afternoon I take the unprecedented step of asking him back to the house. Together we cautiously traverse the pelican crossing that abuts the school gates. Trevor, I notice, walks in the way that off-duty footballers are supposed to walk: hobbling a little on stumpy, overworked legs.

'Nice place you got here, mate,' he says, once installed in the kitchen with a can of lager from the fridge, but I can see his professional's eye glinting with dissatisfaction. Somebody, he cheerfully explains, laid the last lot of emulsion on with a trowel. Plus the cupboards have been badly aligned. Outside the garden is warming up again after the rain. Water drips off the veranda. There is a hint of steam rising from the blackberry bushes. 'Nice spread,' Trevor says, resting a hand on the veranda's wooden rail, but I can see that all this negligence, all this foot-high grass and rotting woodwork, is a grave disappointment to him. On impulse, I ask if he would like to do a little gardening work, tame the long grass, say, and shore up the summerhouse. Trevor squats on his haunches, jabs a white-trainered toe at the fenceposts. He likes to get the feel of a place before setting to work, he volunteers. We agree a fee of £10 an hour that will include the disposal of debris. 'Generous of you, mate,' Trevor says, the optimism he brings to life clearly stimulated by this unsolicited gift.

I continue to take an interest in Ralph Miniver. www.literarynorfolk. com reveals that he died in 1953, leaving two-dozen full-length works: novels, essay collections, reportage. There is even a photograph of a sensitive-looking middle-aged man with centre-parted hair in a suit of plus-fours bending to examine a latch gate. Encouraged, I pay £35 to an online bookseller for a signed copy of *Tillers of the Soil: Studies Among the Labouring Classes of Hingham, Norfolk*. The signature is oddly flamboyant, raging across a quarter of a page, with little curlicues and flourishes. *Tillers*, an early work from 1899, turns out to be the diary of a six-month furlough spent among the agricultural labourers of his father's parish. The average wage is 13s.6d. The families – sometimes extending to ten or a dozen children – at whose blighted hearths Miniver drinks cups of tea and, we infer, dispenses small amounts of largesse, inhabit two-bedroom cottages with no proper sanitation. Violence, incest and disease are rife. The interesting thing about these reports, it seems to me, is their ambiguity. Miniver clearly sympathises with his subjects, wishes them well and yearns to ameliorate their lot. At the same time, you can tell that he doesn't like them, thinks them shiftless, lacking in zeal. 'Surely poverty is no excuse for a child's smudged and sooty face that the merest application of moisture could remedy?' he writes crossly at one point. 'And it cannot be a defective education that allows a mother to neglect an infant lying helpless in its cradle.'

By chance, the TV schedules disclose that *Oslo Night Train* is showing in the small hours on Film Four. The critic in the *Radio Times* describes it as 'uncompromising'. There is some doubt as to whether the piece has survived the censor's scalpel, owing to the inflammatory nature of its themes. I brew a pot of strong coffee and stay up late to watch. *Oslo Night Train* (Norwegian, with subtitles) opens with shots of a girl – blonde, possibly in her late teens – moving briskly around a suburban apartment. Such items as the camera lingers on – a row of Pippi Longstocking books, pictures of horses sailing over gymkhana fences – suggest that childhood is not so very far away. That it will shortly recede over the horizon is confirmed by the items that madam is now stowing away in her attaché case. These include several packets of condoms, a jar of Vaseline and a cucumber-sized dildo. All the while the girl is glued anxiously to her mobile phone, confirming dates, times and issuing sharp rebukes to someone called Jan-Åge. By this point the message of the establishing detail is clear. The girl, whose name is Gudbrod, is a prostitute preparing for business. We next see her, in thigh-revealing skirt and stacked boots, tripping off to the railway station through leprous alleyways and grim underpasses. There is no one about, but occasional rats, feral dogs and at one stage what looks like a small wolf rear up menacingly from their inspection of the garbage cans. Picking her way through piles of spilled refuse and hastening down graffiti-flecked side-streets, Gudbrod arrives at the station, buys a ticket from a clerk whose resemblance to the young Charles Manson must have occurred to many a viewer other than myself, and hops on the train to Oslo.

It is here, on the train, which crashes uncontrollably through the night, that everything starts to turn weird. To begin with the other passengers, though human in shape, have pigs' heads. The conductor, hurtling along the corridors with many a bright remark for those whose tickets he punches, is a space alien. For some reason Gudbrod is unfazed by these apparitions. A slight smile on her luminously pale face, she opts to ignore the crazies who around her and takes out a book entitled *Overthrowing the Male Hegemony*. When each page is done, she tears it out of the book and throws it into the air. Inexplicably, none of the pages descends. Instead they hang at head-level, to be playfully pawed at and snapped over by the pig people, whose hands are now revealed as trotters. All this goes on for what seems like hours. Finally, as the train cruises into Oslo Central, the pig people rise up as one from their seats and sniff the air. By this time Gudbrod's face has lost its serene expression. Plainly, she can't wait to get out of the carriage. There follows a chase sequence, done in a bizarre kind of slo-mo, in which Gudbrod, scattering the contents of the attaché case as she goes, is pursued along endless garishly lit corridors, through a deserted shopping mall, past a butcher's counter, where the display cases are full of human babies, and then cornered on the station steps. The ensuing melee, filmed at ground level, is difficult to follow, but in the end one of the pig people emerges from the press of bodies with what is unmistakably Gudbrod's head in his triumphant, outstretched grasp.

*   *   *

'Did you see that old Tanizaki film?' Stefano asks. His voice sounds more upper-class than ever, aflame with genteel anguish.

'I think it's what they call a challenging piece of work.'

'I thought it was the most awful piece of shit,' Stefano says sententiously. It is 9 a.m., which suggests that what he thinks of *Oslo Night Train* is a matter of some urgency. 'All that feminist symbolism stuff went out years ago.'

'I'm sure you're right.' Beyond the kitchen window, there is bright sunshine falling over the currant bushes. The local paper (PREGNANT MUM'S MERCY DASH) rests a yard away. Stefano, I deduce, is worried about something, over and above the tendency of contemporary arthouse cinema to descend into cliché.

'I made some calls,' he says. 'Apparently *Take Me with You* is due to open in the autumn. "Limited cinema release", whatever that means. The fucking Arts Council are supposed to have put up some of the money.' Like many of the people I come across, Stefano believes that state sponsorship of any cultural activity is fundamentally immoral. 'What I can't work out is who said he could do it.'

'I can see that being a problem.'

A journalist acquaintance of mine, at work on a book entitled *Corporate Rock PLC*, had the bright idea of using the Helium Kids as a case study in the legal-cum-fiscal afterlife of a defunct rock band. After a month of dogged research, he established that a) Garth and Dale were officially managed by Stefano, who had assumed control of their interests after Don's death; that b) all songwriting royalties, such as they were, were channelled through a company called Dangerfield-Halliwell Productions, whose assets had been frozen owing to several outstanding legal cases brought by other members of the band; that c) Dangerfield-Halliwell Productions had at some point sold 40 per cent of these assets to a second organisation which had gone bankrupt and was in the process of being liquidated; that d) there existed a further company, named Helium Kids Ventures, supposedly in charge of the band's interests as a whole, now administered by the great-nephew of the chartered accountant who had originally established it in 1972, which had not filed accounts for seven years; that e) Ian's signature had not been appended to any document sent to him since 1998, thereby rendering any fiscal agreements entered into since that date technically invalid; and that f) there existed a lawsuit, commenced in the mid-1990s but now temporarily suspended, with Don concerning the alleged withholding of half a million pounds' worth of songwriting and image-rights royalties dating back to the early 1970s. My friend had wanted to call the chapter that dealt with this material HOW TO REALLY FUCK THINGS UP, but had been talked out of it by a nervous publisher.

'I haven't given permission,' Stefano says. 'That old tart at Ventures doesn't know anything about it. I rang Tanizaki's production people and they said they couldn't divulge information of that kind to third parties.'

'Maybe you ought to take legal advice.' This is a mischievous suggestion, and gets the response it deserves.

'Look, Nick,' Stefano says wearily. 'There are currently four lawyers up to their necks in this, only two of whom – between you and me – are getting paid. I don't propose to add to their number. If I find out anything else, I'll let you know . . . What are you doing right now?'

'Eating my breakfast. Looking at the garden. Reading a story in the paper about a woman who gave birth to triplets in the back of an ambulance. What are you doing?'

'The fucking house is full of Indian sofa throws. I told Stacia they couldn't shift that stuff at Granny Takes a Trip forty years ago, but what do I know?'

He is right, of course. We are two old men in an age of excited, purposeful young people. What do we know?

There is another old man haunting me. Squinting at the bathroom mirror the other day I saw my father's face staring back. The resemblance is not so much to do with the arrangement of the features as the look: that slightly-to-one-side glance beneath raised eyebrows. An inspection reveals further twitches on the ancestral thread. As well as inheriting his look, I also have his hands: small, bony, blunt-thumbed.

Not much of my parents has survived the years. One or two keepsakes from North Park. The photograph of my mother I found in the box at Echo Beach. When I first came back here I went in search of her a mile down the road at Earlham Cemetery, but the spot where her ashes were buried had been re-dug and the plaque had long since disappeared. I deliberated over the items available in the administrative complex and eventually paid £49.99 for a small square of bronze embossed with the words *Jean Alexandra Du Pont 1.5.1919–13.6.64*, and saw it safely attached to a row of more recent memorials that included various Spaldings and Allmans and Chittocks, but also Quattrominis and Thalanges and Borowcyzks. Like everywhere else, Norwich is changing with the times.

Later on, Gail rings. Have I told you about Gail? Gail is the woman I see. The new fashion, at any rate in newspapers and on TV chat-shows, is to talk about having a 'partner'. You can see why this has caught on. On the one hand, it offers a cheering vision of two sturdy individuals well-nigh heroically confronting the world together. On the other, there is the no-nonsense sheen of a business relationship. Neither of these quite applies to Gail, who – let us be exact about this – is the woman I see. Does Gail think of me as a 'partner'? I have no idea. On the other hand, she is keenly susceptible to the shifts and eddies of contemporary jargon. Who is to know?

'What sort of a day did you have?'

'Oh, you know. A bit *hectic*.' Gail works at the reception desk of the local dentist. Before that she performed a similar role at a beauty salon. 'And then tonight I'm babysitting. No rest for the wicked,' Gail says, as if this is some new and original remark she has spent the afternoon devising.

Gail is in her early forties. She is also, believe it or not, a grandmother, her daughter Tiffany having recently given birth to her first child. The baby is called Kiara-Jasmine. Tiffany's partner – that word again – lives in Lowestoft and is not always around. Indeed, there is a suspicion that he may cease to be around altogether. Gail, with another gesture at the modern word-hoard, is trying not to be 'judgemental' about this.

'Why don't you come over tomorrow night?' Gail suggests. She is in the middle of spooning out some baby food for Kiara-Jasmine, she explains, and somewhat distracted.

'That would be nice.'

'Take care of yourself then,' Gail says affably. There is a thin, twittering noise going on in the background. It is only after Gail has put the phone down that I realise this is Kiara-Jasmine clamouring for her food.

After two or three postponements ('Bit busy, mate') Trevor arrives to start on the garden. Having assumed that his claims to expertise are inflated, I see I have done him an injustice. In fact, he is surprisingly competent. He brings a bag-full of tools to supplement the limited range of spades and forks available in the summerhouse and works for four hours, scything down the bramble hedge that has built up behind the currant bushes, cutting the long grass, ripping out the knotweed that has woven itself through the lawn. The summerhouse will be a tricky job, Trevor thinks. You could probably replace some of the wood, but the stanchions are giving way and the ground may be subsiding underneath. He will have a look and maybe get his builder friend Neil to sink some concrete down there.

At intervals I bring him bottles of water, which he downs in a couple of swigs, hand on hip, before turning back to his work. I am a little concerned that the four hours' labour – 'hard graft', Trevor calls it – will disturb the way we behave to each other, but Trevor doesn't seem to mind. I leave the money – £40 – on the kitchen table, from which he gratefully retrieves it. 'Nice one, mate,' he says, stowing the notes away uncounted in the pocket of his grey sweatpants. His face, burned by the sun, is the colour of tomato soup.

(iii)

The invite comes in an expensive parchment-style envelope. Inside, on a rectangle of pasteboard nearly an eighth of an inch thick, in lines of embossed italic script, the directors of Valhalla Films, in association with Beast Box Enterprises, a subsidiary of Inward Eye Inc., and with the support of three EU-funded grant-awarding bodies, bid me to attend a private screening of *Take Me with You When You Die: The Lives and Times of the Helium Kids: A Romance*, written and directed by Karl Ove Tanizaki, at an address in Dean Street, London W1, a fortnight hence. On the reverse side a frail, half-remembered hand that has a certain amount of difficulty forming its vowels has written *Hope you can make it, GD*. It occurs to me that GD is Garth Dangerfield. I put it on the mantelpiece, next to the taxi flyers, the takeout menus and a business card stamped with the words *T. Liddament, Gardening and Horticultural Services*, which a newly professionalised Trevor has pressed upon me.

By chance, the next morning's *Guardian* carries a profile of Tanizaki. In the quarter-page photograph that accompanies it, he sits at a café table in some cobbled cosmopolitan side-street, a bicycle wheel straying dangerously close to his outstretched leg, staring blindly into the distance. The smoke rising from his cigarette has obscured most of his face: the Viking locks stir in the wind. The *Guardian* has decided that Tanizaki, in addition to being 'the *enfant terrible* of European arthouse', is also 'an enigma'. Of the various interpretations of *Oslo*

Night Train offered up for comment, Tanizaki will only say that it attempts to 'treat bad things in a good way', although 'some of my feminist friends are appalled'. It is doubtless to his credit that, as a self-proclaimed serial monogamist, he has feminist friends. As for *Take Me with You When You Die*, Tanizaki – brought up in Bergen but with a Japanese father – admits to an epiphanic moment when, at the age of thirteen, he discovered a copy of *Cabinet of Curiosities* in a record-store bargain-bin. 'I am thinking immediately that this is a record of enormous power ... And who are the people who have made such a record? I tell myself that I must find out about them. That I must live as they have lived.'

Of the film itself, Tanizaki will say only that it explores 'elements of the Helium Kids' story that require illumination'. He is not sure, and neither does he seem to care, if those portrayed will welcome his approach, but insists that 'it was a film that demanded to be made ... a love-letter if you will, but painful, infinitely painful, and, in its way, you know, cathartic'. His next project, he reveals, is a study of the sex lives of some immigrant workers on the North Sea ferry lines.

Among other affiliations, Ralph Miniver was for a brief period in the 1930s a member of an organisation called the White Knights of St Athelstan. The Knights, according to a book entitled *Fellow-Travellers of the Right*, were a band of genteel homegrown fascists determined that England shouldn't go to war with Nazi Germany. Several newspaper articles written in support of the White Knights are included in *News from the Village Green*, a collection of essays published in 1938. The articles are not, in fact, particularly right-wing – although there is a line about 'those hard-faced Jewish men who would desecrate our ancestral heritage for a mess of potage' – just a series of laments about boarded-up farmhouses and empty fields across whose stony furrows Will the Ploughman no longer treads. All this, though, was apparently enough to get Miniver on a list of Hitler sympathisers circulated by MI5. He resigned from the White Knights early in 1939, declaring that 'its militancy is abhorrent to me'. There is, so I am assured, no further reference to it in his published writings.

Opal, meanwhile, is going from bad to worse. No one in tabloid-land or cyberspace is worried about her meltdown in the Morrisons car park any more, and the intercepted text messages allegedly sent to her cocaine dealer are long forgotten. No, the word on the front pages is that Opal is seriously ill. Pancreatic abnormalities, renal failure and the Big C all have their advocates. An online betting site offering odds on her still being alive in six months' time has been roundly condemned, but is doing good business. Interested parties, naturally, are rallying round. Tyler, her ex-husband, has given an interview maintaining that he is 'there for her whenever she wants me'. The manager of the day-nursery attended by Caramel-Jo and Purple has confirmed that the children are 'coping very well', and the *Star* has begun a petition to encourage Robbie, her current flame, to walk her down the aisle at the earliest opportunity, the implication being that delay may, literally, be fatal.

For once my sympathies are with Opal. There was a picture of her on one of the websites emerging from the biggish but curiously down-market house she shares with pale, thin Robbie – the peculiarity of modern celebrity, to one who was around in the sixties, is how make-do-and-mend it all is – and the look on her face was not exactly of terror but straightforward puzzlement. You can see her point. When you've spent the last half-decade diligently ensconced with the ghost writer from *OK*, near-publicly giving birth – the paparazzi were allowed into the delivery suite a bare ten minutes after Caramel-Jo's umbilical cord had been cut – and jumping into piles of manure on celebrity webcams, the tap of sinister fingers on the existential window pane can come as a shock.

* * *

Gail lives half a mile away in one of the new houses on George Borrow Road. It seems unlikely that the inhabitants have heard of the author of *Lavengro*, but you never know. The buildings, owned by a housing association, are in chunky red brick, like outsize clumps of Lego. Several of the parking spaces harbour 4 x 4s. Gail's baby Renault has come to rest on the kerbside. Stopping to examine the bright pink sticker on the rear windscreen I see that it reads PRINCESS ON BOARD. Everyone is very keen on princesses these days. The small girls you see being unloaded out of their parents' cars to attend children's parties are quite often dressed in tiaras. I gather Kiara-Jasmine was nearly called Princess-Jasmine, until wiser counsels prevailed.

We eat in Gail's small dining room, overlooking her 300 square feet of garden, into which some previous occupant – Gail has been here two years – managed to cram a bed of pinks, a shed the size of a Wendy house and some crazy paving. Coincidentally, we are talking about my own garden, its soon to be refurbished summerhouse and its fast-disappearing brambles, for Gail, it turns out, knows about Trevor. Knows about him and thoroughly disapproves. Trevor, she informs me, over chicken and mushroom soup followed by cheese and spinach flan and chocolate eclairs – Gail's culinary skills are limited, a failing she cheerfully concedes – has, among other conspicuous lapses, done time.

'What for?'

'Witness intimidation,' Gail says, busy with the salt and pepper. 'I'm not one to judge, but . . .'

She has a habit of not finishing her sentences, which I find endearing, not sure whether this trick of cutting off a line of thought betokens indifference or the telepathic assurance that I know what she intends to say.

'He used to work for Laura.' Laura is the dentist at whose reception desk Gail presides. 'But she decided he was unreliable. I think she said some of the garden tools went missing.' She puts her finger up to her scalp and flicks away a tendril or two of corn-coloured hair.

Just now, Gail is uncomfortably poised, halfway between the world she knows and a bright yet uncertain future. The dentist's surgery needs a practice manager. Laura has suggested to Gail that she might apply. On the other hand, there are needy Tiffany (currently residing in a council flat a mile and a half away) and baby Kiara-Jasmine to bear in mind. Gail is torn. Naturally, she is never one to judge, but I get the feeling she thinks that the rest of her family are exploiting her good nature.

'How did Tiffany get on at Lowestoft?'

Gail shakes her head over the outsize patisserie halfway to her mouth, not exactly irritated but concerned. Tiffany's partner, not hitherto known for his proximity to paid employment, is thinking of applying for a job on the oilrigs. I can see that Gail, though supportive of the young people, is faintly bemused by the lackadaisical sheen that covers most aspects of their lives.

'That Bradley? With him it's always one thing one minute and another thing the next. I tell them he ought to come here, and the council will get them a bigger place. And Kiara-Jasmine can have her daddy at home. Not in some bedsitter in Lowestoft. That's what I tell them, but they won't listen,' Gail says, her voice losing its slight edge and returning to a default position in which what those closest to her get up to is always admirable or at any rate acceptable, or at least justifiable. Gail, I have discovered, has bitter experience of Daddy not being at home. Her husband walked out when Tiffany was two. Many of the secrets of this early life I have not yet been made party to. I don't blame her.

'What about you, Nick?' she says. 'What have you been up to?'

And so I tell her about the invite to the screening of *Take Me with You When You Die*. Gail takes a polite but uncomprehending interest. After all, she was all of fifteen when the Helium Kids fell apart. Her preferred listening is Abba, Madonna and some boyband from the nineteen who play endless revival tours. None of this, I suspect, is properly real to her. It is too far away from the dentist's surgery, Tiffany and Kiara-Jasmine.

'You need to be careful of that Trevor,' Gail says seriously, waving her second eclair from side to side, like a conductor's baton. 'Don't let him take advantage.'

Gail, I can see, is impressed by the big house, which she has visited on several occasions. Trevor, according to her reasoning, will be casing the joint. The gardening work, she implies, is simple camouflage. It is quite likely I will come home one day to find the furniture gone.

After supper we adjourn to the front room, where stray beams of evening sunshine frame the photographs in a surprisingly eerie light. Gail on holiday in Tenerife. Tiffany, waif-like yet determined, at her school prom night. Guests at a family wedding, lined up on a leaf-strewn lawn. The men have doughy, near-identikit features; the women are more individual. Gail fits so neatly into their midst that at first it is difficult to isolate her from the pack, but nevertheless there she is, Aunty Gail, smiling eagerly, lost in the moment.

There are occasions when I stay the night at George Borrow Road, to which the author of *Lavengro* gave his name, but this is not one of them. Tiffany, I have already been informed, is going out with some of her 'girls'. Kiara-Jasmine will shortly be arriving to spend the evening with her nan. The girls – these are old school friends – will be heading up to the Prince of Wales Road to sample the local nightlife. Gail is indulgent of these episodes, which go on until the small hours and involve taxi-rides home through the grey, pre-dawn streets. Leaving the house in the twilight to walk the half-mile home, past the usual old men walking their dogs and the lads on mopeds sailing back and forth, I see Tiffany swing towards me in her tiny car, head down over the wheel, like some elfin sorceress out for an evening's haunting.

*   *   *

'I think I may have got to the bottom of this,' Stefano says testily, the following morning. It is about 11.30, more overcast than on previous days. Trevor, encased in a protective leather jerkin ('It's the fucking health and safety, isn't it?') is out in the garden chainsawing a small oak tree found to have a decomposing base.

'Got to the bottom of what?'

'The bloody film, you douchebag,' Stefano says. He sounds unbelievably tired, as if the whole of the night just passed has been spent in pursuing these cinematic threads. 'All down to that fucking Garth. At least someone I know saw him and that fucking Tanizaki at a festival last year. And the accountant said that's who any questions regarding the project should be referred to.'

'So this is the World According to Garth? Have you talked to him?'

'Ha ha, very funny,' Stefano says. 'To be perfectly honest, Nick, I did phone him a couple of times. Tried the place in Haslemere. He's usually there when he's not out grooming his fucking llamas. But all you get is some dozy tart who tells you that Mr Dangerfield is not presently available. Like he was the Duke of Edinburgh or something.'

The noise of the chainsaw is oddly comforting: like a train chugging forward. When it stops there is a brief, artificial silence before the birdsong starts up again.

'Will you be going?'

For some reason this mild enquiry provokes Stefano to something very near fury. 'Of course I'll be going. And so should you. I mean – sorry if I sound a bit upset, Nick – but this is *legacy* we're talking about.'

Of course, we are all of us very interested in legacy just at the moment, those tantalising myths about ourselves that we intend to bequeath to posterity. Judging from the newspapers, Tony Blair and George Bush Jr are positively obsessed by it. But who would have thought that Stefano, of all people, should be so concerned at the prospect of his roistering and doistering being brought to the silver screen?

As I stand by the window pondering all this, Trevor clumps in from the garden. Tiny bits of debris fall from his clothes as he does this. What seems to be half a bird's nest is stuck to one of his boots.

'There's a fucking fox's earth or something under that beech by the summerhouse,' he says. 'Half the roots have gone. It'll have to go before it falls over.'

It occurs to me that this must be part of my legacy: making a bolt-hole in Earlham, where Ralph Miniver once sat and wrote his essays, habitable again.

Afternoon in the garden, thinking about women. Nothing in particular to prompt these thoughts. I just found myself sitting on the summerhouse veranda – Trevor has demolished half of it; the rest is going in a couple of days – with the image of Rosalind in my head. Not from the Westchester years, either, but from further back, in the Phoenix time, eating ice-cream with Marty Knowland or picnicking by the Gila River. The odd thing about these memories is that their intensity never correlates to duration. Susy, to whom I was married for six years in the eighties, I hardly ever think about. Angie, on the other hand, with whom I dallied for a fortnight in a series of Midwestern hotel rooms thirty-six years ago, is very vivid to me. I can almost feel her hip grind against mine, see her corkscrew curls adrift on the pillow, hear her demanding $20 for Stefano's vial of Tuinal. I tried Googling her the other day, but there was nothing. Perhaps she inherited her mother's place in Yonkers and sits there raising cats? Conclusion: that Rosalind was the love of my life; that I should have realised this; that not realising it will always haunt me.

Unlike Angie, Ros is endlessly trackable. It turns out that her husband is being talked up as somebody's running mate in 2008. The website shows a big, grey-haired character with a face the colour of peanut butter. Rosalind stands supportively at his side, smiling but inscrutable, not in the least engaged: a woman after my own heart.

Making preparations for my London trip. Two nights are booked at the little place in Chelsea I frequent on my occasional trips to town. The day that separates them can be spent in bookshops or catching up with whoever happens to be around. Who knows? Perhaps I shall end up in Savile Row looking at gentlemen's tailoring with Ian, or with Keith in Hamleys examining Airfix's latest additions to their range. The garden is three-quarters done – Trevor has finished with the trees and is starting to re-timber the summerhouse – but I give him a door-key to facilitate these endeavours. Plenty of lager in the fridge, I tell him. He can help himself. I ring up the local florists and have Gail sent a dozen roses. The sun continues to shine. The jays screech from the bramble bushes and the invitation card sits on the mantelpiece.

(iv)

'So I said to her, "No one's got a problem with you making a bit of pin-money, darling, but I don't want to fall over a pile of fabric samples every time I walk through the door." And then last week I came home and there's some poof of a celebrity chef being photographed for *Hello* magazine.'

Stefano is not ageing well. In the three years since I last saw him in the flesh his face has begun to fall in, exaggerating the line of his jaw and the pendulous earlobes on either side. There are little vein traceries on either side of his nose. Worse, he has begun to dress strangely. In his green checked jacket and carmine trousers, he looks like a mad squire in one of those TV programmes about rural eccentrics.

'Oh and another thing' – like many people in their late sixties, Stefano has begun to free-associate – 'the accountant reckons somebody wants to do a complete boxed set. You know, all the studio remasters, plus out-takes and any gigs they happen to have in the can.'

'Where are the original masters?'

'That,' says Stefano, 'is a fucking good question. I thought Don had them. That shyster lawyer who wound up his estate says they went back to EMI. There's loads of stuff just ... floating around. I mean, somebody – one of those dealers – told me they bought the tapes of *Smiley Daze* at a fucking car-boot the other month.' At the mention of the car-boot sale, Stefano looks even more mournful. Clearly, the rock heritage industry is letting him down. On the other hand, he fits perfectly into the ambience in which he has opted to remain. Stefano's hotel, down at the bottom of Lower Sloane Street, is one of those places that takes a pride in keeping the modern world at bay. Here in the lounge there are deer heads staring sightlessly from the wall. The occasional tables offer brochures about whisky distilleries. The waiters, gliding silently back and forth, have marked him down as one of their own.

'Nice place this, isn't it?' Stefano says. I can see that in some curious way he feels at home here, that the highly erratic path that has brought him to this lost world of stags' antlers and Talisker single malt has, in a certain sense, carried him home. Unbidden, a waiter brings another pair of brandies. Nodding his head, jacket rising a couple of inches up his sleeve to reveal glossy cufflinks, Stefano looks more than ever like a rustic throwback from the TV docs.

It is just after 7 p.m. Outside, London is slowing down. Footfalls sound in the street. Laughter is blown back on the breeze.

'Who's going to be there?'

'I don't know,' Stefano says uneasily. He takes out a yellow bandana handkerchief and, with maximum ostentation, blows his nose in a series of parping noises. It is difficult to believe that he and I once racketed around America with the Helium Kids or stood in the bowels of Madison Square Garden listening to the tumult erupt above our heads. 'The boys, I should think. There's supposed to be disabled access, so Keith'll probably make it.'

'Tanizaki?'

'At some fucking film festival, guy from the production company told me.' There is something worrying Stefano, I can see, quite beyond the question of who may or may not turn up at the advance screening of *Take Me with You When You Die*, a whole heap of dissatisfaction searching for a lightning rod. The sheaf of light reading material on the tabletop between us contains, I now realise, in among the *Economist*, *Country Life* and *The Field*, a copy of *OK*, from whose cover, flanked by her children and a nattily dressed Robbie, Opal's face stares uncertainly out. Stefano's gaze follows my own.

'Call me a boring old fart,' he says, 'but I don't understand modern music. I mean, that last song she did. Nobody minds some tart not writing her own material. But not even singing on the record . . .'

'Come on, Stef. People used to do that in the sixties.'

'I know. I know,' Stefano says. He is still staring censoriously at the picture of Opal and her brood. 'But they didn't turn round and tell everyone they'd done it. Here,' he goes on, 'you remember that Raff – used to work in promotions? His son used to go out with Opal, way back. *He* reckons she once gobbled him in the toilet of a service station on the M1.'

I shake my head. For some reason I feel protective of Opal. The last thing she needs at this stage of her fraught young life is Stefano dishing dirt about her sexual largesse.

'That's a real dirty girl,' Stefano says, his irritation momentarily quelled. 'I bet she gave that Tyler a terrible time.'

One of the waiters approaches and stands deferentially beneath the nearest stag's head. 'Your taxi is here, Mr Bennington-Smyth.'

Stefano beams so that the shot tracery of veins on either side of his nose grows even redder. Like the green check jacket and the free-associating, his vanity is a new thing. Outside the streets are still aglow in bright sunshine. The taxi takes us up towards Knightsbridge, past Hyde Park Corner, down along Piccadilly, through streets that are full of rapidly pedalling cyclists. The pavements, I notice, are crammed with tourists – Japanese couples in beanie hats and sunglasses sidling modestly along the edge of Green Park, fabulously extended American families with Ma in denim skirt and trainers, Pa camera-festooned and in overtight shorts waddling up to the storefront windows. Just as Stefano professes not to understand modern music, I can't understand modern London. It is too big now, too undifferen-tiated, too out of control. Somebody told me that a house in Egerton Gardens Mews went for £2 million the other day.

For some reason, here in the cab Stefano looks much more his old self. Maybe it is simple locomotion that gives him purpose, takes him back to the days of barrelling tour buses or the Oblivion Express hurtling on through the Pacific night. The briefcase he has been carry-ing around with him since we met earlier this afternoon is pressed fervently against his chest. His eyes stare straight ahead, undeviating in their focus, unmoved by the tourist throng and the surging back-packers, by me and everything in the world around us.

The preview cinema in Dean Street is a modest affair, reached by a grim black doorway sandwiched between a pub whose drinkers are spilling out onto the pavement and a furtive noodle bar. Inside, a tall, bare-legged girl in a micro-skirt ticks us negligently off a clipboard list. 'The name is Bennington-Smyth,' Stefano says huffily as these preliminaries are being concluded. A slatted wooden staircase leads to a room from which floats the bare minimum of conversation consist-ent with there being nine or ten people assembled in it. The noise of the pub crowd below is, if anything, even louder.

And then suddenly here I am, shaking hands with the boys and their attachments, accepting champagne off a brass tray, taking stock of what the years have done. The boys, dressed mostly in black, look like elderly gunslingers in one of those films in which some veteran gang of law-enforcers reconvenes for one final act of vengeance: old, gnarled and faintly resentful. Like Stefano, but in a more flagrant way, Garth's face is collapsing, with all the wrong elements – beaky nose, point of chin – weirdly over-emphasised. Shiny black hair combed up a-top this wreckage, he looks uncomfortably like a jackdaw. Ian, still dressed by Savile Row, has turned grey-haired and frail. Keith sits fizzing in his wheelchair. Only Dale, in biker boots and leather trousers, retains his old jauntiness. With them are their women. Garth – this may be a misreading of the situation – appears to be attached to the clipboard-wielding girl in the micro-skirt. Keith has Kelly to manoeuvre his chair and to lower her head to the level of his jaw when he wants to communicate something. The fourth Mrs Halliwell is a blonde in her early forties with a ripe lower lip. June seeks me out instantly, as if only a week has passed since we sat drinking Earl Grey in the hotel breakfast room in Colorado, and starts showing me photos of her grandchildren. There is no sign of Gary, who has apparently become either a Seventh-Day Adventist or an Infant of Christ. 'We saw him a couple of years ago,' June says, faintly mystified yet comfortable with other people's idiosyncrasies, 'and he says he has to sleep in a tent on Dartmoor lots. But he seemed happy.' What about the rest of us, those not quartered in tents on Dartmoor or Infants of Christ? Do we seem happy? The general mood, so far as I can make out, is fondly reminiscent yet faintly expectant. Stefano looks nervous; Garth slightly mischievous, as if he has some practical joke in train, of whose implications no one else can possibly be aware. Keith, motionless in his chair, is barking the word 'cough' at five-second intervals, which Kelly interprets as a request for coffee. Only Dale is smiling, not especially bothered, alert to comic possibilities. It is all the same to him.

The screening room is reached through flimsy double doors. There are only four rows of seats, erected on a slight incline. A ramp has been provided for Keith. Watching Kelly sweep him expertly into position, I realise that he reminds me of a Beckett character, or even Davros, the Dalek overlord from *Doctor Who*. His features are almost expressionless, but there is the same inflexible will struggling to exert itself beneath the surface. A youngish man in a pinstripe suit whose first language is clearly not English announces that everyone is highly excited by this addition to Mr Tanizaki's *oeuvre*, and they are honoured to have so many of his subjects present at its launch. Garth mutters something to the girl in the micro-skirt, who gives a not terribly enthusiastic laugh. June, seated next to me, is loudly advising Ian of the need to get back to Waterloo in time to catch the 22.17. The lights are extinguished. Without further preamble, the film begins.

It starts with an indistinguishable blueish mass, only revealed as water by a trail of bubbles rising to some far-off surface. Moving downwards, further away from the source of the light, the camera comes to rest on the floor of a swimming pool gathered up in shadow. Here lie various objects – what looks like a child's tricycle, a rocking horse, a television set. A little apart from them, curled up in a foetal ball, is a human body. It is not Florian, a brief glance at his face confirms, but sufficiently like him to make June give a little twitch of alarm. Then, abruptly, the scene changes to what, it takes me a second or two to realise, is the black-and-white promo film made in early 1967 for 'Road to Marrakech'. Here the boys are pretending to play their instruments on what appears to be a magic carpet that undulates beneath them while the sky above their heads alternates at lightning speed from Arctic ice-floes to Saharan deserts. It was shot by a West End advertising man, I seem to recall, and cost all of £2000. There is one slight refinement to the original, which is that the space behind the Lowrey organ, where Florian would ordinarily have stood, has been scrubbed away. In the occasional close-ups you can see the keys being depressed but no hands. Without warning the scene changes again to another promo-clip – much more cheaply made – in which the Kids sit astride the horses of a fairground carousel, rising and falling to what sounds like the strains of 'Mohair Suit'. Again, someone has been tampering with the print, for the horse on which Florian ought to be has a skeleton clinging to its mane.

The carousel ride gives way to black-and-white footage of teeming streets, smoke rising from factory chimneys, swarms of tattily dressed children pressing their faces into sweetshop windows. A caption reads SHEPPERTON, LONDON: 1963. Garth's face appears in eerie close-up, to impart a few salient facts about the early days, the 10s.6d they received for their first appearance, and how they once supported the Beatles at a cinema in Kilburn. There follows some immensely scuffed up film from the mid-1960s: an NME poll-winners' concert at the Empire Bowl; a TV interview in Carnaby Street, where Dale is wearing a feather boa round his neck; several clips of 'Swinging London'. Garth's face appears again, beneath the brim of a floppy hat, in what I remember is a *World in Action* special from 1967 about the 'youth explosion', enlivened by the fact that the subject is clearly under the influence of drugs.

INTERVIEWER: Do you have any particular aims and ambitions, Garth?

GARTH: What I'd really like is to get it together. You know, find some really groovy people I can relate to, who can . . . get it on. Not in any, you know, *dominant* way, but sort of a creative thing.

INTERVIEWER (*clearly appalled by the shambling, inarticulate vista before him*): Is this an exciting time creatively, do you think?

GARTH (*pauses*): Oh yes. Absolutely. It's just so . . . far out right now. I mean, I used to think it was far out before, but things have moved so much further out from there that it's just . . . unbelievable. There's just so much . . . love out there. You go out of your . . . pad in the morning and this great wave rises up from the street and rolls over you.

By this stage it is apparent to all that Tanizaki is bent on one of two aims. Either he is seduced by the myth of Garth as the Helium Kids' all-conquering demonic frontman, an organ-grinder surrounded by his monkeys, or he is determined to submit that myth to some pretty serious scrutiny. It could go either way. All of a sudden, though, we are back in the swimming pool. Not down in its innermost depths, but by its edge. Here, against a backdrop of recliners and potted plants, a long-haired oriental-looking man – clearly Tanizaki himself – is talking to an oldish blonde woman who, for the purposes of the interview, has been persuaded to don an immensely antiquated bathing costume. It takes me a moment to realise that this is none other than Martina, Stefano's very first wife, who in the aftermath of their divorce used to make threatening phone calls to the office on a daily basis until stopped by a court order and what Stefano casually alluded to as 'Don sending someone round to tell her to shut the fuck up.' Tanizaki's interview technique turns out to be stiffly formal. He apologises for intruding on her valuable time. He regrets that certain memories may still be painful to her. Martina, meanwhile, is eyeing up the potted plants as if they might be good to eat, and sagely nods her head as if to confirm that only her duty to posterity is making her pursue this self-lacerating step. At one point, Tanizaki presses her plump, liver-spotted hand. Then, with only a minimal show of reluctance, he gets her to confide that, to her certain knowledge, the last person to see Florian alive was Stefano, who drove down to the farmhouse late at night at Don's behest to instruct him that whatever thoughts he might have of re-joining the band were not worth entertaining. Her then husband, Tanizaki courteously deposes, had what might be construed as a somewhat forceful manner? And Martina nods her head again, as if the thought had only just occurred to her, and remarks that now you come to mention it he did ...

As we hit the late sixties, *Take Me with You When You Die* becomes less of an art project, or an exercise in reparation, and more of a conventional documentary. There is further footage, mostly from

America, including some fooling around with the foxy stewardesses on the Oblivion Express that has June give her meekly attentive husband a sharp dig in the ribs. Garth, a contemporary Garth, apparently filmed in the vestibule of some stately home with a wolfhound lolling at his feet, appears to offer some context for these shenanigans. Again, Tanizaki does the interview himself, and again it is impossible to work out whether he wants information or is bent on getting Garth to expose himself.

TANIZAKI: So it is your understanding that by this period you had reached what I might venture to call a creative *impasse?*

GARTH: Yeah, that's it. I mean, part of me thought, you know, I've got this band as far as I can take them. I mean, there's only a certain number of things you can do, short of playing all the instruments yourself (*laughs*). But then I thought what I if get them to work with me – I mean, they were all really talented musicians, you know – in a new direction. They didn't thank me for it at the time, but you can't disagree with hit albums.

At this point somebody in the audience – the evidence points to Dale – throws a half-full can of Coke at the screen. It hits Garth's celluloid representation square-on. There follows a fair amount of 16 mm footage from the early seventies shows, much of it, it seems to me, discreetly edited to suggest that Garth is performing with a back-up band.

TANIZAKI: The atmosphere at your live performances – what one critic has called a 'sonic cauldron' – must have been very difficult to reproduce in the recording studio.

GARTH: Oh, absolutely. But I was a very sharp operator in those days, very resourceful. I mean, I had to be. Working out the guitar parts. Doing the overdubs.

There are further shots of Garth flinging rose petals from a basket into the front row of an enraptured audience, Garth being mobbed by dozens of pubescent girls in a shopping mall, Garth frowning at a schedule pressed into his palm by a hand that may very probably be mine. Then, as if to counter this exercise in abject narcissism, there is a diminuendo – film of the 1977 US tour showing half-empty amphitheatres, anxious faces assembled in departure lounges – and one final surprise. This is, of all things, an animation, clearly intended to represent the robbing of the safe at the hotel in Boulder. The thief, it has to be said, looks horribly like Stefano, a point emphasised by the reappearance of Martina, no longer bathing-suited but dressed in what Norman Hartnell would probably have called a 'costume', to remark, with an innocuousness that fools no one, quite how well-heeled her ex-husband appeared on his return from America late in 1977 and how little difficulty he had in establishing the business that bore his name.

To conclude, there are four statements to camera.

GARTH: I enjoyed myself. I saw the world. It was a good preparation for what I wanted to do, but it wasn't the whole of my life. Not by any means. Mick Jagger once said to me: 'I mean, it's only music, isn't it?' I think Mick knows what he's talking about.

DALE: We had a good time. We made some records that will stand up. There's no proper pop groups now. But we were. A proper pop group, I mean.

IAN: It all seems such a long time ago. Different times. Different music. But I'm grateful for the opportunity ... (*warmly*) What I really like doing is playing the blues.

(*KEITH does not speak. Instead he stares balefully at the camera from his wheelchair, while Kelly reads from a sheet of paper.*)

KELLY: Keith says he's very much obliged to you all for coming, and he's very glad that a film is being made about the Helium Kids, in which he played the drums for so many years until his unfortunate accident.

The words GARY PASAROLO DECLINED TO BE INTERVIEWED FOR THIS PRODUCTION then flash across the screen.

There is a final piece of film from the sixties in close-up. Shot at the edge of what looks like a small wood, riverbank dimly discernible in the background, it probably dates from mid-1967, for the boys are all at the height of their Beautiful People phase. Garth has been equipped by I Was Lord Kitchener's Valet in the Portobello Road to resemble a cavalry officer of the Napoleonic era. Dale sports a sombrero and poncho combination. Ian's chin protrudes from the high collar of a medieval minstrel's jerkin. Florian is wearing his Elizabethan page-boy outfit. Keith skulks to one side, in flowered shirt and jeans. There is a breeze blowing up, stirring the strands of hair over their faces, agitating the branches by which their pale faces are framed. Garth looks irritated, Dale amused, Ian inscrutable, Keith stolid, Florian lost in some remote, impenetrable world of his own. The breeze continues to blow until the camera leaves them and settles instead for a view of water meadows, dank, receding lawns dappled by summer sunshine. The film ends.

There is a brief interlude before the light goes on. The first person to clamber to his feet is Dale, who stands for a moment patting the pockets of his leather jacket. As in the film from the water meadows, forty years ago, he looks amused, or perhaps only exasperated rather than seriously upset. 'You always were a cunt,' he says, almost conversationally, to Garth. Then his eye falls on Stefano. 'And as for you . . .'

'Not quite sure what to make of that,' Ian says cheerfully from two or three feet away. 'Does it mean Stefano was there when Florian died? Have to say, you know, I always wondered about that.' It is clear that one or two of Tanizaki's subtleties have been lost on his audience. 'Not saying I didn't like it, mind,' he goes on. 'Nice to see some of that old stuff again. Could have done with a bit less of His Royal Highness, though.'

June shakes her head. Garth and the girl in the micro-skirt are still extricating themselves from the chairs in front as June leans forward to bring her hand down on his shoulder. 'You are such a *wanker*, Garth,' she says, and the rebuke is all the more barbed for being delivered in her quiet, grandmotherly tones. 'All those years Ian helped to keep the group together, all those years of you being *stupid* and *unpleasant* and *pig-headed* and going after little girls who should have been in their bedrooms doing their homework. I could tell some stories about you, Garth Dangerfield, but it's too late now. I hope you feel ashamed of yourself.'

'June, June . . .' Garth says vaguely.

'How old are you, anyway?' June demands of the girl in the micro-skirt, who has dimly divined that all is not well. 'Fourteen? Fifteen? That's the age he likes them, you know.'

By this stage the audience is filing out through the double doors into the reception room. Earlier on there was talk of a collective supper party afterwards. Clearly this is not going to happen. Kelly, with the aid of a security man, is already bumping Keith down the long wooden staircase. Ian suggests to June that she may have been over-reacting. The girl in the micro-skirt is giving Garth a piece of her mind. Stefano stands to one side, eyes alert for potential allies, but completely ostracised. When he sees me he says: 'I need to talk to you, Nick.'

'Perhaps you need to talk to a lot of people.'

Still Stefano lingers at the head of the stairs to see if anyone will entertain his company. Then, giving it up as a bad job, he clumps heavily down the steps and out into the twilight. Soho is just starting up, and there are delivery bikes and fast-food wagons clogging up the streets. Stefano, I can see, is searching for a tone in which to address the revelations of the past hour-and-a-half.

'Of course, I shall certainly sue the fucker.'

'On what grounds?'

'Oh, I admit to taking the money. Anyone with any sense could have worked that out when it happened. Let's just say that Don owed it me and there was never any other way I was going to get it back.'

'Did he ever find out?'

'Let's just say' – Stefano's face ripples and sags slightly, as if at the memory of much bygone trauma – 'that he had his suspicions.'

'What about Florian?'

'Florian,' Stefano says. 'Jesus, I can't remember much about Florian. It was a long time ago. I mean, I certainly went down there that night. Don had heard he was trying to get back together with the band. Which was the last thing Don wanted, what with the plans he had to take them away from Ainslie Duncan and relaunch them. I can't remember what I said to him. Can't even remember whether he was sober enough to take it in . . . Might have slapped him once or twice, but I don't think I really hurt him. Of course,' Stefano says mournfully, 'that Martina is going to paint the whole thing in the worst possible colours. The old cow never liked me.'

It is about 9.30 now. Ian and June will be on their way to Waterloo. At this hour, the Soho light has a peculiar quality. Away from the sodium glare of the lamps and the glittering restaurant fronts, there are dense patches of darkness ready to swallow up anyone who crawls into them. What do I think of Stefano? That he took the money and went down to browbeat Florian into not re-joining the band. If that, indeed, is all he did? I get the feeling that at several decades' remove these are matters for Stefano and his conscience – if such a thing exists – not for me.

'You know,' Stefano says – and his battered face is absolutely stricken, almost seared with anguish – 'I don't want people to remember me as a bad person.'

How does Stefano want people to remember him? As someone who tried to do good? Who spent his time diffusing sweetness and light? Who was kind to small animals? I have a vision of him by the poolside in Sussex, there in the pre-dawn darkness, laying down the law – Don's law – to poor, drug-addled, seahorse-faced Florian, who probably has no idea why this man he has never seen before should be yelling at him about something that is apparently no business of his, shortly before the waters close over his head. Just before he died – I read about this in a music magazine – Don endowed a donkey sanctuary on the south coast. His last sentient act was to make the arrangements to attend a pilgrimage of Catholic pensioners to Lourdes. Legacy works in mysterious ways.

'Maybe I shan't sue,' Stefano says, a bit uncertainly. 'Maybe I shall just let the whole thing blow over.'

Just now we are at the bottom of Dean Street, at the point where it runs into Shaftesbury Avenue. I have an idea that, in more than one sense, this is a parting of the ways. Stefano is anxious not to let me go. He puts a forlorn, anaconda-like arm round my shoulder and begins to explain exactly why Martina hates him so much. Three feet away the London night traffic passes in a dense, undeviating stream. Stefano seems not to notice. I have an idea that for him, as for so many of us these days, the modern world no longer properly exists.

For some reason I left my mobile back at the hotel. When I return there are three text messages on it. One, predictably enough, is from Stefano. The second – a shade mysteriously, as I don't ever remember giving him my number – is from Dale. The third (*need 2 tlk 2 U*) is from Gail.

It is too late to call Gail in George Borrow Road. Dale, reached in what sounds like a nightclub, with loud female chatter pulsing in the background, seems delighted to hear my voice.

'It's all bollocks, isn't it?' he says, as jolly as ever. 'I mean, that *Garth* getting someone to doctor the tapes to make it look as if we were the backing band. And there's no point getting mad about it, cos he never takes any notice. Tell you what, though, I'll be taking a very close interest in that boxed set that's coming out . . . And then that Stefano. Can't get my head around that at all. You reckon he had anything to do with what happened to Flor?'

'A bit. Possibly. I don't think he . . .'

'Neither do I. Really . . . Still,' Dale goes on, 'that hasn't stopped Garth sticking it on every website he can find. Never did like the geezer – Stefano, that is. But then, no one ever made a career out of getting people to like them.'

'What are you going to do now, Dale?'

'Just this minute, I'm going to get pissed. Well, as pissed as I can get these days. If you mean longer term, I'm going to do an album. Jack Bruce said he'd play bass. Might even get Ringo on the sticks. No one'll buy it, but what do I care at my age? And you, Nick. You take care of yourself.'

'I'll do that.'

I look at Stefano's text for a long time before deleting it. Then I lie awake for hours in a room full of shadowy half-light, listening to the sound of London – at once quaint, rhythmic and murderous – rampaging on beyond the walls.

(v)

Oddly enough, come next morning it is as if the events of the previous evening never happened. There are no more text messages. One or two of the online celebrity sites are reporting Garth's 'outburst', but I get the feeling that no one is especially interested. It is all too long ago, and the people involved are sunk into that subterranean, twilit world where today's cultural arbiters can scarcely be expected to linger.

I take the train back from Liverpool Street in dense summer heat, oppressed not only by thoughts of Stefano and Garth, and Florian dead on the swimming-pool floor, but by the suspicion that Gail may have been right about Trevor, that Trevor's matiness, his deftly wielded mattock and his cheerful chainsawing might just be a preliminary move in a campaign of wholesale larceny. Now I think about it, I can see exactly what will have happened by the time I get home. The electrical goods will have been taken away in a van and the Hockney print removed from the wall. The bits of *Yellow Submarine* artwork that I bought at the Apple sale will have been shipped off to the memorabilia dealers and the sixties vinyl collection pitilessly despoiled. As the train speeds on across the flat East Anglian plain, through Colchester, Manningtree and Ipswich, on into the patchwork-quilted fields of the Norfolk agribusinesses, the suspicion hardens to certainty. Trevor is a chancer and a crook who will have taken advantage of my absence to exploit my good nature.

But the house, sunk in late-afternoon torpor, turns out to be undefiled. The front door is locked and the keys lying on the mat. Every object on which my eye falls is as it should be. All that lay bundled up and spread out in the fridge when I shut its door behind me remains. Trevor has even left a note, pinioned by a milk bottle, in which he hopes that I've had a good time and invites me to inspect the fruits of his labours. Stepping out into the garden, I discover that the summer-house is near-enough complete, the rotting timbers of the roof replaced, the veranda refurbished, the spilled sawdust and the scythed branches cleared away. The jays, found squabbling on the shiny new handrail, fly away at my approach. What was halfway to a jungle has, in a matter of a week or so, become a sylvan bower. Relief at this transformation is balanced by a feeling of guilt. Meanwhile *T. Liddament, Gardening & Horticultural Services* gets this householder's vote.

On the other hand, not everything is as it was. In fact, at least one apparently durable structure has collapsed into fragments. Gail is not much of a hand at the written word – her preferred medium is the text or the telephone call – but on this occasion she has written me a letter. I find it on the kitchen table, next to Trevor's note. Gail, it transpires, and in the friendliest way imaginable, is breaking off relations. Apparently, Kiara-Jasmine is taking up too much of her spare time. Plus the practice manager's job at the dental surgery will require her full attention. Still, she wishes me well and hopes that we can remain friends. It is an exemplary letter of its kind, of which an agony aunt would warmly approve. I can see her point entirely. With Kiara-Jasmine and a practice manager's job to juggle, who could possibly need me?

It turns out that Opal is dying. This, at any rate, is the implication of the countless medical bulletins and publicists' updates that have been filling the tabloid front pages in the past few days. Apparently, her kidneys have ceased to function and she is spending her afternoons hooked up to a dialysis machine. Hope of a transplant is receding, owing to some vascular irregularity. The online petition demanding that Robbie make an honest woman of her has reached a million signatures. I have signed it myself. Several newspapers previously known for their disparagement of her looks, romantic attachments, parenting skills and singing style are now praising her 'guts', 'pluck' and 'determination'. A *Guardian* leading article, describing her as 'a symbol of some of the worst cannibalising tendencies of the modern media age', has suggested that she is a deeply vulnerable young woman who needs our support. Some online footage from a year ago of her being sick on all fours while attempting to climb into a taxi has received several million viewings.

Autumn in Earlham, and the old routines are reasserting themselves. The footballers are out in Eaton Park. The Black Rat has been raided again. Passing the asphalt pitches that adjoin the school car park, I can see big, brawny girls playing netball. Fallen leaves, anything in colour from bright yellow to tawny, pile up against the kerb and the streetlamps go on at seven. To sit in the garden in the early evening is to feel the first faint chill of winter creeping up from the chalky soil. Trevor, it transpires, is in his element at this time of the year. It is when people start to batten down their hatches, want branches cleared, doors repaired, fences creosoted. *T. Liddament, Gardening & Horticultural Services* has never been busier. And I, too, have a new project. Norwich Millennium Library is sponsoring a 'local studies initiative'. With the enthusiastic support of the librarian, I am organising an exhibition entitled *Ralph Miniver: Norfolk Chronicler*. The library's storage facility, where superannuated volumes are kept, turns out to have several copies of Miniver's early books. It is hoped that these can be part of the display. There will probably not be any mention of the White Knights of St Athelstan. Even better, after writing a letter to the local paper, I have turned up an elderly lady named Mrs Muriel Banks, Miniver's great-niece. Mrs Banks, who claims to remember 'Uncle Ralph' smoking a pipe and talking about his friendship with G. K. Chesterton, is very excited by the prospect of the exhibition. She is also combing the family albums for photographs. I foresee a succession of long winter evenings getting my notes in order and perhaps writing a little pamphlet that visitors to the display will be able to take home with them.

Another thing I did recently was to negotiate for a tiny eight-foot square plot at the local cemetery near to the spot where my mother's ashes were buried. The old man's remains, of course, were deposited somewhere in the Pacific Ocean, but I think he would have appreciated the gesture.

JEAN ALEXANDRA DU PONT: 1919–1964

MAURICE CHESAPEAKE ALBUQUERQUE

SEATTLE DU PONT: 1913–1971

The Helium Kids boxed set, advertised by Stefano at the film screening, is released in October. There are one or two respectful reviews in the music magazines and a highly unflattering profile of Garth in one of the Sunday newspapers. *Take Me with You When You Die* is a source of bafflement to the critics. It is generally agreed that Tanizaki's precise motivation remains obscure.

GIANT INFLATABLES: THE HELIUM KIDS: COMPLETE RECORDINGS 1964–77 (CHERRY RED)

There are doubtless pop completists out there who will have gone grey waiting for a proper Helium Kids retrospective. The two nineties compilations were straightforward 'best ofs', the remastering project petered out halfway through and an earlier boxset, 1999's *Dreams and Responsibilities*, was patchy in the extreme. So diehards will be pleased to learn that *Complete Recordings* means what it says – literally – on the tin: the eleven studio albums, the 1971 live double, two extra CDs of out-takes and alternative versions, plus two DVDs' worth of early promo films and live footage. The latter is mostly from their early seventies Stateside pomp, although someone has turned up an extraordinary 16 mm record of a 1968 Hyde Park concert when the Gary Pasarolo-augmented power quintet was just getting into its stride. In fact, neutrals may very well think it a bit too comprehensive, what with the discarded material from the 1967 sessions that eventually realised *Paisley Patterns*, which consists pretty much of original keyboard player and early casualty Florian Shankley-Walker noodling around on what sounds like a Wurlitzer organ.

Giant Inflatables is clearly a labour of love. It is also not without humour, if not of the intentional kind (check out some hugely vainglorious liner notes, courtesy of Garth Dangerfield). But to anyone interested in the propulsive force of native popular music in the period 1967 to 1972, this is a fascinating aural document, basically the tale of how a middling successful one-time beat group managed, whether by accident or design, to position themselves for glory at precisely the moment when changing musical landscapes – and a changing musical economy – would give them the chance to succeed. To be brutally honest, most of the early stuff is of historical interest only, although some of the early singles (check out 'Girl You Shouldn't Know' and 'Mohair Suit' from 1965) have a certain generic charm. The game-changer is not so much *Patterns*, in which a fair amount of Summer of Love twee-ness is still proudly on display, as 'Agamemnon's Mighty Sword', recorded shortly afterwards, with its raucous guitar and juddering time-changes. Then comes *Cabinet of Curiosities* and that patented late-sixties sound ripe to conquer America: sub-Led Zeppelin *sturm und drang*, maybe, from the vantage point of the early twenty-first century, but just what the doctor ordered back in 1968.

My own personal favourite here is 1970's *Low Blows in High Times*, which may be regarded as what the Stooges might have sounded like if they'd gone commercial. Yes, Dangerfield's occult fascinations are risible in the extreme, and yes (as was frequently the case earlier in their career) they have clearly been listening a mite too hard to a few too many other people, but there is – believe it or not – a subtlety to some of the playing, particularly the blues re-hashes, which allow Ian Hamilton's often underrated bass work to come to the fore.

That the experience of being 'big in America', which they certainly were for a good half-decade, was both their triumph and their undoing is confirmed by 1973's *Street Assassins* – all bluster and rock cliché. Thereafter it was downhill all the way, from prog embarrassments (1974's *Glorfindel*) to rock-and-roll cover albums. The mid-1970s material doesn't make easy listening, and the half-dozen live tracks culled from their final tour are simply the sound of a band grinding to a halt.

So, how should we remember the Helium Kids? One kind of pop historian might say that they were Mods who lost their way. Another kind might venture that they were heavy-metal opportunists happy to ride the wave that had picked them up and deposited them in every 10,000-seater amphitheatre that Nixon-era America had to offer. The truth is that for a short season they were genuine contenders, who burned brightly for a year or three and then slowly declined into a long twilight of vanity and self-absorption which, when you come to think about it, is about the best any of us can hope for.

7/10

Jon Savage, *Uncut*, October 2007

The rain sweeps in over the Norfolk flat and the silent house, where the pictures from those old dead days stare from the wall and the Jim Dine drawing quivers in its frame. In the end, I'm just a boy from the Norwich backstreets. Eaton Park; the gleaming fish in their ponds; the stately trees. This is all I understand.

TOP OF THE POPS

In the old days, 'entertainment' was a red-faced drunk at the mic
Bawling smut about mothers-in-law and kippers
Or a ten-girl chorus-line of beauties in grey satinette
That even the slippered wives at home in curlers affected to like
And a row of talking puppets for the nippers
These days the compass point seems differently set.

All apes aiming to love you up, in their spangled jackets
Short-skirted girls who dance as if scything hay
Pale legs a-gleam. Where once were moons that rhymed with June
Come teen 'sensations' and another kind of musical racket
(in both senses). Take it from me, my sort of thing has had its day
That dodo's world of bandsmen and bowler-hatted jazzers who played
     in tune.

Useless to regret what's gone, of course, the paper-tearers
And the wheezing tenors, 'Signor Enrico' and his spinning plates
(his real name was Smith or Jones), the marching drums that clanged
     like dustbin lids.
In their place are the harvesting girls and the kaftan-wearers
The spruce announcer with the voice that always grates
'And now, all you pop-pickers, without further ado, here are the Helium Kids.'

Philip Larkin, 1969 (attributed)

ACKNOWLEDGEMENTS

Grateful thanks are very much in order to, among those known to me, Marcus Berkmann, Andreas Campomar, Claire Chesser, Cathal Coughlan, Howard Devoto, Pete Morgan, Charles Shaar Murray, Simon Reynolds, Howard Watson and Gordon Wise, and among those not known, Stanley Booth, David Hepworth, Allan Jones, Nick Kent, Andy Partridge, Jon Savage and Louise Wener. Love, as ever, to Rachel, Felix, Benjy and Leo.

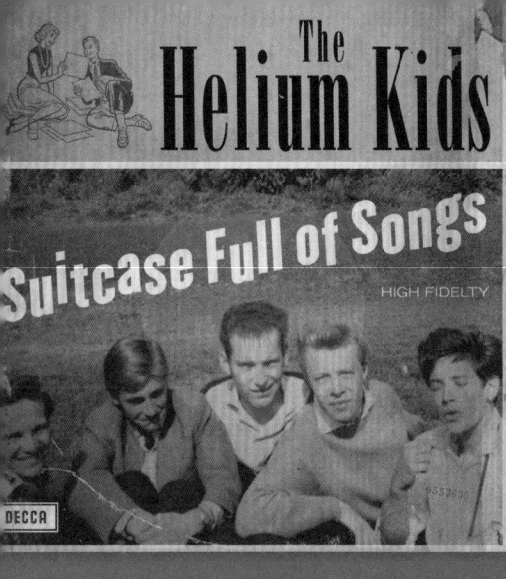

The HELIUM Kids
Suitcase Full of Songs
HIGH FIDELTY

DECCA

The Helium Kids
pumped up

DECCA

THE HELIUM KIDS

JUST SAYING

-4 IX 67

THE HELIUM KIDS
CABINET OF CURIOSITIES

THE HELIUM KIDS

GREATEST HITS

EMI

THE HELIUM KIDS
street assassin

EMI